SOMETHING BLUE

DIANNE CHRISTNER

SOMETHING BLUE

THE PLAIN CITY BRIDESMAIDS

BOOK 3

BARBOUR
PUBLISHING

Other books by Dianne Christner
Something Old
Something New

© 2012 by Dianne Christner

Print ISBN 978-1-61626-233-4

eBook Editions:
Adobe Digital Edition (.epub) 978-1-60742-021-7
Kindle and MobiPocket Edition (.prc) 978-1-60742-019-4

All scripture quotations are taken from the King James Version of the Bible.

This book is a work of fiction. Names, characters, places, and incidents are either products of the author's imagination or used fictitiously. Any similarity to actual people, organizations, and/or events is purely coincidental.

For more information about Dianne Christner, please access the author's website at the following Internet address: www.diannechristner.net

Cover design: Müllerhaus Publishing Arts, Inc., www.mullerhaus.net

Published by Barbour Publishing, Inc., P.O. Box 719, Uhrichsville, OH 44683, www.barbourbooks.com

Our mission is to publish and distribute inspirational products offering exceptional value and biblical encouragement to the masses.

 Member of the
Evangelical Christian
Publishers Association

Printed in the United States of America.

DEDICATION

Many things I love are blue:
beach vacations, sunny skies, faded jeans, my computer
background, and the color of my husband's eyes.
Happy fortieth anniversary, sweetheart!

CHAPTER 1

Brother Eli Troyer groaned and clutched a hand over his heart. The fast, strange sensations escalated as he weeded his wife's vegetable patch. But it wasn't the first time this had happened. Always before, the frightening condition went away on its own. If he told his wife, Barbara, she'd shoo him off to the doctor. He was long overdue for any kind of medical checkup.

He groped for the blue handkerchief in his pocket and mopped his damp brow. He glanced up at the June sun then replaced his straw hat. There were more important things to do than go see a doctor. He couldn't let up when he needed to visit folks who were actually sick. It took time to plan his sermons. Preaching and residing over his little Conservative Mennonite flock was a full-time responsibility, almost becoming too much for him as his energy waned. Why, he would be seventy on his next birthday.

He slowly bent for his red-handled hoe and continued to work his way down a garden row of bushy green beans, fighting against his increasing exhaustion. But he'd promised Barbara that he'd finish the weeding before she returned from her outing, with two other sisters from the congregation, to the discount fabric store in Columbus. Those sisters made up the core of the quilting group, and Barbara was going with them to show her support for their latest project.

Less than ten minutes passed, and he heard the sweet gurgling whistle of a bluebird. He paused to gaze up into the nearby evergreen. Barbara had suggested he put up one of those nesting houses on a pole this spring, the kind that attracted bluebirds. But he hadn't gotten it accomplished. Probably too late for occupancy this year, he decided with regret. The bluebirds would stay around anyway, at least until the blueberries ripened later in the summer. Barbara always planted sunflowers for the birds. And she already had several birdhouses strewn around the yard. She had been a good helpmeet to him over the years, and he now wished he had made that birdhouse for her this spring.

The chest pain returned, harder than before. Maybe it was stress. The last couple of years had taken a toll on him, with some younger members of the congregation pushing for changes. Such notions filled their heads these days. The latest upheaval ended with the men and women sitting together during services. That came after years of segregated seating. He shook his head. Before that, they'd changed the ordinance on the women's prayer covering, allowing women to make up their own minds whether they wore them outside of prayer and worship. But changing the ordinance had kept the congregation from splitting. Thanks be to God for that. He knew it was part of his job to try and understand the younger generation. Sometimes that was hard because he and Barbara had never had any children of their own.

Feeling lightheaded, he decided to call it a day, put away the tools, and head for the house for some of Barbara's homemade lemonade. He started toward the tool shed but only got a few steps when an immobilizing pain seized the center of his chest. He reeled forward, his palms and knees slamming, then sank down to the rich garden soil. Panting, he clutched his heart. What was this? Surely he wasn't having an actual heart attack?

With no one home to help, he wasn't sure if he could make it to the house to use the phone. He crawled a short ways, but the pain was unbearable, making it impossible to draw a breath. He clutched his heart again, realizing his life was in the Lord's hands.

As the painful attack increased, he curled up on his right side, his right hand clawing the soil and dirtying his fingernails. A sudden gust of wind blew off his straw hat, and it tumbled down the garden row and caught on a green bean bush, leaving Brother Troyer's balding head and face exposed to the sun.

Just before the preacher blacked out, he thought, *I'm dying. And I've left a few things undone.* He had no real regrets where his wife was concerned, other than the shock and pain it would cause Barbara to find him this way. But it was a church matter that bothered him most. Had been bothering him for some time. "I shouldn't have put off talking to widow Schlagel. I should have dealt with that." He tried to pray, but his thoughts convoluted, and he forgot all about widow Schlagel, sensing something faint, sweet, and wonderful drawing him. His fingers relaxed in the dirt, and he closed his eyes for the last time on earth.

⁓

"Glory be!" Megan Weaver's black oxfords pitter-pattered lightly across the firm's ceramic tile flooring. She sometimes left off the *to God* in her exclamations, because the rest of the staff at Char Air all knew whom she praised for all the good things that came into her life. Only a few of the employees of the small company she worked for shared her Christian— though not Mennonite—sentiments. She came to a halt and waved a photograph before the face of a middle-aged brunette woman in a beige suit. "Look at this, Paige."

The manager of finance looked up from her computer screen and squinted through her new bifocal contact lenses. "What is it?"

"Remember those bicycles the company flew to Haiti last month? This came with a letter from a missionary near Port-au-Prince. It's a girl with a clubfoot posing with her new bike. This letter says she lives in a remote village and has been walking over two miles to school. Now she can ride a bicycle." Megan studied the girl in the photo. "Isn't that an amazing story? Can you use it in our newsletter?"

"Sure. It's perfect. Thanks." The woman who was in charge of recruiting donations stood up from her desk, which was surrounded on three sides with sleek, chrome-and-gray partitions. Paige stretched then examined the photograph and letter. "I love it. These stories never get old, do they?" She blinked profusely and scanned the letter while Megan pushed a stray blond hair back beneath her prayer covering and waited. Paige placed the items on her file-cluttered desk. "You've sure been busy today."

Megan briefly rested her hands on the waist of her midi-length skirt. "That's because Randy is trying to get caught up before he leaves." As Randy Campbell's assistant, Megan had been careful never to discuss the particulars of her boss's delicate situation with others in the office. Yet everybody knew that the president of Char Air was taking a two-month leave of absence to spend time with his wife in a scrambled effort to save his marriage. Whispered rumors, along with the few details Randy had supplied Megan, led her to believe that his wife would have good cause to leave him but was allowing him one last chance to persuade her to stay.

Paige poked at the watery corner of her left eye. "I hear his brother, Chance, is going to fill in for him. Now he's a feast for the eyes. Too bad I'm happily married."

"I've never met him." Good looking? When she'd first started her job, it had been hard to keep her mind pure while working so close to her handsome, married boss. If his brother looked anything like him, Megan would be spending a lot of time staring at the floor and praying for guidance. As it was, she had already memorized the office floor's herringbone pattern. But now her gaze was on Paige. "I see you're having trouble adjusting to your new contacts. Is it painful?"

"Just bothersome. I'm giving it the rest of the week before I break down and wear my old frames."

Megan nodded, disappointed at Paige's obsession with outward appearance. The other woman was always trying something to beautify herself. Although friendly, Paige wasn't open to any of Megan's advice on that topic. It was obvious from past discussions, Paige considered Megan, with her plain garb and cosmetic-free skin, inept in topics pertaining to fashion and style.

Paige purposefully drew her hand away from her face and straightened her pencil skirt. "He used to work here. He's a pilot, you know. But he's been overseas."

"Really? Doing what?"

"He's a missionary pilot."

Megan's interest piqued as her heart sank. This made the newcomer all the more fascinating. She glanced out the glass wall and watched a flight line technician walk from the company hangar toward a Learjet that was going to transport a local sports team to Atlanta. "Sounds like a nice man." However, she knew that if he was Randy's brother, he was not a Mennonite man. That meant, romantically speaking, she needed to keep up her guard.

Her friend Katy had repeatedly pointed out that working for outsiders was treading a slippery slope. But Megan found her job interesting. If Randy took away her meager paycheck, she'd probably work for free. Not that her job was easy or undemanding. It entailed plenty of patience, making phone calls to smooth over problems with dissatisfied customers, and the constant struggle to find and keep volunteers for the nonprofit flights. Even keeping her hyperactive boss on schedule wasn't a simple task.

"Randy's convinced that Chance can do the job, but I have a hunch our lives won't get any easier the next couple of months." Megan sighed. "But we'll make do."

"I love your attitude." Paige turned toward her cubby. "If you do get any free time, you can help me."

"I thought that's what I just did."

"Oh yeah. Thanks for the photo. And the story."

Megan smiled and went to her desk, a modern cubical identical to Paige's, only located adjacent to Randy's plush, private office. She settled into her wheeled, black leather chair, both anticipating and dreading the arrival of her handsome, temporary boss. Of all things, Chance Campbell was a missionary pilot. *Aye, yi, yi.*

_____

Megan entered her mom's kitchen and donned a blue-striped ticking apron while following a sweet aroma to the black iron kettle, where Mom prepared their first batch of garden sweet corn. Megan's mouth watered. She loved summer nights when their meals consisted entirely of fresh garden vegetables and large slabs of warm, homemade bread and melting butter.

"I'll do the vegetables."

"Slice tomatoes and cucumbers. We're eating early. Your dad has an elders meeting tonight."

"Good because I'm starved. I only had time to eat half my lunch."

She warmed under Mom's approving gaze. Mom placed much stock in hard work, as evidenced by her tidy home and neat garden. But she didn't understand what Megan's job really entailed. Lenient as her parents were, it was probably better that way. She didn't want to worry them about the modern technology and worldly coworkers who surrounded her on a daily basis. Working at Char Air was Megan's first real job since graduating from Rosedale Bible College. Although it might seem like a strange job for a Conservative Mennonite woman, it was the connection with missionary and charity flights that had drawn her. Service and ministry jobs had always sparked her interest.

The house phone rang. Mom wiped her hands and rushed toward the counter. "Hello?"

Megan glanced over, curious, and froze at her mom's growing expression of alarm.

"Oh no. Oh no," Mom repeated, then quietly listened while snatching up a tissue from a blue-flowered box and blotting her eyes with it.

Hurrying across the kitchen, Megan felt her heart pound. "What? What's wrong?"

"Just a minute, Vernon." Mom lowered the phone and whispered, "It's about Brother Troyer. He went into sudden cardiac arrest."

"Will he be all right?"

Mom shook her head and dabbed her eyes again then returned to her phone conversation. Stunned, Megan dropped into the closest chair. Her mom ended the call by saying, "Such a shock. Yes, I'll tell Bill the meeting is cancelled." Mom stepped away from the phone toward Megan. "Barbara went with the quilters to buy some fabric, and when she came home, she found him. I just can't believe it. He died weeding their garden."

"How awful." Megan rose and slipped her arms around her mom's waist. Tears stung her eyes. The last time she'd seen Brother Troyer was at the Memorial Day potluck. He'd told Megan he was going fishing on the Big Darby the next day. He'd seemed cheerful and spry. Normal.

"It's shocking. Poor Barbara. No one suspected anything like this," Mom whispered.

Megan stepped away. "What will we do? Surely Dad won't have to preach?"

Mom's red-rimmed eyes widened.

CHAPTER 2

Megan stood next to her mom. Her nostrils filled with the pungent aroma of mowed grass as she stared at the brown mound of dirt and the freshly dug hole, trying to imagine her life-long preacher actually being laid to rest in it. The grim thought was paradoxical, with his soul alive in heaven. Megan found it hard to release him to God. Her thoughts and prayers remained argumentative, reminding God that they still needed Brother Troyer on earth.

Beyond the road across the pristine, rolling, cemetery lawn studded with neat rows of plain gray headstones—some adorned with flowers—a tributary of the Big Darby gently swirled and cut through the Plain City farmlands. Brother Troyer had spent a lot of time on that river. She tried to picture him fishing in heaven, but it was hard with that pile of dirt and rectangular hole. Yet Christian faith was all about eternal life. That's what Brother Troyer spent his life proclaiming to his humble followers.

The preacher had often turned soil in search of worms for his bait bucket. Megan's mind turned hard ground, poking at this death-life issue, but there was nothing under the clods of her mind besides the image of dead bones and the stark call to *faith* regarding things unseen.

The soft, even whir of the hearse's engine drew her attention, and she saw it park near the grave.

"They're here," Mom whispered.

Megan watched Dad join the pallbearers and carry the plain casket. Off to her left, she heard Barbara's soft gasp and faint whisper, though it was only meant for Barbara's sister. Megan strained to catch the widow's painful words.

"I'll never let the weeds grow on his grave. . .the least I can do. Eli hated weeding. If only I'd not been so proud of my garden." Her voice broke. "He might still be alive."

Megan dipped her head and stared at the ground. By her mom's flinch, she'd caught the pitiful conversation, too.

Barbara's sister, who'd driven in from Indiana, softly replied, "You did for him, too. That's how love is. God must've planned it this way. Eli met his maker in a beautiful garden. Quickly. With no lingering sickness."

Megan was grateful for Clara's calm reassurance, but aye, yi, yi, surely the bean patch wasn't Eli's place of choice. It would've been the riverbank or even the pulpit. Yet he was a kind leader. Devoted husband. Maybe Clara was right.

This was hard. Way too hard to think about. Nothing like when Jake Byler's grandma passed away last winter. Everybody called that a blessing because she was in the last throes of Alzheimer's, not even recognizing her family. But Eli had been so alive. Vital and needed. Megan's heart rebelled against the death and the changes it would bring.

At least Barbara had one living sister who was able to come and be with her during her grief. Mom had pointed out that some elderly people didn't have living siblings. Megan wondered how she could support Barbara in her journey of loneliness. She wished she could weed her garden, but weeds were Megan's dire enemies. Her allergies would never permit it.

"Friends and family. We are here to remember Brother Troyer."

Bishop Heinlein, an overseer of several Ohio churches, had come to help the congregation. Standing between the grave and those gathered, he wore a plain, black, collarless coat. His head was hatless, as was the custom of Mennonite men during worship. In his right hand he held a large black Bible. He cleared his throat and looked out over the mourners, a mixture of black coats and caped dresses. But Megan noticed that prayer coverings and doilies were intermixed with ties and high heels. Amish people and even some outsiders gathered because Brother Troyer was loved and known in the community.

"Psalm forty-six reminds us that God is our refuge and strength."

Earlier at the funeral held inside the meetinghouse, Bishop Heinlein had preached a somber message on righteous living, making the point that nobody knows the hour when they will be called home. But thankfully, now at the graveside, the bishop was quoting a scripture about seeking comfort in the Lord's arms.

"When he will wipe every tear from our eyes. Death will be no more. . . ."

A huge flock of starlings fluttered in and landed nearby, hunting insects in the graveyard's lush lawn. Ugly birds. Megan had a sudden image of rotting flesh and birds pecking Brother Troyer's eyes. She quickly quelled the image.

The bishop didn't heed the birds. "But thanks to God who gives us victory."

The burial ground was just down the road from the church. It was purchased after the original cemetery, adjacent to the church property, had been filled. This one was spacious enough to provide the resting place for several future generations. Megan watched the flock of speckled scavengers. Nobody liked starlings. And she was discovering she didn't like grave-yards much, either.

"It's still lonely." The comment drifted to Megan, and she glanced at the quilters to her right. Their group numbered three to ten and included some widows. The core members were Susanna, Mae Delegrange, and Ann Byler. Although her comment had sounded sympathetic, Susanna Schlagel had her brown, hawk-like gaze riveted on Barbara's back. No doubt the young widow planned to swoop down and snatch Barbara into their group, befriend her as only another widow could. But something about the thought of those two women together made a hard lump in Megan's stomach, about the size of one of their thimbles.

Beyond the quilters stood the young single women. As Megan watched Ruthie Ropp, Lori Longacre, and Joy Ann Beitzel, her thoughts continued on the dark side, wondering how long it would be until she'd wind up in their group. Her two best friends, Katy and Lil, were both married now. And Megan didn't even have a boyfriend. Never had, really. Would there come a time when she would be considered an old maid like Lori, the church librarian who wore too much perfume?

Bishop Heinlein prayed; then Ray Eversole stepped to the front of the mourners and passed out hymnals.

Mom took one to share with Megan. "Surely, we don't need these?"

"It's something to do," Megan whispered. "There's a few outsiders here."

"Then let's pass our book back to them." Mom snatched the book away and turned, motioning for it to be passed back to the visitors.

Frowning at her mom, Megan rubbed her thumb.

The song leader led them in a cappella, four-part singing. And Mom was right—they did know all the words. A beautiful song, surely an angel's song, sweet and melodious. She felt her spirit lift. She'd always felt as if congregational singing was a hug or the Holy Spirit's wings around her. A safe place where she was loved.

> *"When we all get to heaven,*
> *What a day of rejoicing that will be!*
> *When we all see Jesus,*
> *We'll sing and shout the victory!"*

While the message was amazing and stirring, so was Megan's visual. The casket was lowered into the hole. Several strong men discarded their Sunday coats and picked up shovels. Dad helped. Her friend Katy's dad, Vernon Yoder, too. Wrong, somehow, to see them sweat and bunch their muscles in their white dress shirts. They went about their task with somber reverence. As they worked, dust tickled Megan's nose and filled her sinus cavity. With the singing, she couldn't actually hear the dirt hitting the casket.

Each shovelful added to Megan's concern. What would the congregation do without their leader? Would everybody work together, or would this cause the type of conflict that soured Megan's stomach? How would it affect her dad and the rest of her family? Brother Troyer had been the one who united his flock, especially over the past three years when they had experienced so many changes—the seating issue, the revision of the prayer-covering ordinance. And more issues were brewing. She'd overheard Dad talk to Mom after elders meetings. What would happen once the funeral was over?

Megan swiped her wet cheeks. Sniffing, she thankfully accepted the tissue Mom pressed into her hand.

They sang "Amazing Grace." A breeze soughed through the hickory trees that graced the cemetery and lifted the corner of Ruthie's covering. The thin, single brunette reached up a hand to secure her straight pins. The singing waned, and a red-tailed hawk gave a raspy cry and circled above the mourners. Megan wished, like that bird, she could board one of her company's planes and rise above the grief and confusion surrounding her.

Getting a hold of herself, she thought, *Up there somewhere is God. He will see us through this. Bishop Heinlein just preached it.*

The bishop said, "The women have prepared a dinner back at the church. Sister Barbara thanks you for coming. You're all invited to the meal."

Food. What else could take their minds off their despair and the thin veil separating heaven and earth? The men quit shoveling. They weren't finished with the task, but it was time to end the service and escort Barbara and the women back to the church.

"Let's go," Mom whispered, her voice holding the same desire as Megan's.

Megan took a final look at the partly filled hole that reminded them all of their own mortality. They started toward the car. "That was hard. Poor Dad."

"He wanted to do it for Brother Troyer. Helps him deal with it."

"I don't like cemeteries much."

"Yeah well, Brother Troyer's in heaven now. That's just his body's resting place. Until he gets a new one."

Megan's gaze shifted from the grass, where she had been taking care not to walk across any other graves, to the road. Buggies, black cars, and colorful cars made a parade along the narrow country road. Her next inhale was wheezy, probably from the pollen of the tansy and reeds that grew along the creek on the far side of the road. She coughed, trying to clear her throat.

"You all right?"

Megan nodded as she withdrew an inhaler from her black purse. She released medicine twice then returned it to its silky pocket. After several breaths, she replied, "Better."

"That's good."

They neared their car, and Megan heard her name. "It's Katy. I'll just be a moment."

"Take your time."

Megan nodded and turned to wait for her friend.

"Where's little Jacob?"

Katy smiled, and her large, dark eyes lit. "Oh, my mom has him. She's helping to set up the meal." She pursed her full lips. "I hope he's napping for her. He's such a *nix nootz* right now, always squirming to get out of our arms. There's no way we could have kept him quiet."

Megan thought that if Jacob had his dad's ornery ways and was a handful at two months, Katy was in real trouble.

"I'm sure Lil's helping with the meal, too." The third friend in their tight trio attended a different Mennonite church now but had grown up under Brother Troyer's preaching. She was a chef by occupation. Katy was a housecleaner, but wasn't working outside the home since Jacob had been born. Jake's carpentry business was prosperous, and they had settled into a happy marriage.

"I'm sure she is. This is so sad." Katy lowered her voice to a whisper. "I hope working with the search committee won't be too hard on our dads. Mine's still adjusting to his insulin shots."

Megan touched Katy's arm. "I didn't hear about a search committee."

"Mom told me they have no choice but to find somebody quick."

"How?"

"The way she explained it, first the elders elect people to serve on the committee. Then the committee takes suggestions from the congregation and the bishop. Once they narrow down the candidates, they invite them to come and meet the congregation."

"So much is happening. I've spent too much time in my room this week or I would have heard about this sooner." At Katy's curious expression, Megan reminded her, "My boss is getting ready to go on a leave of absence." Katy nodded, her expression filled with concern. "There's been so much to do, that I brought some work home."

"I worry about you."

Katy had always disapproved of Megan's attraction for her boss. Her friend had some bad experiences working for outsiders, and although she'd become more tolerant, she was still skeptical of Megan's position.

"Don't worry. I'm fine."

Jake stepped up and touched Katy's elbow. Ever since Megan had known them—for Jake had been chasing Katy since they were kids—he'd pulled Katy's black ponytail. But after Jacob had been born, Katy started wearing her hair up. Subtle changes, him touching her elbow, them acting like a married couple. "You 'bout ready, Cinderella?"

As she watched her friends head to their vehicle, Megan wished she could have told Katy the truth, that she didn't feel like anything was fine. But she'd always made it her job to make life easier for everybody around her, and she didn't have the heart to trouble Katy now that she'd found her fairytale life.

<hr />

That night in her room, Megan grew nostalgic, thinking about life and friendships. She even found herself on her knees at the foot end of her bed, digging through her hope chest, looking for an old journal. That first one she'd gotten on her tenth birthday. Standing, she wiped her hand across the solid blue cover, though it bore no dust. Her first journal was actually a diary with a key. She lowered the lid to her hope chest and sat on it, leafing through the small book, reading bits of entries long forgotten. Her mouth curved into a smile, and she laughed once until she cried. She paused to read an entry from summer camp:

Dear Journal,
Alone in the cabin, but I gotta write quick before the others come back. They're busy for a few minutes because a spark from the campfire burned a hole in Lil's jeans, and our camp counselor

is outside trying to patch things up with the girl who loaned them to her in the first place. Katy told Lil that the spark probably came from hell because she's sneaking and wearing those jeans. That's what made Lil cry in the first place.

At the campfire, we made a vow. Now I'm sorry I made it. I only did it to keep peace. Lil wanted us to move in together when we grow up and to vow to be each other's bridesmaids. Katy said Mennonites don't make vows, and they don't. But it made Lil sad, so I smoothed it over and got them to agree. That's how I ended up being part of the vow.

Katy wants to marry Jake Byler. Yuck. If I get married, at least, it will be to a missionary or a preacher. Not Lil's cousin!

By the way, I'm going to name you, so you don't have to be a plain old, dear journal anymore. I got the idea when our counselor made us name our group. We call it Three Bean Salad. Katy's the kidney bean, I'm the green bean, and Lil is the garbanzo bean. Lil even made up a garbanzo dance to go with it. But Mennonites don't dance. Maybe Katy's right and that spark was from hell. I hope not.

Here's the names I've thought up so far:

Jo. That's short for journal. It was Katy's idea. Lil thinks I should make up a name that nobody ever heard of before, but it's hard enough to think of ones I have heard of.

Sharon. Because I share stuff with you.

Djibouti. That's a place in Africa. It's fun to say, and I think it would be fun to write.

Maisy. It was my doll's name, but I don't play with her anymore because I'm ten.

Hope Marie. But I really should save that name because it's my favorite.

Phooey, here they come!

CHAPTER 3

Chance Campbell was better at steering the nose of a Cessna through mountains and thunderstorms at zero visibility and landing safely on a runway carved out of the jungle than he was at sitting in a plush leather office chair and pushing a Char Air pencil. He stared at his computer screen with bored eyes, and he'd only been at it a couple of hours.

He'd arrived early, hoping to get in before the other employees arrived since it was his first day filling in for Randy. Only two hours into the job, and he was regretting being persuaded to do his brother this favor. He glanced at the calendar pad that took up the center of his desk. Sixty days. He'd just have to make the best of it. And if he was lucky, Randy would get his act together and return sooner.

But his big brother, normally the reliable one, had gotten himself into trouble and needed rescuing. Usually Chance was the one who took risks and got into scrapes. He hadn't been able to turn down the opportunity to pay his brother back for all the help he'd received from him over the years. Mostly his teen years, but help was help. Randy had intervened many times to keep their dad from finding out about his misdemeanors, even took the rap for him occasionally.

Chance gloated inwardly. It felt satisfying to be the good one for a change. And for the sake of his nephews, he wanted Randy to save his marriage. He was especially partial to the youngest.

A younger brother was in constant competition. Sometimes it took manhood to finally catch up. Chance had. He'd found his glory in the air force. He had even been awarded the Distinguished Flying Cross. But that mission in Iraq, back in 2003, had also been the one that changed his career direction—piercing his heart and bringing his fighter pilot days to a sputter. After that, he had not reenlisted.

Flying was in the family genes, and he could get the same adrenaline high working as a mission pilot. His job, with its life-and-death situations, provided the adventure he relished; only he was helping people instead of killing them. Not that he regretted what he'd done in the air force, because somebody had to do it for the sake of the country. He'd had his personal fill of it and gotten out of it before it resulted in nightmares and a need for counseling. He'd done his part for the country, and now he wanted to invest his talents in something that brought instant gratification—relief and healing for hurting people.

He rose to head for the coffeepot. He hoped that back in Ecuador, the rookie who was taking his place for the next sixty days—mostly to rack up some flying hours for his résumé—wouldn't make too many mistakes. Outside his office, his thoughts and steps came to a screeching halt.

Whoa! Chance slackened his jaw and riveted his gaze on the female headed his way. Who was that babe? As he stood and gawked at the lovely creature, his gaze moved in confusion from the little net cap to her boyish shoes. Why the odd getup? The baggy clothing? It wasn't black or gothic, exactly. His mind scrambled to sift it out, quickly going over his conversations with Randy until it clicked. He remembered, with disappointment, that she must be the chick who Randy had warned him not to touch. The one who was off-limits because she was Conservative Mennonite.

Chance had hardly paid any attention—conjuring up a vision of staid homeliness, similar to an old maid stereotype—even though Randy had been adamant and even made him swear on the Cessna's name that he would leave her alone. At the time, he thought it was just a joke, a jab at his bachelorhood. He'd passed it off without a second thought, assuming the obvious; he wouldn't pursue a Mennonite woman. Not that he knew anything about them.

But *now* he understood why Randy had pushed the issue. If Chance recalled correctly, he and this woman would be working closely together. And Randy had known that this woman's face and figure would rev Chance's engine.

Tall, check. Thin, check. Blond, check. Definitely his type. Only something else was striking about her. An aura of purity. Too much so, for his taste.

His mind backtracked. This wasn't the woman who had gotten Randy's life all entangled? No, that was his previous assistant. But Randy obviously regretted what he had done and was worried, not wanting Chance to make the same mistake that he'd made. But why on earth would he have hired a gorgeous replacement after he'd just succumbed to temptation? The only explanation was their Campbell genes. His father's fault. Women and planes.

The pretty face suddenly reddened. The slim shoulders squared, and the angel started toward him. His mouth went dry.

"I'm Megan Weaver. You must be Mr. Campbell?"

He reached for the feminine hand that was extended toward him. Her touch affected him. "In the flesh," he blurted out, letting his hormones speak for him. And he shouldn't be joking with this type of woman.

She pulled her hand away with understanding and frowned. "Nice to meet you. I am your assistant. My station is right here outside your office." She watched him warily and moved toward it. He followed her, rested his hand on her desk as she placed her purse in her right-hand drawer then looked up at him again.

"Yes, Randy warned—told me," he quickly corrected, "about you."

"Oh?" She straightened her mouse pad and didn't look happy.

"No worries. He said you're very. . .qualified. That you'd be a big help." He was acting like a brainless idiot. Giving a terrible first impression. He took a deep, steadying breath, whipped his hand off her desk and into his pocket. At the same time, he gave her a practiced and usually foolproof smile. "I'll need it, you see. I'm at home in the sky." He shrugged. "Not so much here."

He watched her face. Her cheeks were pale, pale peach with no makeup. They looked soft and fresh, like a child's. Her eyes studied him, unlined, blue, and vulnerable. The way she wore her white-blond hair up in that bun-thing exposed a delicate, tempting neck that definitely didn't belong to a child. That neck would surely provoke him for the next sixty days, but the silly net cap that perched on top of her head gave her a standoffish appearance. Too pious. It was an off-limits warning and would definitely keep her safe from his advances.

She smiled back. "I'm sure you'll do fine. What can happen in eight weeks?"

He knew what he wished could happen. He'd like to see that net cap removed. See what happened then. But he had too much honor to act on that. No, God wouldn't want him messing with His Mennonites. "I was browsing through the mountain of instructions Randy left me, and saw that on Mondays he meets with Tate in Operations. Do you have anything on your calendar for me?"

"On Friday there was a dispute between Jon, director of maintenance, and some of his flight line technicians. You should probably make sure that got resolved. Usually Jon can manage them, but sometimes Randy. . ." He nodded, so she moved on. "I've got some PR calls to make. From there, as Randy says, we wing it." She talked like a businesswoman, only her voice carried a husky accent that he couldn't identify. Possibly a touch of German?

"Great. Do you sit in on the meetings?"

"No. Randy gives me instructions afterward."

"Well today, I'd like you to join us. The two-ears-better-than-one thing. You have time?"

"I'll make do."

"Great. I was headed for coffee. Can I get you a cup? Though I gotta warn you, I made it. It's probably plenty strong for a sweet thing like you." He suddenly stopped, and this time, good grief, he felt his cheeks heat. He was asking a Mennonite about coffee? Calling her a sweet thing? "I'm sorry. Do you drink coffee?"

She arched a blond brow at him. "Yes. And I drive a car, too."

Her tone carried a disapproving sting. Up to this point, she'd been

25

tolerant of his blunderings and his roving, staring eyes. So she was touchy about her religion. "Look. I don't mean to offend you. Why don't you just make me a list, whatever I need to know about you. . .with your"—he glanced up at her net cap.

She tilted her head, studying him as if he were a bug splatter on a clean Cessna windshield then lifted her chin. "My beliefs haven't interfered with my job so far. They won't while you're here, either. But you're welcome to examine my employment application. It has everything personal you need to know. Summer's our accountant. She keeps employee records, too."

Now she was ticked. Women. He raised his palms. "Whoa. I didn't mean to make you mad. That's what I'm trying to avoid, here. We're gonna be working close. I'll need your cooperation, and I'm not the type who even knows *how* to walk on eggshells." He pointed at his shoes. "Big feet." He gave her his smile again, coaxing her to forgive him and get with the program.

Her expression instantly softened, but she didn't smile. "Just treat me normally. Like all the other employees. Really, I don't get my feelings hurt easily. That is, as long as you don't forget the creamer and sugar in my coffee."

"You got it." He winked then turned on his heels, glad to escape to the coffee bar. Just like in the fighter plane's cockpit, it was better to make a hit then zoom it out of there. He needed to regroup was all. She'd caught him off guard. All he'd wanted when he stepped out of his office was a lousy cup of coffee, and then bam, there she stood, looking all pretty and vulnerable and catching him unawares. But that wouldn't happen again. Anyway, there was nothing he liked better than a good challenge. Especially, a pretty one.

—⸲⸲—

Megan glanced at the clock and realized she'd been staring at the speckled texture of her bedroom ceiling for twenty minutes, unseeing and going over every exchange she'd had at work with Chance Campbell. She rolled onto her stomach and retrieved her pen and journal from the top drawer of her nightstand, and started writing:

Jo,

    Chance Campbell has curly, sandy hair, broad shoulders, and a disarming, if not conceited, smile. He's older than I am. Early to midthirties. He looks a lot like Randy. Of course, I won't give in to the attraction.

    I don't have him figured out yet. He's harsh and sweet at the same time. It's sadly amusing, the way he flounders around the office. I can't help but jump in to keep him out of trouble.

    Today I made peace between him and Tate, when Chance wanted him to reserve more planes for the charity flights. Everybody at Char Air knows that although the charity flights are important to the company, they use volunteer pilots and aren't profitable. We need all our charter flights. But I could have hugged Chance, with his love for missions.

    Something underlies his smile and clear blue gaze that makes me scared. It seems to imply that he gets what he goes after. He won't go after me. He treats me with caution, like I'll set off an allergic reaction.

    That first day when he asked me to make him a list, I almost slapped his face. My anger shocked me more than him. I've never felt that way about an outsider's curiosity. For once, I could relate to Lil. When I snapped at him that I drive a car and he could get anything more personal off my employment application, that was straight outta Lil's mouth.

Megan stopped writing when a classroom discussion from her psychology class at Rosedale Bible College came to mind. *Angry because I'm fighting the attraction.* She felt her face heat with the realization that she might be in real trouble. *Aye, yi, yi.* Her pulse quickening, she tore a page out of the back of her journal and tossed the journal in her drawer. She grabbed her Bible. Where was that verse? Then she remembered she'd penned it inside the back cover. It had been special at the time because her dad had been so sweet when he gave it to her. There: *"Be ye not unequally yoked together with unbelievers: for what fellowship hath righteousness with unrighteousness? and what communion hath light with darkness?" 2 Corinthians 6:14.*

It referred to oxen, but she'd been to some Amish pulls. Seen a team of draft horses yoked together. They made a beautiful sight, working together. Her dad had talked to her about it and quoted that verse right before she started college. He had explained that even getting involved with a man from a more liberal Mennonite church would be problematic. She'd taken it to heart. She'd witnessed that with Lil and Fletch. Eventually Lil left the Conservative church.

Chance was a Christian, but he wasn't a Mennonite. That was even worse than Lil's situation. This verse definitely applied. At least, the way her dad had explained it. She thought sarcastically she should make it into a poster and pin it to her wall. Her ceiling. But seriously, she needed a reminder that wouldn't give away her attraction. She tapped her pen against her lips. She needed a place where she could see it every day. On her car's visor!

With summer's glare, she usually flipped it down every time she drove. It would remind her on the way to work when she most needed it. She would meditate on it on the way home from work, too. She would not be unequally yoked, even with a handsome missionary pilot with sandy, wavy hair and gentle blue eyes. Even if he pursued her. Which he wouldn't.

After copying the verse to paper, she jumped up to take it to her car. Gliding her hand along the freshly waxed stair rail, she paused when her feet hit the bottom landing and she heard her dad say, "The professor had a recommendation for a preacher candidate."

Megan knew the professor in question was Noah Maust, a member of their congregation who taught Old Testament at Rosedale Bible College. She crossed the hand-braided rug and quickened her steps. On her way back in from the garage, she'd join her parents and catch up on what all was happening with the search committee.

CHAPTER 4

On Thursday Megan hurried across the hot, sticky asphalt of Volo Italiano's parking lot. It was the swanky Italian restaurant where Lil worked. The establishment was on the airpark outskirts, practically across the street from Char Air. About once a week, Megan got a take-out lunch, always calling first to be sure Lil had time for a quick chat. Time spent with Lil was never dull. She faced issues head on, presenting her opinions quickly and openly. The best part was that Lil was not judgmental.

As soon as the hostess recognized Megan, she went to the kitchen after Lil. Appearing almost breathless in a white chef's uniform, Lil gave her a quick hug and shoved a Styrofoam take-out container in her hands. They went to their usual corner in the foyer, settling in on an imitation stone bench next to the window.

"Hi, Green Bean. How's it going with your new boss? Spill it. You have exactly eight minutes."

Megan giggled, knowing they could cover a lot of ground in eight minutes. "It's been quite the week. I'm exhausted."

"I suppose he's gorgeous?"

"Aye, yi, yi. One of God's masterpieces."

"You're right to say *one* of. You haven't met *your* masterpiece yet."

"I suppose so. But if Chance was Mennonite"—Megan released a dreamy sigh—"I'd snap him up. He's perfect, otherwise."

"Chance? That's an unusual name."

"Suits him though." Megan shrugged. "Work-wise, it was hard at first. It would be easier to do the work myself rather than explain everything to him. But it's getting better. I'm making do." She leaned toward Lil. "He's full of interesting stories about Ecuador. But for that, we need more than eight minutes. We need to get together soon."

"Ecuador! We should swap stories. I'll have you over for dinner before Fletch and I go on our mission trip at the end of the month."

Megan gave a mildly envious sigh, remembering her childhood diary entry that she'd recently read. It hardly seemed fair. She was the one who was supposed to marry a missionary or preacher. Lil hadn't even been interested in such things until she met Fletch. In fact, for a while they'd even broken up over his interest in missions. Lil was into cooking and working at the restaurant. But she'd fallen hard for Fletch.

He was a veterinarian, now involved with an organization of vets who went on worldwide mission trips to teach people how to care for their livestock. So far, Lil had been able to go along. She had made such a favorable impression at the restaurant, that the owner, Camila Battelli, had given Lil permission to take leaves of absence as long as she plugged them into the calendar at least six weeks in advance. The head chef, Giovanni, had a good working relationship with Lil, too.

"I'll miss you."

"I know. I guess there could be a lot of changes while I'm gone. Have you heard anything new about the search committee?" Even though Lil attended another church, most of her family remained at Big Darby Conservative Mennonite.

"They have two candidates. Actually, they'll stay at our house." It didn't bother Megan that she still lived with her parents. It was the norm for an unmarried Conservative woman. She had been fortunate to have gone to Rosedale Bible College, and she had even lived a few months with Lil in a doddy house that they had renovated. But once Lil married, Megan was content to move back home. Being an only child, she'd always had plenty of space and privacy; in fact, right now she had the entire upstairs. And Char Air kept her occupied."

Lil wrinkled her nose. "You poor thing. A preacher at your house?"

"Two. Maybe more." A sudden image of the graveside service shot through Megan's mind, bringing a pang of sadness over losing Brother Troyer and talking about his replacement.

"I'll invite Katy and Jake, too." Lil glanced through some Roman-style pillars and urns filled with artificial greenery toward the back of the restaurant. "I'd better get back to work. I'll see you soon. Thanks for stopping in to see me."

Megan nodded and looked at her food container. "What's in here?"

"Lasagna."

"Yum. Did you talk to your boss yet about not using Styrofoam?"

Already disappearing around the corner, Lil chirped, "She claims it's cheaper. I'll keep trying."

Regardless that promoting the use of Styrofoam made her a poor steward of God's creation, Megan lifted the container to her nose and smiled. She needed to get back to work before Chance got himself in trouble. Her steps faltered. Should she have gotten him something? He usually left the office each day at lunchtime. He might already be gone. This was the first time she hadn't packed her lunch. She shook her head. No. Absolutely not. She wasn't starting that.

—⬡—

Back at the office, Megan barely made it to her desk before Chance's tan, rugged face popped around the corner. "That was fast. Oh. You brought lunch back." He sauntered to her desk, uninvited, and she felt a lump in her throat. Surely, he wasn't going to stand there and watch her eat? If she'd brought him back something, maybe he would have taken it into his office.

"Did you eat?"

"Not yet. I was just heading out. What do you have there?"

"Lasagna from Volo Italiano. My friend's a chef there. You should try it. She's there now. Tell the hostess I sent you, and Lil will give you something special." And she'll get to sneak a look at you.

"I'll do that. As fast as you got back, it must be close?"

Megan scribbled the address on a yellow sticky note, hoping he'd hurry and leave before her own lunch grew cold. Instead, he perched one hip on the corner of her desk. "I'll probably get fat working here. At my real job, I don't eat much. There are usually so many emergencies, I don't get time to eat. He touched his belly. But I guess I make up for it on rainy days. Sometimes I eat at the villages to be polite. If there's time. . ."

He looked trim enough. Not that she'd looked too closely. Most of her evaluations had been snatched while he walked away from her desk. But usually she tried not to watch him at all. She should have read her Bible verse on the way back from the restaurant. She tried to recall it from memory, but her mind wouldn't focus.

". . .But the missionary wives, they cook the best. Whoa. You aren't even listening to me."

"I'm sorry. I like your stories. I've always been interested in the mission field, even though I haven't had many opportunities to participate." She didn't add that she had hoped this job would provide such opportunities, for that wasn't really his problem. It was Randy's, but he had changed since he'd hired her. The promised opportunities hadn't developed yet. She looked up. Chance was studying her intently. "I did go to Bangladesh right after I graduated from Rosedale Bible College."

He questioned her further, and she got swept up in the memories, telling him about the prayer walks through the village. When she finished, he stood, quietly staring at her. She couldn't tell what he was thinking, but he was lost in his thoughts. She fiddled with her Styrofoam container then remembered the sticky note. She tore it off the yellow pad and handed it to him. "I wrote my friend's name, Lil Landis—I mean Stauffer. She's a newlywed."

"You want me to bring you back a replacement? That probably got cold."

"No. It's fine."

"Hold my calls then," he joked, because she fielded all his calls and was handling a fair share of them these days. She heard his departing footsteps and refused to watch him leave.

Megan had only taken two bites when Paige rounded the corner of her wall. "Holding your own, sweetie?"

"Of course."

"Good. Because I came to vent. We just lost a major donor. They said the economy has forced them to cut back. And you know what that means?"

"You have to make a hundred calls? That why you're only wearing one earring?" Megan found it amusing how Paige wore the most unpractical clothing and contraptions.

"Yep."

"Had lunch? I'll share."

"I'm headed to the break room now. I have a sandwich in the frig. I have to work through lunch."

"At least you got used to your contacts."

Paige blinked. "Oh honey, you shouldn't have reminded me. That'll be the next thing. But my eyes are doing better."

She gave her tight suit skirt a twist. "Anything I can get you? Although in my opinion, you've got the advantage, over on this side of the office. Didn't I tell you he's a charmer?"

Megan leaned to whisper. "He's a gentleman, but my workload has doubled again."

"So no ideas on donors?"

"You ask me this every week."

"I know, and you'll keep your ears open, like always?"

Megan shrugged and watched Paige prance away, perfectly poised on three-inch heels. She took a forkful of lasagna. Sure, Paige joked about Chance, and even some of the younger flight line technicians, but she was dedicated to her husband. And as far as Megan could tell, there hadn't been any inter-office flirting. If anything, Paige seemed to watch out for her. Megan didn't like the way men consumed her thinking, these days.

Her friends sensed it, too. Katy and Lil had both told her she needed a boyfriend. The handful of single guys at church had all pursued her at one time or another. She'd had guys interested in her at college, too. But nobody had caught her attention. Except the ones who shouldn't. She put her half-empty container in the wastebasket and picked up her phone. She had calls to make, too. Today she was following up on the corporations who had recently chartered flights. She punched in a number then looked up as Chance breezed back into the office.

"Lil's quite the gal. We hit it off."

Her phone still to her ear, Megan replied, "Great." She couldn't wait to talk to Lil again.

"She told me to keep my hands off you."

"What!" When Megan realized she had blurted *What!* into a customer's ear, she motioned to her phone and turned her gaze away from Chance. *What on earth was Lil thinking?* "Hello. This is Megan at Char Air. I see you flew with us on. . ."

In the background, she heard Chance chuckle. "She also gave away your strategic vulnerability."

Megan glanced back at Chance with narrowed eyes and continued speaking to her customer. "And I wanted to make sure your experience was a pleasant one."

———

Very pleasant, Chance thought, still chuckling and walking into his office. He'd never known that Conservative girls could be so much fun. Lil was outspoken and delightful. Easy on the eyes, too. She'd come straight to the point, warning him away from Megan. But she'd given away enough about Megan for him to realize that there must be some interest in him on her part, or else Lil wouldn't even have heard about him. And the feisty chef had confirmed his hunches about his assistant. Megan was fascinated with the mission field, longing to see other countries and help people.

It gladdened him, because there was nothing he liked better than sharing stories with interested parties. He'd thought Megan was interested, until this morning when she'd tuned him out. But maybe she was just hungry. It would certainly help him to pass the time if he would find in her a willing ear.

And there was nothing he would love more than to show her around Ecuador. As friends, of course. But if he could do something to make those blues of hers light up, he would. For sure, when his two months were over, he would set up a trip for her to visit the mission station in the village of Shell, take her on a couple flights into the rain forest.

He took a taste of his lasagna and figured he'd found his local lunch hangout. There was a sudden rap on his door, and without waiting for him to answer, Paige stuck her brunette head inside.

"Interrupting you? I couldn't help it. I just landed us a huge donor!" She did a little cha-cha shuffle.

He couldn't help but grin at her enthusiasm. "To make up for the one we lost today?"

"Yep, and now I can breathe again. So, I'm headed to the bank. You need anything while I'm out?"

"Nope. But congratulations!"

Just as quickly as she'd popped in, Paige disappeared. The news gladdened him, because his personal goal while working at Char Air was to promote Randy's charity flights. Next he heard Megan's squeal and assumed Paige was passing along the good news. This definitely wasn't South America, but he had to admit, Ohio was growing on him. So was his respect for what his brother had done to promote the charity flights.

CHAPTER 5

On Saturday Megan and her mom went to visit Barbara Troyer. They wanted to help her put up green beans, figuring that since Barbara had found Eli dead in the bean patch, it would be a trying chore for her.

For a parsonage, Barbara's home was pleasant sized with a large yard. Thankfully with Megan's allergies, Barbara set them up in the summer kitchen, which wasn't really a kitchen but a glassed-in porch. Under normal circumstances, it would have been idyllic, the way it looked out over the lawn and garden, edged with tall purple foxglove and a shorter row of yellow snapdragons. The garden contained rows of well-tended vegetables, and a sentry of sunflowers guarded the far end. The view was both beautiful and heartbreaking, given Brother Troyer's demise. Poor Barbara. Megan remembered what she'd overheard at the funeral, how Barbara wished she hadn't asked him to weed the garden that day.

They sat on rush-seated, white folding chairs. The summer porch had slick cement flooring, with only two colorful rugs for covering, one at the door going into the house and one at the outside door. It was the perfect place for messy projects. Each woman had half a bucket of beans—the first crop. It wouldn't take them long to snap off the tips.

"I picked these this morning." Barbara's gray-blue eyes saddened, but

Megan noticed with relief that they weren't misty. "The first thing I did was take the rake and. . .rake the ground where. . .you know."

"Somebody should have thought to do that for you," Mom said.

"No. I needed to do it. It's just that everything reminds me of Eli. The shed, the house. . ."

Poor thing. Megan's throat tightened, glad they'd come.

Mom reached into her pail, drew out a handful of beans, and started snapping. "When did your sister go home?"

"Thursday. Lots of church people have come to see me. I'm blessed with friends. I have enough food to last me for an entire month. Maybe longer. I probably should share it. Must be someone who needs it more than me."

"Don't worry about that," Megan urged. "You going to freeze these?"

"I usually do."

"Ever make three bean salad? Lil has the best recipe."

"Oh?"

Mom laughed. "It's a thing with Megan and her friends. Katy and Lil call Megan *Green Bean*."

Barbara's expression grew animated. "I didn't know that. There must be a good story behind that nickname."

Happy to see a bit of the old Barbara, Megan explained the story. She was ten. They had gone to church camp, and their counselor made them name their group. Lil had insisted they call themselves *Three Bean Salad*. "Katy was furious because she had to be the kidney bean."

Barbara laughed. "I can just picture her."

"I was the green bean because they think Mom stresses good steward-ship a little too much. And me, too."

"Nothing wrong with that," Barbara insisted.

"Exactly!" Mom agreed.

Megan knew Mom had gotten over that insult years earlier, because sometimes her friends still called her *Mrs. Green Bean*. They called Dad *The Blues Man* because his hobby was fixing up old Novas, preferably blue. And because there was nothing dismal or blue about Bill Weaver's personality.

"So Lil was cooking way back then. I'd forgotten that. I should do something different this year. Think I could get Lil's bean salad recipe?"

Barbara's buoyancy impressed Megan. "I'll get it for you. I'll even help you make it."

"How fun. Let's do it in a couple of weeks, when the beans really come in."

After exchanging a smile with Mom, Megan agreed.

They snapped in silence for a while, and Megan gazed out across the peaceful setting. A hummingbird flitted around some pink tubular flowers then zipped into a dogwood tree. Her gaze following it, she was the first to see the widow Schlagel dart past the pink carnations that lined the short sidewalk curving from the driveway. The woman was a bundle of energy who gave out an aura of constant unease and discontent. When Susanna noticed Megan, she gave a jerky wave.

"Susanna's here." Barbara went to the door. "Come in."

Susanna's hand flitted to her upswept chestnut brown hair. "What's going on here?"

"I've put them to work." Barbara unfolded another chair. "Join us?"

"Oh, just for a minute. Can I help?"

"We're almost done. No need to dirty your hands," Barbara gestured at the empty chair. "But sit and visit with us."

Susanna perched with a deep sigh. "This is nice. I miss my garden. Never thought I would. But this time a year, I do. If I could get one of my boys to help in the spring, I'd put one in. But they're all busy with their own lives."

"If you really want one, I'm sure we could get someone from church to help you," Barbara offered.

"Maybe someday." The lovely widow opened her purse and pulled out a small softcover. "Here's the book I was telling you about."

Barbara rose and took the book. "Thanks. I'll just put it by the door and look at it later."

Megan couldn't read the title, but when Barbara turned her back, Susanna exchanged a glance with Megan, causing her spirit to bristle much like it had at the cemetery. She wondered if Mom, who was naturally discerning, felt it, too.

Susanna softened her expression and shifted her brown gaze to Barbara. "I marked the portions we talked about." Abruptly she stood and folded her chair, resting it against the wall. "I need to go, but would you mind walking me to my car?"

"Sure," Barbara said, setting her beans to the side and wiping her hands on her apron.

"G'day." Susanna started to the door and tripped on the throw rug. She righted herself and went outside with Barbara, casting Megan a sour look through the window.

"Did you see that?"

"What?"

"Never mind." How could she explain to Mom how the beautiful widow in all her red plumage reminded Megan of a hawk hovering over its prey?

Barbara returned, slightly out of breath. "Out at the car, Susanna offered to stay nights with me."

"Oh?" Mom replied.

"That's why she dropped by. Well that and the book. But I turned down the offer. It was thoughtful but not what I'm looking for. I can't imagine myself in the widows' group. I've always spent some time with the quilters, but you know that widows' group is a tight circle." She spoke as if she were sorting out the matter. "I do get along well with Ann Byler. She always sees the best in everybody."

And tries to quell Susanna's bitter remarks. Megan couldn't forget Susanna's parting look. The woman was recently widowed, younger than the other widows. Only in her forties. Mom had gleaned from Dad's elders meetings that the woman was bitter and had started several hurtful rumors. Mom felt sorry for her. As a preacher's wife, Barbara must be aware of Susanna's actions, too.

It was kind of her not to mention how Susanna started things, told them to Mae, who spread it around. Mae got the blame for being the gossip. This put the third woman in the widow triangle in an uncomfortable position. Ann Byler tried to squelch gossip. She was on the timid side, so the other two pretty much ran over her. If Barbara entered the group, it would change the schematics. Barbara wouldn't tolerate gossip. But Barbara wasn't ready to join their group.

Megan kept her thoughts to herself. Although Mom occasionally told her about church matters, both of them kept such things confidential. What Dad brought home from elders meetings stayed within the Weaver household. Unless Katy brought up a matter. Since her dad was also an elder, sometimes they discussed things together. It was a small community. News got around quickly, even with the best intentions. But that was different than initiating spiteful rumors.

A clock inside the house chimed twelve times, drawing Megan's attention away from her thoughts.

"Noon. And we just finished. I guess we can go blanch these and get them in containers. Then I'll fix us some lunch from my plentiful donations." Barbara grinned. "Coming, Green Bean?"

Megan smiled back and stood. Moving to the door, she cast a final glance out the window. The lawn needed mowing. She'd mention it to Dad. He could set up something with the churchmen to take turns mowing. The parsonage would need a man's upkeep. Maybe Dad had already handled the situation. But what would happen when they got a new preacher? Surely they wouldn't make Barbara move? Would she even have a garden next year?

⸺ᘒ⸺

Megan handed her dad a wrench and stepped back from the open hood of the classic Nova she drove.

"So what kind of noise was it making again?" he asked.

"I don't know. Just different. Rough."

She fetched a bucket, upturned it for a seat, and watched him work. Knowing that he'd gotten home late the night before from one of his church meetings, she asked, "How's it going with the search committee?" The last she'd heard, in the three weeks since Brother Troyer's funeral, the search committee had gotten a lot accomplished.

"We got it narrowed down to two candidates."

"Really?"

"Yep. The first one is coming to meet the congregation. He arrives this Friday night."

"And he's staying with us?"

"Umm-hm."

"Where's he from? Is he your favorite, since he's coming first?"

"I'm trying to keep an open mind, and if I tell you too much, it'll spoil it for you."

"Not really."

"His name's Joe Zimmerman. He's the professor's suggestion."

"Oh." Megan figured if her stuffy Bible professor recommended him, he'd be. . .well, like the professor. "And the other one?"

"Ben Detweiler's one of the bishop's recommendations."

Both men sounded old. She didn't know what she'd been expecting until she'd felt disappointed. Restless. That's how she felt.

Dad drew his head out from under the hood, sporting a twinkle in his eyes. He was up to something, but Megan had no idea what. "Start the engine for me, will you, honey?"

She climbed into the bench seat and turned the ignition key.

"Purring like a kitten now," Dad boasted. "How's work?"

"Fine." She had no intention of giving him any personal details.

"I suppose it would be fun to work on airplanes. Scoot over and let me in. How about we pick up your mom and go to the Dairy Queen? So I can see how it runs."

Megan quickly moved over. The Nova rumbled out of the garage, and Dad parked it in front of the house. He hit the horn. Soon Mom appeared at the screen door. She placed her hands on her hips.

"What are you two up to?"

"Going to the Dairy Queen." Megan motioned. "Come with us?"

"Oh!" Mom hurried out then turned back and shut the door. "What's the occasion?"

"We're just taking the car on a test run."

When Megan opened her door, her mom waved her hand. "Stay there. I'll just hop in the backseat."

While Dad drove the car, he checked every working part within reach. When he flipped down the sun visor, the Bible verse fell onto his lap. "What's this?" He picked it up and gave it a glance.

"Nothing." Megan snatched it away and shoved it into her pocket. In the future, she needed to learn to do her own tune-ups.

"You got a boyfriend?" The question jolted Megan from her paperwork.

She looked at Chance with contrived annoyance. "Check out my personnel files."

Chance burst into laughter. "Where have I heard that before?"

Her hand involuntarily moved to twist her hair, a habit from years of wearing it long and free. But she'd started wearing it up in a bun at work, so her hand moved through thin air then rested on her skirt. "Why?"

"Just curious. That why your friend Lil warned me off?"

It had been three weeks since they'd started working together and since Lil had warned him to stay away from Megan. He'd never brought it up again. Until now. They had fallen into an amiable work relationship and routine of sorts. At first, she had meditated on her "don't be yoked" Bible verse daily. But after it had fallen from her visor, she'd forgotten to replace it.

"No boyfriend."

"If you did, what would he be like?" He glanced at her prayer covering, a reminder of the dos and don'ts of her religion. "I'm sure he'd drive a car," Chance teased.

"He'd be a Conservative Mennonite guy, if that's what you're asking." This was her opportunity to make him aware that she was unavailable to guys like him.

"He couldn't just be a Christian? Is that why you wear that net cap? To set your boundaries?"

"No." The covering was an object of curiosity for outsiders, but a topic that couldn't be explained without getting into scriptures and deeper Mennonite theology. She didn't think he was after that.

Chance perched on the edge of her desk, in the place that she had intentionally cleared for him after he'd knocked her stapler and plastic inbox on the floor way too many times. "I ever tell you what happened to the first Christian men who visited the Auca Indians?"

With hesitance, Megan repeated, "No."

"The Aucas have been called the worst people on earth. They hated all strangers, lived to hunt, fight, and kill. Even their neighbors—the Jivaros, who were famous for shrinking human heads—feared them. They buried alive their old and sick. Strangled babies with vines—"

Megan threw up her palms. "Please stop. I understand. The worst people on earth."

"Sorry. Anyway, they were territorial and didn't like strangers or intruders. Five men from different mission groups all got the calling to take them the Gospel. They teamed together and studied the language; then they flew over the tribe and made air drops of gifts useful to the Aucas. The Indians knew the gifts came from the men in the planes, who shouted down at them in their own language, 'We like you. We are friends.' The Indians accepted the gifts. So one day the Christians landed. But the Indians viciously killed them and vandalized their plane then ran for the jungle, waiting for other strangers to come and retaliate. But of course, they didn't, and missionaries continued to pursue them for the Gospel. Today about a third of the tribe is believers, and they are more commonly called the Waorani."

"That's a touching story." Megan considered the costs of the missionaries and their families, wondering how she would have responded.

"Don't be an Auca, Megan." Having just searched her soul, she narrowed her eyes and tried to follow his line of reasoning—comparing her to the most awful people on earth instead of the Christian missionaries. "I'm harmless. Please, don't shoot me out of the sky."

"They didn't shoot the plane out of the sky. They had spears and had to wait until it landed."

"That's what I'm saying. I landed on your turf. But I'm not the enemy. Especially if there's no boyfriend itching to pick a fight with me."

How quickly he could twist a story for personal conquest. "Conservative men don't fight." She wasn't giving him the green light, just correcting his understanding of Mennonite men.

"They don't stand up for their women?"

"We are nonresistant."

Chance scowled. "Pacifists?"

Feeling his disapproval, she tried to explain. "Sort of. There's a difference. Pacifists use political means to gain their end."

"You're referring to activists?"

Megan nodded. "They would defend themselves in a lawsuit.

Nonresistance is a submissive term. It stems from peace with God. Pacifists aren't necessarily Christians. While both groups abhor violence, pacifists think more about war and human rights. We would give up our rights to help a neighbor. We are mostly concerned about his soul. There's a big difference."

Chance looked concerned. "Your men don't go into the military, either?"

Megan shook her head. "But during the draft, they served in other ways. Like medical workers and firefighters. And we still help our country by volunteering after natural disasters." She tilted her head, studying him. "What about you? Are you a pacifist?"

"I'd rather be a lover than a fighter." He raised a sandy eyebrow. "Hypothetically speaking, what would a jealous Mennonite man do? Or a protective father?"

She didn't appreciate his menacing question, especially after her lengthy explanation. "Why does it matter? It doesn't pertain. You're not an enemy."

"Then we can be friends?"

"That's not a good idea. You're my boss, and we work together."

"You're friends with Paige."

"Only here at the office."

He gave her a sly smile. "You're forgetting something important. I'm not *really* your boss." He shifted off her desk, and she gave an inward sigh of relief. "Who needs to get back to work. But sometime we should go to lunch. Or let me take you out to dinner. You can tell me why you wear that net cap. I'm really interested in that."

"It's called a prayer covering." She clamped her lips, aggravated that he could easily bait her.

"Even more intimidating. But keep in mind that the Aucas couldn't hold off the Christians forever."

He strode into his office, and Megan stared after him with a heart full of concern. She figured she'd better copy that Bible verse again and tape it inside her desk drawer this time.

CHAPTER 6

By Friday Megan was exhausted and confused from a week of having to fend off Chance's advances. Ever since he had told her the story of the Aucas, he had initiated a campaign to break down her personal boundaries. She had purposefully taken great pains to establish lines that would help her fend off his charms.

Sure her workload had lightened a bit as Chance had become accustomed to the office routine, but not enough to make up for the time he spent perched on her desk or interrupting her for no good reason.

She turned the Nova onto her road, stirring up a trail of billowing dust when she hit a patch of loose gravel. The heat sapped energy from her, too, and she swiped her hand across her forehead. While driving the old car was fun, it had summer drawbacks, such as its lack of air-conditioning.

Weary, she whipped the Chevy into the front circle drive. No need to put it away when she was going over to Lil's for supper. She had looked forward to spending time with her friends all week. Finally she could unwind. It was even a holiday weekend. There were festivities in Plain City, celebrating the Fourth of July.

Chance had tried to worm his way into an invitation to attend some of those events with her, but she'd been able to make valid excuses, until finally, he'd relented. Now she took a satisfied breath, looking forward to a sweet snack and a cool shower. Snatching her purse off the seat next to her, she got out of the car, moved up the steps to the country-style porch, and reached for the screen door. Her hand was already on the doorknob when she heard a familiar creaking sound.

Thinking it was Mom, but surprised that Mom would be swinging this time of day instead of preparing dinner, Megan glanced at the white porch swing. Instead of Mom, a male figure lounged on their porch. She felt a moment of alarm until she remembered the preacher candidate. "Hello?"

"Hi. Hope I didn't startle you." He had a deep-timbered voice.

"A bit." The buckeye tree next to the porch set a deep shadow across his face. She stepped closer and realized that she was speaking to a much younger man than she had expected. "I'm Megan Weaver."

"I know." His voice held amusement laced with triumph. "We've met before."

Something familiar about the voice niggled at her. Confused, Megan took a few steps closer and halted. Her eyes widened when she recognized him. She felt as though she'd walked straight into a living nightmare.

"Micah?" *Aye, yi, yi. Skinny Man?* At college, the name had been a play on *Zimmerman*, and she'd also thought of him as stick man. "You're here about the preacher's position?" Her question came out more disdainful than polite.

He chuckled. "I guess you're not the welcoming committee."

She scowled, having no intention of welcoming *him* into her community or her life. "That would be Mom and Dad. I wasn't expecting you. I was expecting some old Joe Zimmerman."

He grinned. "Sorry to disappoint you."

"Oh no. You didn't." If he was Dad's candidate, she needed to show him some respect. Anyway, disappointment was far too weak for the emotion she was feeling about him. Outrage? But now it made sense that this former Rosedale Bible student would be the professor's recommendation. She hadn't considered one of the professor's students. Dumb. Well, if it had shocked her, his age would be a shock to the rest of the congregation, too.

She recalled the mischievous glint in Dad's eyes when he'd worked over her Nova and discussed the candidates. Bill Weaver probably thought bringing in a younger man was going to be a wonderful surprise for her. He had no idea what he'd set into motion, inviting this man into their home, because he did not know that she had spent her entire first semester fending off his clumsy and dogged pursuit, which had made her skin crawl every time they'd been in the same room.

She forced away the image of him trying to give her a tiny stuffed bear after she'd refused to go to the Columbus zoo with him. The thought of him mooning over her the whole day at the zoo and even bringing her back a souvenir had almost given her the feeling of being stalked. That was when she'd determined to make it clear to him that she wasn't interested. That was right before she'd hurt his feelings.

He stood now, and his smile faded. He towered over her, a Mennonite Ichabod Crane. His brown eyes scrutinized her, not in a suggestive way, but as if trying to pull something out of her soul that wasn't there to give. It had always been that way with him. It gave her the shivers. She'd never been able to understand why his actions disturbed her so deeply.

"As I remember, there was plenty of disappointment. But I'm hoping we can put that behind us."

"Oh that." She lowered her lashes in embarrassment then glanced back up at him. "Sure." As long as he didn't start it up again. He had been a piece of double-stick tape that was impossible to remove, and she didn't want to find herself back in that predicament.

"Good. I—" He sneezed midsentence.

"Bless you," Megan said, and then, her eyes widening, she pressed her finger to her upper lip, trying to ward off a similar impulse. She saw the branches over the swing fluttering and knew that the breeze would bring in more pollen, that she needed to get inside, but her sneeze wouldn't be denied, either.

"And to you," he said softly.

"Allergies. I'd better get inside."

"Wait. Me, too."

Dread engulfed her. So it was already beginning. His trailing her around. Was there to be no peace at home this entire weekend? She'd looked forward to relaxing and having fun. She strode into the kitchen,

Skinny Man at her heels. "Hi, Mom."

"So you've met." Mom beamed and wiped her hands on her apron.

Megan smelled meatloaf baking, which meant her mom was going all out, heating up the kitchen in the summer. She was preparing to cook a big kettle of corn on the cob, too. "Yes." Wanting nothing more than to escape to her room and take a shower, and not get forced into a polite conversation that Mom would initiate with the candidate, Megan quickly added, "You remember I'm going to Lil's for supper?"

"No." Mom looked disappointed. "I'd forgotten."

"You need some help?"

Mom's gaze held a yearning for Megan to stay, but she waved her away, "No, I've got it covered here. Your dad will be in soon. Some others from the committee are coming over after supper to get to know Joe."

Joe. Even his name provoked Megan. Imposter. She didn't want to hear why he was Joe now and Micah at school.

"Thanks, Mom." She glanced at Micah. "See you later."

"I believe I'll freshen up before supper." He followed her to the stairway. She cringed. As they climbed to the second story, he said, "I like your mother. What's your dad like?"

"His nickname is Blues Man." Let him fret over that. Think he was gloomy and mean. It was the only thing she could think of that might give Micah a little anguish before he found out how friendly and good-natured her dad really was.

In the hallway, Micah stopped at the first door. "Megan. Can I call you that?"

Her neck bristled. "Sure."

"What happened at school. . .can we keep that confidential?"

She braced her back against the cream-colored wall with dark-stained moldings. His question carried a lot of weight because she was ready to explode, had already envisioned venting to her friends. "I have to tell Mom and Dad. Otherwise, I'd feel uneasy with you staying two doors down from me." When she saw his expression fall, she tried to soften her words. "Not that I don't trust you."

He glanced down the hall and bit his lip. "I understand."   .

"To be honest, I'll probably tell my best friends, Lil and Katy, too. But they'll keep it confidential. So, yeah, your secret's pretty safe."

He looked at her with resignation. "Thanks for the honesty. This position means a lot to me. It's important that I find a church. Start a ministry."

She nodded. "I understand. But just so you know, Brother Troyer's shoes will be hard to fill. I'm not sure how this will go for you."

Micah softly chuckled. "I know. Nothing like a pair of broke-in shoes for comfort. Thanks for the warning."

She didn't like his flippant reference to Brother Troyer. "I miss him. He's not an old pair of shoes."

"I'm sorry. That was thoughtless."

Realizing she'd snapped when she was the one who'd brought up Brother Troyer's shoes in the first place, she replied, "God's will be done." Inside her room, she leaned against the smooth surface of the door. *Aye, yi, yi!*

꧁

Micah Zimmerman watched Megan disappear, regretting his stupid blunder. Frowning at the awkward incident, he went into the Weavers' pale yellow guest room that Anita had offered him earlier. Megan hadn't changed much, unless she'd grown lovelier. She'd taken the shock of his appearance gracefully, but he'd felt her resistance as strongly as he had that time he'd asked her to the talent show back at Rosedale. He'd quickly discovered her talent was evasion. She did this constant magical act of vanishing into thin air.

She'd refused to accept any goodies from him at the coffee shop, and she hadn't been interested in his disc golf skills either. Her disinterest wasn't merely indifference. She'd been passionate and creative in her snubs and rebuffs. And foolish as it seemed to him now, he'd been just as zealous to change her mind. Only she hadn't given him a chance.

But he hadn't returned to Plain City because of her. It was just the way things had fallen into place. Micah sank onto the yellow-and-blue star quilt, but the soft bedding didn't comfort its guest. He couldn't forget the blond woman who'd given him such a frosty look in the hall, made him feel like an intruder. One whom she feared and disliked. But he wasn't intruding. He'd been invited by Bill Weaver, her own dad, to come to Plain

City for an interview. To stay at this house. Her house.

He'd been looking for a church and praying about his future, and the Big Darby Conservative Mennonite church was the only offer he'd gotten. The recommendation had come from Professor Maust, a man who had been influential in his spiritual growth and education. The offer had both excited him and set his neck hairs on edge. He loved Plain City, Ohio. When he'd gone to Rosedale, he'd enjoyed the area. But he hadn't forgotten that Megan resided in Plain City.

It wasn't like he still mooned over her, but he did remember her on occasion. In fact, to receive the letter from her father had been a shock. He hadn't been positive it was her family, but he certainly hadn't been surprised when she stepped onto the porch, either. Now that he knew her dad had invited him, he wondered if she planned to ruin his chances. He didn't know if he could face yet another humbling lesson. Unless God meant to give him another chance with her.

He leaned back on one of the freshly ironed pillowcases. He couldn't allow that far-fetched hope to niggle away his peace of mind. Perhaps it would be a lesson on denial. He imagined shepherding the Big Darby flock and being forced to stuff his attraction for Megan. To do that would be to give God everything.

When he'd accepted the invitation, he'd determined to do exactly that. It didn't seem impossible at the time. He hadn't seen Megan for more than three years. During that time, his grandmother had died, and his brother had moved away. Megan's rejection was just another major disappointment to add to his string of losses. But he'd survived.

As he considered all this, he realized he was rubbing his eyes. They itched. His throat burned, too. He sat upright and examined the pillows. Down. He wouldn't be able to sleep on them. In fact, he would have to act quickly to ward off a more serious allergic reaction, one that would spoil his evening or even his entire weekend. He rose and fumbled through the zipped linings of his suitcase for his allergy pills. He stuck his head in the hall, figuring he needed to get water from the bathroom. The only thing moving was the floor-length sheer panels from the window at the end of the hall. The bathroom was positioned between his room and Megan's.

The handle turned freely, and he entered, closing the door behind him. Inside he caught a citrus scent. Her scent. He realized she must have recently been in the room. Frustrated in more ways than one, he clutched his collar and wiggled it, unable to resist clawing at his neck a few times. But he didn't want red scratches when he needed to make a favorable impression. Micah willed himself to quit. He popped the pill into his mouth and leaned over the faucet, taking just enough tap water to swallow the pill. He needed about twenty minutes for the medicine to kick in and work. He didn't want to trouble Mrs. Weaver about the pillows and risk coming across as a wimp. If he could get them out of his room, he'd make do without them.

Next he used an inhaler and coughed, waiting a moment for the wheezing to quit. Megan's bathroom was neat. He liked that. Maybe they'd put her belongings away because of his visit. Curious, he opened the medicine cabinet. Inside were some body lotions, a can of hair spray, a bottle of face wash, toothpaste, and her toothbrush. Feeling ashamed that he was privy to the brands she used, he quickly closed it.

Tentatively moving back into the hall, he saw a wide linen closet that he'd missed before. He opened it and peered inside. Mrs. Weaver had told him to help himself to linens. If he removed that one stack of towels, he could store those in his closet and replace them with the offensive pillows. He took the stack of four towels, two hand towels and six wash cloths and turned.

"You giving away souvenirs?"

He froze. Megan stood leaning against the wall with her arms crossed, watching him hauling *all* their linens off to his room. He sought for a witty response, but his brain was feather-deadened, consumed with the fire ants crawling up his neck, and nothing came to mind. Then he remembered that out on the porch, she'd admitted she had allergies, too. Maybe she could sympathize without thinking he was a wimp. How else could he explain toting off all the towels in the entire linen closet?

"Keep another secret?"

She arched a brow. "You're making up a missions packet in there? You just moved into an apartment and have no money for towels?"

"I'm allergic to the pillows. Thought I'd store them in the linen closet. Anita said to make myself at home."

Megan's arms relaxed. "You have down pillows in there? I didn't know we even had any of those left in the house. I'll go tell Mom to get you some others."

"No. Please. I don't want to bother her."

"Oh." She let out an indecisive sigh then admitted, "I'd probably do the same thing. I'm sorry about all the open windows. We don't have air-conditioning." She glanced back at her room, and for one horrible instant he thought she was going to offer one of her own pillows. Thankfully, she didn't.

"I'll be fine."

Her face relaxed. "Good. I'm off to Lil's." She started down the hall then looked back and caught him watching her. "By the way, Dad's nice."

She felt sorry for him. Not the emotion he'd prefer, but he guessed her sympathy was better than loath or repulsion. "Thanks. Have fun with your friends."

She gave him a nod then hurried away.

As he carried the pillows to the linen closet, he told himself it didn't matter what Megan thought about him. But he knew it did. He knew how these small churches worked. Everybody needed to be in agreement for him to take the job. He hadn't been able to elevate her opinion of him at school, and here he was stuck with the same problem.

Her approval mattered to him. When she had stepped onto the porch, every masculine and fleshly desire had been awakened. The attraction was annoying. He'd observed her enough back at Rosedale to discover her weaknesses. She was naive and headstrong. Not exactly the ideal combination for a preacher's wife. He needed a compassionate woman who related to the hurts of others, a woman who was caring and giving. Megan had plenty of passion, but she'd always used it to resist him.

His throat relaxed again, but the rest of his body remained uptight. Megan had made it plain that she didn't want him in her home. And under those circumstances, he didn't want to be in her home, either. Sharing a bathroom with her, for pity's sake. Seeing her pink toothbrush was more than he could handle. And no matter how nice her dad was, once she told her parents how he'd dogged her at school, as if she were a lab specimen, they wouldn't want him as a guest, either. If they moved him to the home of another person in their congregation, questions would arise. In this small congregation, news would spread quickly. It wouldn't be good for his chances. Megan had put him in a difficult and awkward situation. No, he'd put himself there.

Confused and irritated, Micah sank to his knees, clasped his hands together, and rested his forehead against the quilt. *Lord, I'm sorry I allowed my eyes and attention to stray to Megan. Again. She's not my goal here. But You drew me here, so there must be a reason. Something I need to learn that will aid me in my work? Or is this place going to be my calling? My home? Please direct my steps, according to Your will. And help me keep my eyes focused on You. Only You.*

The thought popped into his mind that if his history with Megan became public, it would create a good test, give him a feel for how the people in the congregation interacted. This interview wasn't only about the congregation accepting him. This weekend was about his decision, too. He was suddenly very interested to see what the Lord had in store.

CHAPTER 7

Do you tell Fletch everything?" Megan squirted a drop of detergent in a kettle and ran some water in it while Lil arranged their dinner on serving platters.

"I don't know, why?"

Megan placed a few dirty utensils inside the kettle to soak then turned away from the sink. "I'm still single. I don't know how this works. When I confide in you, am I also confiding in Fletch?"

"Oh. I suppose if it came up, I'd tell him. But he's not all that interested in girl stuff." She eyed Megan carefully. "But if I told him it was confidential, you could count on him."

"So if I don't want Fletch knowing certain things about me, even if I asked you to keep it confidential, you might tell him?"

"Let me assure you. All Fletch can think about right now is his trip to Ethiopia. He can't even remember to take out the trash. I don't think you have to worry about him asking about you. It's not that he doesn't like you. He's just got his own things going on right now. Sometimes he barely pays attention to me."

Megan was shocked at the frustration in Lil's comment. "What do you mean? You're not having problems?"

"No," Lil shooed the comment away with a flick of her wrist. "Is this about Chance? Is he trifling with you?"

"Yes, but it's not about him."

Confused, Lil placed her hands on her apron's waistband. "Spill the beans."

"This is one of those confidential things," Megan started, but just then Katy and Jake arrived.

"This isn't finished," Lil warned, then went across the room to greet the newcomers.

Megan followed her and reached for Jacob. "Hey, sweet boy."

The baby stared at her with bright eyes and responded with gurgling noises. Megan nestled her face into the tiny chest. When she drew away, Jacob's arms flew in the air. "I didn't mean to scare you," she cooed.

As the men conversed, Lil drew Katy to a safe distance. "Megan's going to tell us a secret. And she doesn't want the chump to hear."

Katy didn't flinch at Lil's pet name for her husband, who was also Lil's cousin. And Megan didn't blink when Lil invited Katy into the conversation. "It's just that I made a promise that this wouldn't get around in church, but I'm exploding inside."

Katy's dark, almond-shaped eyes speared Megan. "It's about the preacher candidate, isn't it?"

"Who's staying at your house?" Lil clarified.

"Yeah. Old Joe Zimmerman."

"Dad's meeting him tonight." Katy looked disappointed. "How old?"

"That's my point. He's young. And I know him."

"He's a relative?" Lil asked with confusion.

"No. He's from Rosedale."

Lil untied her apron and slung it across a chair. "That's interesting."

"It's a nightmare." Having their full attention, Megan shifted Jacob to her opposite arm. "It's Micah Zimmerman, the guy who I couldn't get rid of. Remember that first semester?"

Katy folded the apron and replaced it. "Skinny Man?"

"The stick man." Lil covered her giggle.

"It's not funny. Don't you remember how hard it was to get him to leave me alone? Now he's just down the hall. In my own house. What'll I do?"

"You poor thing." Lil tilted her head. "Remember how he slid a poem inside your math book? And didn't he take you to the zoo?"

"No! But he tried."

Katy nibbled her lower lip thoughtfully, "You think he's here because of you?"

Megan shrugged and ran a finger across Jacob's soft cheek. "Professor Maust recommended him. Dad wrote the letter inviting him. But even if he isn't interested in me anymore, it'll be awkward if he gets the job. Worse, if he starts asking me out again." As her voice escalated, Jacob made a pout. Megan attempted to rock him with his arms, but he let out a howl.

Katy reached for him. "If he's staying at your house, you'll get past the awkward part."

"Unless I have to give him another set down."

Lil frowned. "Do your parents know?"

Megan shook her head. "This just happened a few hours ago. Micah asked me not to tell anyone about what happened between us at Rosedale."

"Or didn't happen," Lil corrected.

"I told Micah I was going to tell my parents. He said he understood. But I could tell he didn't like it."

"If this gets around your church, folks'll make a big deal about it."

"I know. It'll be humiliating."

"They won't hear it from me. We're going to be out of the country anyways."

"Me either," Katy promised. "So besides your history, do you think he'd make a good preacher?" Her dark eyes teased. "We already know he's persevering."

Megan rolled her gaze toward the ceiling. "I have no idea."

"And now you have to fend off two guys," Lil remarked caustically.

Hoisting the squirmy baby up on her shoulder and patting his back, Katy demanded, "That Campbell man is still after you?"

"Yeah. He even invited himself to the Fourth of July events."

"Ugh!" Katy scoffed, giving her opinion of the matter. "What did you tell him?"

"I turned him down. Chance Campbell will soon be gone," Megan reminded them. "But what if I have to live the rest of my life with Micah's ogling?"

Katy shook her head. "I don't think preachers ogle, do they?"

"You need some help in there, honey?" Fletch called from the table, where he could see they were merely visiting and not paying attention to his hunger needs.

"No thanks." Lil handed Megan a platter and took one for herself. "Let's go eat. If you want, we'll talk more later."

Megan nodded. Lil was more worried about Chance and wasn't taking the situation with Micah seriously. Anyway, she was going to be out of the country. And Katy wanted her to give Micah a chance just because he was Mennonite. Well, it wasn't like she wanted to intentionally thwart his career.

Using Lil and Katy as a sounding board had sorted out her thinking: The real issue wasn't about how to fend Micah off for a weekend. It was figuring out if they could get along as preacher and parishioner. To find the answer to that question, she needed to get more involved in the process. As much as she dreaded it, she needed to use her influence to sway Micah's decision. If she ran from the situation now, she'd surely regret it later.

⎯⟶☙

Micah—Joe to everyone in the room except Professor Maust—shifted uneasily in his chair and tried to answer the question that had just been fielded at him. *What have you been doing since school?*

The reference to his seminary training as *school* didn't show much respect for his degree and made him feel less than mature around a room full of people two decades older than himself. But he smiled and discussed his work in Allentown with some inner-city kids through a program at his home church. He explained how his love for sports made it a natural fit. He mentioned he'd been given opportunities to preach numerous times. He'd written several articles for *The Mennonite*, a church magazine.

"How long have you been trying to find a church?"

"Not long. I thought it was better to get practical experience first. Also, my grandmother was sick. I lived with her. When she died, it took awhile to settle some family business."

"I'm sorry."

"Thanks."

An awkward silence filled the room, and then Vernon Yoder recapped Micah's past experience. "Since school, you served at your local congregation and did some preaching."

"Yes, sir. I was waiting for God's leading to move forward."

"And you sense that now?"

"Yes. I felt a strong call to come for this interview. But I have to be honest, I don't know if it's a match or not. I want to follow God's will. I'm as interested as you are to see where this goes."

Anita quietly left the room and returned with a tray of desserts. As she passed them out, her husband asked, "Did you know our Megan at Rosedale?"

Micah cleared his throat. "Yes. I met her during my last semester."

The professor quirked an eyebrow, and Micah sensed that his former teacher knew something about their relationship or lack of it. He met Noah Maust's gaze, and there was a definite twinkle in the older man's eyes. Micah redirected his gaze back to Bill. "Your daughter's very charming. I suppose everybody noticed her."

Bill seemed pleased with his comment, but that would probably change once Megan spoke to him and he learned the entire truth.

"Do you have a special woman in your life?" Anita asked, settling into the chair beside her husband.

"No. Honestly, at this point, I'm more interested in my work. I figure if I focus on the Lord, all the other things will fall into place." He could have quoted Luke 12:31—*"But rather seek ye the kingdom of God; and all these things shall be added unto you"*—because he'd memorized it shortly after Megan's rejection. It had become his anchor verse. But he didn't want to come across as overly pious.

"You've plenty of time for that," Bill agreed.

"But you hope to one day marry?" Mrs. Yoder asked. "A wife would be a good asset for a preacher. Help him in his ministry. Our Barbara is a saint."

Micah adjusted his collar, but not from an allergic irritant this time. "I'm sure that's true. When I feel it's in God's plan, I'll consider marriage."

The woman got a glint in her eyes. "Those things just happen sometimes."

Everybody in the room chuckled at Micah's inexperience. He hadn't meant to sound self-righteous. He supposed they'd feel more comfortable with a married preacher residing over them, but they'd known he was single when they invited him. "No girl. No marriage on the immediate horizon."

"We've hounded Joe enough for one evening. We should let him eat his cake now," Noah Maust said.

Though relieved, Micah still needed to clarify one thing. He cleared his throat. "There's something I should probably tell you. Before this goes any further."

Instantly, every eye riveted on him.

"I don't go by Joe. It's Micah." So it was his own fault that he didn't get to eat his dessert, but he hadn't the appetite for it anyways. Next, he found himself telling the story of how he became known as Micah. "So sometimes it doesn't pay to get named after a relative. It's too confusing. After Grandpa died, it seemed disrespectful to take his name."

The conversation shifted to the committee's itinerary for Micah. Being a holiday weekend, the town festivities were mentioned. "When Brother Troyer was here, we had a church picnic every July Fourth to celebrate our religious freedom. What's your opinion on it?"

"While I can't rejoice about bombs bursting in air, I see nothing wrong with attending some festivities. I agree with Brother Troyer's philosophy. We should be thankful for our freedoms. Honor those who died for freedom."

Soon after the cake had been served, people began to leave, making sure to give Micah a personal farewell. When the last visitor had gone, Bill exhaled a deep sigh, and for the first, Micah realized that the man was under a great deal of strain.

"Let me help." Micah straightened some throw pillows and found a cup that Anita had missed and headed for the kitchen.

"Oh, you don't have to do that," she protested.

Bill grabbed the trash and headed out the back door.

"I want to. I always dried dishes for Grandma."

Anita eyed him kindly. "We've peppered you with lots of questions. Enough for one night. But someday I'd like to hear more about your family."

"That's why I'm here."

Anita handed him a dish towel. "You want to go to the Fourth of July parade with us tomorrow morning?"

"I'd like that." But immediately, he wondered who all Anita was including in the *us*.

CHAPTER 8

Megan sidestepped around a family with a child in a red wagon and felt her arm brush against the preacher's. In her mind, she'd started calling him *Preacher*. Her previous nicknames no longer fit him or gave her any pleasure. Instinctively she pulled back and glanced up at him, but his gaze was roving both sides of the street, taking in the small-town, pre-parade activity.

She stole another glance. Micah wasn't as gangly as she remembered him from college. He'd changed. He'd gained some weight so that the sharp planes of his face had softened. His nose fit his face now. Everything about him seemed more solid, even his mannerisms. And he didn't stare at her all the time and make her feel uncomfortable. He seemed almost human. Normal. Still she shouldn't let her guard down.

Or had she magnified her memories of everything that had happened between them at college? She thought about that first day they'd met. He'd been climbing some exterior steps and had actually stopped midflight, turned around, and asked her if he could carry her books. And she had been going in the opposite direction! At that first encounter, she'd been flattered. Who wouldn't have been? At the time, she hadn't taken him seriously. She'd thought he was just clowning around. She'd grinned, shaken her head, and hurried away.

"How's this?" Dad asked. Mom glanced over at them.

"Fine," Megan murmured, feeling almost guilty for where her thoughts had taken her. Was Micah doing the same thing, remembering all their encounters, perhaps even chiding himself? They were both so much younger at the time. Megan lowered her voice and asked Micah, "So how did it go last night, meeting the committee members and their wives?"

"Okay. You missed a good supper. I guess you know your mom's a good cook?"

"Yeah, but so is my friend Lil. She's a chef, was head chef until she got married and stepped down."

He shrugged. "The committee members and their wives were friendly, but it felt a little bit like being in a dunk tank."

Megan smiled. "Are you still interested in the position?"

"I'm more curious about it than ever."

"So what's your plan?"

"Let's see. It goes something like this. Parade. Eat. Meeting. Eat. Meeting. Eat. Preach. Potluck. Preach. Eat."

Megan giggled. "Yes, that's the Mennonite way, all right."

"Oh, and there's a tour of the church in there someplace. Then Monday I leave, and you can breathe easy again."

"Can I?"

His expression grew serious, and he quietly studied her. They both knew that if he got the position, it didn't end on Monday. She tore her gaze away, toward the street. "It's starting now. The children's parade is first. Here comes the baby float now. There's a baby contest, and they even dub a Little Lady and Little Knight."

Megan hoped that sometime during his eat-meeting-eat-meeting-eat stay, she'd be able to figure out what he was really pursuing. If it was her, she'd put an end to it. If it was the job, the situation was more complex.

At this point, the invitation to actually take the job hadn't been extended. But this weekend wouldn't be the end of it. There was another candidate to interview. No matter what happened, the parade might be her only opportunity to find out more about Micah and to get the answers to some of her niggling questions.

A row of four- to six-year-olds twirling batons led a small marching band that was followed by a preschool float. Then a colorful mishmash of decorated bicycles, tricycles, wagons, and floats were followed by a children's choir.

In the short interval after the children's parade, Micah drew his gaze from the street to Megan. "The other afternoon when I first saw you, I assumed you were coming home from work. What are you doing these days?"

"I work at a charter air company as assistant to the owner and also do some customer relations."

"No kidding?" He glanced at her. "That sounds interesting."

She nodded. "It is. Char Air does a lot of charity flights. I've always liked missions, and my boss pretty much promised me there'd be some travel involved."

"How long have you been there?"

Megan glanced across the street at a row of two-stories. Directly across sat a pretty house with yellow siding and an expansive front porch. Next to it stood a neat, brown brick commercial shop. The narrow sidewalk was crammed with onlookers. "Less than a year. I was just getting started in school when you were finishing."

Music drew her gaze farther down the road, where the shops outnumbered the homes. "Here comes the high school marching band." Following that chugged a string of antique tractors and cars. "My dad's not happy about missing the car show for your meetings."

"Does he usually participate in it?"

"Are you asking that question as a preacher, or are you just curious?" she teased.

"Just curious."

"He doesn't participate because he thinks it would be prideful. I'm sure Brother Troyer and the other elders feel the same. But sometimes the show includes cars that he's restored for someone else. He does that as a sideline, makes extra money that way." She drew close and whispered, "He's well known in the entire Columbus area."

"You're proud of him."

She nodded.

A woman leading a pony with a flag-blanket passed them. A dune buggy followed, and someone threw candy into the crowd. Until the next float appeared, all along the sidelines children with plastic grocery bags scuttled to gather the candy.

"I don't know if our congregation's ready for you. I think your age will be shocking."

He looked startled. "Aren't there very many young people in the church?"

"No, there are." She tore her gaze from a Jeep pulling a float of soldiers. "Was it hard to choose a sermon?"

"Not really. Your dad gave me a choice of three topics."

"He did? I didn't know that. What are they?"

" 'Set Not Your Heart on Earthly Things,' 'Going Forward with Unity,' or 'How to Check a Heart against Pride.'"

Megan widened her eyes. Not because of their earlier conversation about pride, but because she remembered Brother Troyer preaching those exact sermons. "I don't understand. Those were Brother Troyer's last three sermon titles."

Micah frowned and glanced at Bill Weaver, whose gaze was riveted to the street festivities. He shook his head. "I wonder why the committee did that? It'll provoke an emotional reaction from the congregation."

Megan understood his frustration and even felt a twinge of righteous anger toward the search committee. Didn't they see that the first candidate would be put at a disadvantage? She wondered if Micah even knew that they were choosing between two men or more for the position.

Most likely, they'd give them all the same sermon choices. But it still wouldn't be fair. The first candidate would be judged the harshest. She glanced at her dad, who was watching the pizza restaurant's float, then back at Micah. "I'm sorry they did that to you."

He gave a broad-shouldered shrug. "Hopefully the other candidates will have the same list. But thanks to you, I'm forewarned."

So he did know that he wasn't the only candidate. "Which sermon did you choose?"

"The first. I figured the older members would be interested to get my opinion of what was worldly and what wasn't. As you mentioned, I'm a young candidate. Obviously, it'll be hardest to gain their acceptance."

She sympathized with him and had half a notion to pay Barbara a call and ask for Brother Troyer's sermon notes. Barbara would understand. Any woman would understand the emotional dimension involved. "That's smart. You're right about that. And that sermon is the oldest of the three, too. Maybe nobody will remember it."

The fire trucks drove past them, drowning out her voice with their flashing lights, firemen, and sirens. A dog rode in the first truck. She felt a hand on her shoulder and turned just as Micah went to whisper in her ear, causing his lips to brush her face. Shocked at the intimate touch, she jerked away and looked at him with confusion.

But he seemed unaffected. "What did you say?"

Micah's question hung in the air, as her gaze took in something even more alarming than Micah's mistaken kiss. "Chance?"

"Huh?" Micah tilted his head and stared at her lips.

Megan felt her face heat as her temporary boss squeezed in beside her, placing a hand at the small of her back. She sensed Micah stepping away, Chance moving closer. The sirens added to her confusion.

Micah was crushed from the velocity of new information and the sudden turn of events. There was nothing fair about what the search committee had done to him, and most likely he would be up all night reworking his sermon. It was reassuring that Megan sympathized with his plight. She'd tried to tell him something just as the sirens blared.

Then he'd leaned forward because he'd missed her last comment, and she'd moved. His lips had touched her face. She'd jerked away as though he'd done it deliberately. It happened just when she'd started to relax around him; the timing couldn't have been worse. Nearly kissing her was an accident, the least of his intentions. About now he could use the hoses attached to that screaming fire truck to put out the blaze that she'd just ignited in him.

And who on earth was the man who had shoved in right after that and wedged his way between him and Megan? The intruder had possessively placed his hand at her waist. But Megan had turned pale as paste. Whatever was going on between them, Micah could tell the outsider was attracted to her.

One good thing, Megan had shrugged away from the intruder's touch. Watching them closely, Micah tried to determine what kind of relationship they shared. The intruder dropped his hands from her waist and jammed them into his jeans pockets. He leaned close to Megan and whispered something. She shook her head, giving him an arched look.

Micah wondered if she was disagreeing with him or refusing him. At least at school it hadn't been necessary for Micah to watch her interact with other guys. To his knowledge, she hadn't shown interest in any of the other students. The flash of jealousy that he felt wasn't a welcome emotion. Especially not now. Not this weekend.

"That's it!" Anita's voice bellowed. She spoke at the exact moment that the fire trucks turned off their sirens. "Well." She lowered her volume. "The best parade yet, don't you think?"

"A beauty." Micah smiled weakly, unable to share her enthusiasm since his mind was on Megan and the stranger. Anita flinched, and Micah knew she'd just noticed the man speaking to her daughter.

"Megan?" Anita stepped onto the street so that she could face Megan and get a good look at the stranger. "Who's your friend?"

"This is Chance Campbell. He's my boss's brother. He's filling in for him right now."

"Oh." Anita's voice carried resignation.

Chance stepped forward and put on the charm, garnering Micah's disapproval. He watched Anita, knowing most Conservative women weren't taken in by showy pretense. He could hardly bite back a smile when Bill Weaver caught on and strode over to get in on the introductions. He was easy to read: *My daughter's a catch, but you better keep your distance.*

Megan's hand flitted to Chance's arm. "It was fun to run into you. But we only came for the parade. I'm afraid we can't stay. But there's more entertainment. You won't want to miss the hot air balloons. There're some sports events planned, too." Her hand fell away, and she gave him a parting wave. "Enjoy yourself."

The stranger's gaze suddenly shifted up to Micah's, as if he was responsible for her swift and unexpected departure.

Micah stepped forward and introduced himself as a guest of the Weavers.

Anita fanned her face. "It's going to be a hot one today. Better find yourself a tall, cold drink, Mr. Campbell. Ready to go, Bill?" She nudged her husband and started in the direction of their car.

"I'll do that. Nice to meet you."

Micah wanted to wait for Megan but knew he had no business doing so and followed the Weavers instead. Before he was out of ear shot, however, he heard some bits of conversation ensuing between Campbell and Megan.

"I thought you were kidding when you said you had plans. I thought you were only trying to ditch me."

"I always mean what I say, Chance. Enjoy your day. And I'll see you Tuesday."

A lot of information was packed in those short sentences. They were on first-name basis. Megan didn't have to work on Monday. It was important to her for Campbell to understand that she always meant what she said. The statement included a warning. The type of knowledge that would have saved Micah a lot of trouble back at Rosedale.

"Is the barn on fire or what?" Megan asked, catching up with Micah and her parents.

Anita shot back, "Sorry, honey. But that man looked like he wanted to settle in and stay awhile. And your dad has a busy day planned. The parade went longer than we thought. It was bigger this year, don't you think?"

Micah liked Anita better all the time. They walked in silence for a while, and when they'd finally moved out of the general crush of bodies, he glanced over at Megan. She seemed lost in her thoughts.

"You said Campbell's filling in for your real boss?"

"Yeah, my boss is on a leave of absence."

Trying to sound nonchalant, he asked, "How long will he be gone?"

"Eight weeks altogether. Five more. I really shouldn't be taking Monday off with all the work I have on my desk, but Chance insisted that I treat myself. Our work routine is finally settling in, but. . ." Her voice died away.

"You're keeping track of the weeks?" Micah gave a contrived laugh. She'd almost said something negative about the situation.

"It's hard not to do. Every time I go into his office, I see a row of big red x's on Randy's calendar. Chance is a missionary pilot. He's anxious to get back to the action."

Their relationship seemed personal, but maybe that was because it was a small, intimate workplace. She'd called her real boss by his first name, too. Micah had no right to concern himself with Megan's relationships. His time with her was limited, and he needed to concentrate on the more important reasons for his stay.

"Megan?"

She looked over, tilted her face with skepticism. "What?"

"You've been a good sport, keeping our secrets. But I've got another favor to ask you." He thought he saw her shoulders sag the tiniest bit.

"Yeah, what?"

"Regarding Brother Troyer's sermon—the one I'm going to preach. Do you remember much about it?"

Given her brief blank expression, she'd forgotten all about it. As their previous conversation came back to her, however, she relaxed. "Sure. If I thought about it long enough, it'd probably all come back to me." Her eyes took on a glint of mischief. "And you want me to tell you about it."

Encouraged by her insight, he confided, "Now that I know what I'm up against, I'll probably be up all night working on my sermon. Do you think we could find some time to talk about it? I could jot down some notes and try to figure out my approach."

"Sure, Micah. I should be home when you get back from your meetings. Just let me know when you want to talk."

"Thanks." Having the promise of her help made the pill easier to swallow. Gave him something to anticipate while he was closeted up with the search committee. He couldn't help but wonder what other surprises they had in store for him.

CHAPTER 9

Jo,

What an awkward day! The preacher tagged along with our family to the Fourth of July parade. I guess I should have expected Mom to invite him. Anyway, I took advantage of the situation. Given our history at Rosedale, I was worried that Micah came to Plain City for more than a job. But after spending the morning around him, I think his motives are good, that he's mostly interested in the job.

Although I never entirely let down my guard, I did relax around him. I actually felt sorry for him when I found out he has to preach Brother Troyer's sermon. And I even agreed to help him. Now I'm dreading it. What was I thinking?

Even more awkward, Chance showed up at the parade. That man's motives are easy to read. He's driving me crazy. The next few weeks are going to be hard because I don't really want to resist him. But I must. The man is off-limits to me. Handsome, charming, fascinating, and definitely off-limits.

Megan heard a door close, which meant that Micah had returned. He'd be looking for her so that they could talk about Brother Troyer's sermon.

With resignation, she slipped her journal into her nightstand drawer and glanced in the mirror over her dresser. She straightened her hair and covering then moved to her door. Hesitantly, she opened it and stepped into the hall. It was empty. The door to the guest room was closed. But a light shone from under the bathroom door. This was crazy. She felt like she was spying on him. She turned and started back to her room. A door creaked behind her.

"Megan!"

Her back tensed at the masculine whisper, and she pivoted. "I thought I heard you."

He ran a hand through his hair. It hit her that he parted it way too deep on the side for her liking. Was that what had always repulsed her? She stared at the part that was at least a whole inch too low. It almost gave him the comb-over effect. Other than that, his hair was normal, or even better than normal. It was about two or three inches long on top. Thick and dark brown. The coloring matched his eyes perfectly. The sides of his hair were short and neatly trimmed around his ears, giving him a boyish appearance. A slight curl or cowlick made his bangs wavy. Probably rebelling from the ridiculous part, they swept across his forehead. He'd need to do something with his hair before Sunday's sermon. When she realized she'd been staring at him, she blurted the obvious. "You look beat."

"A rough day." He glanced at his room and back. "Where's a good place for us to talk?"

Funny. Everybody had been so busy that the opportunity hadn't arisen for her to tell her parents about what had happened between them at Rosedale. Or maybe the threat had lessened somewhat as she'd observed him and realized he'd changed over the past three years. But the prospect of telling her parents was a trump card that could be played at any time. "How about the kitchen table?"

"All right. I have some stuff to do. Fifteen minutes?"

"Sure. See you then."

With relief she watched Micah disappear into his room. He wasn't interested in her at all, just his sermon. And that suited her fine.

The downstairs lighting was dim, and some clattering noises led Micah to the kitchen, where he found Megan standing at the counter with her back to him. She had two empty plates and was scooping a piece of oatmeal cake on one of them.

"Uh, oh."

Startled, she gasped and turned. "I didn't hear you come down. Do you always go around sneaking up on people?"

"Feeling guilty, are you? You one of those middle-of-the-night eaters?"

"No. On both accounts. But I do have a sweet tooth."

"I hope one of those isn't for me." He raised his left hand and started counting off his fingers. "Eat, meeting, eat, meeting. Yeah, I thought so. This is meeting."

The corner of her mouth tilted. "Suit yourself. Mom and Dad are outside on the porch swing. The kitchen seems to be the hub of our house. They'll probably gravitate through here in a few minutes."

Since their initial encounter on the porch, she'd sent prickly warning signals of her distrust, and his radar told him he needed to change that. One way to convince her that she had nothing to fear from him was to keep their interactions impersonal. He'd focus on the real reason he'd come to Plain City. Hopefully she'd see how he'd changed.

Fishing out his sermon notes, he also took a notepad from his brief-case and started a clean sheet. On the header, he wrote his topic-sensitive title: Set Not Your Heart on Earthly Things. He waited for her to settle in at the table with her cake.

"So did you survive the dunk tank today?" she asked.

"Barely."

"Can you swim?"

He needed her to realize that she wouldn't be chasing him away with her subtle threats. "Yes. I swim with the sharks."

Her hand stopped partway to her mouth. "I should have known."

"It's only three hours to the beach. We go to Sandy Hook in New Jersey."

"Who's we?"

"Our family, when we were kids. After my folks died, I went with my brother and some of my friends."

"And the sharks."

"Right. Those, too."

He noticed she'd hardly touched her dessert. "You want to finish your cake first?"

"No, I can talk and eat. Just think how much more you'd accomplish if you didn't have to separate your meetings from your eatings." She scraped her fork clean to emphasize her point.

He looked away from her lips. "Yeah, but I lose my appetite when people ask me questions."

"Lucky for you, I don't." She studied him. "You can't afford to lose any weight."

Her concern amused him. "That why you tried to feed me cake? To make me easier on the eyes?"

She rolled her gaze toward the ceiling. "Sorry. I didn't mean to be rude."

He'd always been thin, even though he ate constantly. Genes, he guessed. And his height. But the last couple of years, he'd had to buy larger clothes. He was comfortable with himself—or had been until she'd brought it up just now. He realized he'd allowed their conversation to veer off course. "So why don't you just tell me what you remember from that sermon. I'll take some notes."

She gave him the high points of the sermon, as she remembered them, and this led to a general discussion about the Big Darby congregation, especially the recent changes.

"I had mixed feelings over the prayer-covering debate. My concern was that the church would split over it."

Grateful to discover that Megan was more open-minded than dogmatic, he asked, "Do you think there're any hard feelings about it?"

"Oh no."

Rosedale represented the Conservative Mennonite Conference at large, and at Rosedale, most of the women didn't wear prayer coverings except to worship. That helped him understand that this congregation was very conservative, yet open to change. He liked that.

He thought his biggest obstacle might be the congregation's longtime attachment to their previous preacher. The position at Big Darby might be a rebound term, bearing the brunt of the congregation's confusion and grief. But most congregations seeking a new preacher would be in some sort of transition.

"Sounds like Brother Troyer was a good preacher."

Megan tilted her face to the side, resting her chin on her hand. "I've been a bit angry that the Lord took him. It's hard to accept."

He thought about his own losses. "These things take time." There was much he could share on the subject, but he remembered his resolve to keep their conversation impersonal.

"You mentioned that you lost your parents. Were you young?"

"Yes. A teenager. I lost them in a car crash. My brother and I moved in with my grandparents. Next my grandpa died. My brother got married and moved away. I took care of Grandma toward the end. Then I lost her, too."

"I'm sorry."

"After Grandma died, my brother wanted me to keep the house. But if I take a post someplace, I'll have to do something with it. And it holds a lot of memories."

"You have a lot of decisions ahead of you—no matter what happens this weekend." She fiddled with her half-empty plate. "Did you feel some kind of call to come here? Besides my dad's letter?"

"A strong call. But just between you and me, I'm not sure if this weekend will lead to a position or if there's just a lesson to be learned through it." He found it impossible to steer away from the personal. Maybe he just needed to be direct. "Even some closure."

She swallowed. "I haven't told my parents that we met at Rosedale. Since you came, there hasn't been time. I don't know if it'll even come up. I guess that depends on you."

Her warning gave indication she wasn't sharing his need for closure. "Thanks for helping me, even though you still have reservations about me. The only explanation I have for what happened at school is—"

Megan's hands flew up. "You don't have to explain anything."

"Please. Let me try."

She nodded.

"When I first saw you, you awakened something inside me. An awareness that you would be significant in my life. I was curious about you. I interpreted it as attraction. I couldn't understand why you didn't feel it, too." He scooted closer to her and leaned forward, lowering his voice. "What if it was a strong premonition? Given your connection with this congregation. Like an affirmation, even before the call?"

Megan's eyes widened.

He feared he was frightening her more than ever and shook his head. "I suppose you think that's dumb."

"No." Her eyes held wonderment. "I'm glad you shared that. I—"

"I saw the kitchen light on." Anita entered the room. She smiled at Micah. "You working on your sermon?"

"A bit." He glanced at Megan with regret. "If you're closing up down here, I can go to my room and finish it."

"We are turning in. But don't move. There's not even a desk in your room. Please stay and use the table. Just shut off the light when you're finished." She tilted her face and studied her daughter.

Megan rose. "I'm going up, too."

Micah watched her go to the sink, where she rinsed her plate and put it in a dish drainer. As she passed him, she said, "I look forward to your sermon tomorrow." She frowned. "You better do something with your hair, though."

Startled, he pushed his hand through his hair.

"For tomorrow."

"Megan!" Anita chided.

He bit back a smile. "Thanks for the advice. Night."

The two women left him, with Anita scolding her daughter as they went up the stairway.

Do something with his hair? For pity's sake, what kind of encouragement was that? Megan was a confusing woman. Trying not to let his mind get distracted, he glanced back at his notes. He'd let Megan get settled then go up and get the rest of his paperwork. He glanced at the coffeepot, wondering if he'd need to make himself a pot. Although Megan's help had given him an idea of how to approach his sermon, he knew he was in for a night of it.

CHAPTER 10

Once Big Darby abandoned segregated seating and incorporated the new custom of families sitting together, Megan had felt like a third wheel if she sat next to Katy. Since then, she'd drifted to the singles section, where she now found her place on their designated pew.

Joy Beitzel shifted beside her. "Isn't this exciting? A young candidate?"

Megan glanced at the woman, dressed in a crisply ironed cape dress. Although Joy's freckles and exuberance gave her a youthful air, she was four years Megan's senior. She gave Joy an unfelt smile. "He's not the only candidate."

Joy waved her hand. "Bosh, I know that. I type the search committee's minutes."

"Yeah, it's exciting." Or nerve-racking. Megan felt almost as anxious as if she were going to deliver the sermon.

She recalled Micah's story of the previous night, about losing his parents and living with his grandma. The sad determination in his eyes had strummed her heartstrings. The most humbling moment for both of them was when he'd admitted that he might have gotten the wrong message about Megan. Although their conversation had been interrupted, she came away from it with a better understanding. Micah was merely trying to follow God's call. He wasn't a timid man, afraid to admit his mistakes. He swam with sharks.

Afterward she'd felt sorry that she'd treated him so poorly at school. Perhaps if she hadn't been so set against him, they could have fostered a friendship.

"I hear he's from Rosedale," Joy Ann whispered.

Megan nodded. But he hadn't been after friendship at Rosedale. She'd had no choice but to give him that set down. Ludicrous as her silly threats seemed now, it had worked at the time. It had been Lil's idea.

In hindsight, maybe Micah was right about their relationship, that it'd all been orchestrated to help him through this sermon, this moment. The idea sent a thrill through her. Maybe God wanted Micah here. She found herself hoping so, even though she hadn't met the other candidate yet.

Her fingers involuntarily fidgeted with her skirt. She glanced around the room. It was no ordinary Sunday. Excitement filled the air. She and Joy Ann weren't the only ones anticipating Micah's sermon.

Joy Ann nudged her shoulder. "There he is."

Megan's eyes went to the pulpit, where her dad introduced Micah. Her heart leaped with delight to see that the preacher had taken her advice. Somehow he'd managed to control his hair. His bangs glistened, not plastered exactly, but sufficiently tamed for the occasion. Her interest in his makeover caused her to miss the introduction. But when her dad left Micah's side, it pleased her that he didn't seem as vulnerable as she last remembered him. Gone was the sad expression. He stood straight with squared shoulders, and his height gave him an air of authority.

Micah cleared his throat. "The Lord is good. Merciful and loving. As I hope you will be with me." There was a titter of laughter. "I was given a choice of three sermon topics: 'Set Not Your Heart on Earthly Things,' 'Going Forward with Unity,' or 'How to Check a Heart against Pride.' I chose the first one."

Good for you, Micah Zimmerman, letting them know. Megan hoped it would affect others as it had her, making them more sympathetic to his plight. Even now she saw folks whispering throughout the room.

"If I were to name this sermon, however, I would've called it, 'What Does it Mean to Set Our Hearts, and How Do We Do It?' The heart is the seat of our affection. It refers to our worldview or beliefs about life. How we set our hearts determines our future actions. Especially in those instances when we don't have time to think about our actions. The trick is to align our hearts with God's heart before we are faced with choices and temptations."

This was new information, something Brother Troyer had not touched upon in his sermon, Megan thought. Joy Ann's eyes remained riveted to the front of the room, as did many others.

Micah lifted his big black Bible with his right hand. "First from Colossians three, verses one and two, 'If ye then be risen with Christ, seek those things which are above, where Christ sitteth on the right hand of God. Set your affection on things above, not on things on the earth.'"

His Bible remained lifted because he quoted the verses from memory. "To better understand what is meant by earthly, we go to Luke twelve, verses twenty-nine through thirty-one. 'And seek not ye what ye shall eat, or what ye shall drink, neither be ye of doubtful mind. For all these things do the nations of the world seek after: and your Father knoweth that ye have need of these things. But rather seek ye the kingdom of God; and all these things shall be added unto you.'"

He set the Bible on the pulpit and stepped slightly to the side. "Of all the things that the Mennonite church has deemed evil, food isn't one of them. Without food, we can't survive. Food isn't the real issue. Jesus participated in many meals while He lived on earth. I've enjoyed lots of good food this weekend. And I understand there's going to be a potluck after the sermon. Some of you are farmers who produce food. Some of you have beautiful vegetable gardens. If Jesus didn't really mean food and drink, what did He mean?"

Megan sucked in her breath. The garden reference reminded her of Brother Troyer's death in the bean patch. Wondering how many minds had drifted to that memory, she glanced at Joy Ann. But the young woman's expression remained griefless. She was mesmerized by Micah.

"We must not set our hearts on our crops or our doctor bills or our accumulating gray hair. If our crops are good, we can fall under the pride that we're able to provide for ourselves. That we don't need God. When our circumstances are bad, if we don't look to God, our faith weakens.

He's telling us that we need to set our hearts to trust in Him and not our circumstances."

Micah stepped back behind the pulpit, which was on the same level as the seating for the congregation. As he moved, the congregation also shifted, many leaning to one side, looking through a gap, attesting to the fact that he had their full attention.

"But how do we set our hearts? Did any of you make Jell-O for today's potluck?"

A few timid hands raised.

"You ladies had to put it in the refrigerator to set it, didn't you?" There were several nods. "Brothers, when you go fishing, you have to jerk your line at just the right moment to catch a fish. It's the same with your heart. God provides the ingredients and the tackle. He gives the Bible and opportunities. But we have to set the hook ourselves. Jesus tells us to set our hearts on Him, beforehand."

Megan related it to Chance. At first, she'd set her heart against dating him. Lately, her heart had become infatuated with him. Chance was increasingly attractive to her. She focused back on Micah's sermon.

"Setting the hook is agreeing with God, with His truth as it is revealed to us. If you don't set your heart beforehand, you will find yourself more receptive to the circumstances instead of the God of the circumstances. It is also a continual thing."

Megan allowed the seed to sink into her spirit, again applying it to her situation with Chance.

"I hope you don't think I've been too vague. It would take many sermons to cover what the Mennonite church calls the doctrine of nonconformity, all the ways we keep ourselves separate from the world. This is a very hot topic. There are more than twenty sects of Mennonites because of various interpretations of this topic. It affects our daily life, business, speech, and our recreation. As the world continues to change, we need to distinguish between the essential and inessential beliefs. I have no doubt that in the years ahead this congregation will face many hard decisions."

Micah looked earnestly over the believers gathered before him. "I know that I can never fill Brother Troyer's shoes. But I am young and enthusiastic. My heart is set to follow the Lord. And just as He is merciful and loving, I felt that from you this morning. Thank you." He stepped away from the pulpit and took a seat in the vacant front row.

⁓

Megan followed Joy Ann into Big Darby's new fellowship hall, her gaze searching for Katy. But her friend wasn't in sight, probably caught behind the crush of those welcoming Micah, or possibly having to change Jacob's diaper. She moved alongside the tables laden with potluck dishes and took some cookies from the dessert table. She quietly surveyed the room.

"Meg! Over here." Joy Ann motioned. They'd barely gotten seated when Joy Ann nudged her. "There he is."

Megan glanced up to see hospitable hands urging Micah to the front of the line. She couldn't help but remember their private joke. *Meeting, eat, sermon, eat.* There was even more food than usual, for everyone was trying to impress him with their generosity.

"I'm not even hungry." With surprise, Megan glanced at Joy Ann's plate, which was at least as heaping as her own. "I just feel jittery inside."

"Why? Didn't you like his sermon? I thought he did a great job."

"Because Brother Zimmerman's so handsome. I don't even know if I can do my job if he becomes our preacher."

The comment shocked Megan on several accounts. First, that was exactly how she felt about Chance. Secondly, she'd better quit calling Micah by his first name and remember to call him Brother Zimmerman, like everybody else did. Until today, it was hard to think of him that way. And thirdly, handsome? Had that been the reason why Joy Ann had stared at him all through the sermon? Megan tried to school her features from her amusement. "Handsome? You think so?"

"You don't?"

Megan shrugged, imagining the petite woman with Micah. She turned to one of the other singles. "Ruthie? What about you?"

The heavyset younger woman wore her black hair in a bun and covered it with a doily. She unconsciously wiped her hands on her denim skirt and nodded. "Yeah, he's cute."

Lori Longacre, the church librarian, leaned forward, her perfume tickling Megan's nose. "Well, I wasn't thinking about his good looks.

But I'm impressed that he's our age. Just think how that could affect the congregation." Megan had to hide her mirth, because Lori was definitely older than Micah or anyone else in their group, nearing thirty at least. She tilted her pretty head. She had a mole on the flange of her nose that resembled one of those studs outsiders wore on purpose. The only time it was noticeable was when she got excited and flared her nostrils. Like now. "So, Megan, he's staying at your place. What do you think?"

Megan tapped her fork on her napkin, while her friends waited for her to reveal something wonderful about Micah. "From what I can tell, Brother Zimmerman's a nice man. He's been through some hard times. I think he's seeking God's will for himself and for us."

"Oh posh." Joy Ann frowned. "You're holding back. You went to Rosedale with him."

Megan didn't know how Joy Ann had obtained that information, but she quickly recovered. "Only one semester. I didn't really know him. I mean, of course, I recognized him." She waved her fork. "Let me tell you something funny. I'd heard a Joe Zimmerman would be staying at our house, and he went by Micah at school so I wasn't even expecting him. It was a total surprise."

"A nice surprise." Joy Ann twirled one of the strings on her covering. "He told the committee pretty much the same thing: you weren't friends, but he'd noticed you. He told your dad that most people noticed you."

"He did?" Megan wondered why Micah hadn't told her about that conversation.

Lori pointed. "Look. Something's going on over there with Brother Zimmerman. I think your dad's trying to get your attention."

Megan tensed at her dad's frantic wave. One glance at Micah, and the way he was clutching his neck and bending over his plate, assured her he was definitely in some kind of trouble. Quickly scooting out of her chair, she hurried to their table. "What's wrong?"

Dad said, "I don't know, but he's wheezing like you do sometimes. It came on him suddenly. I thought you'd know what to do."

Placing a palm on the table, she bent to look into Micah's face. "Are you choking?" He shook his head. "Is it something you ate?" He nodded, gasping and unable to speak.

Megan slammed her purse on the table and rifled through it. Her pulse quickened with alarm, making her all thumbs. Beside her, she heard his short gasps as he struggled for air through restricted breathing passages. Frightened, she tossed out the contents of her purse. The EpiPen rolled onto the tablecloth, and she swiped it up. "Don't worry. This will help you." Her hands shaking, she worked to set it. She placed her left hand on his shoulder to steady herself and knelt down beside him.

His frantic gaze met hers and went to the EpiPen.

"This will hurt. All right?"

He nodded.

"Hurry, Megan," Dad urged.

"I've never done this to someone else." But another glance at Micah's face told her she couldn't procrastinate. "I have to do this right. I only get one try."

Micah looked away, concentrating on sucking in fresh air.

She'd have to penetrate both his clothing and his skin. Setting her teeth, she glanced at him one last time then placed both hands over the needle, positioned it above his thigh, and jabbed hard. Micah's leg jerked up from his chair, but the needle felt solid. "Don't move." She finished the injection, hesitating and examining it closely before she removed it.

Her own legs went weak, and she was appreciative when her dad reached down to help her stand.

Micah placed his elbows on the table, slumped forward, and waited. As they all did, watching the back of his suit jacket heave with each struggle for a breath.

"Do you think we should take him to the emergency room?" Dad asked.

Micah shook his head but still couldn't talk.

"Let's wait a bit," Megan recommended, holding tight onto the back of the chair her dad had vacated. Time had never moved so slowly until finally Micah straightened a bit, his breathing much improved. When she saw that his normal coloring was returning, she asked, "What are you allergic to?"

"Sesame seeds," he slurred, "I didn't see it in my food."

"Oh, that's Inez's famous Chinese Chicken Salad."

Micah took several deep breaths. His speech improved. "Thanks. I don't know what would've happened if you weren't here."

"I was. That's all that matters. But in the future, you should carry one of these." Megan waved the EpiPen and dropped it into her purse.

Micah's hand moved to help her pick up the rest of her strewn items. "I'll reimburse you for your medicine."

"That won't be necessary." She quickly scooped up her billfold, and glancing up at the cluster of observers, snatched her cherry lip balm out of Micah's hand.

"You saved my life," he croaked. And the admiration on his face frightened her more than when she'd first found him sitting on her porch swing.

CHAPTER 11

On Monday after lunch, Micah went to the guest room to clear out his things, but his bag was already packed and waiting. He opened up his briefcase and got out the cheat sheet that he'd been creating to remember Big Darby's members. Not that he'd probably be asked back after his embarrassing allergic reaction. But he needed something to fill in the minutes until his humiliation took him back home to Pennsylvania. He looked over his sketchy notes, jotting down anything new that came to mind:

> *Big Darby Conservative Mennonite Members*
> *Bill and Anita Weaver—Elder. Search committee.*
> *Nova blues man, mechanic. Hosts.*
> *Megan Weaver—*
> *Barbara Troyer—Last preacher's widow, no children.*
> *Leon and Inez Beachy—Search committee, painter, sixties. Feisty wife, hostess committee.*
> *Ray and Emily Eversole—Search committee, song leader. Quiet wife.*
> *Noah Maust—Search committee. Rosedale professor.*

Vernon and Marie Yoder—Elder. Search committee. Middle-aged cabinetmaker. Kids.

Jake and Katy Yoder—Carpenter. Vernon's daughter is Megan's friend. Baby boy.

David and Erin Miller—Farmer with shiny black truck. Married to Jake's sister.

Will and Rose Landis—Farmer. Rose on hostess committee.

Hank and Sara Landis—Farmer. Oldest Landis son. John Deere coffee cup. Little boys.

Stephen and Lisa Landis—Farmer. Youngest Landis son. Curly haired wife. Red-haired baby.

Tom and Michelle Becker—Farmer. Michelle is a Landis daughter with four little girls.

Ivan and Elizabeth Miller—Farmer. Toddler.

Chad and Mandy Penner—Farmer. Easygoing guy. Toddler

Mark and Lanie Kraybill—Sunday school superintendent, carpenter. Wife is taller. Little boys.

Phil and Terri Yutzy—Tall, thin, church groundskeeper. Wife a fancy dresser.

Susanna Schlagel—Widow. Pretty redhead. Inquisitive. Leader of the widows.

Mae Delegrange—Widow. Heavyset with asthma. Talkative.

Barry and Linda Beitzel—Tax accountant with thick glasses. Joy Ann, church secretary

Ralph and Mary Ropp—Builder Supply Company. His shirts match her dresses.

Ruthie—Single, plumpish daughter.

Lori Longacre—Librarian, single, strong perfume.

If nothing else, the cheat sheet would serve as a memory. Someday, he could look back and remember his first interview, his first love.

Megan dipped her hands in hot soapy water, doing the lunch dishes, while next to her Mom lifted the lid to a tin bread box that she'd recently purchased at a garage sale. She removed a loaf of homemade wheat bread and took a serrated knife from the drawer. "Can you get me the cheese from the refrigerator? I want to send a care package along with Micah."

Knowing it would be useless to point out that they'd just risen from the lunch table, Megan quickly dried her hands on her apron and got the cheese. In the meantime, she heard the *plop* she'd been waiting for, coming from the bottom of the steps.

"Please tell him to wait a minute." Mom scrambled to finish the sandwich.

Megan went out of the kitchen and around the corner. Sure enough, Micah stood at the foot of the stairway, his suitcase at his feet.

"Your dad went after the car."

"Mom's fixing you a snack for the road."

Their smiling gazes met. "That's kind. Look, Megan, I don't know how to thank you for everything." He glanced toward the stairway. "Giving up your privacy, helping me with my sermon. But mostly giving me that EpiPen shot. That took a lot of courage. You saved my life."

"I only did what I'd do for myself. I know what it's like. I've had some asthma attacks. But you've got to start carrying an EpiPen for emergencies, Micah. Especially if you end up moving here and everybody keeps feeding you."

He smiled. "I won't forget your kindness." He dug in his pocket and handed her a little card that he had prepared beforehand. "My phone number. If you ever need anything, call me."

She took the card, staring at it as if it were a piece of double-sided tape. She gave a nervous laugh. "Really, you're making too much of it."

"You were my guardian angel. This entire weekend."

She wet her lips then studied him. "I'm glad I got to know you better."

A breeze fluttered in through the open screen door. Micah sneezed. "Excuse me."

Mom burst into the room. "Oh good. You're still here. I packed you a snack."

Megan unsuccessfully tried to resist the tickling sensation that irritated her own nose. Afterward she glanced up at Micah, embarrassed by their allergy association.

But he'd already turned his attention to her mom. "I appreciate that. As a bachelor I feel like a bear that's stored about a month's worth of food this past weekend."

"I promise you: if you come back, you'll never go hungry again." Mom beamed with assurance.

Megan's dad sounded his horn.

"My call." Micah leaned and gave Mom a gentle hug around her shoulders. "Thanks for everything, Mrs. Weaver. You're one special lady."

"I hope you come back," Mom half whispered.

He turned to Megan and clasped her hand, gently yet assuredly, like something a fond uncle would do. "Good to see you again." He picked up his suitcase and started for the door. Just before he stepped through, he added with a sly grin, "Thanks for the use of your hairspray."

The screen door slammed behind him, and Megan broke into laughter. "So that's how he accomplished the impossible."

"Serves you right. I still can't believe you told him to fix his hair," Mom scolded. "Why he could be our next preacher. But I guess you were friends from school."

Megan remembered Joy Ann's comment, that Micah had shared a little about Rosedale with the search committee. She figured it was time to fill Mom in on all the facts. "If you like while we finish the dishes, I'll tell you about the Micah I knew at school."

"Oh, I'd like that. I don't see how the next candidate could be any nicer. Do you?" They went back to the kitchen, and Mom freshened the dishwater.

Taking up the white linen drying cloth, Megan confided, "Micah Zimmerman was my biggest nightmare at school. The only way I finally got rid of him was by threatening to tell my professor, the church elders, or the law if he didn't stay away from me."

"What!" Mom clutched the countertop. "Oh, Megan."

⸺෴⸻

"I thought you said you didn't have a boyfriend?" Chance speared Megan with a glittering, blue gaze.

She picked up a stack of paperwork and tapped it against her desk to align the uneven edges. "I don't. I told you that I don't lie."

The creases around his eyes relaxed. "Then who was that guy with you at the parade? He said he was your guest?"

Megan sighed. "Remember I told you that our preacher died?"

Chance perched on the edge of her desk, knocking a pencil onto the floor. He quickly moved to retrieve it, handing it to Megan. "Yeah."

She pulled her hand away from his touch, stuck the pencil inside her drawer. "Micah is a candidate for the position."

Chance's brows furrowed. "And he's staying at your house?"

"That's right. My dad's an elder. Micah left yesterday. I don't know if he'll be back. There's supposed to be one other candidate."

Chance's left cheek twitched. "Whoa, no kidding? Your dad's an elder?"

"And he's the elder who's also on the search committee, and we've got plenty of room at our house, so he volunteered our place." She didn't know why she found herself confiding in Chance, but she added, "As it turns out, I knew Micah from Rosedale Bible College."

He narrowed his left eye. "So that's why you looked so cozy at the parade."

Megan dropped her paperwork and steeled her own gaze. "Why does it matter? I don't like to bring my personal life to work."

He leaned close. "I've noticed. You purposely push me away. Why do you do that? It's not like I'm not a Christian."

Squaring her shoulders, Megan gave him an honest reply. "I'm just setting my heart."

"What?"

She hoped that if she explained her feelings and convictions to her temporary boss, that God's blessings would surpass her disappointment over slamming the door in Chance's face. "Micah preached about it Sunday. Christians need to set their hearts intentionally, so that when things come up, they respond the way they should."

He stood, squinted at her, and placed his hands on his hips. "You're telling me you're purposely setting your heart against me? And that guy told you to do that?"

"No." Megan blushed. "Not against you. And he wasn't specifically talking to me, but to the entire congregation. You've been to church. You know what I mean."

"Not your church. I don't understand you much at all."

Megan wet her lips. "I'm setting my heart to honor what I've been taught about relationships."

"You're rejecting me because I'm not a Mennonite?"

"Yes," she finally relented.

His face broke into a slow smile. "So you're setting your heart against me because you're attracted to me?"

"Shh! I can't believe you're talking like this. What if somebody hears you?"

He turned and tossed over his shoulder. "Come into my office."

"No." Megan shook her head, just wanting him to go away and leave her alone. "I have a ton of work to do."

He pivoted and hardened his tone. "I'm not asking you, Megan. I'm telling you."

Angrily shoving back her chair, she strode into his office, casting a wary look behind her to make sure no one had overheard them. He reached around her and shut the door then remained standing next to her.

"Do you think this is wise? I don't feel comfortable coming in here to talk about something personal."

"But you don't want everybody at Char Air overhearing our conversation, either. Just relax."

After his showing up at the parade and now his direct questioning, Megan couldn't ignore his personal interest. He wasn't relenting, and they needed to address it. "Fine. But I feel like you're pushing me to go out with you. And I want you to stop."

"It's nice to know I haven't been talking to a wall. Why won't you go out with me?"

She tilted her head with an exasperated sigh.

"We can just go out as friends, if that's what you want. I'll let you set the parameters. Since you're an expert at setting things."

"It's nothing against you personally. I'm not going to date somebody who's not a Mennonite. And going out with you would just encourage you to hope for more than I can offer."

Chance leaned against his desk and crossed his arms. "Why can't you go out with me as a friend? I'm a Christian. I'm a fun guy. And I'm not asking you to marry me."

His comment brought heat to her face. In her thinking, marriage was the object of dating, not friendship. She'd been brought up to believe that intimacies were saved for marriage. Their thinking was miles apart. Conservative Mennonite couples used dating to test for compatibility because marriage was geared to last a lifetime. The more differences, the less compatible, according to her dad and the Bible verse that was once taped to her visor. Swallowing her embarrassment, she asked, "What if I grew to like you and wanted to marry you?"

He grinned. "I suppose that depended on how nicely you asked me." Instantly angry that he mocked her, Megan wheeled and started toward the door. Chance sprinted after her and snatched her arm. "Wait. I'm sorry. I was just teasing. Why are you a good sport about every other topic, but such a gloom and doom about dating? You're the sunshine of this office. What is it about me that scares you?"

Taking a deep breath, she closed her eyes. When she opened them again, he was staring at her and waiting. "Just you. You frighten me."

"Why?"

"Because I like you. And my only defense against you is myself. You're making this hard for me. I wish you'd just forget about me."

"Look, I give you my word that I won't push you into anything serious. I understand about our differences. Just think how we can learn from each other. Become better people for it. I know you're interested in missions. I could take you to Ecuador. Show you my work there. Maybe we were supposed to meet for a reason. Did you ever think about that? Maybe God wants you to see Ecuador."

His reasoning caught her off guard. It sounded similar to what had just transpired between her and Micah. Was there more to Chance than she had imagined? Was he her door to Ecuador? Had she actually been working against God's will? "That's an interesting idea," she admitted.

"Good." Chance smiled. "So let me take you to lunch. Let's go to your friend's restaurant, and we'll talk more about this."

Megan knew that Lil wouldn't be at Volo Italiano. Chance knew it, too. She considered having lunch with him there. It was private and just around the corner. Maybe if she went with him, he'd quit pressuring her. Maybe he wouldn't even like her. But if they left together and returned together, it would start office talk. "No, not lunch."

"Mr. Campbell?" Megan jolted at the voice that blared over the office intercom and interrupted their conversation.

With an angry huff, Chance stepped to his desk and replied, "Yes?"

Megan recognized the voice of the flight technician and turned to go.

"Whoa," Chance ordered her with an upturned palm. Then to the technician, he replied, "I'll be right there." When he returned to Megan, he softened his voice. "You think about it. Give me a place and a time before you leave the office today. We need to get some things straightened out between us. Otherwise, I don't know how we're going to continue working together." He glanced at his desk calendar, with several rows of large red x's. "We've got more than a month."

Megan's heart tripped. Was he threatening her? Could he even fire her? With an abrupt nod, she left his office. How dare he insinuate that she had to go out with him or else? Paige had jokingly mentioned that if he bothered her it was sexual harassment. Or maybe she had been serious. Had Paige noticed what was happening? And now that Chance knew she believed in nonresistance, he assumed she would never press charges against him. She'd opened herself up to his harassment. Or was it harassment, when he knew how much she liked him?

She stared at her computer screen, wishing Lil wasn't out of the country. If she went to Katy with her concerns, she'd probably advise her to quit her job. Although it might be the advice she needed to hear, Megan wasn't willing to do that.

She considered Randy. Upon his return, he'd set everything right again. But as Chance had reminded her, that was more than a month away. The more she thought about Chance's coercive behavior and his ultimatum, the more determined she was not to go out with him at all. She didn't have to date him. She wouldn't.

If he pressed it, she'd tell Paige. She hated the thought of going to an outsider with her problems, but she didn't think she could admit to her

family or friends just how much she was attracted to Chance. And without that information, they wouldn't really understand her dilemma. If they knew the pressure he was exerting on her, they'd be furious. She'd never met anyone as determined as Chance. Except for Micah.

CHAPTER 12

Megan filled canning jars with Lil's three bean salad recipe, while Barbara Troyer fastened lids and placed the jars inside her seven-quart canner. When the second and final batch was cooking, Barbara invited Megan to sit a spell.

Swiping her forehead, Megan eased into the kitchen chair. "That was fun. The bright colors will look pretty on your pantry shelf."

"What's really fun is that every time I open a jar, I'll remember this morning." Barbara went to her cookie jar and came back with a strawberry-shaped plate containing two peanut butter cookies. "Your mom is blessed. For years I longed for a child." She sighed, going to the refrigerator and returning to the table with two tall glasses of milk. "But it wasn't in God's plan."

"I'm sorry. But maybe that's why you made such a wonderful Bible school teacher."

"We must make the best of our journey."

Megan nibbled on a cookie, savoring the sweetness. "Do you think people's paths cross for specific reasons? Even in one-time situations?" Megan was aware that Barbara possessed a wealth of wisdom where practical life was concerned. And she probably wouldn't ask as many questions as Mom before dishing out advice.

"Proverbs twenty, verse twenty-four says, 'Man's goings are of the Lord.' " Barbara nodded. "I believe God's all knowing and enjoys watching His people interact. There are no accidents with Him. But we can miss opportunities. He certainly doesn't twist our arms."

"Do you think that includes relationships with outsiders?"

"Sure. Remember your friend Katy? Her employer had a big influence on her."

"You're right." Megan knew that Katy's struggle with seeing things as black and white had changed when she found out that God used hymns to bless her employer, the same way He did to bless Katy. It had been eye-opening for Katy to realize that outsiders could be Christians. Chance claimed he was a Christian.

Barbara leaned forward, her eyes lighting with excitement. "It's interesting that you brought up the topic of personal journeys. My sister's into genealogy, and while she was here, she got me interested in it, too. For years she's been doing research about our family roots. Did you know that there's a lot of information in the *Mennonite Encyclopedia*? She also has a Mennonite friend with access to a computer."

Barbara's aged hand whipped through the air. "I don't understand it, but she's able to dig into records. She just mailed me a large envelope full of good information. There are photocopies from family trees that relatives wrote inside their Bibles. There're some wonderful faith stories. And these people were our ancestors. It's humbling and wonderful to think how God works down through the ages. I suppose it's a blink of an eye to Him."

Barbara brushed some crumbs into a neat pile on her tablecloth. "I guess when you get to be my age it's natural to wonder if you fulfilled your life's purpose. It's amazing to read some of the stories of my relatives. How they passed their faith on to the next generation. Someday I'll meet them in heaven. Eli might already have met them. But this must be boring for you."

"Are you kidding? I find it fascinating. And I think it's wonderful that you're doing something new. I'm in a bit of transition myself. And I don't have your experience to lean on."

"Oh?"

"As you know, my two best friends just got married. I'm discovering that what I used to share in confidence now gets passed along to their husbands."

Barbara smiled. "That's true. You're smart to realize it. Discretion is important. There should be a sermon on that." She shook her head. "But I interrupted you. Go on."

Megan sighed, glanced at the hummingbird feeder outside the kitchen window. "Lil's out of the country right now, still adjusting to married life. And Katy's busy with little Jacob. And since I started working, I've got this whole new life and nobody to talk to about it. Of course, I'm the only Mennonite in the whole company. I used to tell my mom everything, but suddenly I find myself holding back, not wanting to worry her. I guess I'm afraid she might be overprotective and want me to quit. But I like my job."

"You can always talk to me. It won't go any farther than these walls."

Barbara's walls were a cheery yellow, a reflection of her personality, and Megan trusted her. Chance's remark popped into her mind, too. *It's nice to know I haven't been talking to a wall.*

"What's your job like?"

Megan told her about the charter flights and described her job. She explained how her boss was on a leave of absence and how her temporary boss had generally upset her job and her life.

"Why is your boss on a leave of absence?"

"See, this is the kind of stuff that would upset Mom. Randy was unfaithful to his wife, and they're trying to work through it, trying to keep their marriage together."

Barbara's eyes widened. "That's a big burden for you to carry. It's hard to be thrust into an outsider's world."

"Katy and Lil know about it, but they don't really understand what I'm going through."

"So you're wondering if God wants you at this job? But you don't really want to hear that He doesn't?"

"No, I'm not questioning my job. I guess I'm struggling with how close to get to my coworkers."

"Aha." Just then the stove's timer went off. "I'm sorry. I need to get that. But I've learned that most often, the answer is inside you; confiding in someone just helps you sort it out." Barbara lifted the cage out of the canner and placed it on a cooling rack. "Beautiful!" she exclaimed.

—⌒⌒

That night for supper, Mom served bean salad that Barbara had sent home with Megan. "My mouth's been watering for that all day."

"It was nice of you to spend time with Barbara," Dad noted.

"I like her. Did you know that she's interested in genealogy?"

Dad cut into his savory round steak, browned and simmered in the skillet, just the way he liked it. "No."

"Her sister got her going on it. I think it's a good thing. Like a puzzle, something to occupy her mind. Do you know much about your ancestry, Dad?"

He glanced across the table at Mom and hesitated. Megan noted that he waited for Mom's nod before he continued. "I do. Some of the relatives have traced our roots all the way back to the old country. In fact, we have a few heroes in our line."

Leaning forward, Megan asked, "What do you mean?"

Dad placed his knife on the edge of the bone-colored dinnerware. "You know the story of Dirk Willems?"

"Sure. I learned about him in college." His story had been documented in *The Martyrs Mirror*. He had been fleeing his pursuers when a beadle fell through a frozen river and was in trouble. Dirk Willems had turned back and saved his persecutor. But the beadle had still taken him into custody, and Dirk was killed for his faith. He was a Mennonite hero. "You're not saying *he's* our relative?" Megan looked from Dad to Mom, who focused more on her meal than the information.

"Yep. It's not the Weavers, but through one of the wives, and his blood is definitely in our line."

"But how can that be if he was martyred?"

Dad chuckled. "You're right. Not his. But the same bloodline."

"I can't believe you never told me this before."

Mom got up to take her plate to the sink. While she had her back turned, Dad jerked his gaze in her direction, and Megan realized that he hadn't talked about it for her mom's sake. Mom was adopted. Dad had been protecting her feelings. Mom never talked much about it. In fact, the times Megan had questioned her, she usually closed the topic swiftly.

Feeling sad that her mom had blanks in her past, Megan gave her dad an understanding nod. She'd always wanted to know more about her roots, even before she knew that Dirk Willems was her ancestor. Just hearing his story bolstered her faith. It was a lot like the missionary stories she loved. But she could tell that her dad had closed the topic. If she wanted to know more, she'd need to ask him in private.

Mom returned to the table. "Dessert? Micah's sermon made me hungry for Jell-O."

"Yes," Dad said. "Speaking of Micah, I have news."

Megan dipped up some of the Jell-O, wishing they'd had cookies instead. She'd need a dollop of whipping cream on hers.

"Our second candidate has declined the invitation to come and check out Big Darby."

"Why?" Mom asked, posing her fork midair.

"He felt God wasn't in it."

Megan's mind raced, wondering what this would mean for Micah. "What now?"

Dad took a drink of water then replied, "The committee talked about going to the third person on our list, but then we changed our minds. Instead, we decided to invite Micah back for a three-month trial."

"How would that work?" Mom asked, glancing nervously at Megan.

"He comes as an interim preacher, and at the end of the three months, the congregation takes a vote to decide if they want him to stay permanently. After the vote, he's given the opportunity to accept or decline."

"So the vote itself, whether it's a strong one or not, could influence his decision?"

"Yes."

Mom fiddled with her Jell-O. "I never thought about the candidates turning us down."

With growing alarm, Megan asked, "Where will he stay?" Although she hoped Micah would get the invitation, she didn't want him living just down her hallway for three entire months.

"The committee assumes he'll stay here."

In frustration, Megan blew air between her lips.

"But your mom told me how he pursued you in college. So I'm not happy about him staying with us."

Megan nodded in agreement. "You didn't tell the committee about it?"

"No. I didn't want to bring that to anybody's attention."

She sank with relief. "Isn't there somebody else on the committee who can house him?"

"Unfortunately not. We haven't discussed it recently, but back at the beginning of our search, our home seemed like the only viable option. Unless we rented a place for him. But I came up with an alternative, if your mother and you agree." He leaned forward, and Megan could read the excitement in his eyes. "You know my shop room? We could fix it up for him. I'm sure we could get some folks to help. It wouldn't need much work. I could suggest it to the committee, saying he might feel more comfortable having his own space for that long of a time."

The room was part of her dad's home mechanic shop. But it was separate from his work area. He used it for storage, and it had plumbing.

Megan made a face. "But it's dirty and gross."

"But we could fix it up." Mom caught the vision. "And afterward, it would be a little guest cottage."

"Have you contacted him?"

"No. I'm going to call him tomorrow. I wanted to check with you both before I took the shop idea back to the committee. So what do my girls think?"

"I'm for it. If Megan doesn't care."

"He gave you no indication that he's still interested in you, right?" Dad asked. "Because if he is, then I'm putting my foot down about him staying here."

"No. He's changed. I'm not afraid of him or anything. I guess it would be all right."

"You'll tell us if he does anything out of line? If it's not working out for you?"

"Of course." She shifted her gaze nervously. She hadn't done that with Chance.

"I want to keep my eye on him," Dad said. "I won't let him bother you."

"Thanks. But what's going to happen with Barbara? Is she going to be able to keep her home?"

"We haven't decided what to do about that yet. The church owns the property, but Brother Troyer always paid his rent on time. If she wants to stay there for a while, it seems sad to remove her."

"Especially for a bachelor," Mom observed. "Micah probably wouldn't be interested in keeping up that big garden." She looked at Megan. "Do you think?"

"I don't know much about his interests. I just hope he doesn't live with us forever."

Dad chuckled. "Don't worry. It won't be forever."

"It'll just seem like it." Mom laughed.

A loud bang interrupted their conversation, causing Megan to flinch and look down the hall. The entry door had blown shut.

"There's a storm coming through. I heard on the prayer chain that the Millers have relatives in Indiana, where there've been some tornado warnings." Mom jumped up. "I'd better close the windows. Even if it doesn't rain, I don't want all that dust blowing in."

Dad stood. "I'll help you, honey."

"I'll get the dishes." Megan cast a worried glance out the kitchen window at a menacing sky, glad they hadn't been forced to the unpleasant storm cellar. She stared at her dad's shop, wondering how Micah's presence would change their lives. Would he take all his meals with them? Be constantly underfoot? She hoped it wasn't a big mistake.

A sudden crack of thunder shook the house, and with it came a sense of foreboding. Strange how two men had invaded her life. The look Chance had given her when she left work on Friday still sent chills down her spine. He'd stopped by her desk to make plans, but she'd grabbed her purse and left him standing there. She'd half expected him to follow her to her car, but he hadn't. Would he seek revenge, or find a new way to wear down her resistance?

CHAPTER 13

When Megan returned to the office Monday morning, she put her purse in her drawer and froze. Resting on top of a stack of paperwork was a two-inch rock that she hadn't put there. And it was heart shaped. She glanced at the door to Chance's office. It was closed. But who else would have put it there?

"Morning," Paige chirped, stopping in front of her desk. "That was some storm on Saturday, wasn't it?"

"I know. It took me a long time to get to sleep."

"The wind knocked down several trees on our street, but our property's fine."

"I don't think it did any damage around us either."

Dangling her empty coffee cup, Paige said, "I guess Indiana had some bad tornados."

"Is there a good kind?" Chance asked, stepping into view. He perched on Megan's desk. "You told me that your church helps out after natural disasters. Will they be going to Indiana?"

"I'm sure MDS will send someone."

"What's MDS, honey?" Paige asked, running her finger over the smooth surface of the mysterious heart rock on Megan's desk.

Feeling the heat rise to her face, Megan replied, "Mennonite Disaster Service. They organize volunteers to go in after natural disasters and clean up, repair, and rebuild."

Then Paige asked Chance, "You think this will affect us?"

"Let's make it affect us. I'll get on the phone and see what I can find out. You have time to drum up some donations if I can put together some extra flights?"

"I'll make time just as soon as I get my coffee." Paige gave Megan a wink and started toward the coffee room.

"You have the number for MDS?" Chance asked Megan.

"I'll find it. I know a little about them. I considered applying for a job there, but there wasn't anything local." Randy had never gotten involved with them, but then he hadn't been as motivated in that area as Chance. Mostly Randy handled what charitable opportunities came to him without seeking anything out. But since Chance had arrived, the entire staff had become more charity-minded. Even Paige's enthusiasm was contagious.

"They don't have anything local?"

"Oh, they do. But they work out of Pennsylvania and cover the country in zones." She waved her hand. "It doesn't matter. I'll find the number."

"Good." Chance rose and started toward the door that led out to the hangars.

Megan hesitated, then asked softly, "Chance?"

He paused. "Yeah?"

"Did you put this rock on my desk?"

He came back and whispered, "I can set my heart, too. I put it on your desk. It's to remind you that I won't ask for more than you can give. Just friendship."

As he walked away, Megan felt a lump in her throat. How sweet. He was definitely not firing her. She booted her computer to search for a phone number for MDS at its headquarters in Lititz, Pennsylvania.

Before the office closed at five, Chance had set up three flights that would help with the Indiana tornado disaster. Two would carry MDS volunteers and a third would take in supplies that Paige was rounding up from their own donors. They had also arranged for a press team that would help promote Char Air. And by Friday, two more flights had been arranged. One carrying supplies was scheduled for Saturday, and Chance was going to pilot it.

"I wish you'd go along, Megan. It's your people. And the invitation was given to everyone in the office. Since it's a weekend flight, nobody sees this as a personal thing. It's been a group effort."

But Megan sensed that it was personal. She knew that Chance was motivated to help others, but he'd also made it personal by contacting MDS. He'd opened the door for her, given her a perfect opportunity to get involved, and she wanted to be on that Saturday flight. But she'd had to turn it down because of what was going to happen at her house over the weekend.

"I'd really like to go; it's just that I have an obligation this weekend. I'm expected to do my part because other members of the congregation are coming to help. It wouldn't look good, if all the family wasn't there pitching in with the others."

"But he's not just your preacher. The congregation should do the work. He'll be staying at your house, after all."

"Yes, but it's our property that's getting remodeled. We will benefit from it in the long run, after Micah's gone. It's hard. They're both good projects. But my dad always says God wants you to take care of your family and your own obligations first, and then you reach out generously to others."

Chance arched his brow in disapproval. It sounded rather selfish in Megan's own ears, something was missing from the way her dad always said it. "It's like a circle. You start giving in the core, your family and church, and then it ripples outward."

"That's a different concept for me. My job puts me in direct contact with strangers, one on one, helping the least likely."

"But you came to Ohio to help your brother."

Chance shrugged in acquiescence.

"Now that we have this connection with MDS, I'm sure I'll have other opportunities. But I'm glad that you get to take a plane up on Saturday. I know how you've been missing it. You must be excited."

"I am, and it's your loss, Megan. Just like the Aucas."

Straightening her desk to leave for the day, she ignored his dig because she'd come to realize that he would say anything, no matter how hurtful, if he thought it would persuade her to act according to his wishes. "I admire what you're doing for Char Air." Picking up her purse, she asked, "Have you heard from Randy? How it's going for him?"

"At this point, he still doesn't know if his marriage is salvageable. Tina is bitter. They're having a rough time of it. I hope for the boys' sake that they don't give up."

"I'm sorry to hear that. Have a good trip. I'll see you on Monday."

—⁂—

Chance watched Megan depart then went to his office and shut the door, sinking into his chair with frustration. The woman's will was indomitable. An admirable trait when pressing through a jungle trail, not so excellent when she used it against his advances. Everything he had tried to win her over had failed. She was even becoming immune to his stories, had hardly flinched when he'd told her about the time that he'd spent the night in a tree fending off some crocodiles. And when he'd told her that the green anaconda could reach twenty-nine feet and weigh five hundred pounds and that they had eyes on the top of their heads so they could hunt submerged, she'd asked him if he thought they might be the leviathan sea monster mentioned in the Bible. He'd told her that he wasn't making up some Loch Ness monster, that they were real and sometimes they even ate jaguars. But that hadn't impressed her, either. She'd shaken her head as if she didn't believe him.

It was driving him bananas, and he couldn't get her out of his mind. She'd ruined him now because he didn't even look forward to returning to Ecuador if he had to return without her.

He'd gotten so used to her assistance, her companionship, her sunny smile, and especially her throaty accent. And even though she kept rejecting his overtures, he knew that she possessed a heart that yearned for adventure. He was the man to help her with that.

Chance spent more hours than he cared to admit daydreaming about her being beside him as he flew the sick to Hospital Vozandeson, befriending the missionaries that he transported, making his hovel a home. He could envision her grabbing hold of that life. She'd be wonderful in the field.

If only her family hadn't been occupied with their renovations for that preacher candidate, he was sure she would have gone with him on Saturday. The trip involved her people. And once he got her up in the air and she experienced the satisfaction that came from helping others and the camaraderie of working together, she would understand what motivated him. Realize that he was the man for her. How could anyone recognize the call and not give in to it? It was the fuel in his veins. And he believed that Megan had the same desire for the adventuresome yet simple and practical lifestyle.

Chance had always done what he thought was right. He'd helped his country, and now he was helping others. Surely God had fashioned Megan just for him. Although he'd been a bit of a womanizer, he'd settled down some. He even saw God's sense of humor in handpicking a little Mennonite maiden, prim and proper. But he loved the idea. He didn't care if she wore that net cap. Missionaries came in all flavors. Nothing seemed peculiar in the field where the cosmetics were most often left behind, anyway. In the field, things got real. He was willing to let her keep her identify. He just needed to prove himself to her.

He picked up his stapler, felt the instrument's prickly edge. And if he was willing to accept her, then surely she'd accept him even though they had a few minor differences. Well, major. Especially the one he'd been hiding. Ever since she told him that Mennonites were nonresistant, he'd done some research. He'd discovered that they were adamant against war. If Megan knew that he'd been a fighter pilot, he wouldn't stand a chance with her. If she knew about that mission that earned him a medal, it would be over. That's why he hadn't told her. That was better left concealed until the past was so far behind them that it didn't matter.

But the hourglass was losing sand. If she didn't spend time with him soon, she'd never see his heart, and if she didn't understand his motivations, she would never give him a chance. He replaced the stapler and pulled the red marker out of his drawer. He drew a big red x over the day's date. Only now, he wasn't marking off the time from boredom, but from worrying about the remaining days. So little time was left.

CHAPTER 14

At 6:00 a.m. the sound of Jake Byler's hammer resounded through the air, and the workday began. As Megan set up the coffee table near her dad's shop, she quietly observed the man who had captured her friend Katy's heart, long before Katy had even been old enough to date. The way he handled his tools made them appear to be an extension of his body, all performing together like a well-oiled machine.

"Katy said to tell you that she'll be over after Jacob's breakfast."

"Good. Help yourself to some coffee, and tell the others."

Dad passed by her with a two-by-four slung over his shoulder. "I'm too old for this." He grinned.

"Hardly," Megan replied. "But you might be sore tomorrow."

"Mark's here," Dad told Jake.

Mark Kraybill worked for Jake in the carpentry business. He had a wife and a young son. Megan watched him get out of his truck and don his tool bag. Next he grabbed a tray and headed toward her. "Lanie didn't think she'd be much use today, with running after the baby, but she sent these."

Megan's sweet tooth drooled as she carried the tray of pastries laden with thick penuche frosting. As she placed them beside the coffee, her mom pointed at the sky.

"I don't like the looks of this."

"You think we should set up the coffee inside?"

"Nobody will quit their work to come inside the house for breakfast, especially if rain cuts them off from the house."

Megan glanced toward Dad's shop. But they'd already discussed that option and decided there wasn't enough room inside it to set up the food table.

"No. I don't think it will rain that soon. But from what I understand, lots of donations and furniture will be arriving. We can't just set them around on the lawn and let them get ruined."

"But Dad's got a car inside, and you know how fussy he is about people getting too close to his cars."

"Bill!" Mom called as he made another pass with some lumber. "We need to talk."

"Let me take this to Jake. I'll be right back." But Mom trailed him to the shop's open garage door. He laid the lumber on top of a growing pile. "Something wrong?"

"It's going to rain. My arthritis is acting up. I'm sure of it."

Dad sighed, looked around his shop, his gaze lingering over Chuck Benedict's Nova. While Dad worked on various models at a Chevrolet dealership, on the side he restored only Novas. It was something he did for fun. "I don't like the idea of parking Chuck's car out front. I promised him it would always be protected inside. Anyway, we're going to need our entire driveway for parking." Torn, he looked at the Nova with concern. "It's Chuck's pride and joy, Anita."

"It's drivable?" Megan asked.

Dad nodded.

"Let's take it over to the doddy house. Lil and Fletch are gone, and the Millers have that new carport. It's big enough, and I'm sure they won't mind."

"All right. Let me get a car cover, too. Anita, tell Jake I'll be right back. Megan, run me over?"

"Sure, Dad."

By the time they had returned from the doddy house, Dad's shop looked like one of those garage sales Mom loved, or even a mini relief sale that the Mennonites were always holding. This one would contain mechanic tools and country furnishings. Mom gave Dad a quick hug, assuring him they had done the right thing.

"This is a lot of stuff," Megan said with disbelief. "And it's still early. Don't you think we should leave Micah some space for his own belongings? His room's not very big. If he's going to be here for three months, won't he bring his own things?"

"He'll just have to make do. There's no telling what he'll need. We can't turn down some donations and not others."

"But he owns a house. His grandmother's house, where he's lived for years. Surely he has everything he'll need. And he's driving so he can bring his own stuff."

"But everybody wants to chip in, so. . ." Mom shrugged. "Wait and see. It will work out."

"I guess." Megan wasn't sure why she was objecting to the congregation's generosity. She lowered her voice. "But what about afterward? Will we keep all this stuff?"

Once again, Mom shrugged. "Look. There's Katy. Why don't you bring her inside, and we'll start working on lunch? Yesterday Rose Landis brought over a pork roast, and I need to get it into the oven. The men will be hungry by noon."

Megan helped Katy get Jacob out of the car.

"I think the little outside apartment is a great idea." Katy grabbed her diaper bag. "Are your folks doing that because of, you know?"

Megan nodded. "I'm embarrassed. I'm sure I overreacted. From what I could tell while he was here, Micah's not as awful as I remembered him."

Katy chuckled. "I hope not. He's going to be our preacher. When he preached the other Sunday, I couldn't figure out why you called him Stick Man. He's not much thinner than Jake." She tilted her head. "Probably taller though."

Megan felt her cheeks heat. "He's put on weight since college."

"I think you're off the hook anyway, because from what I heard, it was Joy Ann Beitzel's dad who insisted the committee give him a chance instead of going down the list to the next candidate."

"But Barry Beitzel's not even on the committee. How did he know that the other candidate had backed out?"

"Because Joy Ann's the church secretary. And without a preacher, she's handling some of the paperwork for the committee."

"That's right. She told me she thought he was cute, but that takes some nerve to get her dad to go to the committee and make a request like that."

"Exactly. But from what I hear, she's not the only one interested in your castoff."

"Shh!" Megan reached for Jacob. "Watch what you say."

Katy handed her the baby and lowered her voice. "He's got the attention of every other single woman in the congregation."

"Even after his allergy attack?"

"Yep. So like I said, you're off the hook."

"I have a feeling things are going to get interesting around here."

Before Katy left for little Jacob's nap, Jake and a few helpers had installed a door that would keep the shop's gas fumes out of the new room. They also erected some walls: one partitioned off a bathroom, and one formed a closet. The carpenters had even cut a hole in an exterior wall for a new window. They'd sent one of the men to purchase a window after Jake claimed they needed to be up to code, since there was no exterior door. The fire that broke out in the fellowship hall a few years earlier was still fresh on everybody's mind.

Megan stood at Katy's car. "That window was a good idea. It makes it more like a home. You gotta be proud of Jake."

Katy winked. "More than proud. Can you believe that Jake's general contractor, who doesn't even go to church, donated the insulation and dry wall?"

"He must think a lot of Jake." Megan looked at the sky. "You'd better scat before the storm hits."

Afterward Megan didn't think Katy could have made it home in time, because soon after her departure, the sky opened and the clouds dumped their rain. The yard became soup, and everybody started looking like wet noodles. Especially the women. Susanna burst into the house all aghast and shaking the rain off her clothing while deeming Megan her messenger and errand girl.

Sometime during the day, Mom started calling the new room the blue cottage, and it caught on. At first Megan figured it had something to do with her dad's nickname. But when Susanna sent her out into the storm to find a man to move Mom's sewing machine into the living room, Megan got her first look at the brightly colored walls. The hideous blue paint was leftover from Leon Beachy's latest job. He had admitted, sheepishly, that after he'd bought the paint and done a three-foot wall sample, the customer had changed their mind. He'd laughed, saying he hoped it didn't make the preacher change his mind, too. But it was free. Megan was learning a lot about accepting donations with a grateful heart.

Besides Mom's sewing machine, the quilters brought portable ones that Leon Beachy toted through the storm and set up in the Weavers' living room.

Susanna seemed pleased. She tilted her pretty face with its beak-shaped nose. "Now Megan, don't you just love this material? We're gonna make Brother Zimmerman's curtains. It's the fabric we bought the day that Barbara went with us, the day Brother Troyer passed away in the bean patch. Don't you think that's fitting?"

Megan thought it more ironic than fitting. "It's very nice. I'll just go after that thread you need."

By the end of the afternoon, Susanna had frustrated everyone with her flapping, controlling ways, and Megan vowed never to become a quilter. Susanna had even aggravated Jake when she'd made him lower the curtain rod an inch and a half after he'd used a tape and level.

The singles had shown up and were mostly underfoot as Megan tried to keep everybody happy. Lori Longacre, the librarian with the cute mole on her nose, had brought a few books that she thought would add a welcoming touch. There was personal flowery stationery with it.

"Just a note that explains when the books need to be returned to the library," Lori insisted.

But when Lori took her umbrella and headed outside to see the blue cottage, Megan sneaked a look inside the pretty folded stationery:

I hope I can help you, when it comes to reading material and research books for your sermons. I'm friends with the Plain City librarian, too. Just give me a topic, and I'll be happy to give you a hand. Really, it's no trouble. I look forward to it. Here's my phone number.

"Denim's on sale at the discount fabric store."

Megan jerked her hand away from the stationery and wheeled around. Ruthie Ropp stood watching her. "It is?"

Ruthie eyed her curiously. "Yes. At $3.99 a yard, that's a steal."

"Maybe you should tell Barbara."

"I'll do that." Ruthie left, but she gave Megan a look that let her know she'd caught her reading Lori's note. Ruthie was an expert on denim, owned an entire wardrobe of jean skirts made from the same pattern. She used her sewing expertise to make each one appear a little different. Ruthie had brought a hand-sewn comforter for the preacher's twin bed.

Back at the sewing machines, Ruthie joked that it was out of her hope chest, but since there wasn't much hope left in it, she was ready to part with it.

But Ruthie's friend Joy Ann, the church secretary who was ultimately responsible for Micah's internship, scoffed, "You couldn't get the lid closed on your hope chest anymore. Now that you're such an expert seamstress, you wanted to replace some of the older stuff with new."

Ruthie met Joy Ann's gaze with defiance. "I wouldn't dream of giving the preacher an inferior item."

But all three of the singles had been able to agree on one important factor. They'd been adamant about the need to put a small refrigerator in the preacher's apartment.

At first Mom objected, claiming he'd be welcome to join them at their family meals. That had agitated the singles, giving Megan her first real indication that she'd need to be very careful not to provoke jealousy. They already assumed she'd have certain privileges that they didn't share.

Mom insisted, "I always cook anyways, and I don't intend to banish Brother Micah from the house."

Megan gave her mom the gentle elbow, their signal that Mom was missing something.

She let it go. "I suppose you're right. Folks will want to gift the preacher with food to show their hospitality. I shouldn't be the only one who gets the pleasure of cooking for him." Later she whispered to Megan, "From the looks of things, it's good you didn't set your cap for the preacher. Not that you wouldn't stand a chance, but because you might lose a few friends."

Although watching the singles had been amusing, Megan knew her mom was joking, stretching the matter out of proportion. There was no way that Micah could initiate such a stir. "That's the least of your worries, Mom."

"I don't know. He's a good catch."

Megan glanced at her mom skeptically. "But you hardly know him."

"Maybe not, but I know men like him. Good men."

The singles agreed with Mom because once they were gone, Ruthie's dad returned with a tiny used refrigerator strapped in the bed of his 1980 Ford truck. It almost made Megan feel sorry for Micah. *When a girl's dad got involved*— But Megan broke off her thought. Maybe Micah would be open to the local girls. Maybe he'd be ready to settle down and take a wife. It would be interesting to watch, only she had this awful feeling that just like Susanna was moving in on Barbara, the singles were going to move in on her space. They'd want to include Megan in their circle so that they could find out more about Micah, even control her a bit. And while Megan sat with them in church, she wasn't ready to officially join the group.

At the end of the day when Megan and her parents stood and looked over the work, they were satisfied. The blue cottage was packed with furniture and extra linens and toiletries. Noah Maust, the professor, had furnished a desk and a lamp.

"I guess it's the Lord's room now," Dad said.

Mom sighed. "It's exciting to think about the guests He might send our way."

Megan glanced at her dad. "It's still your room, too."

"I know. I'm all right with it. It was my idea." He smiled. "I guess if the Lord sees fit to keep it filled with guests, to give it another purpose, then maybe I'll have to add on the back of the shop."

Mom smiled. "Yes, you can always do that, honey. There's leftover cake inside that Inez Beachy sent. Anyone hungry?"

"I'm always hungry." Dad moved to shut off the professor's lamp.

CHAPTER 15

He's here!" Mom exclaimed just before the sound of cracking gravel wafted through the open living room window.

Megan set her Christian novel aside on the garage-sale coffee table and followed her mom to the window, keeping discreetly to the shadows of the opened drapery.

The grandfather clock, one of Dad's family heirlooms, chimed twice, and he chuckled. "Good. He's punctual. When I called to tell him about the blue cottage and its furnishings, he calculated that he'd arrive mid-afternoon.

But Mom wasn't listening to him. She'd already opened the screen door and stepped onto the front porch.

"She's in her heights of glory," Dad told Megan with a chuckle. "Loves to entertain."

Megan and her dad followed Mom outside, where the tall, lanky guest was unfolding himself from a dark blue Honda Civic. She exchanged a smile with Dad, who appreciated the irony of such a big man in a small car. That was probably a strike against him in Dad's estimation, but then Micah had surely gained it back when he'd gotten the color right.

Micah's eyes looked a tad road weary, yet radiant. Excited. And Megan felt a tug of happiness for him and his adventure. She believed her mom was feeling the thrill of his adventure, too. Mom gave him a hug, and Megan watched Micah's forearm harden when Dad grasped his hand and cranked it like a wrench.

"Hi." Megan stood back, keeping her hands to her side, and gave him a warm smile.

He held her smile a moment with a matching one. "I can't wait to see the little cottage."

"We call it the blue cottage. You'll soon see why. Come." Mom motioned.

"I should get Miss Purrty out of the car first." Micah's voice trailed off as if speaking to himself. "I hope she doesn't take a notion to run away."

Many things ran through Megan's mind, and she was positive her parents were just as surprised and confused to discover that Micah had a Miss Purrty with him. The three of them instinctively backed away from the car as Micah strode around the back and lifted the hatchback. With a few grunts and some shuffling of belongings, he soon backed out, holding a small, gray animal crate in his hand.

Curious, Megan tried without success to see through the air slats. Micah turned, looking sheepish. "I didn't have any place to keep her. I inherited her. She was my grandmother's favorite cat." Though his face reddened slightly, his voice never wavered, giving the impression that the cat was not an option.

The look on Mom's face indicated that she hoped the cat would wander off and get lost. Mom was pretty persnickety with keeping the house and yard clean. They'd never had any pets, mostly because of Megan's allergies. But now Megan was thankful they'd fixed up the room for the new preacher, because honestly, the last thing she needed in the house was a cat. Of all things.

She wouldn't bring up her objections, though, because she sensed that her parents both harbored plenty of their own. Dad didn't like cats because they jumped up on cars and scratched the paint. And he was into restoring, not scratching. She cast him a tentative glance and saw his eyes widening in undisguised disapproval.

She was sure that Micah saw it, too, because she caught a glimpse of the preacher's doggedness that he had employed so readily at college. Something in the set of his chin and the way he straightened his shoulders.

"Go ahead. Lead the way." His voice was set in defiance, as if there wasn't anything unusual about showing up with an uninvited pet. The way he urged them to lead the way made it sound as if he was inviting them to join him on his great adventure.

When nobody moved, Megan stepped forward. "This way. It's attached to the shop, but you have to go inside the shop to get to it." She found herself babbling, trying to cover the noise of her mom whispering to her dad, most likely trying to calm him from the terrible news that a cat would be prowling around in his sacred shop.

But when she ran out of small talk, her dad's comment was easily heard. "I wonder if Barbara likes cats?"

"Who's Barbara?" Micah whispered through the side of his mouth.

"Brother Troyer's widow," Megan replied.

She saw Micah's shoulders grow more rigid, but he didn't back down, just kept carrying his grandma's cat toward the cottage. Somehow Megan knew that once that carrier was inside the blue cottage, they'd all be bested. There'd be no way Micah was going to budge.

When they reached the shop, Dad riffled through his pockets and came out with a key. "You'll need this. I made an extra. Here's a church key, too." It also worked the lock of a side door, several feet from the overhead garage door that worked with an automatic opener. "Sorry, but there probably won't be any room inside for your car."

"That's not a problem," Micah assured him, accepting the keys and placing them in his pants pocket, while with the other hand, he clamped tight to the pet carrier's handle.

Dad opened the door for them and flipped the switch. A blast of overhead light from the rows of fluorescents filled the room.

"Too bad we don't have a dimmer light of some sort for Micah to use before he gets to his cottage. That could be quite startling at night," Mom noted.

Dad sent her an undeniable dirty look, obviously having reached his limits. "It hasn't blinded me yet."

"It's just temporary," Micah quickly reminded Mom.

She gave a reluctant nod and motioned him to enter the room first.

The moment Micah stepped into the blue room, his face lit with delight. Then a low chuckle rumbled his throat. "Now I know why you call it the blue cottage."

"Leon Beachy's a painter by trade," Megan explained. "He showed up with the paint. Said it's called Something Blue. I'm not sure what the *something* stands for, 'cause I can't think of another thing this color. Hopefully, you can get used to it."

"Actually, it's perfect. It will keep me awake when I need to work on my sermons." Micah placed the crate in the middle of the room. The cat had yet to make a sound or make any kind of an appearance. But Megan thought she caught a glimpse of yellow. Then he turned and gripped Dad's arm. "I won't forget your kindness. I'll do my best to be a good neighbor."

"I'm sure you will," Dad replied, the annoyance already gone from his voice, and his natural good humor returning. "I hope you can work us up some good sermons in here. I, for one, need them."

Megan saw Dad relax a bit and held her breath, wondering if he was going to let Micah get away without setting some boundaries for the cat. Wondering if she should forewarn Micah if he didn't.

"Are you hungry or thirsty?" Mom asked. She also had let go of any irritation toward the cat. "There's some iced tea in your little refrigerator. We expect you to take your meals with us, but the congregation insisted you own a refrigerator so that they could gift you with food, too. I told you that you'd never go hungry."

Micah glanced at the little white frig and the tray of dishes and glasses on top of it. "I remember. I picked up a water bottle in Plain City, though, so I'm fine. I'd like to get the unpacking done and then spend some time on tomorrow's sermon."

"Of course. We'll help you bring things in from the car," she insisted.

At the Honda, he handed some clothing to Mom and a taped cardboard box to Dad. As soon as they were out of earshot, he turned to Megan. "Can you do me a favor?"

"Sure."

"There's a leash on top of Miss Purrty's cage. Can you attach it to her collar and walk her out back some place away from your parents? I don't think I can let her loose yet, and she probably needs to, you know."

Megan stifled her surprise that he'd drawn her into his predicament

114

as an accomplice again. So quickly, he depended on her. Only, she was allergic to cats. Actually, she couldn't believe that Micah wasn't also. But she saw a glint of desperation in his eyes and agreed, this one time. "She won't scratch me then?"

"She's really old. You'll be fine."

Megan grabbed some dress shirts on hangers, feeling a little strange to be carrying his personal items, and headed back to the blue cottage. Micah followed her with what appeared to be a small, wheeled file cabinet. It didn't roll in the gravel, and he ended up carrying the awkward piece. Inside the blue cottage, she fiddled with the clothes in his closet until her parents left to get another armful from the car.

Quickly, she attached the leash to Miss Purrty's collar. She'd never seen a cat walked on a leash before. She soon discovered she wouldn't see it then, either, because the large golden cat balked the moment she got her freedom. Miss Purrty gave a soft hiss and lay down, whipping her tail from side to side.

"Oh, no you don't, missy." Megan gave the leash a tug. The cat gave a sharp mew and looked at her through dark-slit pupils but didn't move. With a sigh, she petted the cat on the head, scratched behind the ears long enough to make friends, then scooped Miss Purrty up and made a dash through the shop toward the back of the property.

Megan looked around their property, figuring the cat would need a place to dig and bury. She didn't want to train her to dig up her mom's flower beds or small vegetable garden. She decided for the old buckeye tree. Nothing grew beneath it except weeds and mushrooms. It was the only bad spot on the property. Mom couldn't even get bulbs to live under that tree.

Megan set Miss Purrty down, and the old cat arched her back and stretched; then in her own timing, Miss Purrty started to sniff and explore. She turned and batted at the leash once, then made the right decision to just ignore it. By the time the cat was finished, Megan had determined that Miss Purrty no longer possessed good digging skills and hoped Micah would clean up after her. Suddenly the cat loped back toward the shop. Pulling against the leash, she continued past the shop toward Micah. Since Megan didn't want to break the cat's neck or get scratched trying to pick her up again, she allowed the behavior.

Micah stopped, and Miss Purrty leaned against his legs, weaving in and out and mewing. He reached down and tickled the white fluff of her neck. "Thanks. If you don't mind, just put her back in her crate for now."

Megan nodded and took the pacified cat, who stared at her with green eyes. By the time she had finished her task, the last of Micah's belongings had been deposited inside the room.

"Well," Mom said with satisfaction, "supper will be at six. Just come on up to the house when you're ready."

"Thanks."

"I'm grilling hamburgers, and Anita makes a fierce potato salad," Dad said, giving Mom an appreciate gaze.

"Great."

And then Megan began her sneezing spree. She gave a little wave and joined her parents, brushing cat hair off her blouse as she went.

*

"Whew." Micah blew out a relieved sigh. "That was tense." He released Miss Purrty from her crate. She walked stiffly and held her head as if miffed. "You didn't make a real good first impression, missy. But they didn't kick you out. Not yet anyway. And lucky for you, I don't believe they have any dogs around the place."

Miss Purrty was not Micah's idea of a pet; he'd never liked cats because he was allergic to them. But this big yellow tabby had been his grandma's baby. And when she had died, she had made him promise to take care of her cat. Just as he'd insinuated to Bill, Micah did it for her. The cat wasn't debatable.

But the cat was a bother because Micah had to bathe her weekly in order to survive around her. To him, washing the cat was like foot washing, a humbling thing you did—not because you enjoyed it, but because Jesus had set the example when He had washed his disciples' feet at the Last Supper. It was something he could do in remembrance of his sweet grandma.

And he'd given the cat a bath right before he'd left, but Megan had still sneezed. Maybe he was getting some kind of immunity to the cat, because the last time he'd been here, he'd discovered that he and Megan were pretty much on the same page—when it came to allergies. That fact and the memory of how she'd whipped out her EpiPen to save his life when nobody else knew what to do formed a sense of solidarity between them.

He moved around, inspecting the small cottage that would be his home for the next three months. He'd been speaking his mind when he told Bill it was perfect. The three-month interim had been an unexpected offer. At first it was less than he'd hoped for, but given the circumstances, it was an appropriate step. Even if he didn't get a permanent position, it would be a learning experience.

And he'd been exceptionally grateful to hear about the little cottage. He wouldn't want to continue on as a guest inside Megan's home, sharing her hairspray for pity's sake. But thanks to her goading, he had learned how to master his hair. He'd used her hairspray mostly to spite her, but it had proved useful.

He stuck his head inside the bathroom and drew back the glass shower door that appeared to be brand new. He grinned, thinking how nice it would work when he gave Miss Purrty a bath. A shower curtain wouldn't have been able to contain her. Bath time was when she recouped all her youthful vigor and ricocheted off the walls like a wet cat-ball. It took her the rest of the week to recover from the ordeal, and by then it was time to repeat the dreaded process all over again.

He opened the medicine cabinet and noticed more storage beneath the sink beside a stack of Anita's fluffy white towels. It reminded him of the pillow incident the last time, the incident that had finally broken the ice with Megan. Yep, he had a great setup with this little cottage. It afforded privacy while he could still take his meals inside and explore whatever it was he felt for Megan.

He went back into the main room. His gaze shifted to the door, which also appeared to be brand new. Just to the right of the door was a beautiful rolltop desk and a lamp with a beaded string. He dragged his wheeled, plastic file cabinet over and found it fit in the corner next to the desk.

The adjacent wall had a twin bed with a spindled wood headboard. He was pleased with the simple, utilitarian style. Although the room carried obvious feminine touches, it wasn't filled with dried flowers and doilies like his own home had been. After his grandma's death, he'd hauled most of that old-fashioned feminine stuff to store in her bedroom, never taking over the master for himself.

Unmatched, medium-sized dressers flanked either side of the small bed instead of nightstands and covered the expanse of the wall. It was disproportionate but practical, yet he would have been willing to give up some storage in exchange for a larger bed. His gaze traveled back to the dresser on the left, which had raised panel drawers with loop bail handles on back plates. The dresser on the right was more decorative with an attached mirror.

Turning the corner brought him to the closet. Its sliding doors glided almost effortlessly. One half of the closet had high-low rods for clothing and was already holding his dress clothes, and the other half had built-in shelving. Nice. Beside it was the entrance to the bathroom, which he'd already explored. And in the small wall in the corner was the little refrigerator. Above it was a hat rack. He smiled to see that it already held a checkered tea towel and a black umbrella with a wooden handle.

Pivoting on his heels, he noticed that the wall opposite the bed had a window with brown paisley curtains. A small table stood directly beneath the window. On top of it were several books. Two small, stenciled, Pennsylvania Dutch chests served as bookends. They felt heavy. Then he saw the flowery stationery. He read the message with a smile, unable to place the librarian from his last visit. He'd have to get out his cheat sheet. He wondered if the tiny chests came from her home.

He carried the pet carrier over and stashed it neatly beneath the library table. "Good fit. There's your bed. And when you aren't sleeping, you can sit up here and look out the window." He cleared a space by moving the books to the dresser closest to the desk. Looking out the window was Miss Purrty's favorite pastime.

On either side of her new nest were mismatched, upholstered wing chairs. The more comfortable-looking one had a matching footstool. A floor lamp stood between the comfortable chair and the door. That would be the light he used when he entered the cottage. He couldn't think of a thing that was missing. Unless. . . His eyes scanned the room again, and he found what he was looking for on the dresser with the mirror. Five o'clock already. He needed to quit dawdling.

Grabbing a stack of clothing and heading for the closet, he said, "We can be comfortable here, missy, so don't get your dander up and get us in any trouble."

The cat walked over to her crate, poked her head beneath the table, and sniffed. Then she lifted her queenly head and jumped up onto the chair without the stool. She curled into a ball and started her motor.

"Well, at least you didn't pick the chair I wanted," Micah said, knowing from experience that aside from the weekly bath, that cat always got her way.

CHAPTER 16

After dressing in a pink shirtdress with tiny pale flowers and donning a new pair of black stockings and her Sunday shoes, Megan took pains with her hair, making sure it was smooth and tidy. She got a freshly ironed covering that she hadn't worn before, even on Sundays. She wasn't doing it for Micah, exactly. But she knew that people would be paying more attention to her family just because the preacher was staying at their place. This wouldn't be one of those Sundays when you slipped in and out without any notice. The congregation would be expecting the Weavers to make a good representation of the entire body of worshippers. Everybody would probably try to put their best foot forward.

She hadn't seen anything more of Micah since their quick supper. He'd been in a hurry to get back to his room, settle in, and work on his sermon. Mom had sent him a plate of leftover pastries that she'd frozen after the workday, and his Honda was already gone by the time the Weavers left for church.

Inside the Big Darby church, Megan stepped into the lobby, jammed full because Micah stood at the entrance to the auditorium. The line to greet him moved slowly, backing up into the lobby. She wondered if church would even start on time. Their congregation was used to Brother Troyer's ability to watch the clock and keep to the required schedule. Running overtime could burn roasts and cut into afternoon naps.

Inez Beachy placed a hand on Megan's shoulder. "Good morning. I hear the preacher's apartment turned out real good."

"Yes, and your husband's paint sure brightened up the place."

Inez chuckled. "He said it was awful—not befitting a preacher—but that it would have to do."

"Brother Micah didn't mind. He said it would keep him awake while he worked on his sermons."

Laughing, Inez replied, "Sounds like he's a man with a thankful heart." Megan took a few steps forward. "I would have come to help, but my arthritis rears up when it rains."

"I'm sorry to hear that. My mom's does that, too."

"She's too young to suffer like that, poor dear."

Megan found herself suddenly facing Micah. She placed her hand in his, and he gave it a firm but clammy handshake, then released it and ran a finger along the inside of his white shirt collar which stood above his dark collarless suit coat. "Megan. Nice to see a familiar face."

Noticing the red welts on his neck, she whispered, "You all right?"

He leaned close, "Just a little itchy."

"You ever get an EpiPen?"

"No. And don't get any ideas. Those things cause a terrible headache."

"All right. But just say the word."

"Now don't go telling this good man how to preach his sermons," Inez chided good-naturedly. "And move along, dear. You're holding up the line."

Megan buttoned her lips and stepped into the main auditorium. As she moved down the center aisle, Joy Ann waved. Cringing, Megan didn't like that Joy Ann was sitting fourth row from the front, up several rows from their normal pew. Instinctively, she shied away from the front pew; being toward the back of a line was the neighborly thing to do. But if Megan didn't go and sit with her, Joy Ann would keep waving and draw everybody's attention. Megan saw her life transitioning in ways she didn't like. She didn't want Micah to think she was a permanent member of the singles' group.

On the other hand, if he did require a shot from her EpiPen, she'd be close enough to pass it up to him. Hopefully he could administer it himself. If he didn't allow himself to get so far gone, and surely he wouldn't if he was standing in front of the entire congregation.

Settling her mind, she lifted her chin to a royal position and moved quickly down the center aisle. The women had spruced up their men, and Megan caught distinct whiffs of shoe polish and discount store aftershave.

She could understand how, as church secretary, Joy Ann would be inquisitive about the preacher. Megan certainly knew what it was like to have a new boss. She probably wouldn't have thought twice about it if Joy Ann hadn't asked her dad to persuade the search committee to give Micah this opportunity.

"Hi." Megan sat and smoothed her skirt. "Why so close to the front?"

"Are you kidding? Without a platform, I have to sit close to see." Joy was a short woman. Brother Troyer never wanted to elevate himself above his parishioners. It was true that sometimes it was hard for everyone to see the preacher.

"But"—Megan caught herself almost calling Micah by his first name, a practice she would have to amend—"Brother Micah's pretty tall. I think everybody will be able to see him."

Just as the minute hand reached the top of the hour, Micah strode past Megan's left side to the front of the congregation. "Good morning," he said and gave his collar a tug. "It's my fault we still have people in the vestibule. Just goes to show how friendly this church is. Let's have a song while everybody gets settled." Micah sat down on the front pew, and a red-faced song leader hurried to the front. It was obvious he hadn't prepared for the extra song and didn't appreciate being put on the spot.

They sang a hymn from memory, and then the service took the usual order of things. When Micah moved behind the pulpit again, the congregation hushed. He cleared his blotchy throat. "First, I want to thank everybody for inviting me to be your interim preacher and for allowing us time to get to know each other. I think it's a perfect plan. And I also thank you for the little cottage at the Weavers' place. I hear that a lot of people chipped in and made donations. It'll make a wonderful home for me and Miss Purrty."

That brought a soft rumble over the people. "The cat I inherited from my grandma at her passing."

Smart, Megan thought. He'd just made his stance about the cat. Surely there were as many cat lovers as haters in the congregation. But his statement brought more murmurs because everyone knew about Dad's penchant for restoring cars and understood his sacrifice.

"This is a generous congregation. It's been brought to my attention that July has brought Ohio and Indiana some storms, and since I know you're going through your own storm of changes, my sermon's entitled, 'Weathering Unexpected Storms.'"

He thumbed through his Bible and read a verse about God's protection. "Though I'm young to some of you, I've experienced some storms of my own."

Megan noticed that everyone settled in and really listened to his story. He told them the same story he'd shared with her. As he spoke, his hands flitted occasionally to his throat or his eyes, and she could tell that he was really struggling with an allergic reaction.

Soon, his eyes became mere slits in puffy sockets. She squirmed, wishing there was something she could do.

"What's wrong with him?" Joy Ann whispered.

"Allergies."

"Is he going to need your shot thing again?"

"Not as long as he can breathe."

"The poor man. What a hard life. And now he's broken out in hives. How's he going to make it through the potluck? I really wanted him to taste my lemon meringue pie. You know I have the knack for meringue. You think we need to get a list of the foods he's allergic to?"

It was true that if anybody could give Lil some competition in the food department, it was Joy Ann. "I don't know," Megan whispered, keeping a close eye on his face and breathing. Though he wasn't struggling in that area, she knew he was terribly itchy.

Micah, however, continued through his sermon, using his doggedness to prevail, and didn't cut it a minute short either, from the sound of it. Her heart warmed with sympathy and admiration.

As soon as the service ended, he strode straight to Megan.

"That was a comforting sermon." Joy Ann stepped in, causing Megan to squirm uncomfortably.

"Thank you." He turned to Megan. "Could you tell your dad I have hives and ask him to go to my apartment and find my antihistamine? It's in the medicine cabinet."

"Of course. I'll go right away."

Joy Ann offered, "I'll be sure to pick up an extra bottle to keep at the church. What brand do you use?"

"That won't be necessary. . . ."

Megan left them and hurried to find her dad but didn't see him anywhere. Making a spur-of-the-moment decision, she thought it would be faster if she just went after the medicine herself. As she hurried over the gravel roads at just a few miles over the speed limit, she wondered what set off Micah's hives, but nothing came to mind. A pothole made the car shudder.

At home she got her dad's shop key off the hook by the kitchen door and ran across the lawn, hurrying through the shop and into Micah's cottage. She opened the door and let out a shriek when the forgotten cat leaped across her path. Placing her hand over her heart, she wondered where the cat had been. Miss Purrty had flown across the room airborne. Megan hurried past the animal and into the bathroom, found the right bottle, and started back out. But the cat had situated herself in front of the door and was now taking a spit bath.

Megan hesitated, wondering if she should get the leash and put Miss Purrty in the cage lest she take another unexpected flight and escape through the open door. Since Micah had given his pet the run of the cottage, Megan opted to do that only as a last resort. Tentatively, she grabbed the door handle and tried to move the cat with her foot. The cat swatted her leg, catching a claw in Megan's new black stockings.

With a gasp, she tried to shake the cat off her leg. At the same time, Miss Purrty tried to back away, but her claw caught and put a run in Megan's stocking.

"No! Stop!" Megan squatted down and caught the cat by the collar and then tried to untangle the claw. By the time she'd finished, the cat had ruined her stocking. "Now look what you've done. Phooey! You naughty, naughty thing!"

The cat hissed and backed away, whipping her tail.

"Now I've got to change my stockings," Megan huffed, as she opened the door.

But the moment the door opened, the cat leaped past Megan into the shop. With a shriek, Megan flew after the cat. Miss Purrty disappeared under Chuck Benedict's Nova.

"Aye, yi, yi," Megan bemoaned. She stomped back into the cottage after the leash, wishing she'd listened to her intuition and caged the animal from the beginning. *Next time I won't feel sorry for the dumb thing.* She returned to the shop and gasped. The cat had jumped on top of the Nova's hood, the very thing they'd all wanted to avoid. "Don't move. Oh please, don't move."

Megan tried to think what to do. What would create the fewest number of scratches on the Nova's shiny paint? She started by lowering her voice and going for a soothing tone. "You are a nuisance. Nice kitty. Nice kitty." She took a step closer. The cat stood, made a complete circle, and slightly arched its back.

With each feline footstep, Megan flinched. Yet she continued to woo the cat in a singsong voice. "I can't believe you're doing this, Miss Purrty. Don't you know this is the worst thing you can do for yourself. For Micah?" When Megan got close enough to touch the little imp, she warned, "I'm just going to pet you behind your ear." She reached out slowly. The feline accepted her touch and pressed its yellow head into Megan's hand. "You're an unpredictable creature. Nice kitty."

The cat took cautious steps across the hood of the car toward Megan. "If you're going to live here, I think you may have to get declawed. Nice kitty, kitty." The cat reached the edge of the hood and leaned into her. Megan lifted Miss Purrty by her tummy and snapped on the leash. At the sound, the cat stiffened. Megan hurried back into Micah's apartment.

"Sorry, kitty." Megan tossed the cat into its cage. When she reached inside to remove the leash, Miss Purrty bit her hand.

"Ouch!" Megan jerked away, banging her hand on the inside of the cage. When she examined it, she saw no blood. It was more of a feline warning. "Fine. Keep it on then."

Megan secured the cage door and hurried out of the cottage, running toward the house. She ran upstairs and changed her stockings. Tried to brush cat hair off her dress, and then hurried back to the car. Inside she checked to make sure she had remembered Micah's medicine. Thankfully she had it, so she steered the car back onto the gravel road.

As she drove, she thought about the cat's claws on the Nova's hood, wondering if her dad would be able to spot any damage. If he did, she would need to take the blame.

When she reached the church, the fellowship hall was bustling with voices and activity, and it took her awhile to spot the preacher. He was seated at a table with Jake's sister, Erin, and her husband, David Miller. Megan greeted the younger couple and, as discreetly as possible, handed the medicine to Micah. She noticed his face was blotchy and his eyes had narrowed into even thinner slits.

"Oh good," Erin said. "It's getting worse."

"Where's your dad?" Micah asked, gulping down two pills and some water.

Megan sensed a hard edge to the question. "I couldn't find him, so I went after your medicine."

"You've been gone at least an hour."

She didn't think she'd been gone that long, but it probably seemed like an eternity to Micah. She sympathized with his agony and felt some admiration that he'd been able to keep his hands away from his face.

"I need to talk later, about your cat."

"Miss Purrty?" His eyes widened every so minutely.

"She's fine. We'll talk later." Megan turned away and asked Erin, "Is there any food left?" But in reality, she'd lost her appetite.

—❦—

Micah gazed around his cottage through slotted eyelids and didn't see anything amiss. Then Miss Purrty mewed, and with surprise he saw she was inside her cage. Probably what Megan wanted to explain. He bent to let her out and was irritated to see her leash twisted around one of her legs. When the cat favored the leg, anger flared up at Megan. Why would she leave Miss Purrty unattended with a leash that could have wrapped around her neck? What sort of trouble could an old cat make, anyway?

All he'd wanted, those agonizing hours of the potluck, was to kick off his shoes and flop onto his tiny bed. But first, he needed to take out the cat. Monday he'd get a litter box. He picked up Miss Purrty and started toward the back of the property. Irritably, he scratched at his neck and set the cat down. It walked over to a nicely turned flower bed and made itself busy.

"Micah? You feeling better?"

Flinching, he turned. "Nope."

"I'm sorry."

"When I got home, my cat had its leash knotted around its paw. Why did you cage her? And why did you leave her leash on?"

Megan took a deep breath, allowing for the fact that Micah wasn't at his best.

"Because your cat dashed into the shop and ran under the Nova. So I went for the leash, and when I returned, it was on top of the hood. Dad will have a fit when he finds out, especially if there are any scratches on it. He restores cars, Micah. He sees every little mark. Maybe you need to get Miss Purrty declawed."

"She's too old to go through that. Why didn't you send him after the medicine like I asked? The way he protects his cars, he wouldn't have let the cat out."

"I was only trying to help."

"Now Erin and David Miller think that you go in and out of my cottage. I don't know them. Will they spread gossip? As a bachelor, I can't have you going into my room, Megan. I thought that's what the cottage was all about." Megan clenched her jaw. He made it sound as if she were some tramp. "I have just two things to say to you, Brother Zimmerman. First, quit expecting me to get you out of your scrapes. Secondly, Mom won't be happy that your cat just uprooted one of her pansies." Looking furious, Megan turned on her heels and started to the house. But then she stopped, wheeled back, and said, "Actually, there's one more thing. You owe me a pair of stockings."

His gaze naturally dropped to her legs. They looked fine to him. When he raised his gaze again, her face had reddened. "Just so you know, buying women's stockings does not come under the definition of discreet." He reached in his pocket and pulled out his billfold. "How much do I owe you?"

"Oh, phooey. Just forget it." She stomped away.

The only good that came out of it was that sometime during their heated conversation, the cat's leash had fallen away. The feline had curled up in the pansies. It appeared Miss Purrty had no intention of running away. But Micah just might.

CHAPTER 17

Megan sliced cold meatloaf, feeling miserable and wondering if Micah would make an appearance for supper. No routine had been established, and she noticed her mom casting nervous glances out the kitchen window, which was in a direct line with the cottage.

"I hope he's doing all right. I wonder how long it takes to get rid of hives?"

Megan shrugged. Thankfully it'd never been a condition she'd experienced. She hadn't told her parents about their altercation. "I imagine he's sleeping it off." Hopefully his foul mood, too.

"If he doesn't come in, I'll send Bill out to him with a sandwich."

Megan doubted Micah needed food, doubted he wanted to see any of them about now, especially her. At least he hadn't been required to preach that evening. She felt miserable for snapping at him. It was not like her, and she needed to apologize. Only the matter about the cat and the car still bothered her. If Micah didn't tell Dad, she'd need to do it. It was her fault.

The Weavers had just sat down to their meal when Micah tapped on the kitchen screen door.

Mom shot out of her chair. "Oh, you don't need to knock at mealtime.

Just come in. I hoped you join us, but I didn't want to bother you."

He took an empty seat and waited while Mom brought a fourth plate and set it in front of him. Micah dipped his head in silent prayer.

When he was finished, Mom asked, "Are you feeling better?"

"Some." It was easy to see that the symptoms hadn't completely vanished. Micah started to make a sandwich.

Megan felt her face heat, not sure if she should apologize in front of her parents or hope for an opportunity in private.

From the corner of her eye, Megan watched Micah fork out one of Mom's homemade dill pickles and cut his sandwich in half. But instead of eating it, he placed his hands on his lap. He seemed to be struggling about the incident. "I need to apologize for some things that happened today."

"No, I do," Megan quickly objected.

She felt her parents' surprised gazes darting between them.

Micah gave her a smile. "Please, let me go first."

She nodded.

"Bill. Anita. I'm sorry about my grandma's cat. It was not part of our bargain. And today there was an incident. Well, two. She got into the shop and jumped up on the Nova. And later she messed up the flower bed."

Dad's fork clattered to the table and his gaze went to the screen door. The color drained from Mom's face, whether from the news of her flower bed or the scene that was playing out, Megan couldn't tell.

To Dad's credit, he didn't run out to the shop to check on his baby but remained to face the discussion. "It's not my car. Usually the Novas out there belong to owners who trust me to keep their cars in mint condition."

"I understand that."

"It was my fault," Megan blurted, unable to allow Micah to shoulder the blame. "I let the cat out of the cottage when I went after Micah's pills. I shouldn't have been out there in the first place. He asked me to get you, Dad. Instead I went myself. I didn't think about how it would look to the church members." She saw her dad's shoulders sag.

"Maybe I need to find an apartment someplace else. Is there anything in Plain City for cheap?" Micah asked, looking extremely sheepish. "I don't suppose Barbara has an extra room? Maybe I could help her out?"

"No!" Mom lifted her chin. "Everybody pitched in to fix up the Blue

Cottage. It's better not to stir things up. We will work this out on our own." She turned her gaze to Dad. "Bill?"

Dad clasped and kneaded his hands. He swallowed. "I appreciate your honesty. It's no secret. I don't like cats. We will all have to be more careful. We're just getting started, and we've got three long months ahead of us. But I'm sure we'll work this out."

Megan felt a rush of relief that Dad forgave them.

"The congregation's watching us," Micah replied.

Mom nodded. "My point, exactly."

"It was my fault. I went to Megan instead of coming directly to you, Bill. I could've gone home myself or carried pills in my car. The hives were unexpected." Now he turned his gaze toward Megan. "When we talked earlier, I shouldn't have put the blame on you. It's just that I didn't think you understood my situation. Being single, I have to be careful how I interact with women." He shrugged. "But I shouldn't have expected you to think about that. This is your home, and you're used to having the run of the place."

Dad turned to Megan. "He's right. Even though we all know that you and Micah are only friends, you can't be going into his cottage."

"I understand. I'm sorry. But surely with time, everyone will figure out that we're not interested in each other. That we're only friends."

Micah nodded with clenched jaw. "I'll get a litter box and try to keep Miss Purrty out of your flowers, Anita. I replanted the one she tore out, but I don't know if it'll survive."

Mom gave a nervous laugh. "How much damage can one cat do?" Dad quirked his eyebrow, and she quickly amended, "I mean in the yard? Now everybody, the food will get cold."

"It's cold meatloaf, Mom." Megan grinned.

"Oh, right." Mom was clearly flustered. Megan knew Mom wanted to be the perfect hostess for their important guest and felt uncomfortable caught between pleasing him or her husband.

After the meal, Micah passed on dessert and excused himself, starting to his apartment. Megan jumped up and fled after him. "Wait, Micah. I know you don't want to be alone with me, but I need to tell you I'm sorry I snapped at you. Everything you said was right."

Micah smiled. "I started it."

"Only because you were in pain, feeling miserable."

His expression saddened. "Today was a poor start. The entire congregation saw my weakness. I guess God wanted to humble me."

"You're not weak at all." Even at Rosedale, she'd seen his strength, his ability to persevere. "If God wanted to humble you, then He must have big plans for you."

He nodded. "You're right. Good night, Megan."

She watched him turn and walk toward his cottage, wishing there was more that she could do to encourage him. But today, she'd hindered him. When she stepped into the kitchen, both her parents stared at her.

"I just needed to apologize."

Dad reached out and took Megan's hand. "I still don't like the idea of having a cat in my shop, but I'm glad he came to us with the truth."

"The windows are open," Mom reminded them. She whispered, "He had a rough day."

"We all did." Megan squeezed her dad's hand and released it, taking their plates to the kitchen sink.

⁓ↄ

Megan watched a plane roll up to the hangar then brought her gaze from the glass window behind Chance and focused on their conversation.

"Randy had a rough weekend. He got in a big fight with Tina." Chance kept his voice low. "He came to my apartment, ready to leave her."

Megan was sorry to hear it. "What did you do?"

"I persuaded him to give it another try. He texted me a little while ago that they're going to book a cruise if I'll stay longer."

This news brought Megan conflicting emotions. "Longer?"

Chance laughed. "Don't look so mortified. Yes, you're stuck with me two extra weeks."

Two weeks wasn't so long. "We'll make do."

"That's the spirit," Paige said, stepping into view from somewhere behind Megan. "I swear, she's the most positive person I know. But one of these days, her desk is going to sprout wings on it, the way you always perch here like it's your personal cockpit."

Megan felt her face heat as Chance stood. "You're right." He leaned close to Paige's ear, but Megan could hear his rebuff. "I don't like being cooped up in there."

"Just two more weeks," Paige said.

"You keeping count?" Chance appeared insulted.

Paige shifted her files to her other arm. "It's not hard. Every time I put invoices on your desk, I see those big red x's, and the yellow highlighted square that is your last day."

Megan rubbed the side of her head with the end of her pencil then got it caught in her hair. Working to free it, she pointed out, "That yellow square has changed. He's staying two extra weeks."

"You are?" Paige laid her files on Megan's desk and moved to help her, then handed Megan back her pencil. "I guess we can carry him for two more weeks, right honey?"

Rubbing the sore spot on her head, Megan nodded. "That's just what I was saying when you walked up. We'll make do."

Paige picked up her files and parceled them out. "One for you, honey, and two for you Mr. Campbell." Then she strode back toward her desk.

Chance tucked the files beneath his arm. "I love to irritate that woman."

"Love to irritate women, period," Megan corrected, but then when he turned back and perched on her desk again, she wished she'd kept quiet and let him have the last word.

"Speaking of, I'm taking the Cessna back to Indiana on Saturday. Want to go along?"

Her heart raced. After the last trip and Chance's report of actually getting involved with a rescue, she'd regretted missing it. She glanced at her desk. Interesting as the man was, she had a list of calls to make. She didn't want to waste another half hour arguing about his question. "I'll think about it. When do you need to know?"

With surprise, he stood. "Thursday or Friday."

"Thanks for the offer."

With an expression much too hopeful, Chance smiled. "You're welcome." Finally he strode back to his office.

Megan glanced out the huge glass windows, watched a plane gliding out toward the runway. This was the opportunity she'd been waiting for.

It wasn't Ecuador or Djibouti, but it was going up in a plane, helping with MDS. She really wanted to go. But would Chance misinterpret her actions if she agreed?

_ᘓ

That afternoon when Megan pulled her Nova into the driveway, she noticed Micah sitting on the porch swing. Parking next to his Honda, she followed the shrubbery then clipped the corner of the lawn to the front sidewalk. She was already climbing the steps when she remembered she was not supposed to be hanging out alone with him. She hesitated.

He waved her forward, as if he'd forgotten, too.

Megan plopped her purse next to the screen door. "Hi."

Micah laid his Bible beside him on the swing. She wondered if it was intentional, to keep her from sitting beside him. She eyed it. "It's kinda funny. I used to be the one fending you off, now you're trying to keep your distance from me."

He looked stricken. "That's not true."

She waved a hand, "It's all right. Makes me kinda relieved. At least at home, I can drop my guard. Let you worry about that."

"Oh? But at work, it's different?"

"You're perceptive." At least he was perceptive when he didn't play dumb, like he had back in college. Or when he'd muscled the cat in, despite the disapproval he felt from her dad.

"Part of the job, I guess," he said.

"No, I think it's a gift. Mom has it, too."

"So what's going on at work?"

"Oh, Chance asked me to fly with him on Saturday. He's working with MDS, taking supplies to Indiana for victims of the recent tornado. Char Air does a lot of charity flights. And I've always wanted to go on some of these flights. I just don't want to give him the wrong impression."

Micah ran a hand through his hair, started to say something, then refrained, his expression looking pained as if it was hard to remain silent.

She glanced at the buckeye tree then at Micah's Bible. "I told him I'd let him know at the end of the week." She saw Micah's jaw twitch. He probably didn't realize he was tapping his leg. "Any advice, Brother Micah?"

"You asking me as your preacher?"

"Sure."

"It's a good cause. MDS wouldn't be able to keep going without volunteers."

She picked up his Bible, scooted in beside him, and dropped it on her lap, careful not to move his marker. She sank back against the swing's back, allowing the slight movement to ease away the day's stress. "Would you give me the same advice as a friend?"

She heard him sigh. "I'd agree that you needed to be careful not to give him the wrong impression. All men are easily encouraged."

She fondled the soft leather cover. "As a preacher, you say yes, but as a friend, you say no? That leaves me without any clear direction."

The swing creaked, filling in the comfortable silence. She wondered if this was what it was like to have a brother. Heaven knew she needed another friend, what with Lil gone and Katy busy with her little family.

"Some things you have to decide for yourself."

Her legs gave in to the soft swaying movement of the swing. "That's exactly what Barbara told me."

"You talked to her about this?"

"No. But I talked to her about Chance."

"I'd like to get to know her."

They fell into silence except for the rhythmic creaking. "I see you got rid of your hives."

"Yes. I went into the office today. Joy Ann says she needs a witness to count the offering. But I don't think the preacher should see the checks. I'd rather not fall in a trap of judging people by their donations. I'm going to suggest that a treasurer assist her with that."

"Good idea. How often will you go to the office?"

"Joy Ann says Brother Troyer went in every morning. I'll try that. She only comes on Mondays and Fridays. She cleans house the other days. Joy Ann told me you're friends."

"Yes, but not close friends. I think she's trying to impress you."

He sighed. "I was afraid of that. Guess I better talk to your dad about not being at the office alone with her. I suppose it wasn't an issue with Brother Troyer. But things are different these days." He continued telling her about his day. "On my way home, I picked up a litter box. And when you pulled up, I was thinking about next week's sermon topic."

"What is it?"

"I don't know yet."

Megan patted his arm and rose. "How about something like 'How to Hear God's Voice' or 'How to Follow God's Leading'?"

He laughed. "You'll have to make up your mind about the flight before Sunday's sermon."

"True, but there's always next week and next week's problems."

"You're right, Megan. There's always that."

CHAPTER 18

Do you know how to make hot dogs?"

Megan looked up, her gaze following the aroma of french fries and the masculine voice that was hard to resist. She laughed at Chance's serious expression. "Sure. That's not hard. They're not healthy, though."

He shoved a red fast-food container toward her. "Want one?"

She looked at the fries. "No thanks."

"Hard to eat these without the hot dogs. In Ecuador, they have what's called *salchipapas*, french fries with little hot dogs on top."

"Can't you make hot dogs?"

"I could if I had a grill. But I'm not staying in the States long enough to buy one."

"You can boil them in water."

"I tried microwaving one, but it blew up. The woes of being a bachelor." He wagged his eyebrows at her.

"Now that's the way to charm a woman." Megan mimicked his voice, "Come make me some hot dogs."

"Yeah? Nothing else is working. And it's really too bad, because you would love Ecuador. It's beautiful from its sky to its jungles. It has cliffs and waterfalls. And the weather is perfect. Always in the seventies, perpetual spring. I'm telling you, Megan, it's the life. Sure beats asphalt and high-rises."

"Plain City doesn't have any high-rises. And I thought you said it rained a lot and the runways were gooey."

"But that's what makes it the rain forest. Gorgeous."

"You miss it."

"Yes, but I'm going back. You, on the other hand, will miss out altogether unless you let me take you over." He opened a ketchup packet and squirted it inside his cardboard container. "You should go before all your shots expire."

Megan smiled. "What kind of work would I do? I'm not a nurse."

"The hospitals need employees to keep records, too."

"Tell me about the hospital."

"There's more than one. The Hospital Vozandeson is on the edge of the Amazon rain forest and has twenty-eight beds. They do surgery and treat snakebites and tropical diseases. Oh, and they deliver babies. There're a couple of houses in Shell, mission hubs for missionaries, translators, supplies, pilots. I'm sure they need help running those places, too. I don't suppose you'd want to get your pilot's license?"

"Hardly. What you just described, are these voluntary positions?"

"Most. But not all. I'm telling you, once you visit, you'll fall in love."

Megan smiled. Yes, she would. She'd already fallen in love with his irresistible smile. It was hard enough in a sterile chrome and glass office not to give in to his charms. What would it be like to be with him in his Garden of Eden?

"But first, you should go with me on the MDS drop on Saturday. See what a safe pilot I am, build a little trust that I can deliver what I promise." It was certainly tempting. He'd promised that if she claimed his friendship, he wouldn't press her for more. But he hadn't promised to protect her from her own feelings and desires.

Just then Paige and Tate entered the office. "It's nonstop lunch and break time with you two, isn't it?" Paige plucked the last french fry out of Chance's hand, stuck it in her mouth, then smacked her red lips. "Too much ketchup."

Chance shook his head, handed Megan the empty carton, and fell into step with Tate. "What's the story on that cargo plane?"

But Paige lingered at Megan's desk. "The only thing that man understands is power. He respects it. That's why I boss him around. Keeps him from bossing me around."

Megan rolled her gaze to the ceiling at Paige's weird philosophy and tossed the french fry carton into her trash. Brushing her hands, she looked Paige in her contact-covered pupils. "I'm not after his respect; I'm trying to repel him."

"I knew it." Paige hit the desk with her fist then leaned close. "Don't give in. Not a sweet thing like you. I can give you some tips."

"That's what I'd hoped."

"Over-laugh at everything he says."

Megan snickered. "That's your advice?"

"No, seriously. I just read this article about the best ways to repel a man. When you said repel just now, it reminded me of the article."

"Why were you reading that kind of article?"

"Getting my hair done and it sounded interesting."

Megan could see how a laughing hyena might deter a man. "What else?"

"When you're not laughing, cry for no reason. Talk loud. Nag him." She stood, straightened her pencil skirt. "If those don't work, then don't wash your hair. Got it?"

"Sure. Just be generally obnoxious?"

"You have any better ideas?"

Megan shook her head.

Paige shrugged. "Then try obnoxious. And if that doesn't work and you get yourself in a pickle, just scream. I'll be across this room in a flash. He'll never know what hit him."

"Thanks, Paige. If nothing else, you know how to lift my spirits."

After that, Megan buried herself in her work, which must have been why she didn't notice how the sky had darkened until Chance strode through her office. "Look outside!"

Megan lifted her eyes and saw an ominous sky. "Aye, yi, yi."

Chance's mouth quirked, but his smile didn't reach his eyes. "There's a storm heading in. And now there're tornado warnings. I'm closing up shop. Everybody goes home early."

Tornado warnings! Megan leaned over her steering wheel and squinted between strokes of the windshield wiper for a better look at the sky, scanning for any indication of funnel clouds. It was too dark to tell. Plain City didn't usually get tornados, but she couldn't dismiss the severity of the storms that had recently ravaged Indiana. She fiddled with the radio, but the antique only hissed static.

Sheets of rain blurred her vision. Wind whipped the car, and she fought the steering wheel to keep it in its proper lane. By the time she'd taken her exit on the down ramp, her nerves were fraught. Between blinding bursts of rain, visibility cleared enough to reveal some new obstacles. Her eyes widened at a row of telephone poles that had been snapped like matchsticks. "Aye, yi, yi."

She clamped the steering wheel and drove another mile, and then the wind suddenly quieted. The rain quit. The wipers screeched against the windshield, but she didn't have faith to turn them off. Drawing in a breath of relief, she searched the sky to see if it was just a lapse between storms. It looked like she'd have a clear road now, and she was almost home. The worst was over. Still thinking about the telephone poles, she glanced in her rearview mirror.

Back in the distance, a swirl of dust moved across a field. How could it be dusty after the downpour she'd just driven in? She glanced in her rearview mirror again, unable to take her eyes off the peculiar squall. It bounced. . .and spewed things!

Frantic again, Megan rolled down her window and jerked her side mirror. Then she saw what was feeding the whirlwind. A small funnel cloud hovered over the field, touching the ground, scraping it, and sending splatters of destruction back into the sky. Oh no!

With a groan, she stomped on the gas pedal and held it to the floor. The car bucked and slid. She whipped the steering wheel and the tires straightened and gripped the road. It took all her concentration to keep the Nova on the road, and she couldn't see much out the rearview mirror except that the tornado was gaining on her.

With a prayer of relief, she braked just enough to make the drive, spitting gravel and hitting the brakes. Her car slid sideways and barely missed Micah's Honda. Her hands trembled so bad she couldn't get her car door open. But it suddenly burst open. Micah grabbed her arm.

"Hurry!"

"There's a tornado!" she cried.

"I know. I've been out at the road watching for you."

She must have driven right past him. Clutching her arm, he dragged her toward his cottage. She stopped and shrugged him away. "No. We have to go to the root cellar. This way."

She broke into a run, assuming Micah was behind her, and yelled over her shoulder. "What about Mom?"

"They're at your grandparents. Hurry."

They'd reached the corner of the house, and she led him past the kitchen door to a smaller one with a wooden bar. A downburst drenched her in seconds, and she fumbled with the bar.

A hand clamped on her shoulder. "Let me."

Megan danced to the side, and Micah jerked the door open, revealing a dark, cavernous hole. She'd never liked the root cellar, hated when Mom sent her after canned goods. It was smelly and full of spiders. Once they'd even had a snake.

A roar filled Megan's ears, and her heart lurched in fear. "It's coming."

"Are there steps?"

"Yes."

He nudged her. "Hurry, Meg."

She jerked the string that dangled from the ceiling. A light switched on. She started down. "Can you close the door?"

"Yes, I've already got it bolted."

She'd hit the bottom landing and swung around. She grabbed his shirt. "What about the cat?"

He placed his hand over hers and squeezed. "It'll be fine."

She looked into his eyes. They brooked no argument, so she nodded.

He gave her a grim smile. "We will be, too." His gaze swept over the small cellar.

As the roaring sound grew louder, the electricity flashed off, pitching them into complete darkness. Megan gasped and clutched Micah's shirt tighter.

He drew her close against him. "Let's go beneath the stairs. It's the safest place."

They couldn't move unless she released her hold on him. He was right about moving under the stairway. Reluctantly she eased out of his arms, and they felt their way around the stairway.

"Let's sit down." His calm voice was an anchor in the storm.

"All right, but it's dirty."

He laughed. "The least of our worries."

They eased down and braced their backs against a wall that probably had spiderwebs. She hated the brown recluse that occupied dark corners. When Micah's arm slipped around her, pulling her close, she burrowed into his protection. The winds howled, and he softly prayed something out of the Psalms. Her fingers curled around the front of his damp shirt.

A loud crash rattled the wall near the entrance. He patted her hand. "Shh."

She hadn't realized she was crying. She gulped, embarrassed. "It was an awful drive home. The funnel cloud chased me. I didn't know if I could outrun it."

Beneath her hand, his chest rumbled with low laughter. "I saw you coming down the road. It was amazing the way you handled your car."

"I couldn't even get out of my car. Thank God you came for me." He'd been the best sight of her life.

"I've got you now."

She hiccupped. "After all your blabbering about being discreet, here we are alone together. In the dark."

" 'When it is dark enough, you can see the stars.' "

"What?"

"Ralph Waldo Emerson."

"I don't see any stars. I highly doubt stars are out there tonight."

"Maybe not tonight, but tomorrow."

"But—"

"Listen! Hear that? It's letting up."

She let out a nervous laugh, grasping at the hope that the nightmare was ending. "My grandparents have a basement. Is that why Mom went over there?"

"She was visiting them when your dad came home. He wanted to go over and help your grandfather get ready for the storm."

"He doesn't get around so good anymore."

"Your dad was worried Anita might get caught on the road in the storm. He was worried about you, too, but I told him I'd keep you safe." He relaxed his hold on her. "Maybe I should go up and look around. Where do you keep a flashlight?"

She hated to be in the dark cellar alone. "In the junk drawer in the kitchen, but I want to come with you."

"Wait here for now." He disengaged himself from her, and she heard his footfall on the steps. She heard scraping, a thump, and a groan.

"What's wrong?"

"The door won't budge. It's probably that loud noise we heard. Something's blocking it. There's a hole and water leaking in, too."

Panic tamped up her spine. "But we can't stay down here."

Several stair steps creaked, and he sidled in beside her again. "We have no other choice. We'll just have to make the best of it."

"How?"

He stroked her cheek. "If you don't think of something, I will."

He meant to kiss her! For an instant, she wanted it, too. But then she came to her senses. "I guess you could practice next week's sermon on me."

His touch fell away, and his laughter rumbled through the darkness. "That would be my second-best idea."

She tried to straighten against the wall and not humiliate herself by clutching him like a frightened bird again, but it wasn't nearly as comforting. Especially when the storm continued to brew overhead. He mumbled something about dealing with pain. His sermon did little to warm her, and she shivered. He moved closer. She felt the hard planes of his side and leaned against his strength.

⁓ও⁓

Megan awoke with a start, stiff and hazy-minded. Her face was pressed against a beating heart. She went rigid as the night's events came back to her. Lifting her head, she gently pushed away and swiped at her hair.

"Your dad's back. But he had to go after help."

"What time is it?"

"Still the middle of the night, I think." Micah pushed up and started up the creaky stairway.

"He was here earlier?"

His voice grew more distant, coming from overhead. "Yeah, you were sleeping."

She didn't want him to leave her alone in the dark. "Is everybody all right?"

"Yes."

Megan stood and bumped her head on a step. With a groan, she rubbed it. The cellar was too dark to see much until her eyes adjusted. She swiped at her clothing and moved to the bottom of the stairway.

"Stay put for now, Megan. When they remove the structure, there could be a cave in."

"Cave in?" She backed into a row of canned goods.

"Micah! I'm back."

"I'm here." Micah returned her dad's shout.

How had she slept through his first visit? The floor was flooded. Had Micah kept them dry? She was embarrassed that she'd slept while he kept vigil.

Dad gave Micah instructions, and Micah backed partway down the steps again. There was a big commotion, and suddenly, the door burst open. Megan scurried up the steps behind Micah, and he helped her out the splintered opening.

Dad pulled her into the safety of his arms. "Thank the Lord you're safe."

"I'm fine. Where's Mom?"

"I made her stay inside. She's worried. Better go in to her."

Megan stepped out of his embrace and into the predawn. She swept her gaze over the property, portions dimly lit by the headlights of Will Landis's tractor. The only major damage she saw was the tree that had smashed into the cellar door.

Will grunted, pushing debris out of her path.

"Everybody all right at your place?" she asked the farmer.

"Yep. We won't be able to tell what's happened till morning, but I haven't gotten any calls that anyone's in trouble. 'Cept you."

Micah stepped up beside her. "Looks like we picked the most dangerous spot on the property."

Bill tugged his dripping ball cap. "You did the right thing."

Megan looked up at Micah, who'd been her mainstay. She couldn't think of words to express her deep thankfulness. Awareness of their intimacies burned between them. "You coming?"

"In a minute. I'm going to check on the cat."

Almost relieved, she rounded the house to the kitchen. While Micah's embrace meant everything in that dark, dank hole, she feared once the sun broke, matters would take a different spin.

CHAPTER 19

Bill used the chainsaw, and Micah dragged away limbs and tossed debris into a trailer that Will Landis had loaned them. Bill hadn't said much, other than to thank him for keeping Megan safe. The night spent in the pitch-black root cellar with Megan dominated Micah's thoughts. The way she'd clung to him for protection had crashed his defenses so that all he had been able to think about was shielding her from harm.

When he'd seen the funnel cloud chasing her car and met the desperation in her eyes as she drove unseeing past him, instinct launched him to her side. He'd every heroic intention to sweep her up into his arms and to the shelter of his cottage. But she'd summoned her wit for the both of them and run toward the root cellar instead.

That night, the cellar became a world within a world, a journey to a place where time fell apart and set them on the cusp of reality. Everything material and inconsequential fell away. Everything dear and true became monumental. All that mattered in the darkness of the storm was Megan and God.

When she'd quieted in his arms, everything was pure and right. There with Megan and God, he had been satisfied and fulfilled. But then the storm ended, and Bill's voice from the other side of the trappings thrust him back into the harsher, outside world.

Micah heaved an armload of debris. It thudded into the trailer. He pulled himself up over the side rails and stomped down the trash, oblivious to the pain of sharp branches and prickly brush. He hopped out again and strode toward Bill.

The kitchen door opened, and Megan stepped into Micah's view. She looked pretty and fresh, calm and collected as if it were any other normal day. She stopped beside her dad and commented on the damage. "We'll miss that tree, won't we?"

"Yep. It's going to expose your Mom's garden now. Coulda been worse, though."

She looked at Micah with a heated gaze that validated his own feelings. For them, normal had evaporated and rolled away with the clouds. They would have to redefine their relationship.

She looked away. "I gotta go."

"Micah and I are going to Barbara's and the other widows' after we're done here."

"Good. I'll see you both tonight." She started toward her car, off to the pilot and everything that drew her away from him.

—⟲—

That afternoon Megan drove home, sadly observing the tornado's hit-and-miss destruction. Some barns had been damaged and trees downed. The road was washed away in places, but from all she'd heard, Plain City had missed the brunt of the storm. Still, she found it hard to shake off the vivid memories of the funnel cloud and the terror that had clamped her chest and stolen her wits. Through it all, Micah had been solid and strong, tender and reassuring.

She flicked down her visor to ward off the afternoon's glare and flinched. The paper with the words *Do not be unequally yoked* was pinned to her visor with a prayer-covering pin!

Her mom must have found it in her skirt pocket. A pang of guilt struck her that she'd completely forgotten about it. Her conscience recalled how she'd earlier memorized it and meditated on it throughout her workday. But Chance had broken down her guard with his constant presence. It was hard to think about Bible verses when he was perched on her desk, painting her pictures of his jungle paradise.

She removed a sticky note from her steering wheel and stuck in on top of the verse then glanced back at the road. Just before she'd left the office, she'd returned to her desk from the ladies room. That's when she'd discovered the sticky note. Chance had placed it on her computer screen. It read:

MDS needs you. So do I. No hot dog making required.

She remembered snippets of their conversation, his concern for her well-being during the storm. Tomorrow was Friday, and she still hadn't given him her answer about the flight to Indiana. She needed to make her decision tonight. She had thought up an excuse she could use, flimsy as it was. Lil and Fletch were returning tomorrow, and she was anxious to see them again. Chance would know it was the truth, since he still dropped in at the restaurant, but there was no reason Megan had to see them on Saturday. Flimsy.

She pulled into the drive and noticed that Will Landis's tractor and trailer were gone. Aside from the ugly gap where the tree once stood, things looked pretty normal. Her gaze swept across the garden and froze when it found Micah. He stood with his back to her and his shoulder pressed against the scaly trunk of a surviving hickory tree. She should talk to him and get it over with before things got more awkward. Slinging her purse over her shoulder, she shut her car door.

Micah startled and looked over his shoulder. "It's that late already?"

Starting toward him, she replied, "It's been a long day for me."

He kneaded his arm muscles. "Couldn't be as rough as mine."

She shrugged. "I kept thinking about the storm. How's Barbara?"

"She's fine. Nobody got hurt. The men have been cleaning up all day. I helped out at Lori Longacre's this afternoon." He touched the back of his neck. "Did I mention how sore I am?"

"I took the hint." The muscle flexing was hard to ignore. She tried by fixing her gaze on Miss Purrty. The cat rolled in the litter at the edge of the woods. But when silence prevailed, Megan's thoughts rushed out. "Thanks

148

for everything last night."

The rascal's mouth quirked up in the corner. "It was my pleasure."

Hers, too, but she wouldn't admit it. Now in the daylight, the way she'd clung to him was pitiful. But her embarrassment clearly amused him.

"I thought if I was going to meet my Maker, hanging onto the preacher's coattail was the smartest thing to do."

He arched an eyebrow. "I did notice your attachment to my shirt."

She smiled. "Your sermon was good, too."

"Just doing my duty. Protecting Bill's little girl."

She felt her face burn.

Micah bent his knee and propped one foot behind him on the tree, studying her, trying to draw something from her that she wasn't willing to reveal.

"So Lori had some damage at her place?"

"She lost a tree. She wants to pay me back by helping me with my research." He scratched his head and brushed away bits of bark. "Usually librarians are sweet old widows. But Lori's young and smells good. I like her. But I don't know if I should take her up on the offer."

It galled her that his statement was worded like a question, seeking her permission. Was he talking about Lori so Megan wouldn't consider the root cellar incident anything more than a man doing his duty? It irritated her how swiftly he went from helping one woman to the next. Their night together obviously hadn't affected him like it had her. She hadn't been able to work through it yet, but this conversation was adding clarity.

She kept her voice nonchalant. "I can tell you what I know about her. Normally she doesn't chase men. I don't recall her helping Brother Troyer. But maybe I just didn't know about it. Although she's not old-old, she's older than you. So maybe she's just trying to be helpful."

Micah laughed sarcastically. "She's not old. And I don't want to give her the wrong idea. I need to stay focused on my goals."

Megan couldn't tell if he was warning her off or if he was only talking about Lori. She knew what it was like to fixate on the wrong person. But Lori was a good Mennonite woman. "She's smart, even progressive in her thinking. Maybe you should just give her the I-have-to-be-discreet speech you gave me. Tell her the truth."

He looked out across the garden and fell quiet. Megan was just ready to end their conversation and go inside when he asked, "Did you know that church secretary is a volunteer position?"

Confused, she replied, "Sure."

"The elders told Joy Ann they're getting somebody to help her."

Why was he dragging all his female admirers into their conversation? "Safety in numbers?"

"Right. Anyway, when they told Joy Ann, she didn't bat an eye and recommended her friend Ruthie Ropp."

"That's surprising. I figured Ruthie would be her competition, interested in you herself."

"No. Ruthie's not interested."

So there was one woman he hadn't smitten with his Ichabod charms? Megan saw her chance to get under his skin. "Maybe I can help. I can give you Paige's sure-fire ways to repel a man. Maybe they work for women, too."

His lip twitched. "Repellents? Are these the tactics you used on me at college?"

"Hardly. I didn't even know Paige then. I work with her. She recommends over-laughing at everything. She read this article. It also recommends nagging."

"Men don't nag." He lowered himself to the base of the tree, placed his back against its trunk, and motioned for her to join him. "But this is amusing. So your friend Paige does these things to fend off men?"

Megan set her purse on the damp ground and joined him, tucking her skirt around her bent knees. "She's happily married, and if anybody gets out of line with her, she clobbers them with her list of donors. She employs power and conquest. And perhaps the element of surprise. Oh wait"—her hand flew to his arm—"I remember another one." She glanced at his wind-tousled hair. "Don't wash your hair. Leave it all *stroobly*."

His hand instinctively went up to his hair. He brushed it off his forehead and asked, "Or use hairspray?" Then he laid his head back against the tree. "No. I won't do anything that puts me in a bad light."

"But according to Paige, you have to make yourself less attractive."

He leaned forward and scratched his head. More bark chips showered down his back. "That won't be hard for me."

Megan thought she'd teased him long enough. "My mom says you're a real prize."

He burst out laughing. "I'm sure you set her straight."

"Just because I don't want to date you, doesn't mean I don't think you're a prize. You were there for me last night. If I'd had a brother, I'd have wanted him to be just like you."

He picked up a piece of bark and tossed it in front of the cat. It switched its tail. "But when it comes to the romance department, you're looking for somebody more like Chance?"

She draped her arms across her skirt and shrugged. "Maybe."

"What's he got over the rest of us?"

"You've seen him. He's fun. Likeable. Has this vulnerable side to him. Kinda like a teddy bear."

Micah made a disgusted face. "I thought he seemed aggressive. Arrogant. More grizzly than teddy."

She tilted her head thoughtfully. "He's sure of himself, all right. There was something in his confidence that scared me at first. Not anymore." Megan narrowed her gaze, followed the cat's movements as it stalked a sparrow.

"If he's like every other air-breathing man, you'll have to draw him a line in the sand. He won't stop until you show him that line."

Megan smiled at him. "I can't wait for you to meet my friend Lil. She'd tell you that's a good thing. Lil's draws her own lines."

"Maybe. When does she get back?"

"This weekend." The cat gave up on the bird and inched across the lawn toward them. She strode snootily past Megan and stepped possessively, one foot at a time, into Micah's lap.

"Maybe I'll take your advice. I'll go on that MDS flight and set some boundaries."

"If you're not too swept away by the entire experience that you forget to do that."

Megan grew weary of the topic. She reached out and touched the purring cat's head, scratching her behind the ears. "So are you still worried Miss Purrty might run away?"

"Not really. I was worried about her getting lost in the woods at first. But she doesn't seem to want to get too far away from me. And now she knows that the cottage is our home. I think she's adjusting."

"I guess if Miss Purrty's so attached to you, she's got her competition cut out for her," Megan said, rising and brushing off her skirt.

"Nope, she's the only female for me."

Laughing, Megan picked up her purse and left him to go into the house.

⁓☙

Micah scooped up the tabby and headed for the cottage, watching Megan retreat to the house. He wished he could tell her how foolish she would be to go on that plane ride with a conceited outsider who wanted to despoil her. What else could the man be after? At the least, he wanted to despoil her soul, wanted her to give up her religion for him. It made Micah's blood boil, made him want to drive over to Char Air and spin the man's propeller.

But if he did that, he might drive Megan away forever. And probably drive her right into Campbell's undeserving arms. He tossed Miss Purrty onto the floor, and she instantly leaped up onto her favorite chair, settling herself in for another spit bath. Micah slumped in the chair on the other side of the table and crossed his long legs on the footstool, his insides jumping more than they'd been during the storm.

It irked him that Megan would choose a man like Chance over himself or another good-hearted Mennonite man. He'd been foolish to attribute her actions in the root cellar to anything other than fear.

If he'd never chased Megan in school, would she look at him differently now? The question had little bearing on Megan's infatuation with her boss. He'd just have to trust that she'd remain faithful to her convictions. Even though she'd spurned his own advances, he wanted the best for her. Chance Campbell was not the best.

Megan knew the right thing to do. But people made foolish decisions all the time. He went over their conversation again, and then he remembered something she'd told him. *"If I'd had a brother, I'd have wanted him to be just like you."* He snarled his lip. She thought of him as a brother. He liked the idea of Lori and Joy Ann, or even Ruthie, thinking of him as a brother. It was the exact image he'd hoped to create. But Megan feeling that way made his heart sink into gloom. Before a day had passed, their relationship had been redefined.

CHAPTER 20

As Megan approached the white-and-green-striped Cessna Caravan waiting on the tarmac, excitement tramped up her spine. Chance guided her to a right rear air stair, and soon she was inside the small cargo plane. She leisurely took in the plush cockpit then glanced back at the cavernous cabin, the exterior of which was now partly filled with boxes of supplies. She knew some had also been stored underneath the cabin.

"Make yourself comfortable while I do a few last minute things," Chance said with a smile and eyes that mirrored the excitement churning in the pit of her stomach.

"Sure." Her eyes traversed the plane's features, ten times more luxurious than her Nova. As she waited for her pilot, she gazed out at the familiar tarmac, easily visible because of the plane's high wing position, and reassured herself about her decision. She worked for a charter flight company. It made her a better employee to experience a real flight. It would be foolish to turn down the opportunity when it was the reason that she took the job with Char Air. Barbara claimed that paths cross for a reason. She couldn't be obstinate just because her pilot was attractive.

She'd done everything to persuade him that she wouldn't veer from her convictions. Now she needed to give God the opportunity to show her why their paths had crossed. She was merely taking supplies to MDS volunteers. And she would do her share of the workload. It was more worthwhile than anything else she could have done with her time.

"All set." Chance moved into a plush beige leather seat and touched the W-shaped yoke.

Megan glanced at the control columns on her side of the plane, amazed at all the dials, levers, and the three large screens. As Chance did his job to prepare to taxi and take off, she fastened her restraints. She watched through the tinted glass cockpit as they moved down a taxiway and then sped down a runway. When they lifted into the sky, her stomach did a little flip, but she gave Chance a huge grin.

"You're a natural." He smiled at her then gave his attention to piloting.

She glanced at his headgear. After all the stories she had heard about surviving impossible landing scenarios and storms and near misses, she now felt confident to have the plane in his competent hands. "Don't you think it's a little early to tell?"

"I can tell."

She relaxed and settled in for the flight. The cabin was quieter than she had expected, but Chance wasn't all that talkative while he worked. He did point out various landmarks such as the Wabash River that wound through square quarter sections of farmland. The time went so quickly that she could hardly believe it when he was pointing out the recent tornado's destructive pathway.

"Looks like someone ran their finger through the sand," he said.

From the air, that's exactly what it resembled, only instead of sand, it was housing communities and forests and fields. Looking at the destructive power of nature brought back the terror of trying to outdrive the funnel cloud. What would she have done if she'd had to spend the night alone in the root cellar? Her heart clenched with fear, even though the incident was behind her. She tried to hide her anxiety from Chance. She hadn't told him the entirety of what had happened. She knew he wouldn't approve of her time alone with Micah.

She looked down, took some deep breaths, and tried to focus on God's creative and sustaining power. When they dropped to a lower elevation, she was able to peer into homes as if they were dollhouses without roofs, their contents strewn and trees uprooted. Her heart instantly filled with compassion for the people who had not been as fortunate as she had. They had lost so much. "It still looks bad. As if it just happened."

"They work first to set up temporary housing, do the search and rescue. But now they're ready to start cleanup and rebuilding. It all takes time. There used to be a trailer park down there." He pointed. "I saw a lot of devastation the last time I was here."

Now the stripped lot with twisted metal looked more like a junkyard. Megan tried not to imagine what the occupants had experienced. Chance spoke to the control tower and turned the plane. "Prepare for landing, Megan."

She glanced over at him, wondering what it would be like to join him for a day in Ecuador. In his paradise, there would be mountains and rain forest instead of corn and soybean fields and cities. The plane gave a little bounce, but mostly it was a smooth landing; then Chance steered the Cessna to a specified taxiway. At the ramp, they were immediately met by a handful of MDS volunteers.

The married couple in charge stepped forward and introduced themselves. Danny was a retired farmer, and his wife, Cindy, was a friendly woman who told Megan, "The UPS driver should be here anytime. That company's been a Godsend the way they activated an action team and provided trucks and services."

"Whoa. There he is now." Danny waved the driver over.

Chance quickly raised the cargo doors on either side of the plane and pointed out which were the lighter boxes. They lifted the boxes out of the plane and dollied them to the van. The group worked for a good hour moving boxes of gloves, first-aid kits, bleach, shovels and rakes, trash bags, tarps, and food and water. Perspiration had collected on Megan's brow by the time the last box had been loaded inside the brown truck.

Cindy thanked them and hugged Megan. "We can give you a ride to the shelter, where they divvy out the supplies."

Chance thanked her. "We need to get the plane back this afternoon so that it can get serviced. It's booked for another flight. This one was barely squeezed in."

"Well, it's much appreciated."

Megan watched the older couple and other volunteers get into a white van and drive away.

"We do have time for a bite to eat," Chance said. "There's a restaurant within walking. Nothing fancy like Lil's place."

"Sure."

He locked things up, talked to some flight techs, and led Megan through a side door. The restaurant was more of a fast-food cafeteria for the working crews.

"All this just to get your hot dog?" Megan teased.

Chance laughed. "They have some deli sandwiches and salads."

"I'll have whatever you have. Hold the onions."

"You got it."

Megan found a small booth by a huge window that looked out over the airport apron. When Chance returned, she took a long drink from the soda he had provided. "Seems even hotter here," she remarked.

"Farther south." He gave her a look of admiration. "You worked hard today."

"You worked harder."

He shrugged, took a bite of his hot dog. He swallowed. "All day, I kept seeing you with me in Ecuador."

She felt a sharp intake of breath. "I thought about it, too. What it would be like to drop down into the jungle instead of an airport."

"It's not Indiana. It's dangerous. There are no UPS trucks with helpful drivers."

"Just the other day I learned that one of my ancestors was a hero."

"I'd love to hear the story."

"His name was Dirk Willems. He was a Dutch Anabaptist, before we were called Mennonites, who had been imprisoned during the Reformation."

"The 1600s?"

"Yes. Many were getting burned at the stake for their beliefs. Anabaptists believed in baptism for adults instead of infants, and the state church called them heretics. Anyway, Dirk tied strips of cloth to make a rope and escaped from a prison tower. As he ran across the countryside, a guard chased after him. They came to pond covered in ice, and Dirk took the risk and crossed it safely. But his pursuer broke through the ice and was doomed. Dirk had to decide if God was securing his escape or if he should go back and help the man. He decided to go back. But the guard took him back to the prison, and Dirk was later burned at the stake."

"It sounds like the missionaries who helped the Aucas."

"Yes."

"And he's your ancestor?"

Megan leaned forward. "I just found out from my dad. He doesn't talk much about these things because it troubles Mom. She's adopted, and I guess she has some blank spots in her background."

"But she's Mennonite?"

"Of course." Megan took a sip of her drink and hit bottom. Then she pushed it away. "The point of the story is that I read about Dirk Willems in college. His story is in a huge book of Anabaptist martyrs called *The Martyrs Mirror*. These stories always stir up my faith. And now to find out that this man I always admired is a relative just makes me a stronger person. I have to wonder if his mother prayed for her descendants, what ties connect us."

"But if he died, then how—"

She laughed. "That's the same thing I asked. Not him, per say, but his bloodline."

"I see." Chance glanced at his watch. "Maybe this stirring in you is a calling. Think seriously about Ecuador. It could be the reason we met."

Megan's pulse raced, and she wondered if it was true. She wouldn't have to marry Chance to go to Ecuador.

"I have a DVD at home I'd like you to see."

"I don't watch television or movies," she objected, reminded of her conversation with Micah. She had told him that she could use this trip to draw the lines in her relationship with Chance.

"I think you could make an exception for this one. It's called *The End of the Spear*. It's the story of the missionaries who were killed by the Aucas. And the scenery is representative of Ecuador."

"It wasn't filmed in Ecuador?"

"No. Colón, Panama. On the Panama Canal much farther north. It's more touristy, but the movie gives a true picture of what it's like."

"I'll think about it. Maybe I should ask our preacher if this would make a good exception."

Chance bristled. "Preacher? As in the guy staying with you? Are you two getting chummier?"

Embarrassment fell over her to think of the night she spent with him in the root cellar. Chance would definitely consider that chummier. "We're friends. Having him around is like having a big brother."

"Just because you view him as a brother doesn't mean he sees you as a sister. Better watch how chummy you get with him, unless you want to be a preacher's wife." Then he finished off his hot dog and glanced at her paper cup. "You want a drink for the sky?"

"No. I'm fine." She wished she hadn't brought up Micah. Just when she'd thought that Chance was acting reasonably, he'd gotten jealous. She mulled this over as they returned to the plane. She might not get another opportunity alone with him to draw the line in the sand.

Just before takeoff, she turned to Chance. "Are you jealous of Micah because I said he's my friend and because I'm cautious about my relationship with you?"

"Do you blame me?"

"Micah's a Mennonite preacher. Even if a friendship with him deepened, it would be acceptable."

"So you're considering a relationship with him?"

"No. That's not what I'm saying."

He nodded. "Fasten your seat belt, Megan."

Frustrated, she prepared for takeoff.

As the flight progressed, his irritation vanished. Megan was able to relax and enjoy the trip. Once she looked over and caught his gaze. "Thanks for today. You kept your promise. And I appreciate that."

He knew exactly what she meant. "I'd keep my promise if you stopped by my place and watch that movie with me, too. I'd be a perfect gentleman."

Megan nodded. "I'll think about it. Right now, I just want to enjoy this plane, the flight."

"I get that. This baby is sweet from spinner to rudder. A little bigger than my Cessna in Ecuador, but sweet just the same."

"Very sweet," Megan agreed.

"How was your flight?"

Startled, Megan whirled and whipped her hand to her pounding chest. Her purse dropped back onto her car seat. Micah stepped out of the growing shadows, his brow creased in apparent worry. "Great. It was very exciting."

"No regrets?" he pressed, studying her carefully.

"No. Chance was a perfect gentleman. Actually, he doesn't talk much while he works." The observation suddenly hit her as amusing. He must not consider the office work, the way he talked nonstop there. Smiling, she determined to tease him about it.

Micah shook his head. "Your dreamy smile is not a good sign."

"No." She waved her hand through the air. "I was just thinking something about work."

"No doubt. And MDS? Were you impressed with them, too?"

"Yes. We actually never left the airport. They came to us with a UPS van. But we worked hard to get everything unloaded and into the van. They were appreciative for all the supplies." Megan reached back inside the car for her purse and inclined her head toward the house. They started walking. "I was able to see the devastation from the sky. It's really unbelievable. It lifted houses off their foundations."

Micah fell into step with her. "I was on a volunteer team once. Pretty heart wrenching."

"Exactly." She glanced over. "You have your sermon ready?"

"Yep. I was just putting an antihistamine in my glove box for tomorrow when I heard you drive in."

"I hope you don't need it."

"It's good to be prepared. My day was more boring than yours, so bear with me if I ask too many questions. What kind of a plane was it?"

"A Cessna Caravan, single engine. The Caravans are cargo planes. They can even put those floatie things on them for landing in water. I learned quite a bit about planes today. That can't hurt my job. I'm glad I went."

Micah grinned. "You learned about 'floatie things'?"

"Fine. Pontoons. But we didn't need them."

"Never been in a small plane."

She glanced at him. "You'd like to?"

He shrugged. "Wouldn't turn down the chance."

She stopped walking. "How thoughtless. I should have invited you along today. Would you have gone?"

"Probably."

"I'm sorry. Next time just tell me."

"All right. But my curiosity's not satisfied."

Megan started walking again. "Yes?"

"What I'm wondering is what did Chance do after you drew the line in the sand?"

"He was a perfect gentleman." Reaching for the screen door, she asked, "Any more questions?"

"What's for dinner?"

"Taco salad," a voice chirped from inside the kitchen.

Megan jumped. "Aye, yi, yi! Mom, you scared me." She frowned at Micah. "You two in cahoots or what?"

Micah threw up his arms in a gesture of denial.

"What do you mean?" Mom asked.

"Oh nothing. It's just that Micah scared me, too, out by the car."

"Maybe you're just jumpy." Mom's piercing gaze held a strange glint, causing Megan to wonder how much her mother had heard of their conversation about Chance.

Jo,

    My heart's full of hopes and dreams and questions. Barbara claims nothing is an accident with God, that people's paths cross for a reason. Chance wants me to take a trip to Ecuador. I have no idea how this would be arranged. But Randy will owe Chance a big favor, and Chance could probably make this happen for me.

    I know flying is not a Conservative thing. But on the mission field, it's necessary. Chance understands me, the stirring I feel.

    Then there's Micah. He's become like a big brother protector. The night spent in the cellar with him was confusing and special, bringing us close. Though we both continue to make light of it, I think he feels it, too. It's nice to know I have a friend. I don't blame Lil and Katy for being busy with their own lives.

CHAPTER 21

On Sunday after his sermon, Micah tried to figure out why he'd gotten hives again. Speaking in front of a group didn't make him nervous. He'd earned As in speech class. He liked research and Bible study. Loved the writing process and hoped to branch out in that area.

Micah savored the intimacy that his sermon preparation created with God. All week long, the Lord gave him spiritual insights and affirmations. He even relished the times when God convicted him of sin.

But the ultimate fulfillment came during his sermon and afterward, when he saw how the message touched people. Eyes shone with revelation. Faces softened and sometimes sorrowed with repentance. All in all, it blessed him to shepherd a soul into God's truth. He knew he'd never tire of it.

So why when he was doing what he loved did he get hives again? Was it some allergy that had nothing to do with his spiritual growth? Or was it God speaking to him? He supposed a man could learn from every experience. But how could he do his job when all he could think about was clawing his face and throat? And it was becoming more difficult to concentrate on his conversation with the librarian when his mind was fixated on the antihistamine bottle in his glove box. He thought grimly that he should have put a capsule in his pocket for good measure.

"I love the quote you used in your sermon from *The Problem of Pain*. 'Pain provides opportunity for heroism; the opportunity is seized with surprising frequency.'"

"Yes, thanks for the book. C. S. Lewis is one of my favorite writers."

Lori smiled. "You're welcome. I also liked the part that age has nothing to do with pain. I know I've had my share."

Micah scratched the side of his neck, and his nose started tickling from her perfume. "I'm sorry. Glad you found comfort in the sermon."

"Oh, I did."

Across the vestibule, he saw Megan speaking to a petite brunette and wondered if it was her friend Lil. When Lori moved on, he went over to introduce himself.

"Fletch Stauffer." The brunette's husband offered a handshake. "I'm sorry we haven't met earlier, but we've been out of the country."

"So I heard. Where did you go, again?"

"Ethiopia. Taught some classes at the university."

"I'll bet you came back with some great stories."

"Lil invited some people for lunch today. Can you come?"

Micah didn't miss the frantic note in Lil's glance, though her smile affirmed her husband's invitation. The guest list had to include Megan, but he didn't want to push his way into her circle of friends.

She touched Lil's arm. "Micah and I've become good friends."

"Oh. We'd love to have you, Micah."

Fletch gave some quick directions to the doddy house; then the couple departed.

"You have hives again." Megan made it sound like he'd done it purposely.

"Yes, but I have medicine in my car. I'm headed there now. I'm going to swing by my cottage and make sure it settles down first."

"Take your time. Lil won't have the meal ready for at least half an hour. I'll see you there."

"Oh, Brother Zimmerman?"

Micah pivoted, colliding with Joy Ann's smile. "Mom wants me to invite you to dinner if you don't have plans."

"I'm sorry. I just accepted another invitation."

She furrowed her brow. "From Megan? But you eat with her every day."

Micah bristled at her resentful tone. "Fletch Stauffer just returned from a mission trip. I'd like to get to know him." He tried not to sound defensive, but he shouldn't have to explain his actions.

"But they don't even go to our church anymore. Not since they got married."

He hadn't remembered that. "Will you give your mom my apologies? Maybe I can take a rain check."

"Put us on the waiting list then." She gave him a flirtatious smile. "Hopefully we're at the top."

"Yes. You are." Now would be the perfect time to employ some of Megan's woman repellants, only he couldn't drum up so much as a solitary chuckle. It erupted into an impatient cough. He had a growing inkling that he would end up hurting Joy Ann's feelings.

"I'll see you tomorrow when we count the offering."

He needed to tell her that the elders had taken his advice, and a treasurer would be helping her with the offering in the future, but he didn't want to detain her any longer. He was one-tracked, needing to get to his car and get relief for the fire ants that marched up and down his neck.

⁓

Megan folded the quilt they would use for the picnic while watching Lil's animated expression.

"The trip was so good for our marriage. We'd gotten off track, you know." Lil placed dinnerware in the picnic basket that had once been her grandma's. "Just a lot of adjustments, and with both of us working, we were getting snappy. So on the long plane ride, we came up with a plan to keep our relationship exciting. Romantic picnics. Our first date was a picnic. So we're going to plan them around our work schedules."

"Nobody said anything about this being a *romantic* picnic."

Lil waved her gloved hand then took the ham out of the oven. "Silly. This is just a fun day with friends." She shook her head. "I've missed you."

"Chance goes to Volo Italiano all the time now."

"How's it going with him?"

"He took me up in a Cessna, yesterday."

Lil momentarily froze. "You're kidding. Why?"

"While you were gone, Indiana had some tornados. MDS went in to help. We flew in some supplies. I didn't help with tornado cleanup, just helped unload the supplies. But the plane ride was amazing."

"Wow." Lil eyed her with skepticism. "I didn't really like flying over the ocean." She got a knife and carved the meat.

Megan made sandwiches. "So what was Ethiopia like?"

"It's in the Horn of Africa. Mekelle's one of its largest cities. The market had rows of palm trees. I got some recipes from the locals. You know the recipe book I'm working on?"

"Yeah?"

"Since I'm going to be traipsing around the world with Fletch, I thought I'd add an ethnic section. It'll give me something to focus on while he's doing his thing."

"What was his thing?"

"He lectured at the university about gross parasites. The place is known for their cows and honey. I brought you back some."

Megan shivered. "I hope you mean honey and not parasites."

Giggling, Lil touched her arm. "I'm glad to be home, Green Bean. Did I tell you I invited Ivan and Elizabeth? The babies are close in age, and I thought it would be nice."

The doddy house was on Elizabeth and Ivan Miller's property. The young married couple occupied the big house. "Our lives are branching out, aren't they?" Megan smiled. "Soon you'll have children, too."

Lil leaned close. "I wonder. I thought by now. . ." She sighed. "It's all right. I'm enjoying the restaurant, but watching Katy and Elizabeth, the idea of becoming a mom is growing on me."

"Katy seems very busy."

"But I've never known her to be happier. She makes it look easy. Back to Chance. So the flight was strictly work related?"

"Yeah, but he wants me to go to Ecuador next. Thinks I can find a job there."

"What?" Lil looked stricken.

"It's just an idea."

"I'd hoped to keep you here. But after Ethiopia, I understand you a little better."

Katy stepped into the doddy house and hugged Lil's shoulders. "This is so fun. What can I do to help?"

"Did you see if Elizabeth had the table set up yet?"

"She does."

Lil closed a plastic container that held the sandwiches they'd just prepared. "Let's start carrying the food out."

As they moved onto the porch, they saw Micah drive in. "So you and Micah are friends now, too?"

"Yeah, the night we spent together in the storm cellar pretty much cemented our friendship."

Katy's eyes widened. "You what?"

"When the tornado came through. We got trapped in there when the tree fell on the house."

"Dad told me about rescuing you guys," Lil admitted. "Said Bill wants to keep it quiet."

"What happened?" Katy asked.

"I was so scared, but Micah protected me. He's like a big brother."

"If you're looking for a brother, you can have one of mine," Lil scoffed.

As Megan helped spread the quilts on the ground, she saw Elizabeth leading Fletch their way. "Let's drop it for now."

Fletch clamped Micah's shoulder. "You're just in time to say grace."

During the meal, Fletch shared stories about his work in Ethiopia. Lil kept an adoring eye on him and interjected colorful tidbits. Megan nibbled one of Lil's cookies and rubbed little Jacob's back until he drifted asleep on the quilt.

When Micah finished eating, he swept up Elizabeth's fussing toddler and took him a safe distance from the sleeping baby. He tossed the child in the air until he giggled.

Katy watched him. "You've missed it, Lil. Regardless how brother-like he is, Micah's caused quite a stir in the community."

Lil glanced at Megan as if she'd been holding back on her. "He's single." Megan shrugged, as if that explained everything to Lil.

Katy traced a finger across the back of sleeping Jacob's neck. "I believe Joy Ann has set her cap for him."

Lil pierced Megan with a gaze that demanded honesty. "But you're not interested in him?"

"I'm very interested in him. As our next preacher. I'm probably his biggest supporter."

Lil's gaze swept back to Micah. "From what I see, I like him."

"We like him, too," Elizabeth chimed in. "It's time for somebody younger to take over the reins at Big Darby."

Jacob stirred, and Katy withdrew her hand. "When we were kids, you always said you wanted to marry a preacher."

"Or a missionary," Megan reminded her friend.

"Lil got the missionary. But there's an available preacher who's watching you with interest."

"Elizabeth, don't pay any attention to these two."

The other woman grinned. "Here he comes now."

"Shh!" Megan warned them.

"The little guy's strong." Micah lowered the toddler and watched him run to Ivan.

At some point, Micah had unbuttoned the top of his white shirt. He didn't know it, but when he'd been roughhousing, his shirttail had worked out of his trousers. A light breeze ruffled his hair, disarraying its absurd, deep side-part. A tender, protective feeling welled up in Megan. He was much better looking than she'd ever given him credit for. She could understand why Joy Ann and Lori were smitten.

He must have sensed her watching him, or else he'd known that the women were talking about him. He brushed her with a soft gaze and quirked the corner of his mouth. And Megan couldn't deny being his biggest supporter.

After Micah left the picnic, Ivan took the men to the barn to look at some new farm equipment. Katy and Elizabeth put the babies in strollers, and the women took a leisurely walk past cornfields and ditches covered in spires of purple loosestrife. Although Megan's nose tickled and a dull headache settled in behind her eyes, she kept it to herself. She didn't want to spoil one of the rare moments when the friends could all be together.

CHAPTER 22

Megan's headache had increased by the time she returned home. Deep in her thoughts, she entered the house through the kitchen and walked toward the refrigerator.

"Just look at the floor! And I mopped it yesterday."

Megan whirled, following her mom's gaze. "Was that me? I'm sorry."

"Not just you. Everybody!" Mom exclaimed. "And I suppose you're hungry now?"

Megan took out a pitcher of iced tea. "No, I was just getting something to wash down a painkiller. I told you I was going over to Lil's, didn't I?" For the life of her, Megan couldn't figure out why her mom was acting snippy.

"Yes. You told me. Guess nobody else is hungry, either." Mom placed her hand at her temple. "I didn't mean to snap. I'm sorry you have a headache."

"I'll be fine, but are you feeling all right?"

Mom's face reddened. "'Course I am. I was thinking about making some homemade ice cream tonight, but we're out of rock salt."

"You always work hard. Why don't we go to Dairy Queen later? I'll treat."

"That would be nice, honey. I got a new *Country Living* magazine. Think I'll just go sit on the swing and relax a bit. Your grandparents are coming over later."

"I'm going to wash my hair. We went for a walk today, and Lil's road is so dusty. There must be some pollen in it, too."

"That's the same thing Micah said. He sure does get hives a lot."

Megan nodded and went upstairs, glad to get away from her mom's bad mood. As she washed her hair, she wondered if having Micah around all the time was starting to wear on Mom. She'd always enjoyed having friends over, the relatives, too. Often she hosted the holidays. Megan blotted her hair on a towel. Everybody was allowed a few grumpy days. She just hoped there wasn't anything wrong that Mom wasn't telling her.

By the time she'd finished, the bathroom was steamy. The summer heat always rose and made the upstairs hotter than the rest of the house. Megan opted to dry her hair on the porch and give her mom a chance to redeem herself.

"Can I sit with you?"

"Sure, honey." Mom scooted over, gave her a wary glance, then turned the page to her magazine. "See this quilt advertisement? It's machine stitched. Now why would somebody want to buy this when they can make one themselves—a much better one, too?"

Megan drew the hairbrush down through her long, straight locks. "Don't know, Mom."

"You ladies trying to solve the world's problems?" Micah asked, stepping up onto the porch and obviously not realizing the tension surrounding the women.

Feeling his gaze on her hair, Megan self-consciously tossed it behind her back and dropped the hairbrush onto her lap.

"No, I was just asking Megan why somebody would want to buy a machine-made quilt when they can make a better one."

"Probably for convenience."

"I suppose. But shortcuts don't make things better."

"Unless it's Dairy Queen," Megan teased.

"You don't like my ice-cream recipe? Honestly, Megan. You're a piece of work right now." Mom rose. "I'm going to ask Bill which he'd rather have. There's still time to make a batch before your grandparents get here."

Thought we didn't have any rock salt.

—◌—

Micah watched Anita go into the house. On the porch, Megan sighed.

"Sorry. Guess I have bad timing."

She stared at the screen door. "It's not like Mom to be rude. Something's bothering her. We used to be able to talk about things. But lately. . ." Her voice trailed off.

"She's withdrawing?"

Megan shrugged. "Maybe it's me."

"I talked to her this afternoon. She seemed stressed. I hope it's not me. Or the cat."

"Phooey. Mom loves to entertain and play the hostess. She always enjoys having my grandparents over, too. Whatever it is, I'm sure it'll pass." She glanced at him and patted the swing. "Sit?"

"I'm good here." He lowered himself to the top step.

Megan shrugged. "I'm glad you could spend time with my friends."

"You all grew up together except for Fletch?"

"Yes. Katy and Jake loved each other since first grade."

"Jake told me how he helped fix up the doddy house. It reminded me of my cottage, here."

"Believe me, the doddy house needed more than a day's work. It was a major project."

"So you girls lived together?"

Megan fiddled with her hairbrush. "Katy and Lil moved in together while I was still at Rosedale. I couldn't afford my share of the rent until I graduated and got a job. I lived at the doddy house with Lil for a while, but then she got married and took it over."

"You sound disappointed."

"Not really. It was Lil's dream. And she loved the place. After she met Fletch, her dreams changed." As Megan got invested in her memories, she involuntarily drew her half-dried hair to the front of her shoulder and ran her hairbrush through it.

Watching her made Micah's mouth go dry, and he struggled to push away his own dreams, the ones of Megan with the silky long hair. It was good the root cellar had been dark; it had helped him maintain his self-control.

She tilted her head, realized what she was doing, and shook it back over her shoulder. "You all right?"

"I'm fine," he managed.

"Good. I saw your sneezing fit at the picnic."

"I saw yours, too."

"I know. It's weird how we're allergic to the same things. Except I don't have any food allergies."

He clamped his arms around his bent knees. "You don't get hives every Sunday morning, either."

Megan leaned forward and waved her hairbrush. "Why do you think that is?"

He gave a harsh laugh. "If I knew, I'd put a stop to it."

"You think it's something at the church? It's only on Sundays," she reasoned aloud. "Could it be stress or nerves or something you wear?"

Micah shook his head. "I've been stressed and nervous before. Never had hives. But something I wear? Hmm." His eyes widened. "I did get my suit coat dry cleaned just before I came to Plain City."

Megan eyes sparked with excitement, "That's got to be it." Then her shoulders sagged. Beautiful shoulders that were making it hard to concentrate on their conversation. "No. That can't be it. You wear it more often than Sundays."

He stood, rubbing his clammy hands on his trousers. "No, I have more than one. I think you just solved the mystery." As difficult as it was, he needed to put some physical space between them. "Enjoy your ice cream."

"Don't you want to stay for Dairy Queen? At least let us bring you back something."

"Thanks for the offer, but Anita's already stressed. And your grand-parents just pulled in the drive. I'll give you some family time."

Megan stood. Her pale hair fell forward and caught a shimmer from the sun that was dropping low in the west. "All right. 'Night, Micah."

" 'Night." He curled his fists and strode to his cottage. His cat leaped from the window seat to greet him, rubbing against his trousers. "She's an angel, Purrty, and I feel like the devil."

Megan went to Volo Italiano for lunch. "All week long, Mom's been snippy and withdrawn. She goes to bed early, and Dad's been spending more time in the shop. Micah must have sensed something's wrong, because he'd grown scarce, barely taking any meals with us. I don't know what he thinks of us," she bemoaned.

Lil touched her friend's arm. "I know what you're going through." She referred to her own mother's long, painful bout of depression two years earlier. "I never dreamed it would happen to Anita. You better talk to her. Try to get at the bottom of it, before she slips into a downward spiral."

Lil wasn't helping matters. Megan hadn't felt this scared since her frantic drive with a funnel cloud barreling after her. Her heart clenched as though destruction was peeking its head in her rearview mirror and gaining momentum, even as they spoke. "I'll talk to her."

"Good. Or I could send my mom over."

"No, not yet." Megan pushed the idea away, almost sorry she'd brought up the matter. "Did you have your romantic picnic this week?"

"Tomorrow. Fletch doesn't have to work. At least, as far as we know."

"Has it been hard getting back into the grind?"

"Not bad. Giavanni's patient."

"A good thing," Megan teased. Lil had tried the patience of every boss she'd ever had before Giavanni. Of course, that was back when Lil's mom was going through depression. The thought of her own mom having that condition troubled Megan.

"I only saw Chance once this week. He hasn't left yet?"

"No. two more weeks. His stay got extended." Megan debated asking Lil's opinion about the movie that Chance had pestered her about all week. But when she saw Lil glancing toward the kitchen, she knew their time had ended. She pushed up from the stone bench. "I'm glad you're back. Thanks for the penne."

"I'll pray for Anita." Lil pushed up and straightened her black slacks. The two friends hugged, and Megan left the restaurant with a heavy heart.

That evening, Megan fidgeted through an uncomfortable supper.

"I can't believe I burned the potatoes," Mom apologized.

Micah examined the food on his fork. "Parsley potatoes are supposed to be crispy, aren't they? And if they aren't, then you're on to something good with these."

"A little charcoal's good for the liver," Dad teased.

Mom tossed her napkin on the table. "Don't patronize me."

Soon after that, Micah slinked away to his cottage. But there was no place for Megan to go. This was her home. It used to be happy. "I need to know what's going on with you two. Nobody will look me in the eyes anymore. Mom?"

Mom grabbed some plates and went to the sink.

Dad sighed. "Come back here. Sit down and tell her."

An army of dread marched up Megan's neck. Dad hardly ever spoke sternly.

With slumped shoulders, Mom set the plates on the counter and returned to the table. "It isn't a pleasant story." She clenched her lips.

"Dad?" He shook his head, and Megan looked back at Mom.

"You know that I'm adopted."

Megan nodded, nearly numb with fright. Surely they weren't going to tell her she was adopted, too.

"What you don't know is that I know some things about my blood relatives on my birth mom's side. They come from Reading, Pennsylvania. They have kept in contact a little bit."

Relief swept over Megan, and she strived to understand. "Do I have grandparents that I don't know about?"

"No, they aren't living. But you have a great-aunt."

"Did something happen to her?"

"No." Mom's jaw tightened. "She's coming for a visit."

A boulder of burden rolled off Megan's shoulders. "But that's wonderful!" So Mom's irritability was worry about meeting her relative? She wasn't depressed, and her parents were still getting along? Only relatives visiting. It was a good thing. But Mom didn't act like it was good at all.

"Not so wonderful. Let me tell you the rest."

The weight returned and pressed heavily. Megan kneaded the base of her neck.

"I didn't tell you about your relatives before now because I thought it was something we could brush under the rug. But it refuses to stay where it belongs. Now I wish I'd told you about them before."

Dad's eyes shone with sympathy. Folding her hands on the tabletop, Megan whispered, "So tell me now."

Fidgeting with the cloth napkin, Mom nodded. "Your great-aunt is English. I come from a family that is not Mennonite, never was. My blood mother was not even a Christian."

An ocean of shock washed over Megan, disabling her movement and speech.

Mom dabbed her eyes with her napkin. "I'm an imposter."

Dad reached across the table and stilled Mom's hand. "That's ridiculous. You're a wonderful woman. You may have been born into the world, but you were raised Mennonite. Megan and I don't have any regrets."

Megan struggled filled with confusion and frustration. "Not Mennonite?"

"Of course she is," Dad maintained. "She was baptized in the church just like you were."

Truth strangled Megan's neck. "Then I'm not Mennonite, either. I have the outsider's blood." Tears pressed behind her eyes. She stumbled to her feet and clutched the table. "This is a shock. But I have to know. Who are we?"

Mom blew her nose on her napkin. "If I hadn't been adopted, my name would be Lintz. My mother's family was Witherspoon."

The word *adopted* reminded Megan that none of this was her mom's fault. Mom couldn't help that her parents had been killed in a car crash, either. Megan softened her voice. "How do you know they weren't Christians? Did you meet them?" She refused to believe that her mom would secretly stay in contact with her family and keep it from her.

Once Mom opened up, the story spilled out. "My parents weren't even married. My grandparents attended some church, but my mom didn't want to have anything to do with their faith. She went wild and lived with my dad without the blessing of her parents. I don't know much about the Lintz family. When the accident happened, my grandparents rejected me."

"Maybe they were too old to raise a child?"

"Not that old. They knew about the Mennonites through a friend's housekeeper. They made some inquiries and found a home for me." Her voice glittered with resentment. "One that was far away, in a different state. So they could hide their shame. But now they're gone. My aunt Louise wants to bring me some of my grandmother's things."

"Did she tell you all this?"

"No, Mom told me."

Megan knew her mom referred to Grandma Bachman, the woman who had raised her. With Dad's parents gone, she was the only grandmother Megan had ever known. "When?"

Mom gripped Dad's hand. "When I was about your age, Mom told me about my background. It was hard for me to accept their rejection. Now this Louise is sticking her nose in where it doesn't belong. I told her not to come. She wouldn't take no for an answer. She's bound and determined to drag up my past. What good can come of it now?"

Feeling as though she were crawling out of a dark shroud and viewing the light for the first time, Megan blinked. "Who all knows about this?"

Mom shrugged. "I suppose most of the older folks in church."

Resentment that she'd been kept in the dark, Megan cried, "I can't believe nobody ever told me."

"It's one of those things that died down."

"You know that everyone loves your mom." Dad patted Mom's hand. "And they adore you. I know it's a shock to discover some genes you didn't know about, but these people gave you and your mother some good genes. A cheery disposition, for one."

Megan pushed in her chair and gripped its back, disgusted by how he could refer to an entire clan of living people—her people—as a gene pool.

He explained, "You can't discount the good just because a young girl made some poor choices."

"When is our aunt coming?"

"Next month."

Megan forced a smile. "Don't worry about it, Mom. Somehow, we'll make do."

Mom's expression filled with gratitude. She shot to her feet and pulled Megan into an awkward embrace. Megan woodenly patted Mom's back. But inside, she felt broken, as if everything she'd always believed in had been snatched away from her. She pulled back. "Thanks for telling me. I'm tired. I think I'll go to my room now." She shifted her gaze to the kitchen sink.

"Go on to your room. You don't need to help with the dishes."

Megan didn't have the strength to argue and sprang up the stairs and down the hall. In her room, she slammed the door and crumbled.

CHAPTER 23

The skeletons in Megan's outsider closet rattled their bones, making sleep elusive. She squinted at the digital clock. It was barely after midnight. Anger and resentment added to the clatter in her brain, and after hours of struggle, she threw back the covers. She tossed her legs over the side of her bed.

Her room was hot and oppressive. She snatched up her robe and stole downstairs. Mom claimed lemon tea helped her occasional insomnia. In the kitchen the demons of the conversation she'd had with her parents haunted the air. Through the window, the cottage light glimmered. Her lips formed a grim line to think that she'd once considered Micah repulsive. In truth, she was the faulty piece. With her outsider genes, she was no longer a prize for any decent Conservative man.

The whistle of the kettle drew her from the window. She quickly removed the teapot from the burner, lest she awaken her parents. She didn't want to face them or their sympathy. With resentment she fixed her tea and bought the steaming cup to her lips. Micah's light twinkled into the surrounding darkness. What had he told her in the root cellar? *"When it's dark enough, you can see the stars."* She bent and looked up toward the sky, but it was blocked by shrubbery.

She padded barefoot onto the front porch, flinching when she heard the creaking chains of the porch swing. "Micah?"

"It's me."

She hesitated. "What are you doing here so late?"

His soft voice was laced with amusement. "Probably the same thing as you. I couldn't sleep." His brown gaze swept over her night robe.

"Sorry for disturbing you. I better take my tea back inside."

"Is Anita upset with me?"

"No. It's nothing to do with you."

"Are you sure?"

His pleading tone beckoned. With brief hesitation she rationalized that even though she wore a robe, her body was fully covered. They had survived the root cellar without causing a scandal, and he was the preacher. Her bitterness scoffed that her good name was already smirched, anyway, so she sank down beside him. "I found out what's troubling Mom."

"I don't mean to pry, but it's obviously upset you."

With her forefinger, she twisted her hair. "Mom's adopted. I always knew that, but tonight I found out that she kept some things from me about her real family. We have an aunt who's coming to visit us. Mom's been worried about the visit and also about me finding out the truth about her family."

"That explains her behavior."

Her bare feet fell into sway with Micah's tennis shoes, and the story flowed forth in hypnotically bitter waves. "We're not sure why my great-aunt wants to meet us. But I found out that my mom's family is not Mennonite. They aren't even Christians. Funny, Dad just told me a couple weeks ago that Dirk Willems is in our blood line." She laughed bitterly. "I was so proud of it. And I didn't even know who I really was."

Micah gave a short whistle. "Dirk Willems *is* a hero. I heard the story in college. It stirred me, too. It's easy to believe that a man like him would be in your bloodline."

She pulled a sarcastic face. "Hardly."

"Regardless of your mom's people, he's still one of your ancestors."

Megan lowered her gaze, and her hair fell into a silky curtain that veiled her shame. "No. I'm lucky if I got any of those genes. Don't you see?

178

I've been living a lie. I'm so angry at Mom for not telling me sooner. I feel so deceived. Confused."

Micah removed her cup from her hands and set it on the ground. Then he folded her hand in his, intertwining their fingers. "Despite what you're feeling, this doesn't change who you are. God holds each of us accountable for ourselves, according to our talents and our own faith. That hasn't changed."

She tightened her grip. "Hasn't it? For nearly two months, I've fought off an attraction for Chance." Her throat constricted painfully. "Just because he's not a Mennonite. But he's a Christian. If he knew about this, he would despise me for my hypocrisy."

Micah caressed her hand with his thumb. "How could he, when you just found out? But you're still a Mennonite. You haven't changed just because you found out some things about your relatives."

She pulled away from his touch and thrust her hand up in anger. "I can't just slough this off. If something like this came out about your family, do you think you'd still feel confident about your job at the church?"

"First of all, I'm not confident about it. Secondly, maybe your aunt is coming to help you work through it."

Megan shook her head. "Mom says she's coming to stir up the past."

"Anita's a typical parent, trying to protect you. She's probably afraid that if you visit these people, you'll see something you like and be tempted to leave the church."

"What if she's right?"

⎯☙⎯

Micah saw that Megan's faith was being sorely tested. Doubts and emotions were blurring the truth that had been the foundation of her faith. The timing of this news couldn't be worse. Anita couldn't have known about Megan's infatuation with Chance. It was up to him to place Megan's hand back on her anchor.

"Being Mennonite is a way of life that reflects certain beliefs. It's not something genetic. Now more than ever, you need to pull strength from your beliefs. Let them ground you."

"I've been thinking about this all night. It's like a ripple that widens into eternity. I can't comprehend how it's going to affect my life. But I know one thing. It was wrong for Mom to keep this information from me. People at church knew about this and didn't tell me, either. Don't you understand how betrayed I feel?"

"I'm sure nobody wanted to intentionally hurt you. They probably saw your mom's adoption as a blessing. The church family was an extension of her adoptive family. Then when she married a man of the church, her grafting in was even stronger. All that was set in place before you were even born. Your family is a strong unit, providing leadership in the church."

"Whenever I asked Mom about her real family, she always made some comment that made me believe she didn't know anything about them. How could she cut off ties with her real family and assume that I wouldn't want to meet them?"

A night owl hooted. Another owl gave answering calls. Micah's heart melded with the mournful music and Megan's pain, seeking to ease the latter. "She'd already weighed everything and made those choices before you were born."

"My grandparents are dead. She made the choice of shunning them. And because of that, I never knew them."

His own grief identified with Megan's pain. "That's hard. I loved my grandma." He still missed her cheery hugs and gentle guidance. She'd been good-natured like Anita. He hoped this disclosure hadn't caused a breach in Megan's relationship with her mom. He asked tenderly, "Did you have an argument with your mom tonight?"

"No. She was upset. I wanted to think through everything before I said something to upset her even more."

"That was a smart thing to do."

Megan tossed her hair over her shoulder. The simple gesture aroused a physical reaction that he tried to tamp down. Everything about her affected him, but lately it was becoming a natural habit to gravitate toward her need as much as her desirability.

"Chance thinks I can find a job in Ecuador."

Her bitter remark splashed cold water on his foolish hopes and drove a knife into his reckless heart, but he understood what drove her. The sifting and weighing of her faith had shattered her self-control and caused her to lash out at the restrictions of her upbringing. His frantic heart leaped, willing her to realize that her life didn't have to drastically change.

She hardened her gaze, ineffectively warding off his unspoken intervention.

Her world had tilted, giving Chance a small window of opportunity to step into this new realm of Megan's life and prey on her vulnerability. When Micah saw his words were powerless against her instability, he slipped his arm around her, anything to anchor her to the Conservative world, his world. "Don't run from your family, from the people who love you."

Megan wiggled out of his embrace and pushed to her bare feet. She narrowed her eyes into thin glacial slits. "We shouldn't be out here."

He gave a sad sigh. "I suppose. It's just that I want to protect you."

"Thanks. But I need to figure this out myself. And I need to tell Chance the truth."

"Do you think that's wise?" She swept her chilly gaze over him as if he was from an enemy camp. "All I meant was you shouldn't do anything rash. Give yourself more time to think things through."

"Chance invited me to his place to watch a movie about the Aucas. It will help me work through my new identity. Spending time with him and learning more about Ecuador will help me make some decisions so that I *don't* do anything rash."

"I understand that. But proceed slowly while you're still emotional."

"We don't have much time until he leaves the States again."

"Surely you can take a few days?"

"Fine. I won't talk to him about it until the weekend, when we watch the movie."

Balling fists of frustrated energy, he pressed, "You shouldn't go to his apartment while you're feeling confused."

"Micah, how is it any different than being alone with you, like we are now? Don't you trust me?"

"It's different because you're not attracted to me." Rays of moonlight revealed her embarrassment.

"What if the timing of Mom's news was meant to make me more open-minded toward Chance's offer?"

"And what is his offer? Has he offered you marriage?"

Megan eyes glittered. "My blood grandmother wasn't married when she had my mother."

Her unanticipated slash drew blood, but it only made him more obstinate to play the hero and shield her from her own foolishness. He parried, "Or maybe God sent me to Plain City to keep you from ruining your life."

She placed one hand on her hip, looking regal in her white night robe. "Now you're just being manipulative."

"I'm being your friend. If our friendship means anything, then at least consider my advice."

Tears glistened, softening her eyes. She sucked her bottom lip between her teeth.

"Meg," he breathed. He drew her close. She melded into his embrace, clutching the back of his shirt. She sobbed against his chest. If he had manipulated her, it was for her own good. But his conscience licked wildly at his ears. And he wrestled with his scruples, as he comforted the object of his desires. A broken barefoot woman wearing a robe with her hair immodestly streaming down her back. He struggled with the impulse to whisper that she didn't need to go any farther than her own porch to find a man who would love her and help her find her identity. Instead he whispered, "Your identity is in Christ. Be sure to pray about it." And then he released her.

Megan nodded. "Of course. Thanks for listening. For everything." She bent and picked up her tea then gave him a wobbly smile. "Don't lose any more sleep over it, Micah."

He smiled and watched her disappear into the house. Sleep was the last thing Micah had on his mind.

—◌—

"You look terrible." Paige tilted her face, studying Megan. "Like you cried all night."

"Personal problems," Megan muttered.

"Wanna talk about it?" Paige lowered her voice and leaned over Megan's desk. "Is it about Chance?"

Megan shook her head. "No. And I don't want to talk about it. But if

I fall asleep at my desk, bring coffee."

"Sure thing, honey. Hope you work things out."

Megan had gotten to work a few minutes late, and the door to Chance's office had already been closed. Until she talked to him about the movie, she wouldn't be able to calm the restless river that flowed through her veins, making it difficult to concentrate on her work.

As soon as Paige left, Megan scooped up a stack of paperwork and knocked on his door.

"Come in." She pushed the door open and allowed it to close behind her. Chance looked up with pleasant surprise. "Hi."

"Can we talk?"

He nodded toward a side chair. "Sit down."

Megan slipped into the welcome support of a masculine leather side chair. "I'm sorry I was late this morning."

"No problem. Usually you're early. Everything all right?"

Now Micah's warnings were sharks circling her mind and confusing her, but she couldn't break free from the promise she'd made him. She clutched the files and drifted into unchartered waters.

"Something wrong?" he repeated.

She wet her lips with her tongue. "Some personal stuff that I don't want to talk about right now. But I wondered if the offer still stands about viewing your movie *The End of the Spear*?"

Chance's face lit with undisguised pleasure. "Of course, Meg. Do you want to do dinner first?"

She drew a line in the sand. "Oh. Just the movie, if you don't mind. And could we do it during the day?"

Chance acknowledged her wishes. "Sure, no pressure. We can just watch the movie." Then he tried to gain control again. "You want me to pick you up on Saturday? Two? Three o'clock?"

"If you give me the address, I'll drop by around two."

He quickly scribbled the address on a yellow sticky note, and she exchanged the address for her files. "Thanks. These need signatures."

Accepting the paperwork, he replied, "Let me know if I can help. With the other."

"I think you already have. I'll explain it on Saturday." Relieved to have maneuvered the situation to her satisfaction, Megan stepped out of his office. But her brief buoyancy fled when she saw Paige waiting near her desk. The other woman's gaze narrowed as if she saw right through Megan's intentions. "I don't advise crying on his shoulder."

"That's not what I was doing." Megan resented the way everybody interfered, treating her as if she wasn't an adult capable of making her own choices. If her mom hadn't been protecting her for all these years, she wouldn't be feeling so rotten now. "Why does everybody want to run my life? Do I need to wear a No Trespassing sign on my back?"

"I guess you never heard the story about Little Red Riding Hood?"

Slipping into her chair, Megan rolled her gaze toward the ceiling. "Yes. A lot of wolf stories are circulating, but thinking about them doesn't get my work done."

Paige gave a sulky toss of her head and departed.

CHAPTER 24

Megan stood at her bedroom window and looked down over the peaceful country landscape, but it did little to ease her internal restlessness. She'd spent the remainder of the workweek consumed in private thoughts, feeding the idea that she needed to explore the part of the world that she knew so little about. Fifty percent of her genetic background came from the outsiders' world. She couldn't just ignore it like her mom had done.

She had to find out if those genes were responsible for the unexplainable stirrings she sometimes felt. She needed to identify the source of her restlessness so that she could determine if they were God-given or sinful urges. She had no intention of shucking her Christian faith, but she needed answers. Now that her eyes had been opened, she was rethinking her personal destiny. Was she still to follow the Conservative road or did another road beckon? The mission field? More specifically, was God calling her to join Chance in Ecuador?

Just as she released the gauzy curtain to move away from the window, she heard the sound that could be none other than Lil's old rattle clap. A quick look verified it. Only Lil never dropped by these days, not since her marriage. They always met at Volo Italiano or the doddy house. She hurried downstairs and moved with haste to answer the door.

"Hi. You busy?"

Easily sensing that something had occurred to upset Lil, Megan drew her friend inside. With a warning finger to her lips, they snuck past the hall, almost losing Lil to the aroma of freshly baking cinnamon rolls.

Upstairs in Megan's room, Lil sank on the bed with a sigh.

"What on earth's wrong?"

"Fletch cancelled our picnic. He has to work again. I thought my dad had the market on pigheadedness, but I was wrong. My husband thinks he's always right about everything. I always have to give in."

"Fletch had an emergency?"

"Vic had an emergency, and Fletch feels like he has to cover for him at the clinic."

"Why don't you just take the picnic to him?"

"I didn't think of that." Lil shook her head. "The picnic's off now. He's mad because I second-guessed his decision. And according to him, I'm *never* supposed to question his decisions. I'm not in the mood for a picnic."

Although Megan hated to see Lil angry and upset, she had a strong inkling that it wasn't a coincidence that Lil had stopped by. "I don't know about *never*. But this time, I think he made the right choice."

"What?"

"I think I'm the reason Fletch has to work today."

Lil looked at Megan as if she'd lost her marbles or wasn't following the conversation at all.

"Because I need you to go with me this afternoon. I thought about asking you anyway. First I thought about asking Micah, but that wouldn't have worked." Micah would have gone with her to watch the movie. But after telling Chance that Conservative men were nonresistant, putting those two men together would have been setting a foolish trap for Micah. After nixing that idea, Megan had thought of Lil. And here she was, delivered right to her doorstep.

"Slow down. Go with you where?"

"I'm going to Chance's apartment to watch a movie with him."

Lil jumped off the bed and grabbed Megan by the shoulders. "What? You aren't even allowed to watch movies. And going to his apartment is asking for trouble. Have you lost your mind?"

"Not my mind. Just my identity. Sit down. It's a long story."

Lil drew her brows together in concern. She eased onto the edge of the bed. "Okay, spill it."

The story unfolded more easily the second time around, and Megan only strayed from it long enough to answer a few of Lil's well-placed questions. "And this is your aunt?"

"My great-aunt Louise. My instincts tell me that her visit is going to reveal some things that could change my life. There has to be a reason why she's coming to visit us now, after all these years. Although Mom's skeptical, I want to hear everything my aunt has to say."

"But what does this have to do with going to Chance's house?"

"I want to weigh all my options with an open mind."

"Your mind may be open, but your emotions are all over the board."

"You sound just like Micah."

Lil arched a brow but didn't press. "Don't worry. I'll keep you accountable."

"Then you'll go?"

"Of course I will."

"I'm probably not the friend to advise you about husbands and marriage. Katy would have more experience in that department. Sometimes I even feel sorry for myself, that you are both married. I'm sorry I've been so engrossed in my own life that I haven't noticed your struggles."

"You drop in at the restaurant all the time. If I needed a shoulder to cry on, I would have told you. I came today, didn't I? And I don't want you thinking we have marriage problems. I'll admit we both have self-control issues. But if God led me here today, then I owe Fletch an apology. I haven't been a very understanding wife." Lil leaned close. "Fletch really is pigheaded. But then, so am I."

Megan smiled.

Lil grinned back. "Movies aren't forbidden at the church Fletch and I attend. It'll be fun." Lil suddenly giggled. "I can't wait to see Chance's face when I walk into his apartment with you."

Megan laughed. "Poor Chance. It will be a surprise."

⟶੧

Chance shook his head and burst out laughing. "Of course you brought a friend." In a sense, he was relieved. He didn't want to do anything to chase Megan away, and she'd come up with the perfect solution. One that made her feel safe to set foot into his bachelor apartment. He didn't know why he hadn't suggested it himself. "Come in, both of you."

As Lil passed by him, she whispered. "Just remember I'm watching you."

His smile deepened, and he whispered back, "I think I can take you." Then he flinched, for he'd almost referred to his air force experience. Revealing that information before he'd won Megan's complete trust would have shot their relationship out of the sky, sending them in a downward spiral with no recovery.

Lil flounced by, and Megan shrugged. "Lil showed up at my house today, and I thought she'd enjoy the movie, too."

"Believe me, I understand. I'm glad she came."

Megan gave a slight nod and entered his apartment, which he'd spent the morning cleaning. He knew that she kept a tidy desk, and by the way her hair was always perfectly swept into that bun and net thing, he was pretty sure she even bordered on the neat-freak side.

His gaze swept over her, as hers took in the results of his cleanup campaign. Megan usually carried herself with confidence, but today her shoulders were soldier straight. Normally her serene expression and pale skin gave her a feminine appeal, but as she perused his apartment, her face tilted upward, revealing a strong square chin and a don't-mess-with-me attitude.

To Chance, it was a challenge. He watched her move about the room. She wore a dark print dress, black stockings, and black shoes. Her clothing was always too baggy for his preference. He figured she did that on purpose to hide her figure.

"In Ecuador, is your apartment this sparse?"

"Small and sparse. Except for my tapestry collection. My favorites are a gray elephant print and a blue tree of life."

"What's an elephant print?"

"The design has rows of elephants." He thought how to best describe it. "Along the lines of an Egyptian motif."

Megan nodded.

"I'm sure they're nothing like the quilts we're used to," Lil interjected.

"Do you hang them on the walls or use them as rugs?" Megan asked.

"Both. I hope I can show them to you someday."

She glanced at the floor of his apartment—a short-piled, neutral carpet—and back up at him. He saw a glint in her eye that made his heart race, but he tried to keep his voice casual. "Sit down, ladies. Can I get you something to drink? I have soda and water bottles."

Megan and Lil shared the couch, and he brought them water. As they made small talk about Lil's recent trip, he watched the petite brunette with the stylish haircut swing a jean-clad leg. Not for the first time, he wondered about the women's friendship. They both had the same Pennsylvania Dutch huskiness to their voices. Were they relatives? After listening for a polite period of time, he asked, "How did you two become friends?"

Megan replied, "We grew up in the same church. After Lil got married, she started going to a different one, with fewer restrictions."

A spark of righteous anger flared up in him, he turned to face Lil. "Then why are you so dead set against me? You do realize I'm a Christian?"

Lil replied, "I was never satisfied in the Conservative church. But Megan is."

He caught a flicker of disagreement in Megan's gaze. His pulse raced to think that she no longer felt that way. "But it's her choice. I know she's interested in missions, like you. That's why I invited her to see the story of the Aucas."

"Um, I'm sitting right here," Megan interjected.

Lil ignored her. "My husband is the one interested in missions. But I support him in it."

Still feeling that Lil's attitude was a bit duplicitous, he took the DVD out of its case. "I'll start the movie."

The picture began, and vivid jungle scenery flashed onto the screen. As the plot escalated, it contrasted the beauty and dangers of the jungle, focusing on its hostile tribes. It delved into the missionaries' faithfulness to their callings, no matter the hardships. Chance couldn't help but get caught up in the wonder of the story again, feeling a strong desire to return and continue the work he loved. A glance told him that the women were swept into the plot, oblivious to their surroundings, and he wasn't surprised to see them cry when the missionaries were killed.

After the movie concluded, the women sat in brooding silence until Chance sought to lighten the mood. "It had a good ending, don't you think? In real life, the grandson is now a Christian and works with the missionaries."

Megan's voice was huskier than usual. "Grandson?"

—☙

"Yes, although the grandfather was heathen, the grandson has helped to reach many souls," Chance explained.

"That's good to know." As dismissive as Megan's statement was, the idea was momentous, taking root in her mind: the grandfather was barbaric, but the grandson became a Christian. It was as if God whispered in her heart, *"You don't have to follow in your grandmother's steps."* It wasn't the direction she'd expected from God. And after viewing the hardships the missionaries incurred, she wasn't so sure about the jungle lifestyle, either. Swiping her eyes, she gave Chance a tremulous smile. "This movie touched me. But I need time to think about it."

His expression told her he understood she was talking about more than the plot.

When Megan stood, Chance tried to detain her. "You ladies don't have to rush off. Let me take you to dinner."

Megan needed more time to process her thoughts. Before she came to his apartment, she'd had every intention of telling Chance the truth about her background and even revealing her feelings for him. She was growing to despise secretive behavior of any kind, lest it fester and spread its malignancy to the unsuspecting. But the movie had planted some reservations in her about rushing forward with her earlier plans. "Dinner? No thank you. Perhaps another time. Lil needs to get home to Fletch."

"Yes. I also have a cat, a basset hound, and a rabbit to feed. Fletch is a vet, and he came to me with an entire entourage of animals."

"I won't keep you then." But when they reached the door, Megan felt his touch on her arm and turned into his low growl. "What if I want to spend some time with you?"

"Lil?"

Megan's accountability partner arched a warning brow. "I'll meet you at the car."

As soon as Lil was gone, Chance joked, "She packs a big wallop for her size."

"I don't know about that, but she's a good friend."

"At work you mentioned a personal problem. The preacher's not bothering you, is he?"

Thinking that Micah's advice was more detrimental to their relationship than anything, she shook her head. "No, nothing like that." Micah meant well. Why, he'd opened his arms to comfort her even though he lived beneath the congregation's microscope. If her dad had walked onto the porch and misunderstood, Micah might have lost his position at Big Darby. No, Micah wasn't bothering her, but his harsh advice sometimes presented a nuisance. Both men found pleasure in cutting the other down.

"Then what?"

"It's a long story, and Lil's waiting in the car." But she owed him an explanation. "I'll keep it brief. You see, I've always known my mom was adopted. But this week, I found out that none of her relatives are Mennonite. Or even professing Christians. I always thought I had a strong Mennonite heritage. I was wrong. I came today looking to find some answers."

His eyes rounded with understanding. "Because this sheds new light on our friendship. I've known all along that you were attracted to me. And now you're wondering if there's a way that we can be together?"

His quick assessment set her pulse racing. "Pretty much. But I'm not ready."

He placed his forefinger beneath her chin, tilted her face upward so that she could look into his yearning gaze. "We're running out of time. Soon I must return to Ecuador. You must come with me. Find your answers in Ecuador. Like I did."

"What do you propose? Exactly?"

"Whatever you need. A trip to Ecuador. Friendship. Love. I want it all, but I'll take whatever you can give me."

She watched his earnest expression, waiting for the word marriage, but it wasn't uttered. Realistically, it was too soon for him to consider it. They hardly knew each other. But Megan had to make sure the word was in his vocabulary.

In her hesitation, he urged, "I hope it's love." His gaze darkened, and he lowered his head and brushed his lips against hers. His arms encircled her and drew her close. The kiss was surreal. With it, many things went through her mind. He kissed her again and tried to deepen it, but she drew back with a slight gasp. "But are you the marrying type?"

He smiled. "I dream of sharing my life with you. I'm not opposed to marriage, but I see it farther down the road for us. Somewhere after dating. I believe the more appropriate question would be, are you willing to take the next step?"

She placed a hand on his cheek. "I know you have to go back to Ecuador soon. But I'm not ready to give you an answer. If our feelings are real, they'll last. My aunt's coming to visit. She wants to tell us about the relatives we never knew. I'd like to hear what she has to say before I make a decision."

Placing his hand over hers, he assured, "I'll wait. I'll give you whatever time you need."

The doorbell rang, and Megan withdrew her hand. "Lil." His smile held disappointment. "I'll see you Monday."

Inside the car, Lil apologized, "I'm sorry about the doorbell. I just wanted to give you a way out."

"Don't worry about it. It was perfect timing."

Lil started the car and glanced sideways. "So what happened?"

Megan sighed. "I told him about my mom's real family. He asked me to go to Ecuador with him. I asked if that included marriage. He said yes, that he dreamed of spending his life with me. Oh. And he kissed me."

"All that!" Lil shook her head. "He's fast. I'm glad I didn't leave you alone with him any longer."

Megan smiled. "I kind of cornered him when I asked him if he was the marrying type."

Lil burst out laughing. "Good for you. But let me tell you that the marrying type needs plenty of patience."

Megan burst into laughter, feeling lighter than she had in weeks.

As the city turned into countryside, the Ecuador decision tiptoed back into Megan's mind. Gazing at the fields and mailboxes that held names of lifelong friends, she asked herself if she could really leave the familiarity of Plain City. The movie imprinted her with a fresh perspective of a missionary's life and hardships. It wouldn't be like her college mission trip. The sacrifices she'd make for Ecuador would be permanent. Life-altering. If not Ecuador, then some place similar; for she was certain Chance wouldn't be comfortable living in the States. He thrived on adventure and blue skies.

Pulling into the drive, Lil pointed. "What's Micah doing by his car?"

Megan craned her neck. "I'm not sure."

"Do you think he's the marrying kind?"

Megan sank back in her seat and rolled her gaze toward the car's peeling ceiling. "How would I know?"

"Just asking. I imagine that's what your entire congregation is wondering."

"I suppose. But there's no sense putting the cart in front of the horse." Yet their midnight rendezvous flashed across her mind. "Micah's a nice man. He deserves a good woman. I'll miss him when he moves out of the blue cottage. It's been nice to have a friend so close at hand."

"When I wasn't there for you."

"I didn't mean that."

"All I'm saying, Chance isn't the only fish in the ocean. And there're probably even more where Micah came from, too. Remember how the Lord brought Fletch right to my door?"

With a sad sigh, Megan replied, "I wish you liked Chance."

"I'm sorry. I'll try harder. My family didn't like Fletch. Yet you helped us get together. You were the one who convinced me to give him a second chance. You deserve the same support from me."

"Thanks. It means a lot to me. And thanks for going with me today." Megan reached for her door handle. "Coming in?"

"No, I'm going home to make myself presentable for Fletch. We have some making up to do. Anyway, I think your preacher friend is lingering over there, hoping to talk to you."

Megan threw Lil a kiss and backed away from the car, waving. Then she saw Lil was right. Micah was watching her.

CHAPTER 25

Micah curiously observed the women, not that it was any of his business where they'd been. When Lil finally drove away, Megan started toward him.

"What are you doing?" she asked. "Hopefully not packing up your car?"

"You probably wish I was. But no, I'm cleaning it. It was filthy." He straightened and tossed his drying rag over his shoulder like a tote, noticing that she'd shed her heavy spirit. "You look happier."

"I am. I learned something today."

Micah crossed his arms. "I'm all ears."

"Lil and I went to Chance's apartment to watch that movie I told you about."

Relief washed over him that she'd not gone alone, like he'd imagined. "I'm glad you took someone along. That was the smart thing to do."

"I figured you would think so. Anyway, as I told you before, the story was about the Aucas natives who murdered some missionaries. It turns out that a native who threw one of the spears had a grandson who became a Christian. Now he tells people about the Lord. I felt God showing me that it doesn't matter what my grandmother was like. I can be whoever I want to be. It doesn't answer all my questions, but. . ." She shrugged.

Micah's arms relaxed to his sides, and he quietly thanked the Lord for answering his prayers. "That's what I've been trying to tell you. But we probably shouldn't judge your grandmother, either. Usually the rumors or hearsay about someone is worse than the actual truth."

Megan nodded thoughtfully.

"So what did you think about Ecuador?" Micah chose to ask that instead of what he really wanted to know: After seeing Ecuador, was Megan still interested in the missionary pilot? Was she planning to run off with him?

"The film wasn't actually in Ecuador, but in a place with similar climate and terrain. It's jungle. Very primitive. I enjoyed my college mission trip, but I'm not sure if I want to live permanently in such a wild and dangerous place. If I'm interested in Chance, it's my only option. He's committed there. That's the kind of life he's offering me."

Micah clenched his fist and snapped his towel off his shoulder, running it through his other hand. "So you talked about marriage?"

"Sure."

His jaw hardened with jealousy.

"He wants me to go to Ecuador and spend time with him, take it slow. He's not opposed to marriage."

He blurted, "Not opposed?" His throat released a harsh objection. "That sounds like less than you deserve, Megan. You do realize that?"

"How do you know what I deserve?"

He tore his gaze from her hurt expression, focusing on the towel. Reminding himself that he possessed no rights to Megan beyond those of a friend. "I think you deserve a clean car. Want me to wash it for you?"

Her resistance slowly melted away, and she looked at him with gratitude. "Yes. But only if I help."

He twisted his rag and lightly snapped her skirt with it. "That depends on your skills, missy."

"Ouch! Hey! Do not call me after your cat." Tossing her purse aside, she tried to snatch the rag away from him, caught the end of it, and held on. "I think I'd better be the drier."

Enjoying their tug-of-war contest, he started to reel her in. His breath catching, he wondered what she would do if he reeled her in close enough to kiss. But when their faces got within inches of each other, she released it so fast that he stumbled back.

"You don't play fair," she pouted.

"And you need to play more."

"Is that so?" With a mischievous glint in her blue eyes, she grabbed the half bucket of sudsy water and started toward him.

Micah's hands went up to shield his face, allowing the towel to slip from his hands to the ground. He made a pass for it, but missed. Megan eyed the towel, too, and he could tell she was undecided whether to make a move for it or to drench him with her pail of water. His gaze shifted from the towel to Megan, trying to anticipate her moves.

She darted forward, letting the pail go. It rocked and sloshed but remained upright. She snatched the towel off the ground and dashed after him with it.

He dodged her and went back after the bucket. Megan understood his intentions too late. He started toward her, holding the bucket while its contents slopped sudsy water onto his shoes.

"Oh, no. No you don't," she said, backing away. Micah stopped advancing just as she backed into something solid. With a shriek, she turned. "Dad!"

"Is it recess?" he asked.

Feeling foolish, Micah explained, "We're just in the middle of car washing." He glanced toward the shop, referring to Bill's Nova. "Want us to wash yours?"

Megan brought the towel close to her face to cover her grin.

"No, thank you. Carry on." With that, Bill strode toward the house.

As soon as he was inside, Megan keeled over in laughter. When she could finally speak again, she said, "He'd never let us touch that car. Did you see the expression of stark terror on his face when you asked him?"

Micah set down the bucket and thrust his finger at her. "Young lady, you were born to get me in trouble." Then he motioned, "Come on. Let's see how good you are with that rag."

He pushed his damp shirtsleeves above his elbows and reached into the bottom of the soapy bucket, retrieving a sponge. He washed, and Megan dried. As they worked, he tried to concentrate on the task and not the woman beside him.

They were partway through Megan's Nova when she said, "You must have your sermon ready."

"I do. And I took my suit to a new dry cleaner. Hopefully tomorrow will go better."

"You deserve a good day."

He cast her a flirtatious glance. "And how do you know what I deserve?"

"Oh, it's easy to see into your heart, Micah. Because it's so big."

Her remark couldn't have been further from the truth. Because if she really could see into it, she would see her own reflection.

Late Sunday afternoon, Megan quietly read in the living room, keeping alert for a familiar creaking that would signal Micah's presence. She wanted to return his straw hat to him. She eyed it on the floor by the door. About halfway through Chapter 5, she heard the chains groan, so she laid aside the novel. She swept up the hat and stepped onto the porch. But Micah's slumped posture faltered her steps. "Excuse me." His head snapped up. "Oh, hi."

"You left this on the swing the other day."

"Thanks."

Megan seated herself on the top step. "Why so sad?"

"Have you been to Joy Ann's house for Sunday dinner?"

Trying not to laugh at his expense, she admitted, "Not lately. She made you do the dishes, huh?"

"I'd have gladly done the dishes. Instead, it was a checkers competition, but more like a ploy to spend an hour alone with her while everyone else found excuses to leave us alone. The looks she kept giving me. . ." He shook his head and ran his hands through his hair.

As she watched him, Megan wondered when she had quit noticing how his hair was parted way too far on the side. Suddenly it seemed important to her to fix it, and it was all she could do to keep her hands out of the brown, haphazard mane. She looked away, stared at the crooked floorboard planks. She kept her gaze diverted until she'd counted three missing nails. When she looked back up at him, the anguish she saw made her sorry she had joked about the situation. "Poor Micah." His hands dropped, and she had his full attention. "Could you like Joy Ann, if you weren't focused on your job? You know, later after you get settled in?"

He shook his head. "No. But I don't want to hurt her."

"Well, if you're not worried about burning any bridges with her, I think honesty is the best policy." She remembered telling him that before when they discussed the librarian, but he hadn't had the stomach for it.

"Back at Rosedale, you told me the truth, but I wouldn't listen."

Megan sighed, remembering their encounters at Rosedale. "Everybody responds to rejection differently. You just get more obstinate."

"I'm not obstinate."

"Yes, Micah, you are. You also have the gift of perseverance."

"Well, this isn't about me. You don't think I'd hurt her?"

"I think it's more likely you'll make her mad. But you can't keep leading her on."

"She's leading herself on. But you're right. I have to do something. The way things went today, I'm going to have to say something to her this week."

Megan nodded, having already experienced what he was going through. It hadn't been easy to give him that set down. And now that she knew him, she felt even worse about it. Scrambling for something to brighten his mood, she said, "At least you didn't get the hives during your sermon."

His gaze darkened. "But did you hear what I said?"

She'd forgotten all about that. Now she covered her mouth to keep from laughing at the gaffe he'd made at the end of his sermon. He'd told the congregation to "go home and breed the Gospels." When she thought she could keep a straight face, she said, "Well, at least it's not on tape. At Lil's church, they record the sermons."

"Right." He rolled his gaze toward the porch ceiling. "I didn't even realize what I'd said until I heard people snickering; then when I sensed something was wrong, I backtracked in my thoughts. I could still hear the phrase floating in my brain. So I tried to cover it by saying, 'go and have a good day,' which really brought down the house. More than one man asked me how to"—he cleared his throat and cut off his remark, as if remembering he was speaking to a woman.

"Don't be so hard on yourself. You're doing fine."

"Oh yeah? Did you know that your dad told me after church that the search committee is going to call monthly meetings?"

"No."

"Yep. They want to discuss how it's going. Give me their perception of how the congregation's responding to me. Bill tried to make it sound like the meeting was for my sake. But I don't believe that for a minute. It's for their protection."

"Whose?"

"The point is, it wasn't part of the original agreement. I already meet with the elders regularly. I expect the search committee wants to give me some specific dos and don'ts. Or a hand slap."

"Honestly! Sometimes I wonder if my mom doesn't give Dad any advice at all." Megan released an angry sigh. "I'm sure the committee doesn't mean to be disrespectful."

Micah propped his elbows on his knees and leaned forward. "It's not that I blame them. But I have to believe that it's a sign that I'm failing."

"You don't know that for sure. Let's think about something else. Remember how my friend Paige came up with those man repellents?"

He eyed her warily, leaned slightly away from her. "The ones that didn't work for you? Yeah?"

She moved closer. "I have one that might."

He gave her a reluctant grin. "I'm listening."

"If you parted your hair about a quarter-inch deeper on the side than you already do, like this—" She reached out and ran her fingers through his hair, making a deep and even sillier part than he normally wore. Then using both her hands, she brushed the rest out of his eyes.

He froze at her touch, but she ignored it. She leaned back and bit her bottom lip, studying him. A few wisps stuck straight up. She carefully brushed them into place. Releasing her lip, she smiled. "Then our worries would be over."

But Micah didn't return her smile. His eyes narrowed and darkened. "And what about you, Megan. Would that chase you away?"

Feeling confused and slightly embarrassed, she snapped, "No. If your hairstyle mattered, I'd already be gone. Honestly, you can use my help."

His gaze took on a glint. "If I repel one woman, I might repel them all.

What if I don't want to repel you?"

"Don't be ridiculous. I'm trying to help. It's just that you part your hair way too deep. And if you didn't, you'd be rather handsome. But either way, it doesn't affect me."

He snatched her wrist and scowled. "Are you sure?"

She jerked her hand away, wretched that he'd felt her racing pulse and saw the truth that curled deep in the pit of her stomach. She wanted to see him at his best because she actually enjoyed staring into his face. Disconcerted, she wheeled and started to the door, tossing over her shoulder, "Or wear it the same. And everybody will just make do. 'Night."

Behind her, he got in the last word. "I'll think about it. Don't want to make any rash decisions. We must guard our steps, Megan. One wrong move, and life can become a jungle."

Her face now burning, she stepped into the darkening room, snatched up her Christian novel, and headed upstairs. Maybe she needed to take Micah's advice and draw a line in the sand. For him! Because she didn't want to hurt him again. But mostly, she didn't want to get her own heart broken. Yet she might. If Micah didn't get the position at the church, she was going to miss him. Unless, of course, she was living in the jungle.

⁓

That night Megan prayed about her future but remained torn. Every time she envisioned Chance's hopeful smile, the way it had been when she'd left him on Saturday, Micah's sad expression chased it away. She knew she'd hurt him badly. Wished she could turn back the time. Wondered why it bothered her almost as much as her indecision. What was it about Micah that disturbed her?

Was it the way he'd pinned her with his black scowl, after she insisted that she wasn't affected by his looks? He'd almost sneered when he'd asked, *"Are you sure?"*

She flicked on her lamp and went to the foot of her bed. She knelt in front of her hope chest and opened the lid, taking in the scent of cedar and the pull of nostalgic dreams. A pang of regret saddened her, to think of the many ways that Ecuador would change her life. How would her parents react if she married Chance and moved out of the country? The news would be shocking. She was their only child. Folding back her grandma's quilt, she searched for the journal she'd kept in college, the year she'd known Micah.

It was beige with green vines. She took it back to her bed and slipped under the covers, thumbing through its pages, looking for the entries pertaining to Micah. As she read, she felt ashamed. The entries were no longer humorous. She must have hurt him deeply. Why had he been so obstinate? That's what she'd called him today. It was true.

Otherwise, he'd never have returned to Plain City. She let the journal drop onto the covers and lay back on her pillow, staring into the past. Once he'd told her that she had awakened something inside him. She felt something similar. She wished her dad and the search committee weren't making things difficult for him. She hated to see him despondent. Even if she moved away, she wanted to think of him happily ministering at Big Darby. She sat up and reached for her other journal. Lately prayer had replaced her journaling, but she'd missed it. Still, she found herself unable to do anything more than jot down her prayer requests:

1. *Direction regarding Chance.*
2. *Forgive Mom.*
3. *Accept whatever Aunt Louise brings us.*
4. *Micah getting the desires of his heart*
5. *Randy being able to save his marriage*
6. *Lil getting along better with Fletch*
7. *Be with Katy and Jake*

CHAPTER 26

Megan drove into Char Air's employee parking lot and parked in a partially shaded area about sixty yards from the front of a row of sleek buildings. When she opened her door and stepped out of her car, the sight of Chance striding toward her sent a surge of alarm. Dread curled in the pit of her stomach because he would press her to go to Ecuador. A longing pushed her toward the thrill of his kiss and the remembrance of his sweet promises.

"Does this old girl have air-conditioning?" His admiring glance swept over the Nova then rested on her.

"No. Sorry to say." She reached back for her purse. "So why does something old and classic have to be a she?"

With a shrug, he admitted, "If it's something appealing to a guy, it's usually female. No air-conditioning and yet you always look so pretty and fresh." He leaned close and brushed a kiss on her ear.

Megan shivered. "Better not do that here."

"But we only have ten more workdays until I leave. And if you go with me, then who cares?"

Megan studied him regretfully. "Ten days isn't long. But you did remember that my aunt is coming to visit?" Did he really think she'd pack up her life in two short weeks?

"Yes. You want to talk to her before you decide about Ecuador. But what does that have to do with us?"

Megan drew her purse strap over her shoulder as they started toward the office building. "It's just a mystery that I have to explore."

"So she's coming this week?"

Her steps faltered. "No. Late next week, and we don't know how long she'll be staying."

Chance grabbed her arm and wheeled her around to face him. "But I'll be leaving."

Reading the alarm in his expression, she softened her voice. "If you really care, you'll make do." She remembered saying something similar in his apartment, feeling as though they'd already had this conversation once.

"I know. I'm just disappointed."

"Chance! Hey. Wait up, buddy!"

Megan flinched at the unexpected intrusion. A quick glance revealed Randy and his wife Tina walking toward them.

Almost protectively, Chance whispered, "Go on ahead."

His words yanked her out of the clouds and dropped her back to her lowly station, where she was merely a Char Air employee. Thinking she'd do well to remember it, she nodded. She gave the approaching couple a little wave and went on toward the entrance of the office building. With a soft grunt, she tugged the long door handle and entered the building. Why were Randy and Tina here? The question troubled her, because it was the first time she'd seen Randy since his leave of absence.

"Hi, Summer." She passed the receptionist. The hallway opened into a space with several modern cubbies. Her space carried an uncomfortable feel now that she'd been to Chance's apartment. There was nothing safe about it. He had invaded every inch of it with his smile and his adventuresome style. She felt like she had lost her grip and was now only along for the ride.

If she bailed, he would still fly off to his jungle, letting her crash. And when she hit the ground and crawled back to her space, she'd find it vacant and meaningless. She sank into her chair. She could always buy a plant to place on the corner of her desk where he liked to perch. She could go on a vacation. No, Randy would need her.

"Hello, Megan."

Megan snapped her head up and quickly pasted on a smile. "Tina." It felt awkward to be addressing Randy's wife, given the private knowledge that their marriage was falling apart. "Good morning. Can I get you some coffee?"

"Oh no. I already had some." The tall, thin woman gave a little wave with a tanned, manicured hand. "We stopped for breakfast on the way over. Randy just needs to pick up his passport for our cruise." Silence pervaded for a few moments. Tina said, "It's my first one. Randy's always been too busy for getaways. But you know how everybody raves about cruises?"

Megan dropped her gaze, for the people she knew didn't go on cruises. Mostly they worked for people who went on cruises. When she looked up again, she noticed that Tina's eyes bore more sadness than anticipation and wondered if the cruise could restore the happiness the couple had lost.

"How's work going?"

"We're keeping Randy's customers, but I can't deny that he'll have a few pieces to pick up when he returns."

Tina tucked blond hair behind her ear. "Yes, he's been doing a lot of that lately."

Thankfully Megan didn't need to respond to the bitter comment because Randy and Chance entered the office and strode up to her desk. Randy paused long enough to give Tina a peck on the cheek before heading into his office. Outside the door, Chance hesitated. He gave Megan a tender expression that assured her everything was fine.

Her blue eyes suddenly glittering, Tina stared at Megan. "I can't believe what I just saw."

"What?"

"You two." Tina narrowed her eyes. "There's something going on between you guys."

Megan knew exactly what the other woman meant. She had just lumped Megan in the same category as Randy's previous assistant, whom Tina detested. Her expression shot sparks of blame as if Megan was responsible for her marriage problems.

"It isn't what you think," Megan defended, but it sounded like the cover-up it was, and she knew that eventually the truth would surface. It always did. For all she knew, at that very moment, Chance could be spilling out everything about their relationship to Randy.

"I don't know you that well," Tina continued, her eyes spewing accusation, "but when Randy hired you, he assured me that you were chaste because of your religion."

Chaste! Anger bubbled up Megan's throat like bile; one kiss didn't make her promiscuous. And her personal life wasn't any of Tina's business. She fought for control of her tongue. *I can't fly into the boss's wife. She's hurting and pathetic.*

"Anyways, I thought Mennonites were some sort of pacifists."

"What?" Megan's head spun from Tina's baffling and unjust allegations.

"I'm just shocked that you'd lower your morals and fall for an air force fighter pilot. That's all."

Stricken by the words *fighter pilot*, Megan clutched the underside of her desk. Her thoughts swirled to make sense of Tina's rebuke. *Fighter pilot?* She panted slightly then felt her heart clench. When she could speak, she repeated, "Chance is a fighter pilot? He told me he was a missionary pilot."

"Now he is. But he served in the air force. Even received a medal."

Megan read the truth in Tina's eyes. "I didn't know that."

Tina lifted her chin in justification. "I see. Let me tell you something for your own good. Women are fools around men. But not me. Not anymore. Don't be a fool, Megan."

Looking up through burning eyes, she nodded. "Thanks for the tip. If you're sure you don't want coffee, I'd better get back to work."

Tina tapped her flamingo-pink fingernails on Megan's desk. "I'm serious. If he lies to you once, he'll do it again. Anyway, he's not the settling-down type. Never has been."

The door to her husband's office opened. Randy and Chance stepped into the room, oblivious to the undercurrents. Megan watched Tina's gaze turn icy, before she averted her own. The bitter woman had pushed her out of the plane, and she was plummeting, but Megan determined not to crash until she was alone. With wooden movements, she changed her calendar and pulled out her to-do list.

"See you soon, Megan. I've heard some glowing reports about you," Randy said.

Megan felt Tina's smirk and gave her old boss a weak smile. "Just doing my job, sir." She lowered her gaze back to her desk.

When the space around her cubicle grew silent, Megan lifted her eyes. Randy and Tina were gone, and Chance had disappeared into his office. She stared at his door, feeling belittled and deceived. When Tina shoved her out of the plane, her decision about him and his jungle had been made—the painful way.

Her phone rang, bringing her thoughts to the present. She answered it and then worked frantically for the next hour, refusing to dwell on the painful disclosure, because if she did, she'd crash. Megan didn't want to do that at work. Didn't want to see the sympathy in Paige's eyes. Didn't want to hear, *I told you so.*

Megan went through an entire stack of paperwork before she stalled. When she did, she was unable to proceed. As much as she fought it, her mind sank its teeth into the information that Tina had divulged. Chance was a fighter pilot, turned missionary pilot. How little she knew about him. Tina's loathsome words held merit in Megan's case: *"Women are fools around men."*

Shame burned her cheeks to think how she'd succumbed to his advances. He'd taken advantage of her inexperience. He'd wrapped her around his little finger, while she blindly turned her eyes from the truth. No matter how much outsider's blood she possessed, she was a Mennonite at heart, and she could never fit in or feel at ease with him. He must never have intended for their relationship to be permanent. It had all been a game with him. For if he loved her, he wouldn't have taken her into the sky without a parachute.

She recalled the conversation where she'd confided in him about her nonresistant beliefs. He'd scoffed, putting down Mennonite men. Now she understood that he'd only probed into her beliefs so that he could skirt around them. He intentionally kept his military past a secret.

She clasped her head, shaking with anger so that she couldn't focus on anything but the man who'd played her like a fool. Pushing back her chair, she strode to his door. She squared her shoulders and knocked.

"Come in."

Megan stepped into the room and gave the door a shove. It banged behind her. As she stood trembling, Chance's eyes went from surprised to wary.

"Megan?"

She strode to his desk and speared him with her furious gaze. "When were you going to tell me that you were a fighter pilot?"

His eyes closed and fluttered opened, filled with regret. "That was a long time ago. I didn't think it mattered."

"I don't believe that. You knew it mattered. You purposely deceived me."

Chance rose and came around his desk. Megan jerked away from his touch. His hand moving upward in appeal, he explained, "When we first met, I thought we were like night and day. But the more we worked together, the more we connected. And lately, it seemed that we might be able to meet somewhere in the middle and actually have a wonderful future together. I was only taking it one day at a time. Just like you were."

An image of rows of red x's flashed into Megan's mind. With it came the idea that he'd been bored, using her to while away his time. She pushed him aside and ripped off the top page of his calendar. She crumpled it with her dreams and flung it at him. "That's what I think of your one day at a time!"

The wad hit his chest and bounced onto the floor. Chance stared at it then looked back at her. "Whoa. You're way too angry to think clearly. You need to cool down."

"I won't be deceived."

His hands went up in appeal. "Look. I meant it when I said I dream of us together making a happy life in Ecuador."

Happy when she let go of her beliefs and blended in with him and his lifestyle. "You knew I didn't want to date you. But you pursued me anyway. You took advantage of me because I work here. I'd no place to go to get away from you, and you were relentless. You wouldn't take no for an answer. What kind of boss is that?"

"When you say it that way, it sounds bad." He shrugged and gave her a contrite smile. "I couldn't help it. You're irresistible."

"That's sick. Just admit it. It was only a game for you."

"All right. Maybe at first I was curious. But I fell for you." He touched her again, and she was too exhausted to pull away from his pathetic appeal. "You make it sound as though we're finished. We can work through this, just as we have every other difference. This is no game, Megan. It doesn't matter if I made mistakes getting to this place. Now we're talking about our future life together."

"Futures are built upon honesty and respect. You played a dangerous game. Couldn't you see that there would be no winners?"

"There aren't any rules with love."

"Tell me, Chance. Have you changed since you were in the air force? Are you now nonresistant?"

"I won't lie to you, I'm not. But yes, I've changed. That's why I resigned from the military and use my career to save lives instead of to kill. We're both Christians, and we can disagree on a few things. People do that, you know."

He had killed. Even if she could forget that, given their personalities, she'd be the one who'd always have to adapt. The fight went out of her. She took a calming breath. "Look. I respect what you're doing with your life now. But today's broken the spell and opened my eyes. I see you differently. I know that going to Ecuador with you won't make me happy." She shrugged. "I've been starry eyed for a long time. It wasn't your fault."

"Meg, honey. You're just emotional. Don't say anything more until you've had time to really think about this. It's not about who we were then, but who we are now. Together. We make a great team."

"That's what I'm telling you. We aren't a team. We're finished."

"Two weeks. Don't decide yet." The irresistible charmer now came across as a spoiled, begging child.

She thought about how she'd threatened Micah she'd call in the church elders if he didn't quit pursuing her. It seemed childish, too, but it was proof that she could have resisted Chance. She had chosen to encourage his advances. If anything, she had courted a dream. "I'm sorry I led you on." She pulled away from his touch and stepped away. "I was wrong to give you hope."

He shook his head and advanced. "I'm not letting you go."

"Then I'll go to my desk and write Randy my resignation." She started to go.

"Wait."

She hesitated, her shoulders sagging.

He released a loud sigh. "You're really serious?"

"Yes."

"Don't resign. You stay, and I'll go."

"What about Char Air? And what about Randy?"

"I won't stay here and pretend to ignore you and your pious little net cap. Now get out before I change my mind."

Stung, Megan lifted her chin and marched out of his office. She sank into her chair, sick to her stomach, waiting for his door to fly open again. She expected him to storm past and make a dramatic departure. What would Randy say when he found out that she'd chased his replacement away? Would the cruise get canceled? Would she lose her job, anyway, because she'd caused such a fiasco?

But when the door finally opened, Chance emerged looking repentant, without his briefcase. He perched on the corner of her desk, squashing her imaginary plant and looking at her as if it was business as usual.

Megan tensed, hoping he wasn't going to beg.

Lines tugged the corners of his mouth down, and even his voice sank. "You go home. Take a couple sick days. Come back on Thursday, and I'll be gone."

Her mind leaped at the opportunity to escape, but his kindness flung a shackle of guilt around her ankles. "I really do feel sick."

He rose into a stance that made her wonder how she could have missed his military background. "The war changed me. You changed me, too."

"We've both changed." She lowered her gaze and heard him walk away.

With a burst of adrenalin, she moved toward flight. In a few strokes, she tidied her desk and grabbed her purse. On the way out, she told the receptionist that she felt ill and was going home. "Chance said he'd take care of things for me."

"Take care of yourself, honey."

"Yes. That's what I'm doing."

Micah had just stepped outside his cottage to exercise the cat when he noticed Megan's Nova pull into the drive. His brow furrowed, thinking it wasn't like her to come home in the middle of the day. When she got out of the car with a lowered gaze and sagging shoulders, it confirmed his suspicions that something terrible had happened. He darted across the yard toward her.

"Megan?"

She stopped, looked up in confusion, staring at him with vacant, red-rimmed eyes.

"What's wrong?"

She shrugged, and pain replaced the emptiness in her eyes. "I just came to my senses." He could only hope she was referring to the pilot. Her gaze flitted briefly over to the kitchen window. Sensing she didn't want her mom watching them, he nudged her elbow. "Come with me." He guided her around the front of the house past the porch to the buckeye tree that would shield them from public view. "Megan?"

"I broke it off with Chance. I found out that he had an entire past that he'd kept secret from me."

Images of a wife and family back in Ecuador came to Micah's mind. He had an un-Christian urge to place his hands around the man's arrogant neck, but instead he tried to remain calm.

"He had a military career. He was a fighter pilot."

"Hmph." That was the last thing he'd expected to hear. But it didn't surprise him. Although they were nonresistant, Micah didn't think Chance's military career was that shocking. She'd known all along that he was a man with feet firmly planted in the outside world. Micah wondered why, in her mind, his military career overshadowed his current mission work? And then it hit him, it was the timing of the deception, so soon after her mom's disclosure.

"He kept it from me. And I had dreams of marrying him. But when I heard that, I realized he'd manipulated me. I let him draw me away from my faith. I set my heart in the wrong place. What was I thinking, Micah?"

"We've been praying for God to reveal His will to you."

"I know. But it doesn't make this any less painful. I wanted him."

Her confession cut through the freshly laid scars of his never-healing heart, but he gently kneaded her shoulders and whispered, "I'm sorry." And when she eased into his arms, he comforted her, placing his chin on the top of her golden-spun hair. He closed his eyes to their merging pain. They both ached because they loved somebody they couldn't have.

"He told me to take some sick days. When I go back to work, he'll be gone." She clutched his shirt and mumbled, "I'm sorry I keep crying all over you."

He drank in her citrus scent. "I understand."

She released him. "Thanks."

He wiped her tears with his finger. "I admire your strength and determination to do the right thing."

She squeezed his hand and stepped away. "Thanks. I gotta go." Then she brushed past him and went into the house. Feeling exasperated, he stared at the door. The cat mewed. He looked down and scooped up the feline. *Why do I want her when she only wants him? I'm such a fool.*

—⁂—

Later that evening, Megan poised her pen thoughtfully.

Thank You, Lord, for revealing that Chance is not the man for me and Ecuador is not the place You want me to go. It hurts, but I accept it.

She scanned her other prayer requests and added:

1. *Heal my pain.*
2. *Direction for my job at Char Air.*
3. *Healing for Chance.*

She set her journal aside to read from her Bible, pausing at Job 17. Verses 11 and 12 jumped out at her. "My days are past, my purposes are broken off, even the thoughts of my heart. They change the night into day: the light is short because of darkness." It was so similar to Micah's quote: *"When it is dark enough, you can see the stars."*

CHAPTER 27

Micah pulled his blue Honda Civic into Big Darby's parking lot. Sometime during the night, he'd realized that Megan's crying all over him had been a good thing this time. It'd been the last and final straw, opening his eyes to reality. Sure he was glad that she'd finally made the right choice. But the depth of Megan's feelings for the pilot had created an impenetrable wall. It was time he realized she was still inside the walled fortress of her own making, desperately needing to heal. Micah had been prowling and pacing around its perimeters, ever since the Fourth of July parade, waiting for a breach. It was sickening. Disgusting. It needed to stop. And it would.

He stepped out of his car and strode purposefully to the church building. He resolved to give his job the priority it deserved. He opened the door and moved down the hall. If he didn't confront Joy Ann, then he was treating her no better than Chance had treated Megan. He'd face the situation head-on and wouldn't be soft. She'd survive rejection. He was living proof it wasn't a fatal disease.

Inside the secretary was already busy at her desk. He was positive that Joy Ann had started arriving early merely to create a private time with him before Ruthie's arrival. Today that worked in his favor. He paused at her desk. "Morning, Joy Ann."

"Hi, Brother Micah. I guess you don't want to see yesterday's bank deposit slip?"

"You're right about that. My job doesn't require knowledge of church finances."

"I can see that, but—"

"But you don't like change?"

"I thought I did. But I guess I fell into the same mind trap as everybody else."

He saw that as his opening. "You're just trying to do a good job."

She involuntarily dusted her phone buttons with her fingertips. "Thanks."

"Sometimes you even go beyond what's expected. Take, for instance, how you always come to the office early."

Her face glowing, she explained, "I like to get things set up before Ruthie arrives."

"I understand, but I need to ask you not to do that anymore."

"What? But why?"

"This is a little awkward for me. It's because it doesn't look good for us to be here alone together."

Misinterpreting his caution light for a green one, she fingered the edge of her caped bodice. "I suppose it wouldn't do for people to start talking about us, especially before you hire on for good."

"Exactly. People might get the idea that you and I have something going, even though we don't." Joy's face reddened, whether with embarrassment or anger, he couldn't be sure yet. "I have a one-track mind right now. Focused on my work, you understand."

"Oh." He saw that she didn't understand. And she wasn't going to let it drop until she pushed him for more clarity. "So for now, we should. . ." She looked up at him with frustration.

"Joy Ann. There's no we."

She blinked furiously.

"I want to keep things strictly business at work, and outside of work, I'm not looking for more than friendship with you."

Her lower lip drooped for a second before her eyes darkened into stormy slits. She pushed back from her desk and stood. She planted her hands on her hips. "Just because I'm nice to you, doesn't mean I have my cap set for you. Preacher or not, I think you're a little big for your britches."

"Maybe I was out of line. But when we were playing checkers, I got the distinct feeling that—"

Her hand flew up. "Just stop. Just—" Her voice broke.

Micah touched her arm. "You're a great secretary."

Joy Ann lunged at him, burying her face against his shirt and slipping her hands tight around his waist. Micah froze. Not again. Did every woman think he was their weeping pole? He must be the only preacher who got himself in these scrapes. Joy Ann shuddered. He glanced toward the hall, wishing he'd closed the door, yet that would've been even more inappropriate. And what he saw in the doorway made him cringe and quickly pry Joy Ann's arms from his waist. Susanna Schlagel was staring at them with astonishment and pursed lips.

—⁂—

The next morning, Megan strolled through her mom's flower garden, pausing to enjoy the rugosa roses that were blooming after the third or fourth flush of the season. After crying on Micah's shoulder the previous evening then telling Mom the entire story, she'd spent hours alone in her room engaged in prayer and contemplation. Now she was positive that she'd done the right thing by ending it with Chance.

She also felt strangely tranquil in the certainty that God would guide her in the days ahead. She set down her weed pail and placed her gloved hands on her hips. Despite her lingering grief, she was unable to ignore the way the honeysuckle danced against its white trellis. She caught the scent of lavender and vowed that when she had her own home, she would plant a garden like this one. The scents and colors were healing to the soul. She envisioned imaginary conversations with her mom, comparing techniques and varieties. She followed the flight of a butterfly, amazed that she'd been so willing to exchange all that she was familiar with for an outsider's jungle.

Her mom had urged her to spend the morning in the flower beds, acting like they needed urgent care, but she'd known it was a ploy to cheer her. Megan's gaze lifted farther out to the big garden with its routine upkeep, which was now focused on tomato worms, squash borers, and flea beetles in the eggplant. As precarious as their relationship had become this summer, Mom remained kind and giving.

Pushing back her long hair, still wet from her shower, Megan knelt and began picking faded flowers and seed pods and ungainly stems, tossing them with soft thuds into a metal pail. As she worked, she began to hum the chorus of "Great Is Thy Faithfulness." She snapped off some ungainly stems and moved farther down the row, when unexpectedly an exuberant male tenor provided words to her tune: "'All I have needed Thy hand hath provided, great is Thy faithfulness, Lord, unto me.' I need that assurance right now, too."

Smiling, she paused from her work to look over her shoulder. "You have a nice voice."

"And you have a pleasant hum."

Megan softly laughed. "Hardly. But what are you doing back from church so soon?"

He knelt down. "It was too awkward at the office after my talk with Joy Ann."

"Oh. How did she take it?"

"At first it was hard for her to accept."

"She got angry?"

"Yes. She cried. But worse than that, she latched onto me just as Susanna Schlagel showed up at the office."

"Latched onto me"? Had he felt the same way when she'd clung to him after breaking up with Chance? When she'd cried about her outsider genes. When she was wrought with fear in the root cellar? She flung a sprig of hardy ground ivy into her pail. Brushing off her gloves, she asked, "So Susanna saw the two of you?"

"Mm-hmm. After that things went downhill. Let's just say I'd rather be pulling weeds than back at church cleaning up the mess I made."

"Actually, this is therapeutic. Even if it does kick up my allergies."

"We can't let the sniffles keep us from living." His gaze traversed the length of her hair, followed it all the way down to her waist. Then his jaw hardened, and he looked away.

Feeling his disapproval, Megan wished she'd braided it instead of enjoying the nakedness of sun and breeze. She didn't even have on her covering. The whole conversation had reminded her that he was more than a friend. He was a man. And he was a preacher; one who didn't appreciate women latching on to him. She'd do well to remember that. "So there's the pail. Help yourself to some therapy, while I go in and fix us a soda."

Yanking out some quack grass, he called after her, "You better come back. I hope this isn't a trick to get me to do your work."

She composed herself and returned with her hair primly bound beneath her prayer covering. Although she was sure he'd heard her approach, he kept working until she offered him a tall glass of the iced beverage.

Thoughtfully, she sipped her own cool refreshment. "I'd like to have a garden like this someday."

"I can picture that." He stood and brushed the soil off his pants. "A man could be happy with a property like this."

She wished happiness for him. "Dad is, but his cars have something to do with it. If you stay, the parsonage has a big property. Enough to enjoy the outdoors, but not enough to keep the preacher from doing what he's supposed to be doing."

Micah seemed thoughtful, almost distant. "Sister Barbara seems pretty attached to her place."

"I know. I wonder how the elders will handle that? Have they mentioned housing to you at all?"

"No." He pointed toward the apple trees and changed the subject. "Does your dad spray those?"

"Yes, he does."

"I can do that for him."

"You like gardening?"

"I've been keeping up my grandma's place for a long while. My place," he softly corrected.

Megan felt a tug of sympathy. She looked into Micah's eyes, and before he schooled his gaze, the depth of compassion and sadness she saw almost made her feel like a trespasser. But he quickly schooled it, and next he flung a tiny clod at her. It hit her skirt and fell to the ground. "Yes. I like gardening."

The boyish gesture beckoned her. Her lip curled, all intentions of revering her preacher fled. She was just about to pay him back good when she noticed the change in his appearance. Her mouth gaped in astonishment. She squealed with delight. "You did it! You parted your hair in the right place." She made a slow and complete circle around him. He rolled his gaze skyward in minimal toleration. She smiled. "If you're not careful, next you'll be almost average looking."

"Megan!" Mom appeared from nowhere, shaking her head. "Remember, you are talking to our preacher."

Waving her hand through the air, Megan dismissed manners. "Oh, Mom, you know we're old friends. Brother Micah," she mocked, "our lunch must be ready." She turned her back to him and strode toward her mom. "He wants to spray the apple trees next."

Mom called, "You coming, Micah?"

"I have some leftovers in my cottage. Thanks anyway. But when you're finished, you can show me where you keep the spray."

"Oh, sure."

At the screen door, Mom paused. "You sure you and Micah are only friends?"

"I'm sure. Micah just makes me feel better."

Mom nodded. "I just thought. . .never mind."

CHAPTER 28

The next day Megan awoke rubbing her eyes, a hangover from her gardening spree. Grabbing a tissue from her nightstand, she wondered how she could fill the hours of another day with no work. Then she remembered the promise she'd made to herself at Brother Troyer's funeral, to spend time with Barbara. Somehow since then, she'd gotten caught up in her own affairs and neglected that promise. Megan's romantic disappointment had to be minor compared to the older woman's loss of a lifelong companion.

At breakfast while she and Mom lingered over coffee, Megan brought up the matter. "I'd like to go see Barbara this morning unless you have other plans for me."

"That's a great idea. If you're up to it. You don't look so good."

"It's just allergies. I took a pill, and I'll be fine."

"Would you mind stopping at the store for me on the way home?"

They made plans, and an hour later, Megan found herself ringing the parsonage doorbell, while juggling a small watermelon Mom had sent along.

Barbara's eyes lit with delight. "Nobody can grow those like your mom. Come on in."

They set the fruit on the countertop and settled in at the kitchen table, where Barbara's Bible lay open.

"How are you doing?" Two months earlier, Megan wouldn't have had the nerve to ask the older woman anything so personal. But given all her own soul-searching, the question came out so naturally, it almost asked itself.

"I have moments when I feel sorry for myself. But even though I'm lonely, there are new blessings every day. To think that a young thing like you takes an interest in an old widow like me. Well, that's a blessing."

"I'm not so young." With all she'd experienced since she started working at Char Air, life had caught up with her.

"Something's happened." Barbara pushed up from the table. "I've been cooped up all morning. Let's take a turn around the garden. I want to show you my hydrangea bush. Then you can tell me what's going on."

Not bringing up her allergies, Megan followed Barbara's spry steps, thinking that her back was more stooped than usual. When they reached the eight-foot-high bush, equally large in diameter, Barbara plucked a stem with a pink cluster. "Just look at this. Did you ever see anything happier than this bush?"

Biting back a smile, Megan took the happy bloom in her hand, gave its stem a twirl, and brought it to her nose. It was fresh and sweet smelling. "Mom had me weeding her flower garden yesterday. The lavender smelled so good we took some inside. We added some roses to the bouquet."

"It sounds lovely. But shouldn't you be at work?"

"I'm taking a break from my boss."

"And he pays you for this?"

Megan laughed. "He told me to take a few sick days." She briefly filled Barbara in on what had happened with Chance. The widow listened without batting an eye. Megan was in the middle of explaining about her great-aunt Louise's portending visit when she was silenced by a series of sneezes.

Barbara snatched the stem from her hand. "Oh honey, I forgot about your allergies."

"It's probably because I was in Mom's garden yesterday. I should've known better."

"Well, let's go inside." A bluebird swooped into a blueberry bush. "I wanted Eli to build me a bluebird house, but he never got around to it." Inside, Barbara placed the stem in a tall, narrow vase of water and bent to rearrange her refrigerator to make room for the watermelon. "I guess you see how this melon is white on the bottom? A sure sign it's ripe and sweet. Sometimes, life is like that. I think you're still on the vine, honey, but very soon now, things are going to change for you."

Later at the store, Megan got the few items on Mom's list, while going over the strange conversation with Barbara. The widow enjoyed hinting at things, as if she was privy to some prophetic insights. While she was there, Megan should have asked her if she thought that Micah would get voted in as permanent pastor.

—⟋⟍—

Micah heard the low din of male conversation drowned out by his own footsteps clattering across the linoleum hallway. When he got close to the doorway, he heard a cough followed by dead silence. Stepping into the meeting room, the hair on the back of his neck bristled at Vernon Yoder's guilty expression. Micah took the remaining chair and folded his hands on the sterile gray, rectangular table.

He nodded at the five men who had assembled to discuss the state of his interim pastorship. Bill sat on his immediate left. Vernon and a grim-faced Leon Beachy sat across the table. The painter had some white speckles on his wrist that he must have missed when he'd showered. *Normal people just like me,* Micah tried to reassure himself.

Next to Leon was Ray Eversole. They were on good terms since Micah had learned not to put him on the spot, asking for songs that weren't on the agenda. To his right sat Noah Maust, the professor who had recommended him for the position.

Bill cleared his throat, which wasn't necessary since the room was already quiet. "Vernon, you wanna pray?" There were a few mumbled *Amens* when the prayer was completed, and then Bill turned his gaze toward Micah. "Do you have anything to share with the group? Want to tell us how it's going?"

Being the specimen on display, Micah sought for something that would put himself in a good light. "I still believe God led me here, no matter the outcome. It's been humbling to break out in hives two Sundays in a row, and then make that embarrassing blunder last week. . . ." He had to pause when they broke into laugher. "But I've also been blessed with affirmations. Brothers and sisters telling me how the sermon touched them or spoke to their needs. I see God in it."

Bill nodded. "That's true. People come to me with good things to say about you."

There were some affirmations along that line, and then Bill continued, "I've probably gotten to know you the best, and I respect and admire you as a godly man. I'm quick to always put in a good word for you."

"We think he just wants to keep you around to spray his apple trees," the professor teased. Micah had learned back at Rosedale that the professor had a good sense of humor when he felt like applying it.

The song leader smirked. "It isn't all roses over there, from what I hear. Not with a cat in the shop."

The men chuckled at Bill's weakness for nice cars without cat scratches.

Bill winked at Micah. "Let them have their jokes."

Micah figured it was best to remain silent and keep them in good humor.

Bill yanked at his button-down shirt. "All in all, the committee feels positive about your preaching and your character. But some rumors have reached us. We'd be at fault not to bring them to your attention."

Assuming he knew where the conversation was headed, Micah nodded. "I understand."

"So Leon, why don't you tell Micah what your wife heard this week at the quilting."

"Sure." He turned his gaze onto Micah. "My Inez, she doesn't gossip. Just so you know. But she overheard the widows talking at their corner of the quilt, pretending to keep their voices low, but Inez said she thinks everybody heard them when Susanna Schlagel told Ann Byler that she went to the office on Tuesday and saw you and Joy Ann Beitzel in a heated embrace."

"Where was Ruthie?" the professor asked.

"She hadn't arrived yet," Micah interrupted. In spite of the committee members' startled gazes, he continued, "Let me explain. I thought Miss

Beitzel had a crush on me. I believed that's why she always managed to come in early before Miss Ropp. I saw the infatuation from the start but wasn't sure how to handle it, not wanting to hurt her or offend anybody. I've tried to show her that I wasn't interested, but after Sunday's dinner invitation at her home, I realized I was going to have to be more direct with her. On Tuesday she was there early again. So I explained as kindly as I could that I wasn't interested in a relationship with her. She didn't accept it. I tried to explain that I appreciated her as a person and a secretary. That made her even more upset."

Several eyebrows lifted, and Micah was certain that if the men knew Joy Ann at all, they were imagining her reaction. "At first, she argued. Then she cried. Before I knew what had happened, she clapped her arms around my waist. I didn't know what to do and looked up, frightened that somebody might see us, and sure enough, there stood Susanna Schlagel in the doorway."

Leon shook his head. "That explains it. Bad timing, that's for sure."

Micah felt beads of sweat on his forehead. "I disengaged Joy Ann and went to the door to speak with Susanna, but she stormed off and wouldn't listen to my explanation. After that Joy Ann returned to her desk. She was embarrassed, but we were able to speak more calmly about the incident. I affirmed her work again, and then I went into my office until Miss Ropp arrived. After that, I left the church because the atmosphere was strained."

"Too bad," Leon repeated. "But there's more."

With surprise, Micah jerked his gaze to the painter. "More?"

"The widows claim that you stare at them while you preach. They want to know why you stare at them."

"I don't stare at them!" Micah objected, feeling a flash of resentment toward the widows, Susanna in particular.

"They claim it makes them uncomfortable and self-conscious, wondering if you are trying to lay some conviction on them. It makes them feel like the congregation is watching them."

Micah wanted to say, *if the shoe fits*, but instead he shook his head. "I'd never single out a person and preach at them. If I had something to say, I'd tell them privately to their face."

"Good." The professor quickly came to his defense. "The incident with

Joy Ann verifies that."

The other men nodded thoughtfully.

"Like I said, my Inez doesn't gossip. Trust me on that. But if I were you, I'd make sure you don't look at the widows' section anymore when you preach. Leastwise, until this settles down some."

Vernon cleared his throat and spoke for the first time. "The real issue's not your character, Micah. I hope you don't feel like you're on trial. We can only hope that the congregation's ready for a single preacher. It's a tricky situation. A big change. But the younger folks are behind you. Katy and Jake have nothing but good things to say about you."

"There's still time for the congregation to settle in and accept the idea," the professor replied.

Bill interrupted. "I'm not sure this will die down on its own. I'd like to take this information to the elders committee. They may have some helpful advice. The last thing we want to do is embarrass any of the women if we can help it."

After that, Micah wondered if he was capable of doing his job in a way that would exhibit the constant decorum and discreetness that it required. All that came to mind was the many times he and Megan had spent time alone together, how they'd embraced. And how he secretly loved her. If someone confronted him about that, there would be no way to deny it. In a sense, Susanna wasn't that wrong about his character, only she'd attributed his weakness to the wrong woman.

⁓

When Megan returned to Char Air, Paige wasted no time to single her out in the coffee room. "Feeling better?"

"Much better."

As they prepared their hot drinks, Paige waited until they were alone and then probed. "I guess Chance must of caught whatever it was you had."

"Did he?"

"That's what I'm asking you."

Megan sighed. "If I tell you, can you keep it to yourself?"

"I always told you that I'm here for you."

"We were getting close, and he asked me to go to Ecuador with him."

Paige's face stretched in disbelief, partly horrified yet greedy to learn more. "All that right under my nose! I'm getting lax."

With a wry grin, Megan replied, "Maybe you should trade in those contacts for some reading glasses." Paige swiped the air with her hand. "Anyway, he was relentless, and I was even considering it."

"I guess my man repellants didn't work? Nor my big bad wolf speech, either?"

"No."

"So what happened, honey?"

"The other morning when Randy and Tina came to the office, she told me that Chance was a fighter pilot."

"Well, yeah. I thought you knew that."

"No. Actually, we'd talked about my beliefs, and he purposely held back that information. It helped me understand that he wasn't being honest and open with me. It wasn't all his fault, but it helped me understand that we needed to end it."

"So you did have the same thing."

Megan nodded grimly. "It's my own fault. But it's going to be dull around here without him."

"I don't like dull, either, but I can tell you from experience. Sometimes dull is restful. I know you have a sweet tooth. Maybe you should put a dollop of whipping cream in your coffee today and an extra spoonful of sugar. That'll help."

"Do you see whipping cream?" Megan joked. "No thanks, but I am going to Lil's restaurant for lunch today. Want to come along?"

They started walking out of the coffee room. "Maybe next time. I need to get my work in order for the real boss when he returns after next week." Before Paige returned to her own desk, she shook a manicured finger at Megan. "Now I know why you snapped at me the other day. You need to trust me more."

"I'm sorry about that. I did confide in someone who I thought would give me good advice."

"Who?"

"The preacher who lives in our little guest cottage."

"And did he?"

"Yeah."

"Well, I'm no preacher or even a saint. That's for sure." With a huge chuckle, Paige left for her own cubicle.

On Megan's desk were stacks of work that Chance had organized for her before he left. Brief sticky notes topped each one. She peeled off the first one and brought it up to her face. *Dead ends.* Rather fitting. Was he on a plane now headed for Ecuador? How long would he think of her? With a sigh, she grabbed the stack of files and headed to the file cabinet.

The morning went surprisingly fast, and she soon found herself at Volo Italiano, confiding in Lil. This time, Lil had taken her back into the employee's snack and lunchroom, and they ate together.

Lil waved her sandwich. "You're a strong woman. I'm proud of you for sticking to your beliefs. I like the part about how God opened your eyes and you just knew."

"That was amazing. I'd been struggling for so long and didn't seem to be getting any direction at all, but at the office that day, I just knew." Megan frowned. "Is that a peanut butter sandwich?"

"Yeah. I like them." She leaned closer. "Get tired of pasta every day."

"Last night Dad said that Joy Ann resigned from her secretary duties. Ruthie did, too. And guess who's going to be the new secretary?"

"Not you?"

"No. Barbara."

Lil smiled. "That's perfect."

"I know. At least it'll keep her from weeding Brother Troyer's grave plot."

"She still does that?"

"Mm-hmm. And I think they'll make a great team."

"I hope it works out for him. Maybe Barbara will put in a good word for you."

Megan sighed. "Let's not go there." Everybody wanted to match her up with Micah. No one understood how numb she felt. Even if she grew interested in the preacher, there was no way that he would forget how she'd cried over Chance.

CHAPTER 29

The next week sped by because both Megan and Paige had more than their normal amount of work to do with both Chance and Randy out of the office. Megan was glad because it helped her not worry about Great-aunt Louise's scheduled visit that weekend.

After lunch on Saturday, Mom replaced the tablecloth on the dining-room table three times, finally settling on the antique white with the scalloped edges. The center of the table bore a beautiful bouquet of lavender and roses that Megan had refreshed. "It's beautiful," she tried to reassure her mom. "But she probably won't even remember anything about our house. She's coming to look at us."

Her hand going up to her hair, Mom gasped. "I see a car in the drive now. It must be her."

"Don't worry. It'll be all right."

Only moments later, their aunt had swept in and taken control of the get-together. "Louise means *warrior*, you know. But don't let that bother you. I'm a warrior for the real King." She pointed toward the sky.

"I'm happy to hear that," Mom replied, but Megan could tell that she wasn't happy at all. Mom was pure nerves. Megan herself wasn't much better off.

Seated together on the sofa, they faced their warrior aunt, who leaned forward from the edge of the chair that was a garage-sale purchase. Louise had short, bottle-blond hair and bright blue eyes, which openly studied them. "I suppose you're wondering why I waited all these years to contact you?"

Mom's hand fidgeted with the sofa pillow. "You mentioned something about my grandmother passing."

"Yes. My sister, Mary, rest her soul. A good woman."

Things were not going at all as Megan had envisioned. Warrior for God? Good woman? Where were the wild ancestors? Surely she hadn't conjured up that vision? No, Aunt Louise hadn't mentioned Mom's birth mother yet.

Mom placed both feet firmly on the floor and leaned forward. "You don't know what it feels like to be given away. It doesn't seem like something a good woman would do. In my church, we take care of our own."

Her finger dancing through the air, Louise said, "Mary knew that the Mennonites were good people, and that's why she allowed them to adopt you. About the time you were born, there was so much strain between Mary and her daughter. Janice broke Mary's heart when she left the church and rebelled against all she had been taught. Mary was going through a bit of depression herself at that time. Then when Janice and your father were killed, Mary grieved because she wished they hadn't broken ties."

"Yet she was willing to break ties with me."

Louise flicked her tongue in and out as if it stoked her thoughts. "She regretted it once the depression lifted. It was a sad time. Mary and I were close as two sisters could be."

"We wouldn't know," Mom quipped.

Louise tilted her head and glanced at Megan with confusion.

"Mom was an only child. I am, too. But I have two close friends so I understand the type of relationship you are describing."

Louise looked back at Mom, who finally shrugged.

"I'm here for Mary. I want to bring a piece of her to you. So I've collected some things that I thought you might want to keep."

"So Mary didn't really set these aside herself?"

"Now, Anita, your grandmother didn't want to bring you pain by stirring things up and thought it best she not contact you. But I found your address among her belongings. I'm sure she put these things together for you."

"She sounds like you, Mom," Megan noted. "Not wanting to stir things up."

"But not me." Louise thrust her fist into the air. "I forge ahead, and I felt God tugging at me to do this, so here I am." She settled her gaze on Megan. "You resemble our family."

"I can tell."

"You both do, but Megan even more so. You look like Janice."

That would be the rebellious girl. And maybe she did carry some rebellious genes that had been handed down to her, but she'd already made her choice to resist them. "What about you? What's your life like?"

"I am at that stage in life where I'm defying my age. I do that by traveling. I have a widow friend. We go to wonderful places. I even put my house up for sale. May I send you tokens from my future travels?"

"No! Yes!"

"Well, you'll just have to share yours with your mother then, dear."

Mom looked contrite. "You've come a long way. My manners have been poor. May I get you something to drink? I have cookies."

"Oh, no. I'm fine on those accounts." Louise stood. "Now, if you'll follow me to the car, I'll show you what I've brought."

They followed Louise to her rental car, and she pulled a hinged velvet box out from the passenger's seat, handing it to Mom. Then she riffled through her purse for paper and pen and jotted something on paper. "Megan, here's my address. Let's stay in touch."

"I'd like that." Megan didn't dare glance at Mom.

"Good. Anita, I know that my sister would want you to have those things. Mary must be smiling from heaven even now."

"She was a Christian?" Mom asked.

"Oh, yes. A Methodist!" Louise spread her arms to include their property. "This is a pretty place. God must have planned all this for you. Nothing gets by Him, you know."

Megan admired the twinkle that brightened her great-aunt's eyes when she spoke. She admired her zest for life and God.

"But I speak for the entire family when I say that without you, something was missing. We all missed you. And you'll never know how much it blesses me to see you. If, after you look through those things, you have a change of heart, I'd love to stay in touch."

Megan held her breath, hoping that her mom didn't refuse to accept the box. More than anything, she longed to see what was inside.

"We have your address," Mom replied. "Thank you for your good intentions."

Louise smiled. "You're welcome. Now, may I hug you both before I go?"

Reluctantly Mom allowed the gesture, but Megan meant hers. "Thank you for coming." She wanted to say more, to say that having Louise contact them had changed her life. But it might be better to write her a letter instead. Tokens of affection seemed to matter a lot to this sweet little warrior woman.

They watched the car until it drove out of sight. "Did that really happen?" Megan ventured.

With a deep sigh, Mom said, "Let's go inside and see what's in the box. What she thought was so important that she had to cause all this trouble."

Megan's heart leaped joyfully. She hoped it would contain something that would ease Mom's pain.

They took the box to the dining-room table. Mom ran a shaky finger across the stitched ribbon edging. Slowly she opened its hinges. The lid was lined in red velvet on the inside, too. The first thing she removed was a small Bible.

"It's worn, like she used it," Megan said hopefully.

"A Methodist!" Mom imitated Louise's comment, and when they both laughed, some of the tension left the room.

"Open it."

Mom opened the cover and gasped. On one of the cover pages, Grandma Mary had made a hand-drawn family tree, and Mom's name was there: *Anita Mary Lintz.*

"They gave me my dad's name."

"Mary never knew you, but she loved you," Megan reminded her.

But Mom's eyes darkened. "It's just a name, says nothing about love.

Love is what your Grandma Bachman did for me. For us."

"I know that. But Grandma Witherspoon carried the loss in her heart. Surely, she did." Megan examined some photographs of her mom's parents. "They were so young."

"Young and foolish, I suppose."

They took turns studying the photographs, trying to decipher any resemblances.

"We should have asked about your dad's family," Megan said with disappointment.

"Please, don't ask about that. I'm not ready for that yet."

Nodding, Megan decided in her heart that someday she would ask Louise. She had a right to know, even if her mom didn't want to deal with any more information.

Next Mom drew out a lacy handkerchief. The antique was tiny and delicate. She unfolded it and smoothed out its creases. It looked yellow against the white tablecloth. The handkerchief was trimmed in blue and had hand-embroidered blue initials on it. Suddenly, Mom's hand fluttered at the side of her face. "Do you see it?"

"What?"

"It has your initials."

M.W. "It does."

"You must have this. If you want it?"

"Oh, yes." Mom handed it over, and Megan drew it to her face and took a deep breath, inhaling the musty sweet smell. "What does it smell like?"

Mom found a sachet and brought it to her nose. "Roses."

"I'll bet that's hand sewn, too. I'm glad Aunt Louise brought these, aren't you?"

Mom whispered, "Yes."

"Do you think you'll ever go to Pennsylvania?"

A sarcastic laugh quickly replaced the tender moment. "No. My family is here. This is all I need." Then her hand went out to touch Megan. "But you may stay in touch with Louise. That would be nice."

"Thanks, I'd really like to do that. But what is that bundle of papers?"

"I don't know if I'm ready to find out."

"May I?"

Mom hesitated then nodded.

Megan removed the ribbon that bound a two-inch stack of stationery. She unfolded the top paper. "It's a letter." Silently she read then laid it down and took up the second. "Mom, they're love letters between Mary and your grandfather. His name was John. They must have had some sort of long-distance relationship."

"But we shouldn't have those."

"Why not?"

"Let me see it. I believe you're right. Listen to this. 'Dearest Mary, I can't wait to see you in two weeks. I'll take you for a ride in my convertible. I love to see the wind blow through your blond hair. You look like an angel.' " Mom stopped reading. "It doesn't seem right to read this."

"I'd really like to look through them."

"Fine. You can have them. I need to go start supper."

⎯ↄ⎯

The next week Randy returned to Char Air. When Megan got to work the first day of his return, there was a note on her desk:

Come into my office.
Randy

Not knowing what to expect, she wasted no time, but grabbed a note pad and knocked on his door.

"Come in."

Megan stepped inside. "Welcome back. We missed you."

"Oh. Did you?" He didn't meet her gaze. Rather, he kept it averted to the legal pad on his desk—on top of the blank calendar that wasn't on the right month because she'd wadded it up and destroyed it. "Chance left me some notes. Sit down and we'll go over them."

Sliding into the leather side chair, she felt her face heat at his rebuff. He went through the list so quickly, that she could hardly keep up, scribbling notes as they went. He never made eye contact until they were finished. Then he studied her. "Now that my playboy brother is gone, are you ready to get back to work?"

She met his gaze, feeling resentful because she hadn't loafed, but carried a heavy load in Randy's absence. Yet he made a valid point about her foolish behavior. "Yes."

All week long, Megan was bombarded with an almost impossible workload, and she had to wonder if Randy was trying to break her, push her to quit. Or maybe it was Tina who wanted her gone. But she was determined not to give her boss another good reason to fire her. If she left the company, it'd be her choice.

In spite of his gruff behavior toward her, it was obvious Randy had missed, possibly even mourned, his job. His enthusiasm drove him to be everywhere at once, righting things and even pushing Paige harder to drum up new business. His thirst was unquenchable. Yet there were isolated moments when Megan caught glimpses of turmoil on his brow, sad determination in his eyes. Generally speaking, he'd aged. She had no idea if he was still with Tina.

Their most personal conversation had been minimal, when Megan had asked, "Did you enjoy your cruise?"

Randy had set his jaw and replied grimly, if not sarcastically, "Had the time of my life." And the look he'd given her indicated the conversation was finished forever—unless she was masochistic, and she wasn't.

There were no lunches with Lil. Megan dragged herself home every night, too tired to field any questions her parents or Micah wielded at supper. After helping with the supper dishes, she excused herself and went straight to her room. She wrote in her journal and read her great-grandparents' love letters. She discovered that her great-grandfather loved to quote poets and well-known love sayings. Among her favorites was a quote from Elizabeth Bowen: *When you love someone, all your saved-up wishes start coming out.* Her great-grandparents' letters were the bright spot of Megan's existence.

CHAPTER 30

Thursday evening on his way home from work, Fletch stopped at the Weavers on Lil's behalf. He invited Megan to join them for a picnic and softball game at the doddy house. On Friday Megan held her breath, hoping that Randy wouldn't ask her to work on Saturday. He didn't.

Lil set up the picnic much like she had the one earlier in the summer. After the meal while the toddlers napped, Fletch numbered off the guests to form softball teams. Gleeful that it wouldn't be like in grade school, when Megan was one of the last to be chosen, she joined Fletch's even-numbered team. Ivan and Elizabeth were on her team. Each team had two couples and a single person. Micah joined the Yoders and the David Millers.

Lil was first up to bat. "Get it over the plate, chump," she taunted her cousin.

"And what good will that do you," Jake shouted back, "if you don't know how to hold the bat?"

But Lil did know, and she met the ball with a loud crack. Her bat sailed through the air as she hastened to first base, nearly knocking Fletch's feet out from under him. When she saw she was safe, she did the garbanzo dance to the amusement of everyone, even their opponents.

"You shouldn't throw your bat like that, honey," Fletch admonished, stepping up to take his turn.

"Sorry, sugar," she replied with a sheepish grin.

He brought Lil in, and the score was 1–0.

Next, it was Megan's turn. She warmed up her swing then waited for the perfect pitch. To her surprise, she connected and even sent it over Micah's head at second base. When she saw Fletch go for home, she made a bad choice to try for second base. She heard her teammates' groans, but there was no turning back.

"Run, Megan!"

She sped up, even though she saw she couldn't possibly make it. Micah planted himself over the base, and she barreled into him.

"Oopfh!"

The man was a brick wall and had barely budged. His free arm had even snagged her and kept her from falling at his feet. When he saw she was steady, he lifted his glove and cried, "Out!"

Breathing hard from the sprint, she looked up. His eyes were hidden behind dark sunglasses, but his lips quirked just before he repeated more softly, "Out."

She jerked her arm away, wanting to wipe off his silly grin.

"Watch out how you act around the preacher," Lil warned.

Megan sloughed it off and joined her on the grass. "Whose side are you on?"

"Yours. I missed you this week."

"It was rough. Randy came back with a chip on his shoulder. I get the feeling he regrets hiring me. I'm not sure if Tina wants me out of there or what's going on."

Jake's arm improved, and Ivan and Elizabeth both struck out. The girls pushed to their feet, and Megan walked toward the outfield. Beside her, Lil adjusted her glove. "I'd miss our lunches if you ever left your job, but sometimes change can be a good thing."

Megan wasn't so sure. She hated job hunting. "I'm all right. Since my great-aunt Louise came to visit, Mom's back to her old self. I think her contentment is rubbing off on me."

"Oh yeah? You looked pretty intense out there with Micah a minute ago."

"He was laughing at me."

"I know. We all were."

"It's just that he's always so capable." And she was always the needy one, hanging on his shirttail or using it to wipe away her tears. "Sometimes his perfection is just plain aggravating."

"I know exactly how you feel. It gets even worse after you marry them. But loving Fletch is better than hanging on to my pride." Megan was glad Lil was happy, until her friend put in a parting jab. "I see you and Micah drove separate cars. A waste of fuel, if you ask me."

Megan rolled her gaze skyward, but she had to admit that she would've enjoyed riding over with him because they hadn't talked all week. Unless you counted a few snippets over supper with her parents in the room. She hoped he didn't think she was avoiding him. But if she recalled correctly, he'd missed a couple of meals, too. Her gaze traveled over the Millers' yard until it located him, standing in the home team area, trying out various bats.

He wore jeans, which in itself was an unusual sight. More often, she saw him in his dress clothes. He also had on a solid gray, pocketed T-shirt and a pair of sunglasses that prohibited her from knowing where his gaze was focused. As he made some test swings, his shirt lifted a bit, revealing a small waist. She felt a strange sad yearning, but it was as fleeting as it was strange. As his legs found their stance, his strength drew her interest. He had fascinated her from the moment he'd stepped onto the Weavers' property. Now his arms bunched under his shirt as he took several fake swings. Finally he took his place at home plate. Tapped the plate with the tip of his bat.

Ivan's first pitch was outside, and Micah let it go by. Fletch was catcher. He lopped it back to Ivan. The next pitch was good, and Micah drew back. He hit the ball high into centerfield. Megan's gaze followed it, until she saw that it was going to fall behind her. Both she and Lil ran for it, but it hit the ground beyond them. Lil scooped it up first, probably because she could run faster in her jeans.

Panting, Megan bent slightly to catch her breath and watched Lil toss it into the infield. It was an overthrow that sailed over Ivan's head. Micah rounded third, his long, churning legs never slowing. Megan watched the play unfold, found herself rooting for Micah even if he was aggravating and playing for the opposing team. He hit the ground and slid, uprooting some grassy clods, his feet hitting home just before Ivan finally recovered the ball and threw it to Fletch.

Micah stood and clapped Fletch on the arm, both men grinning. Then Micah brushed off his jeans and looked up, and although she couldn't be certain because of his sunglasses, she thought he caught her staring. Quickly, she dropped her gaze and returned to her position.

"We're tied," Lil called over with disappointment.

But in Megan's estimation, Micah's home run outshone anything their team had done. Her admiration diminished, however, when the odd-numbered team's runs began to stack up against them, inning after inning. And when the babies woke up and the game ended, Megan was glad to be finished with it.

Lil and Fletch served homemade ice cream topped with strawberries, and Megan was content when Micah stretched out on the grass beside her quilt. "You're good. Did you play in school?"

"No. Just lucky," he replied.

She didn't think so. "Normally we have a church picnic and ball game on Labor Day weekend."

"Really?" Micah got excited. "No one's mentioned it."

"Only the men play ball," she clarified. "It's always been the last hurrah before school starts, kind of an early harvest celebration."

"Why should this year be any different? I think we should do it. Who plans it?"

"Brother Troyer and his wife always did."

"I'll talk to Barbara about it. A church ball game might ease some tension."

Megan nodded, wondering what tension. She took a spoonful of ice cream, felt his gaze on her.

"Do you think I stare at the widows?"

Almost bursting into laughter, she asked, "What?"

"When I preach?"

She saw he was dead serious and tried to envision his last sermon, when suddenly her eyes lit with understanding amusement. "I believe you do. But I always thought you were watching the clock."

"Of course." He shook his head, and a clump of bangs fell playfully over his sunglasses. He gave it a quick brush of his hand. "That's it."

"Guess you'd better put a watch on the pulpit."

"Now I can give the search committee an explanation." He rubbed his chin thoughtfully, and she noticed that he had ice cream under his lower lip.

It was all she could do not to reach out and remove it. She quickly glanced away, watching Katy scoop up little Jacob. Why was she always wanting to fix him? Help him when he was already practically perfect? The idea troubled her. "Glad I could help. I need to go talk to Katy." She stood and brushed her skirt. "I'll be on the swing later if you want to drop by and gloat about getting me out on second."

His voice sounded grave when he replied, "It's tempting."

As she strode toward Katy, she felt her face heat and wondered how she could be so bold, but she missed him and their quiet talks. From the start of Micah's return to Plain City, God had drawn them together. She found rest in his quiet strength.

She was certain he would never offer anything other than friendship, like everyone seemed to hope. He might wish to, but he wouldn't. She had ruined her real chances with him when she had acted the fool over Chance. No, Micah was too honorable, too perfect to make that kind of mistake. When had she started thinking of him as perfect? That night in the root cellar? Certainly not back in college.

"Megan, have you heard what Jacob did last night?"

She tore her attention away from the preacher and saw the joy in Katy's eyes. Marriage and motherhood agreed with her. Megan fondled the baby's soft squirmy arm and shared in Katy's delight. "No. What did he do?"

⁓

Micah pushed his notes aside. How could he study his sermon when Megan might be waiting for him on the porch swing? Had he really caught her staring at him throughout the ball game? Or did she merely need another sounding board, a tear blotter. If so, he'd be smart to think ahead and stick a hanky in his pocket and keep her off his shoulder and out of his arms.

Megan had been distant all week, which had suited his desire to quit chasing her. But he'd been disappointed that she hadn't been there for him when he'd needed to vent after his search committee meeting. Today, however, she'd redeemed herself, by solving the mystery about why the widows thought he stared at them when he preached. Not only that, she'd told him about the annual church picnic and softball game.

With a touch or a word, she made things right, providing the exact type of encouragement he needed. He sighed and laid down his pencil, hating to admit that she'd helped him as much, if not more, than he'd ever helped her. And surely her motives were purer than his own.

With things intensifying at church, he didn't need the extra stress of Megan messing with his emotions. She didn't realize how she affected him. Her naïveté was deadly.

What he needed was his grandmother's sweet advice. She'd been more than motherly, she'd been a saint. The past week, working with Barbara, those memories had returned. He could hardly face the idea of failing at Big Darby and having to return to live in the quiet old house alone. It would stir up the sad memories of her last weeks. He knew that he would need to go back and deal with the house sometime, no matter what happened.

His traitorous thoughts returned to Megan. Why had she asked him to meet her on the porch? With a disgusted sigh at his male weakness and one-track thinking, he pushed back his chair. Scooping up the cat, he went toward the door. Once he was outside, he'd be able to tell if Megan was there. Usually his body came to alert anytime she was on the property. He'd know, all right. He'd take the cat out, but he wouldn't sit on the porch and wait for her, for pity's sake.

Miss Purrty meandered toward the back of the property, and something akin to static electricity danced across his arms. But his heart throbbed with a dull pain, like arthritic joints before a rain. Megan was his rain. She was nothing if she wasn't bittersweet. He paused, listened. Smiled at the swing's groan. Stuffing his hands in his pockets, he gravitated toward the rain.

When he reached the porch, he saw her hair was backlit by the moon, giving her face an ethereal appearance. "Hey."

She looked up. "Fireflies will soon be gone."

"Like me."

"You're in a bad mood for being on the winning team."

He didn't ask for permission, just slipped onto the seat next to her. Oddly, she didn't slide over, like he'd expected, which left their shoulders lightly pressed against each other. He already regretted their touch, and he would suffer from it. But if she wasn't going to move first, he certainly wasn't going to go wimpy. He'd already done that earlier in the afternoon, when he'd gotten a sneezing attack the second time he was up to bat. He'd made it to first, and as he'd waited for the next batter to hit him around the bases, he'd heard Megan sneezing in the outfield. Though his allergies always made him feel less than manly, it gave him a perverse sense of satisfaction that she shared his symptoms.

"I saw your light. Working on your sermon?"

"Mm-hmm. It's about patience."

"You're good at that one, aren't you?"

"Not so good."

"I'm anxious to hear your sermon. But lately, I have this feeling. . ."

"What?"

"That everything will turn out right in the end. Is that patience, you think?"

"Sounds more like faith. Was it something your aunt said? Did she leave you with an inheritance or something?"

She ignored his sarcasm. "I think it had more to do with finally agreeing with God, instead of resisting Him. The past two weeks seem like years. Another lifetime, actually. I don't think I loved Chance." She turned, searched his face. "Do you think that's fickle?"

He wanted to kiss the fickleness right out of her lips, help her find her way. But she trusted him with her shoulder snuggled against him. "Nope." When her eyes widened, he realized he'd said that out loud. "No. Not fickle. I know what it's like to lose someone. Feel disappointed and confused. To receive God's peace in the midst of it. I understand."

"Your grandma?"

He missed her dearly, but he was thinking about his struggle to get over Megan. It was exhausting, so he directed their conversation to a safer place. "I don't want to lose this position." Had he really agreed with God, as Megan finally had? Or was he still resisting Him?

"What can I do to help?"

Kiss me. Keep your distance, and for crying out loud, don't be inviting me to meet you on the porch swing. He glanced at her moonlit face, wondering if he could tell her that. Would she understand if he explained how hard she was making it for him to concentrate on his job? Or would it frighten her and make her loathe him for pretending friendship when he really loved her. She looked at him, waiting expectantly. "Just be a good sport and hold my hand, I guess."

She took him literally and slipped her hand in his. "I'm glad we're friends."

He eased away. "We are, Megan. But difficult as it will be, we need to quit meeting like this. Like you said before, we need to agree with God, not resist Him, and I don't think our actions honor Him."

She rubbed her rejected hand down her skirt. "I guess. But it feels right. I don't understand why I feel so comfortable with you? Do you?"

He wished he could say the same. But comfortable didn't quite fit the bill for him. He clamped his knee so he didn't give in and put his arm around her. He heard Purrty's mew, and knew that their moment was ending. That he had to take his stand against the pull of the flesh. "I'd better get back to my sermon." She turned, looking hurt. Somehow, he found the strength to say, "I'm glad that we could get over the awkwardness of college. I appreciate all you've done to help me. Your friendship, your kindness. But we're not children, and we can't play with fire, Meg. We need to keep our distance, for both our reputations."

"Is this what you told Joy Ann?"

Surprised to hear the edge in her voice, he studied her eyes. Even softened by moonlight, they held flashes of anger. "Of course not. But if you really want to help me—"

"Stop," she interrupted, as she stood. "I get it."

"I don't think you do. You don't realize how you affect men."

"Are you insinuating that I enticed Chance?"

"No. I'm just saying I can't go around protecting you." He sighed, ran his hands through his hair. "I need to practice what I preach. In all honesty, we both know we need to grow up."

Her head dipped. He hoped she wasn't going to cry again. Because he refused to comfort her the way he had in the past. He waited. Slowly she raised her head. There was a trace of moisture in her eyes, but thankfully, she kept her composure.

"You're right. I've been selfish. It's impossible to continue this way. But I hope you won't think badly of me if I see you staring at the clock tomorrow and make a face. It won't do, you know, to keep staring at the widows."

Grateful for her brave attempt at humor, he whispered. "I'd be honored for your help."

"It's late. 'Night."

He scooped up the cat and headed for his cottage without even attempting a reply. He wanted to get as far away from his temptation as possible. He knew there'd be some kneeling time before he could get back to his sermon. But he felt good about taking a stand. It was up to God now to give him the strength to abide.

—⸱—

Added to everything else that had happened, Micah's rejection devastated Megan. She'd never expected him to give her the brush-off. She deserved the humiliating set down for using him the way she had. She'd been selfish and horrified when he told her to grow up. But worse was the loss of a valuable friendship. Kind, gentle, perfect Micah, always trying to do the right thing. He was not a weakling. He was the strongest man she knew. And she'd driven him away.

Rolling onto her back, she stared into the darkness and pulled the covers up under her chin. She was positive that he still cared about her, but he'd been man enough to resist her. He wouldn't settle for less than what he deserved. Someone who adored him, some pure-hearted woman who could share his life and bring honor to his position as head of the church. Who would he choose? Lori Longacre? He admired her and found her attractive. It was painful to imagine the two of them together. Why had it taken her so long to realize Micah's worth? She'd been such a fool. Twice over.

She would take his advice to heart, as if it was from God Himself.

Micah was her preacher, after all. She would pick herself up and be a better person for it, even if he did marry the librarian. She would do everything in her power to help and not hinder him. He deserved that much from her.

She thought she understood the quotation in the latest love letter by her great-grandfather that she'd read: "There is no remedy for love than to love more"—Henry David Thoreau.

CHAPTER 31

The next morning at church, Megan watched Micah preach his best-ever sermon, his gaze never veering toward the clock or the widows' section. Afterward, he announced his plans for the church picnic and what he now called the Brothers' Baseball Outing. At the announcement, a general buzz fell over the congregation. On one hand, she was happy that his idea was being accepted, but on the other, she was a bit disappointed that Micah presented the idea with enthusiasm and didn't appear to have lost any sleep on her account.

"Clever name, Brothers' Baseball Outing," Inez whispered to Leon.

When the general din waned, Micah surprised the congregation further by delegating those men seated on his left to be on the white-shirt team, and those on his right side to be on the blue-shirt team. He encouraged them to choose their own captains. As she listened to Micah's plans, she was surprised to hear that Joy Ann and Ruthie were organizing some games for the children. And Barbara was working with the hostess committee to plan the food.

After the meeting, feeling generally left out and disagreeable, Megan started across the parking lot to find Katy, hoping little Jacob would lift her spirits. She'd only taken a few steps when she heard David Miller planning to recruit Chad Penner, who was home sick with a cold. She wondered if Micah's new method would foster unhealthy rivalry and contention amongst the men. But with Micah's rejection still heavy on her heart, she didn't have it in her to warn him about it. *Men. Let them work it out.*

"Hi, Katy. Can I hold him?"

"Of course. He loves you."

Megan bounced Jacob until he giggled.

"I have news. Elizabeth Miller is thinking about taking a job, and I offered to babysit for her if she does." Katy's dark eyes flashed with joy. "Won't that be fun?"

Megan kissed Jacob's cheek. "I thought you hated that nanny job."

Tucking a strand of black hair beneath her covering, Katy quickly explained, "That was different. Those children were raised differently and I didn't know how to handle them. I've also developed a little patience since then."

Megan's mind went to Micah's sermon on patience, but she quickly reined it in. "From living with Jake?"

Katy laughed. "That, too. But enough about me. I heard Randy's been rough on you. I've been praying for you."

"Thanks. I'm not sure what I'll do if things don't change soon."

"Have you talked to Micah about it?"

"No. He doesn't want to have much to do with me, either." Megan didn't wish to turn Katy against their preacher candidate, so she quickly added, "It's not his fault. Our friendship isn't really appropriate, right now."

"Are you still unwilling to admit it might be more than friendship?"

Trying to speak while Jacob poked her cheeks, seemingly fascinated with adult speaking mechanisms, Megan replied, "I was foolish to tell him about Chance. Now I wish I hadn't. He knows everything, and I don't think he can get past that. He needs somebody with a good reputation, somebody like Lori."

"Oh." Katy's dark brow suddenly quirked in warning, just before Susanna swooped in and landed beside them.

"Young ladies, the quilters are helping the hostess committee with the picnic. Isn't it exciting? Anyway, I wanted to ask you, Megan, if you'd bring that three bean salad that Barbara raves about."

"Of course. But it's really Lil's recipe."

Her arm swept a graceful but fierce wing through the air. "Well, work it out between you. Hopefully Lil will come and bring something a little more. . ."

"Scrumptious?" Katy supplied, and Megan's feelings weren't in the least bit hurt.

"Exactly. We certainly don't want to tie her hands, now do we?" Susanna's laugh croaked. But when she walked away, Megan asked, "Did she hear us talking about Micah?"

"I don't think so, but then her hearing is extraordinarily sharp."

Micah watched the tender scene transpiring across the parking lot, how Megan gave Katy a friendly hug and then lifted baby Jacob into her arms. It caused a bittersweet pang, knowing that Megan would make a wonderful mother.

"Brother Micah?"

He quickly tore his gaze away from Megan and rested it on the pretty brunette woman facing him. "Yes, Lori?"

"I believe that resurrecting the picnic and ballgame was the perfect thing for the congregation. How do you do it? Always anticipate the needs?"

"I sense a *but* coming next."

She smiled. "See what I mean?"

He waited, curiously. Lori had been helping him with research for his sermons. He no longer worried about her stepping out of line. She was easygoing, and in working with her, he'd learned that her advice was usually timely and valuable. It was too bad her perfume always tickled his nose.

"There's a cold bug going around and a few families traveling to family reunions. I overheard some men scheming to snap up the better players upon their return. There's some competition brewing. And I was just wondering if you were going to let them get away with that?"

"I can tell that you have a different idea."

"I do." She urged him closer with her finger. "I think I can help."

He leaned close, strangely intrigued.

⁃ᥫ

The following Sunday, Megan slid into the pew next to her mom and watched Micah deliver a sermon on peace, another fruit of the Spirit. She jotted down a few notes but often found her mind detouring, fixed on the way his jaw hardened when he stressed a point. It was his tendency in the next breath to soften his jaw by allowing his lower lip to droop into a bit of a smile. She knew him well enough to recognize it as one of his pleading smiles. Often he admitted his own shortcomings to the congregation. But his humility only made him more loveable.

She crossed her arms and wished his smile wasn't the last thing she thought about before she fell asleep at night. She'd tried to tell herself that she was only attracted to him because he was a preacher, just like she had been attracted to Chance because he was a missionary pilot. After all, weren't God's men the most appealing?

But it wasn't his occupation at all. He'd wiggled his way into her heart, little by little, revealing his true nature. And now when she looked at him, that's what she saw, not the gawky outer shell she remembered from Rosedale. His physique had become pleasing as well. Now her competition was plentiful.

She uncrossed her arms, took a tissue from her purse, and blotted her forehead. Maybe this fascination with him was the result of reading her grandparents' love letters every night before she drifted off to sleep: "To love another person is to see the face of God"—Victor Hugo. What better way to describe what she felt for Micah?

He sneezed twice, drawing her from her private thoughts. "Anyone wishing to play softball who wasn't here last week when we designated teams can draw his team placement from a jar in the library. Lori Longacre will monitor the drawings after the service and each week until the event."

Megan frowned at the affectionate look he shot Lori.

"In fact, I'm headed there to draw a team for myself after the Doxology. This way the teams will be formed in a fair manner, even if they end up lopsided, for I'm sure the team who gets me will be at a disadvantage."

There were a few chuckles. *Hardly a disadvantage*, Megan thought, remembering how he'd hit a home run the day they'd played at the doddy house. Micah went on to stress that this was first and foremost a friendly competition.

Suddenly Megan felt the forewarning tickle of a sneeze. She brought her tissue up to press under her nose, hoping to ward off her irritating connection to Micah. When she felt it was safe, she lowered her hand, and her gaze involuntarily followed those of the majority of the congregation's to Lori Longacre's pew. It shocked Megan to see the woman's undisguised admiration directed straight ahead toward the pulpit.

Clearly, Lori and Micah had conspired to come up with that plan. It tugged painfully at Megan's heart to imagine him going elsewhere for advice. She'd recognized the admiration they shared for each other from the beginning. She certainly wouldn't go anywhere near the library after the service. Let them have their fling!

⸺☙

After that day, Megan intentionally kept out of Micah's way. As if in un-spoken agreement, he followed suit, accepting more food offerings, keeping to his cottage most evenings. If her parents noticed a change, they didn't comment to her about it.

Megan's workload lightened. One noon she dashed over to Volo Italiano. Two men standing beside a silver SUV eyed her Nova as it rum-bled into the parking lot, and she felt their gaze follow her all the way into the restaurant. Inside it seemed busier than usual.

Lil darted around a corner. "Just a minute!"

"Sure." Megan turned to the hostess. "Seems busy today."

"A conference. Bunch of engineers."

"Think Lil's too busy for me?"

"I doubt it. They made reservations, and we increased our staff today."

Lil strode up, tucking some straying hairs back into their pins. "Sorry about that."

"Just when I get a break, you're busier than normal."

Lil brushed a hand through the air. "The worst is over; it's mostly some stragglers left. I was glad when you called. So Randy's off your case now?"

"He's eased up. But work's different. It's just a job now. You know what I mean?"

"Sure. The honeymoon's over." Megan glanced at Lil to see if her comment was a jab at Fletch, but it didn't appear to be. Especially when she added, "That's not always a bad thing."

" 'There is no remedy for love than to love more.' "

"Huh?"

"Henry David Thoreau. From my great-grandpa's love letters."

"I like that. I guess you could say there's no remedy for work than to work more."

Megan laughed. "You're right about that, too. Tina dropped by the office this week. She acted like we were old friends. It's weird. But at least now I know they're still together. That's a good thing." Megan shrugged. "Did your family tell you Big Darby's having their annual picnic and softball game?"

"Yeah, Mom mentioned it."

"You and Fletch should come. See the old crowd. It'll be fun. Susanna hopes you'll bring something scrumptious."

"Susanna misses me?" Lil glanced over her shoulder. "Before I go, I've been thinking about something. Remember when Fletch and I were dating? We broke up for a few months because he needed time to work things out so he knew what he had to offer me."

"I remember. It was a hard time for you."

"Maybe that's what's going on with Micah. He needs to concentrate on his job now. Some things are worth the waiting. You know, like my veal spinach ravioli."

CHAPTER 32

I t rained the night before the Big Darby picnic. By noon the sky remained ominous, but the grassy field at Inez and Leon Beachy's home had dried somewhat. The congregation held the annual softball game and many other church outings at the Beachys' farm.

Years earlier, before the couple's children had left the vicinity, Leon made a ball diamond with softball dimensions. It became a community gathering place. Leon finally gave up trying to fill in the bare spots. Though weedy, it could easily be resurrected for a game just by mowing the sparse grass lower than normal.

Inez, a starkly conservative but take-charge woman, knew how to set up for an event. When Megan arrived, several of the women's black tied shoes had already stomped down the grassy area in and among the folding tables. Megan quickly jumped in to help them with the tablecloths.

Inez twisted her mouth, placed her hands at her hips, and studied the picnic site. A breeze swirled the hem of her skirt and her covering strings. "This will never do." She pointed. "See those small rocks at the base of that tree?" Megan shifted her gaze. Tree roots twisted through an undergrowth of wild ground ivy, but she saw some stones protruding from the tangle. "Those can secure the tablecloths."

Susanna lifted her hawkish nose, which presided over her oval face, and sniffed the humid air. "I'm going to make some quilts to use at these events. They'll be heavy enough that we don't have to use dirty old stones."

"Nonsense! Where do you think our food comes from? The ground." Inez huffed. "Anyway, they'd get ruined."

"It wouldn't be any different than using white tablecloths." Susanna lifted the hem of the closest cloth. "You know these have seen their better days. We'd only need four or five at the most."

Inez swiped her hand through the air. "I suppose it might work."

Megan left the bickering women and washed the stones at a nearby water faucet, making sure to put one at the ends of each table.

A huge cloud rolled in over the farm, cooling and darkening the air. Susanna shook her auburn head. "This is going to be a disaster."

"Maybe so, but the food's arriving. You head up the dessert table," Inez instructed the widow. "I'll arrange the main table, and Rose can handle the drinks."

Megan eyed the dessert table regrettably, but followed Rose to the drink table, knowing that when Lil arrived, she'd pitch in and help there. Wooden sawhorses with planks supported crocks of lemonade and iced tea. Coolers were stuffed beneath the tables and emptied of their contents. Side dishes and cold salad arrived in heirloom dishes to fill Inez's tables. Crowd-sized roasters contained sliced or shredded meats. Susanna hovered over the desserts of fluted, flaky pie crusts baked to perfection.

Lil arrived carrying homemade bread, and Susanna intercepted Fletch. "What do you have there, young man?"

"Lil's veal spinach ravioli."

The widow lifted the foil and eyed it greedily. Then she pointed. "Take it to Inez. Over there."

When Fletch returned, he said, "Hon, I think it cut the mustard. I'm going after our lawn chairs."

Megan looked away from the tender exchange and watched guests vying for places to set up their folding chairs. Her gaze took in the bright old quilts strewn across the ground and the sports equipment propped up against rough-barked tree trunks. But the person she'd been longing for was still missing. She scanned the cars that lined the dirt driveway, some all the way out to the weed-fringed, faded barn. The rickety structure still held some old farm antiques, but was mostly used for Leon's paint business. And then she saw it. Micah's Honda.

Quickly scanning the yard again, Megan spotted him with a small cluster of men from the search committee. They were all glancing skyward. Megan looked up, too. Though there had been moments of sunlight, the sky was mostly hidden in fast-moving clouds.

Lil nudged her. "What's so interesting?"

"Nothing."

Lil quirked the corner of her mouth. "Right. Hey, there's Katy. Let's go over."

Megan followed Lil, and they dropped to the quilt where Katy had laid Jacob. "Where's Jake?"

"Tossing a ball with Ray Eversole. They're taking this game way too seriously to suit me."

"Really?"

Katy's sulky lips thinned. "The men were not happy to be mixed up."

Although Micah had gone to everybody but Megan for advice, even after the picnic was her idea, she still came to his defense. "He didn't know about the tradition. That they already had teams."

"I know. But they don't like change."

"Nobody does. But it doesn't matter who the next preacher is, there's going to be change. We all knew that."

A loud whistle rent the air. Megan looked to her right, and her heart gave a sad twinge. Oblivious to the undercurrent of complaints, Micah's face was wreathed in enthusiasm. He stood on a stump and waved his hand as the din around them quieted. A few childish squeals broke the silence. Then as parents drew the youngsters, hyped from their first week back at school, to themselves, a reverent hush fell over the group.

Micah prayed, thanking the Lord for Brother Troyer's years of service, dedicating the day to his remembrance, and asking for strength for his widow Barbara. There arose a soft murmur of affirmation. Afterward, he told the group to enjoy their meal and fellowship and, Lord and weather willing, they'd assemble for the game around 1:30 p.m. Megan knew he was rushing it a bit, hoping to beat the storm.

"We'd better get to play," Ray Eversole shouted out, "I hope I haven't conditioned the last couple of weeks for nothing."

Hoots of laughter came from the men. "What kind of conditioning?" Mark Kraybill asked.

"I'm not giving away my secrets," the song leader replied.

"Better just go and fill your plate. You'll need your strength," Mark urged.

Megan got in line next to Joy Ann. "So what do you have planned for the children?"

"We're having some relay races. I bought some pencils and prizes they can use at school."

"That was thoughtful."

"It was Brother Zimmerman's idea to get the prizes. I was happy to do it." She pushed her glasses higher on the bridge of her nose. "Ruthie's helping. And some of the young moms."

Somehow Micah had made his peace with Joy Ann, who now took a plate and turned her attention over to her choices. Megan made sure she got some of Lil's veal spinach ravioli before Susanna cleaned the platter. When they'd lived together in the doddy house, she'd seen firsthand how painstaking the recipe was, with Lil making everything from scratch. She noticed with a bit of glee that her own bean salad was also getting devoured—word must have gotten out that it was Lil's recipe.

Megan took her food to join her friends. Their men assembled nearby, and Elizabeth's little one toddled back and forth between his parents. He took bites and shyly watched the older children who would rather play than eat.

"Jake got rained out early yesterday, and I ended up doing an extra load of laundry last night to get rid of all the wet clothing. That man can make a mess. But after the baby went down, he surprised me with a new Christian novel. We stayed up late reading it, when we really should have been studying for our Sunday school lesson."

"I love hearing Ivan's perspective on the lesson. You can always study tonight," Elizabeth said. "Isn't that what Saturday evenings are for?"

"If nobody has a sick animal emergency," Lil piped up. Then coloring a bit, she quickly added, "I'm not complaining, just saying."

Megan couldn't help but feel left out, getting such vivid imagery of her friends' married home lives. The three young couples seemed settled in like old shoes, yet she could see by the sparkle in their eyes that there was still plenty of romance in their relationships. The honeymoon wasn't over, as Lil had insinuated. Micah ate with the Kraybills, while jostling one of their little ones on his knee. He was good with kids. Megan remembered that he had worked with teenagers back in Pennsylvania. She had no doubt about his reading and Bible study abilities.

Passively listening to the conversation, Megan's plate emptied first. "I'm going for Mandy Penner's blackberry pie before it's all gone." The young woman worked at the well-known Berry Farm on the Mitchell-Dewitt Road.

"Could you bring me a piece of blueberry?" Jake called over.

"Sure." Megan grinned, amused how the men honed in on their conversation when it involved food. She brushed off her skirt and went to the dessert table. Her gaze went over the rows of glass pie pans, searching for the mouth-watering blackberry. A familiar scent tickled her nose. She froze at the sound of a recognizable male voice. She had been unaware that Lori Longacre and Micah were inching together along the opposite side of the table. How had he moved so quickly from the Kraybills?

"Those lemon bars have to be yours," he purred.

Megan lifted her gaze. Not seeming to notice her, Micah placed a lemon bar on his plate, his head bent.

Feeling the heat creep up her neck and scorching her temples, she would have slunk away if she hadn't promised Jake his pie. She quickly got two clean dessert plates and filled hers with the blackberry and then moved to the blueberry tin.

"That's right. I baked some for you when you first arrived. I'm surprised you don't waddle by now."

He had plenty of room on his sharp bones, Megan thought. Even called him Stick Man at Rosedale. Keeping her gaze down, she hurried to get done with the pie and away from the sickening conversation.

"I don't waddle. I do worse things. I. . ."

Megan's pie slipped off the spatula. It plunked onto Inez's starched white tablecloth. "Aye, yi, yi!" She stared at the mess she'd made.

A masculine hand touched her arm. "Let me help. You hold the plate, and I'll serve the pie."

"What a waste." Lori dipped her finger in the glob of blueberry and licked it off with pleasure. "I'll go get something to clean it up before it stains."

"I'll do it," Megan argued. *Tablecloth's seen its better days anyway, according to Susanna.*

"I don't mind."

In resignation, Megan held the plate, trying to keep her hand from shaking. Micah slid a perfect piece onto Jake's plate. "Thanks." She couldn't help but glance up and was even more distressed to see the crinkling around his eyes. Returning his look with one of low toleration, she hurried back to the refuge of her friendly circle.

But Micah followed her and lowered himself next to Jake, balancing his plate of Lori's lemon delights on his knees. "Who's ready to work off their meal?" he asked the men.

Megan turned away, so that her back was to the other quilt. She stared at her pie. Her appetite had vanished. Obviously she wasn't as ready as she had thought to give Micah over to Lori. And even though her eyes couldn't watch the intruder, her heart felt his presence, and she felt naked and vulnerable as if everyone could interpret what was churning inside her.

But Lil was giving Katy tips on pasta sauce. And Elizabeth was chasing the baby, who'd gotten bold enough to finally venture after the older children.

Megan took a forkful of pie, willing herself to taste it. Took a second bite and soon found herself scraping another empty plate. Lori was right. A waste of good food. The image of Lori's slender finger dipping into the blueberries made her set her plate on the grass beside her. She shouldn't resent Lori's quick reaction, coming to her rescue. But everything about the librarian irked her lately.

Behind her, she heard rustling and the general din of men, clad and divided by white and blue shirts, doing their manly maneuvers to prepare for the game.

"Let's move the blankets closer to the game," Lil suggested.

With Megan's dad and Fletch on the same team with Micah, she was able to cheer for the white team without embarrassment. By the second inning, her dad had struck out twice, but Fletch was usually able to get on base. In the fifth, Micah lost a ball in the outfield and scored a home run. The game lagged in time out as several men combed the field of grass and wildflower to recover the ball. The fuss Micah received was more than Megan could bear. She jumped up. "Want some lemonade, Mom?"

"Sure. Thanks, honey."

Megan strode purposefully toward the house to fetch it. The man was good at everything. Sure, there'd be complaints and lots of change, but he'd overcome. She, on the other hand, might not. She placed her cup beneath the crock's spigot.

"Too much excitement for you?"

Megan flinched and pivoted. "Just parched. And you?"

"Actually, I'm good." Lori smiled at Megan.

"How nice."

"But I might as well get some iced tea while I'm here." Lori filled her cup, swirled it, then gazed at her with sympathy. "I don't need a man to make me happy."

Megan narrowed her eyes and set her cup on the table. "What's that supposed to mean?"

"Don't be blind, Megan. Micah's all yours. But respect God's timing. Micah has more important things on his mind these days."

Even though Lori was her senior, the unbidden advice hit Megan as condescending. "Oh, yeah? You two seem chummy."

"Really?" Lori's mouth twisted in disgusted sarcasm. "That's just the sort of rumor that could ruin Micah."

"No kidding."

Lori's anger vanished as quickly as it had been stirred. "It's true we share a friendship, but there's nothing romantic going on between us. If it appears that way, then I'll be more careful."

Megan blinked back unwanted tears. "I'm sorry. It's none of my business. You've done nothing wrong. I don't want to hurt Micah."

The librarian's touch gentled Megan further. "Really, my life is complete without a husband. I'm not desperate for a man." Lori lifted her chin. "I've had offers."

"I didn't mean it that way."

Lori's hand fell away wistfully. "If I married, I'd have to give up the things I enjoy. My freedom. My books. I'm one of those people the apostle Paul talked about. Sometimes the single life is best."

Megan bit her bottom lip, taking in the other woman's sincerity. "Thanks for sharing that. Maybe I should consider a single life."

Lori smiled. "Or maybe you should be more patient toward the right man. Micah's been preaching on patience, hasn't he? I hope he gets the position. We need young thinking. I'm using all my resources to help him."

Lori had always been progressive in her thinking. Some of her family had moved to churches like the one Lil attended. Her candid honesty warranted Megan's respect. She was ashamed over her jealousy. *There is no remedy for love than to love more.* "You've given me a lot to think about."

"Looks like the game's starting again."

Lori's perfume lingered after she'd left. With a sigh, Megan filled her cups and trudged back to the sidelines.

"I thought you'd gotten lost," Mom chided.

Shifting the attention away from herself, Megan pointed. "Look, Dad's up next."

When her mom turned her interest back to the game, Megan quietly pondered the unusual conversation with Lori, wondering if in time Micah could forgive her for chasing after Chance. Could he let go and allow himself to fall in love with her? But then Lori didn't know about all that. Or did she?

"Look!" Mom pointed upward.

Almost instantly, the sky cast a dark shadow over them. Even the ball players fidgeted as the stormy wind caught several loose lawn chairs. Inez jumped, grabbed her skirt, and ran toward the tables.

Micah raised his hand. "We better quit now. The women could use our help."

"But it's mid-inning. It's not fair!"

Some of the men ran in from the field and huddled around Micah. Megan saw some gesturing and a glove slammed down to the ground. Although she couldn't hear the hot debate, she saw Micah plant his feet and shake his head in that obstinate way of his. Soon after that, the players formed a line and shook hands.

Fletch walked over to Lil. "They're calling it a tie."

"But the white team's a run ahead," Lil argued.

"Yeah, but it's mid-inning. It's only fair."

Megan hoped that was the general consent, but she didn't wait to find out. She went to help with the food. The wind whipped the tablecloths at every unsecured edge. Megan spit hair from the corner of her mouth and tried to tuck it behind her ear and secure her covering, but the effort seemed useless. Inez rushed bundled tablecloths to the house, and Megan went to help Katy and Jake get the baby and all their belongings to the car.

She was amazed at how quickly everything cleaned up and everybody dispersed. Hastening her gait to a near jog, she started toward her own car, giving a few final waves. She'd parked on the far side of the lane, and before she'd made it the barn, the real downpour began. It drenched her and made it hard to see more than a few feet ahead.

"Megan!"

CHAPTER 33

Micah lunged for Megan's hand and drew her into the shelter beneath the barn's overhang. "It's dry here."

"Whew! I guess I was too slow."

"I saw you helping back there." He leaned his back against the rough barn wall. "Let's just wait it out a little. Maybe it'll let up in a minute."

With a shiver, she backed up against the damp wall next to him. Overhead, water dumped on the barn roof and ran off the eaves. Her hand fluttered around her face, tucked a wet strand behind her ear. "I'm already soaked."

"I know. But you might get run over out there." Thunder rumbled above the roar of water. "Or hit by lightning."

"I can't even see the driveway."

All he could see was the woman next to him. Dripping as if she'd just taken a swim, Megan was totally fetching. She silently watched the rain, her damp bodice still heaving from the run. Sudden blasts of pinpricks occasionally peppered them, but mostly they were sheltered. In fact, too secluded for his raging testosterone. Water cascaded off the roof, creating a wall between them and the elements, a paradise for the two of them—Tarzan and Jane and their own private waterfall. He tried to focus on something other than Megan and his junior-high novel reading list, turning to the obvious. "Looks like Leon needs to fix his rain spouting."

She grinned. "You offering?"

"I should. He's on the search committee."

Her smile widened, revealing fine even teeth. "Is there anything you can't do? Or won't do?"

"Yes. There is."

She lowered her gaze as if reading his mind. Lori had warned him that Megan was jealous earlier. After that, he'd hardly been able to concentrate on the game. He supposed it was foolish to hope that Megan could grow to care for him as more than friends. Ever since he'd pushed her away, for his own sake, he'd missed her. As their silence prevailed, rivulets of water transformed the ground around their feet.

"You're a home-run hitter," she said softly. "Next thing to a hero."

"Hardly. Most of the men don't like the way I handled things. And I even dented Professor Maust's car. I'm thankful it wasn't your dad's."

"You did? I must have missed that when I went to get lemonade. Wasn't he the one who gave the search committee your name?"

"Yeah. So I wonder what he needs fixing around his house?"

Megan laughed softly, tucked her hair behind her ear again. "I don't think it's going to let up, Micah. Maybe we should make a run for it."

"Not yet." He reached for her hand. "I've missed you."

She gave a soft gasp. "Remember what you said? About playing with fire?"

His own words boomeranged, hitting him as sharply as they must have struck her, earlier. He regretted them, but they reminded him of his good intentions. He dropped her hand, and his voice came out harsher than he intended. "You're right. Give me your keys. I'll bring your car around for you."

"You don't have to do that. I'm already soaked."

He reached out and touched her shoulder. "Please, Meg. I want to."

She nodded and silently riffled through her purse. Keeping her lips grim, she thrust them at him. "Here."

"I'll be right back."

"Brother Zimmerman? Would you get my car, too, while you're at it?"

Micah froze. Watched in horror as Susanna inched her body carefully around the corner of the barn then blinked her eyelashes at him. Her unwelcome appearance brought him back to that day in the church with Joy Ann Beitzel. And it was obvious by the cunning look in the widow's gaze that she'd heard every word that had just transpired between him and Megan.

—⟲

Megan watched Micah turn pale and angry, but he left them without uttering a word. The moment he was gone, Susanna looked down her dripping beak. "Cozy under here, isn't it?"

Feeling like a rodent stalked by a capable hunter, Megan squirmed under Susanna's brown gaze that held the same fiery highlights as her hair. "It's not what it sounds like."

"Sounds like a lot of first names flying around." The thin lips pressed together in accusation.

"We knew each other at Rosedale College. It's hard to break old habits. We're just friends." Megan inwardly cringed at the partial lie. "As you probably heard us talking, Brother Zimmerman pointed out to me a few weeks ago that even though we're friends, we need to be careful around the house not to tarnish his. . .our reputations." Megan bit her lip, regretfully setting up some imagery for the widow's sharp mind.

"Or his chance for the position he's after? I didn't just fall out of the nest, young lady. I was married. I know exactly what playing with fire involves."

The rapturous widow circled, fearsome with her extended claws. Megan squeezed her eyes closed, trying to think of something that would keep her from shredding Micah to pieces. "But you didn't hear our earlier conversation. Brother Zimmerman merely pointed out to me that because I was naive, I was too trusting of men. That even though I could trust *him*, I shouldn't. That I needed to show more discretion."

"Such as not kissing under the barn eaves?"

Megan gasped. "Kissing? Susanna. We never!"

"Then why is your hair all messed up?"

"Because it rained. And yours is messed up, too!" Only the widow's ruffled appearance made her all the more frightful. Megan heard the approach of her Nova's rumble.

"At least he had the sense to bring your car around first."

Megan bit her tongue. She'd already fueled the woman's cruel imagination and ruffled her feathers. She would've been better off to just keep quiet like Micah. "I'm sorry if I was rude, just now. I don't want to cause any trouble for Brother Zimmerman."

"That's obvious, dear. You had to remind *him* not to play with fire?" She patted Megan's arm. "I commend you for that. He needs to be stopped before he ruins someone else. First poor Joy Ann Beitzel. And now you. Who will be next?"

Micah suddenly appeared, and Megan clamped her mouth closed. Looking distraught in his wet clothes and with water streaming off his hair and down his face, he urged, "Hurry."

"Thanks." Megan gave him an apologetic look then made a dash to her car. She slammed the door, all thoughts of the weather gone. Her windshield wipers were already swishing, so she put the car into DRIVE and prayed for Micah and what he had yet to endure.

⸺◌⸺

His career at risk from Susanna's barbed threats, Micah changed into dry clothing and grabbed his umbrella. The downpour continued as he sprinted across the Weavers' yard to the main house. When he stepped into the kitchen's warmth, Anita turned in surprise.

"Micah! Come in. I just put on a pot of coffee."

Closing the umbrella and propping it against the door, he went to join Bill at the table.

"Too bad about the rain. We woulda beat them," Bill said. "But I suppose the tie warded off bad feelings. Probably the best thing, in the end."

Although the men's competitive fervor was an earlier concern, now Micah's worries had shifted. "Yeah, you're right about that. Is Megan here?"

Bill's voice filled with suspicion. "Yeah. She's upstairs changing. Why?"

"I need to talk to you."

Anita brought both men steaming mugs of coffee. "That's the same thing Megan just said."

"Does this involve her?" Bill probed, his expression starting to resemble the thunderclouds.

"Yes."

"Well, what happened?"

"It's probably best to wait for her to join us."

Bill glanced at his wife. "Why don't you go check on her."

Mrs. Weaver wiped her hands on a striped linen dish towel and scurried from the room.

Meanwhile, Micah didn't feel like making idle conversation so he took some fortifying sips of the dark, strong brew. After weeks of sitting as a guest at their table, one of the refrigerator magnets that Anita collected from her garage sales had driven home its message taken from Walt Whitman: "Either define the moment, or the moment will define you." Regardless, when Anita quickly returned with Megan, he hardly knew where to begin. "There's been an incident."

Bill shot a gaze at Megan, whose wet hair had been slickly brushed back into semblance.

"Back at the picnic during the confusion of the storm, I found shelter under the barn's overhang. I'd only been there a few moments when I saw Megan running for her car. I called out for her to wait it out with me."

"I could hardly see the road in front of me," Megan interjected, fiddling with the sleeve of a soft gray sweater. "It was lightning, too."

Anita plopped another cup of coffee on the table and pushed it toward her daughter.

Micah continued. "We were only under there for a few minutes. We didn't know it at the time, but Susanna Schlagel was also taking refuge there, just around the corner of the barn. We found out later that she overheard our entire conversation."

Bill's hand moved away from his cup and swiped through his wet hair. "What exactly did she overhear?"

Micah met Megan's gaze. "I think we need to tell them everything."

Her voice held resignation. "I was going to anyway."

Bill's jaw clenched. If there was a refrigerator magnet to describe the emotions on Bill's face, it would have read. "Nobody messes with my daughter."

"What's going on?"

Anita's hand went out to stay her husband. "Now, Bill. Micah's trying to explain. I'm sure it's not what you're thinking."

He shrugged away from her touch. "How do you know what I'm thinking?"

She tilted one eyebrow reproachfully. "After all these years? Believe me, I know what you're thinking."

"Please," Megan interrupted. "It's not."

"What is it then?" Bill's eyes snapped angrily.

"When I first came to Plain City, Megan was one of the few people I knew. We quickly became friends. Remember how she saved my life with her EpiPen? Sometimes I need someone to talk to, and we hang out."

"Hang out?" Bill's voice was harshly judgmental.

"We talk on the porch swing."

"Micah is always full of good advice," Megan explained. "I talk to him about work."

Bill's nostrils flared. "Sneaking around right under our noses, taking advantage of our hospitality."

"We did give Micah the run of the house," Anita reminded.

Bill shot his wife a withering look.

"But a few weeks ago, I was convicted about it. I warned Megan not to be so trusting around men." Micah sighed and plunged into what might be his defining moment. "I told her our behavior was ultimately playing with fire. So we quit meeting like that."

"That's why you don't come in to supper anymore?" Anita shifted her gaze from Micah to Megan. "And why you've been moping?"

"Mother! You know I've just been extra busy at work."

"So what exactly did Susanna hear?" Bill's voice was somewhat calmer but filled with dread.

Micah exchanged a glance with Megan, and she gave an encouraging shrug. "Like I said, we were just there at the barn a few minutes. Megan wanted to make a run for it, but I asked her to wait. Told her I'd missed her. She reminded me of my own words, how we shouldn't be playing with fire. I knew she was right. So I offered to go get her car for her."

Megan jumped into the story. "Then Susanna came around the corner of the barn and asked Micah to get her car, too. We knew she'd heard everything. When Micah went after my car, Susanna accused us of kissing." Her face reddened. "Which we didn't, of course. I probably said all the wrong things to her, but she's coercive. The last thing she said was that she didn't blame me. That it was Micah's fault, and she hoped he didn't ruin any other girls. I'm sorry, Micah."

Bill slammed his fist on the table. "I trusted you, young man. And now you've embroiled my daughter in one of your escapades."

Even Anita looked at him with disappointment.

"Susanna's trying to stir up trouble," Megan said. "Can't you see that?"

"Of course I do. But if Micah's foolish enough to play with fire. With my daughter. Under my own roof. Then maybe he deserves to get burned!"

"Dad."

"No, he's right," Micah replied, then shifted his gaze from Megan to Bill. "There'll be trouble. I wanted you to hear it from me first."

Bill folded his hands on the table. "What are your feelings for my daughter?"

Micah met Bill's unflinching gaze. "I admire her. And I respect her. I'm not blind. Megan's an attractive woman, and I've felt fortunate to become friends with her."

"If you respected her, you wouldn't have gotten her involved in this."

"But he was doing the right thing by me," Megan argued. "He was protecting me. Giving me good advice about Chance, too."

"At the barn when you were ready to go, he asked you to wait. Was that the right thing? Tell me. Do you love him?"

"Dad. Don't do this."

"Are you willing to let Susanna smirch your reputation? If you two are falling in love, then the logical step would be an engagement."

—⟶

Megan had never seen her easygoing dad so obstinate. "People don't believe everything Susanna says. And if you ask me, the elders need to talk to her about her gossiping."

Brushing that aside, Dad said, "First, I need to know Micah's intentions."

Humiliated that Dad was backing Micah into a corner, Megan jumped up and gripped the edge of the table. "But I'm not ready to get married."

"Engaged," Dad corrected.

"And it's the farthest thing from Micah's mind, too."

"So you've talked about it?"

"Sir," Micah interrupted. "I'm not sure that friendship and attraction are the basis for a good marriage. As you know, my heart's set on preaching and ministry. I need to marry the right woman for all the right reasons." He turned his gaze to Megan. "As much as I like you, I'd rather get voted out than do something we'd both regret."

"Yes, you can leave Plain City. But Megan has to stay and weather this through. This may ruin her chances to marry a good man."

Megan lifted her chin. "Maybe I don't even want to get married. A woman doesn't have to get married to be happy. Today at the picnic, Lori Longacre and I were talking about that very thing."

"Nonsense!"

Megan restrained herself from arguing further.

"You were right about one thing, Micah. You were both playing with fire. I'll call the other elders tonight. See what we can do."

Megan mumbled, "Thanks." She gave Micah an embarrassed glance then went to her room. Fighting back anger toward Susanna, she moved to the window and drew back the curtains. The rain enveloped her in a wall of sound. How long ago it seemed since that Christmas season when she stood at this window with Katy and Lil. They'd watched the snow with high hopes of moving into the doddy house. So much water under the bridge since then. Now both her friends were married. And she was floundering, making a mess of her life.

Micah couldn't have made it any plainer. He'd reinforced what she'd already known. He was attracted to her, but he would marry the right woman for all the right reasons. He would stick to his convictions. And she'd become an old maid like Lori, that is if Micah didn't marry Lori. Megan had been nothing but a jinx on Micah, creating problems for him. She placed her forehead against the window pane, remembering the John Dryden quotation in her great-grandparents' latest love letter: "Love is not in our choice, but in our fate." She was fated to misery.

CHAPTER 34

The next morning, Megan would have preferred to skip church. But on the other hand, she didn't want to mope at home while Susanna spread gossip. Mom encouraged her to face the situation and get it behind her as quickly as possible, so Megan made the choice to go. But poor Micah had no choice. He had to face the congregation.

Megan slid into a pew as inconspicuously as possible. Mom followed her, leaving a space at the end of the pew for Dad to join them later. Megan opened her church bulletin and noticed the topic was faith then scanned through the announcements until the opening hymn.

After the singing, Micah stepped to the front of the congregation. He took a sip of water and cleared his throat. "I apologize for my voice. I've caught a bit of a cold." Megan conjured up the image of him bringing around not only her car, but also Susanna's, and then running after his own. "Today's topic is faith." Micah raised the Bible in his left hand and recited from memory. "Hebrews ten, verse thirty-eight says, 'Now the just shall live by faith: but if any man draw back, my soul shall have no pleasure in him.'"

He coughed and took another sip of water. "Fruit is an agricultural term. The Christian life is not based on the fruit we bear but on the Lord who gives the vine its fruit. When we walk in His Spirit, He produces fruit in us. He gives us the measure of faith we need for our circumstances, as we need it. Some may only need a cherry, and somebody else might need a watermelon."

The congregation chuckled, and Megan figured she definitely needed a watermelon.

"This varies from day to day. I lean on faith, same as you. I trust God for my future. You trust God for the future of this congregation. The day is coming when you must decide if I will be your permanent pastor. If we follow God, we can trust Him for our best. Remember faith is unseen, but not unfelt." He paused and looked over the congregation. His gaze rested briefly on Susanna, included Megan, then moved away.

He ended his sermon with an admonition. "In Acts, the church gathered together to talk about God. The early church gave us an example of what we should be doing. When we leave the auditorium, we should be sharing how God answers prayers, reminding each other of the glories of God, building each other up in the faith, and not tearing each other down."

"A good reminder," Megan whispered to her mom.

"Yes." Mom stood. "Your dad's got a five-minute meeting with the elders. I'm going to go invite Barbara for lunch."

Megan watched Mom leave and made her own way to the center aisle, catching up to Katy. Everyone was talking about how the storm had brought their church outing to a screeching halt. When they stepped outside, Katy whispered, "I have something for you."

They stepped aside so others could pass, and Katy dug in her diaper bag and then handed Megan an envelope. "Micah asked me to give this to you. What's it about?"

"I don't know." She drew Katy off to the side and briefed her about Susanna.

"Oh no. I'll pray for you. But I wonder if it has anything to do with the envelope? Are you going to open it?"

"Not here."

"I understand." Jake waved, and Katy frowned sympathetically. "Stop by the house or call if you need to talk."

"Thanks. I'll keep in touch."

Inside her car, Megan tore open the seal with shaky fingers, removing a note card of the masculine persuasion:

Megan,
    "When it is dark enough, you can see the stars"
—Ralph Waldo Emerson.

                                    Micah

Her lips formed a sad smile.

—❧—

After the Weavers' Sunday noon meal was finished, Dad offered to help Mom with the dishes, so Megan took Barbara outside to the porch swing.

"I always wanted one of these. Guess it's one of those things we never got around to. I've driven by a few times and seen Micah here studying. Usually, he's so caught up in what he's doing, he doesn't return my wave. It's been nice working with him at the church. Reminds me of when Eli and I first started out. There wasn't any church secretary, and I helped him a lot."

Megan's legs fell into rhythm with the older woman's. "I'm glad that's working out for you."

"Your mom's a good cook. Micah has it good here. After he leaves, you think your parents would consider taking on a permanent resident?"

"Why, I'm not sure. It all happened pretty spur of the moment. They seem open about it."

Barbara's shoes scuffed the floorboards as her blue gaze traversed the Weavers' yard. "I love my home, but someday it's going to be too much for me to take care of."

"I've heard Dad talk. The men don't mind helping out at the parsonage."

"Oh, I know. But it seems impractical, don't you think? I'm sure they don't want to boot me out, but I sure don't want them to think they have to wait around for me to die."

Shocked, Megan shook her head. "Nobody's thinking about that. Everyone loves you. You've served the congregation in many ways. For a long time, too."

"Exactly, I'm no spring chicken."

The swing creaked, filling in a gap of silence, and gradually Megan understood. "You want to move into our cottage?"

"I'd do my part. I'm no slacker."

"That's the least of anyone's worries. Do you want me to talk to Mom and Dad?"

"Not yet. After the church votes in Brother Zimmerman, then I'll talk to your dad."

"So you're asking me to keep a secret?"

"You might as well get used to it if you're going to be a preacher's wife." Before Megan could object, the older woman asked, "You think Anita's bringing our dessert out here, or do we need to go back inside?"

Megan jumped up. "You stay here. I'll go see."

But the moment Megan was inside, she paused to compose herself. Preacher's wife? Was Barbara actually prophetic? She'd seemed so sure that Micah would be voted in. By the abrupt manner in which Barbara changed the subject, the topic was closed. Perhaps the old woman was more brilliant than senile.

─────

Relieved that he wasn't the first to arrive at Susanna's two-story, gray-sided residence nestled beneath large evergreens, Micah harbored mixed feelings about the meeting. The elders were bringing the barn incident out into the open, and they wanted both Micah and Susanna present.

He needed to be there to stand up for himself. But his honesty was apt to provide more fodder for Susanna's voracious appetite. At the least, it would aid her justification. He'd already reckoned with the fact that he deserved whatever might come, but he also knew that God was merciful and forgiving, even if Bill Weaver wasn't. There was no turning back. The incident needed to get resolved. Especially if by some miracle of God's grace he ended up being Susanna and Bill's preacher. Megan's.

The air smelled of damp soil, stringent from the recent storm. He couldn't help but notice that Susanna's yard needed lots of work. The storm had broken some tree limbs, and the flower beds were weedy and rampant with decaying litter. The porch, however, was freshly swept.

Susanna answered the door and curtly invited him in. He wasn't late, but he was the last to arrive. He took his place at the end of one sofa beside the professor, who gave him a brief pat on the arm. On the other side of him was a round end table, shined to perfection so that he could almost see his own trepidation. A glass lamp and a Bible were the only items on top. A mean thought struck him—that Susanna would profit from reading the holy book.

She came to hover over him. "Would you like some tea? Or are you a coffee sort?"

A quick glance told him that the others had already taken her up on refreshments. "Coffee, if it's no trouble."

She speared him with a look that assured him, he was extremely troublesome. But she went into the kitchen and returned shortly with his beverage. She placed a tray of snickerdoodles on the coffee table. "Please help yourselves. I miss cooking for Charles, you know."

"How long have you been a widow?" Micah asked curiously. She was young for a widow, couldn't be any more than in her early forties and still carried a trim figure. In spite of the earlier incidents with her, he hadn't heard her story.

She went to the fireplace mantel and returned with a framed photo, which she handed Micah. "Two years now."

"He was a handsome man. I'm sorry for your loss."

She nodded, took the photo, and placed it back on the mantel. Then she turned and placed her hands on her dark skirt. "I have a hunch what this is all about."

"I'd feel more comfortable if you sat," Micah said, not liking the way she presided over the room.

She snapped her gaze in his direction. "I'm not really concerned about your comfort, young man."

Bill leaned forward. "That's hardly the way to speak to one of God's anointed. Actually, we're all your church leaders. And we'd all feel better if ya relaxed and took a seat, Susanna."

She transposed from gracious host to a red-tailed hawk ready to strike at its nearest victim. Eyes glittering, she perched on an antique side chair near the hearth, keeping herself separated from the men. "Perhaps you should have brought your wives along. I feel like a cornered rabbit."

It was all Micah could do not to roll his eyes at her dramatization. It was more like she was the bird of prey and they were all the rabbits.

Bill replied, "We could have done that, but we felt this was a personal matter that didn't need to go any further than the people in this room."

"Hmmph. There's one woman already missing who was involved. And are you telling me that your Anita doesn't know about Micah's behavior?"

"Let's pray before this discussion goes any further," Bill said.

Thankful, Micah bowed his head.

Afterward, Bill returned to the previous conversation. "It's true that Micah and Megan came to me after the picnic and told me and Anita what had happened. Perhaps we should start with your perception of what you saw and heard that was so troubling."

Susanna repeated the conversation she'd heard and gave her perception of how loose Micah was around the single women, bringing into it the earlier incident with Joy Ann Beitzel.

"What you claim to have heard validates Micah and Megan's story. As an elder board, we urge you to consider the fact that Megan and Micah knew each other from Rosedale. Because he's staying in our guest cottage, they've spent time together in our home. After the incident, I asked them if they've any intentions of marriage. Neither of them has thoughts along those lines. All they've done is have some private conversations. Even then, either Anita or I was at home. They haven't done anything wrong."

"Micah specifically said they were playing with fire."

"Which is pretty smart for a man his age," the professor interjected.

Micah flinched and quickly whipped a handkerchief from his pocket and sneezed into it.

The professor restated, "We all think Micah's mature beyond his age."

"Well, you're allowed your opinions," she said.

"And it is the consensus of the elders that you need to look inward and examine the source and motives of your opinions."

"Well, I never! Brother Troyer would never have acted like this. This church is going to pot."

"With your husband now gone, we're here to encourage you in your walk."

"I'm sorry for the misunderstanding." Micah was almost embarrassed over the staunch support the elders gave him. He supposed his set down was coming later.

Susanna gave Micah a cold look. "Noah is right. You're young. Maybe this has taught you a lesson."

"You're right," Micah said, pretty sure it hadn't taught her anything edifying.

"The snickerdoodles are tasty," Bill said, bringing the meeting to a close. "One of my favorites."

"Yes, we all have our favorites." Susanna rested a calculating gaze on Micah.

Outside Susanna's house, Bill followed Micah to his car. "Guess we didn't have to drive separate."

Micah wasn't positive Bill was ready to make jokes about the situation, but he couldn't resist. "Wouldn't want you to show any favoritism."

Bill smiled. "Look. I'm sorry I jumped down your throat last night. You caught me off guard. And Megan's our only daughter."

"I expected and deserved everything you said."

"Anita and I were talking about it afterward. Sometimes women have better insight into these kinds of things. We see what's going on between you and Megan. The undercurrents. We think it would be a healthy thing, if you'd take meals with us again."

"Undercurrents?"

"Don't get the wrong idea. We're not trying to matchmake. We're not pushing Megan off on you. I'm talking about your friendship. We all miss you." Bill shrugged. "Anita suggested it. She's usually right."

"Tell Anita I'll be in for supper tonight."

"Good."

Micah got in his car. While he was sitting in Susanna's living room, the Lord had whispered in his heart what he needed to do regarding the widow. He wasn't looking forward to it, but he was going to be obedient.

After that, when Bill had walked him to the car, he'd been expecting another set down. Bill's change of attitude was a mystery. Was it godly forgiveness or was it because of those undercurrents he'd mentioned? He said he wasn't matchmaking, but it seemed like that to Micah.

He remembered Megan admitting that she'd talked to Lori. It had almost sounded like the two had conspired against him, with their anti-marriage sentiments. But maybe that had all been a bluff. Because Megan was warming.

He started his engine, never having imagined an hour earlier that he would leave the widow Schlagel's house with a grin on his face and a dinner invitation. Indeed, God was merciful.

—⟶

As Megan set the table, her mom said, "Be sure to set a place for Micah."

"I doubt he'll come in tonight."

"Your dad invited him, and he accepted."

Megan swung around as her mom took a berry cobbler out of the oven. "Why would he?" Then she shrugged, answering her own question. "I suppose we all need to make amends."

Mom kept her gaze lowered. "Something like that."

Moving to the cupboard above her mom's slow-cooker chicken and dumplings, Megan got the extra plate. She'd just placed it on the table when her dad came in from the shop with Micah. Amazingly, the two men bantered as if Saturday had never happened.

Micah took a chair then sneezed into his handkerchief.

"Sorry about your cold," Mom empathized. "You taking anything for it?"

He shook his head, stuffing it back into his pocket. "I think it's allergies. And just when things had settled down for me."

"Oh, probably the start of fall allergies," Mom said. "Your resistance is probably low. Maybe from the storm?"

Micah looked at Megan. "You don't have any symptoms?"

"Not yet."

Micah frowned at her as if she was letting him down. Her lack of sniffles had probably been his basis for assuming it was a virus.

"Medicine makes me drowsy."

"Work makes me drowsy," Megan quipped back, but when she saw everyone's gaze rest on her questioningly, she quickly added, "But it's getting better, now that Randy's back." The incident had left its mark, making her feel as though she were walking on eggshells, afraid to say the wrong things. But when Micah didn't react negatively, she relaxed. Maybe everyone had gotten past Saturday's argument after all.

Mom speared Dad with her gaze. "Can't the newspaper wait till after supper?"

"Oh sure." He folded it up and handed it to Megan with a sheepish grin. "I'm tired, too."

Megan took the newspaper to his favorite chair in the living room, and when she returned, everyone was waiting.

After Dad's prayer, they passed the food. "Good sermon," he said.

"I didn't get it," Megan differed. "Is faith something we have to do? Or something God gives us?"

"Both," Micah said. "You inhale to breathe, but air is a gift from God."

"How do allergies fit into your analogy?"

"Or exercising?" Mom arched an eyebrow.

Micah grinned. "They're darts from the enemy."

"Amen!" Megan said, grinning back.

Across the table, Mom smiled, too.

Dad shrugged. "What? When dinner's so good, who's got time to breathe?"

CHAPTER 35

Micah drove into Plain City, down Madison Street, to a small house in the heart of the village and parked on the street. He made his way up the rippled sidewalk and climbed three stairs to the exterior stoop. Then he rang the doorbell. He waited, staring at the floor and noticing it was in bad need of paint. When he didn't hear any stirring, he rang again. This time, the door opened.

"Micah. What a surprise. Come in."

"I've been meaning to stop in, sir."

"Glad you did."

Micah followed his professor into the adjoining room that looked more like a library than a living room. One corner of the room held bookcases. Beneath a window was a massive desk. But Noah Maust took Micah to a set of masculine armchairs.

"A wonderful room," Micah observed.

"Yes. For years I studied back in one of the bedrooms. Then one day, I decided to make myself comfortable. Most of my visitors feel more comfortable in this atmosphere, anyway."

"Yes, sir. I could certainly make myself comfortable here."

"It's time to dispense with the titles. If anything, I should defer to you now."

"That doesn't seem right. How about first names?"

"Done. So what brings you here, Micah? Making your rounds?"

"No. I came to find out how much I owe you to fix your car."

Noah brushed his hand through the air. "No need. I'm more concerned about function. Your ball didn't destroy that."

"You don't intend to take it in for body work then?"

"For one little dent? Don't be ridiculous. I'm just glad to have the ballgame behind us. Never relished playing."

"But you did fine. You got on base several times."

"It's not something I enjoy, but I do my part."

"It's tougher than I imagined trying to fill Brother Troyer's shoes."

"Nonsense. Lori Longacre says we need young blood. And all that bluster with the widow will soon blow over."

Micah studied the professor thoughtfully. "You and Lori talk?"

Noah laughed. "Women love talking better than anything."

"I'm discovering that. Talking and crying."

The professor laughed. "Lori's the studious type, and we have a lot in common. We're actually kind of in cahoots, trying to put in a good word for you whenever we can."

"You two are friends," Micah repeated. "So you think men and women can just be friends? I'm finding bachelorhood is getting me in trouble."

"Even though I never married, I enjoy several female friendships."

"If you had to do it over, would you stay single?"

"Good question. It's lonely. But my job at Rosedale places me around people all day long. So home is my retreat. I like it. I'm used to it. I know what Bill said at the meeting, but is it really over between you and Megan?"

Micah felt Noah's probing gaze. "I can't believe I'm so transparent."

"Something tells me you didn't come here to talk about my car. I'm sure it's lonely for you in your position. I make a pretty good sounding board."

Micah met the professor's gaze and decided he was good as his word. "I could use a mentor. I talk to Bill, but not about Megan. I can't get her out of my mind."

"How does she feel?"

"Even though she despised me in college, we've become close. When

I first came, she was in love with her boss. She came to me for advice. She gave him up because he wasn't a Mennonite. She cried on my shoulder. Actually, she does that a lot." Micah decided to omit the information about the night in the root cellar.

"So you don't know if she's over him?"

"She's over him. But I don't know if she could ever think of me as more than a friend."

"That's complicated. I understand your thinking. You're a perfectionist. And now your idea of the perfect woman conflicts with reality, especially because you weren't Megan's one and only."

"I hadn't admitted that to myself. Of course, I live by grace and extend grace to others. But maybe you're right. Maybe it bothers me more than I thought."

"On the other hand, you love her. Marriage would make your job easier, and from what I hear, there's not a perfect relationship out there."

Micah gave the professor a half grin, wondering what a bachelor like Noah really knew about love or marriage. "Is that why you never married?"

Noah's gaze drifted up to his left toward the window. "I proposed once. A long time ago. Obviously she refused. But I didn't regret it because it freed me to get over her. And if you're going to live in Plain City, you either have to marry her or get over her like I did and move on."

"You're right. But I don't want to rush her."

"Again, the perfectionism. Waiting for the perfect time. But from what I hear, you can't rush a woman, anyway." The professor gestured toward the adjoining hall. "Can I get you something to drink? I'm a pretty good cook, too."

Micah rose. "Next time. Thanks for listening. Now, what would be a good day for me to show up with my paintbrush?"

"Excuse me?"

"I'm painting your porch floor."

Amusement crinkled the corners of Noah's eyes. He studied Micah almost long enough to make him squirm. Then he finally replied, "Any weekday, now that college is back in swing. Just be sure it's dry before I get home. And make sure it matches the siding. Oh, and whatever you do, don't show up with any of Leon's leftover blue paint."

Micah laughed. "It's a deal."

"You don't owe me for anything, except taking so long to get over here."

"I wish I'd come sooner."

Micah saw himself out, whistling all the way to the car. The professor was right; he should have visited him when he'd first arrived in Plain City. It was his own loss that he hadn't, for an hour with his old mentor had revealed many things.

—⌒○

Megan arrived at work, glanced at the clock, and saw that she was fifteen minutes early. As she waited for her computer to boot and did a few rote tasks, she wondered what it would be like to move into Barbara's parsonage with Micah. Was the woman really prophetic? Or had she made her observations while working alongside Micah? The idea of supporting Micah in his ministry put goose bumps on her arms. She rubbed them, thinking Barbara wasn't the only person pushing her toward the idea.

Lori and Lil saw her and Micah together, but insisted the timing was wrong. If that was true, Megan needed patience. She bit back a smile, thinking that the other night at the table, she should have asked Micah about patience rather than faith. She imagined him catching her hidden meaning and taking great pains with his explanation, even throwing in a love quote or two. No, she'd been reading too many of Great-grandpa's letters. That wasn't real life, not her life anyway.

She didn't even know when she'd fallen in love with Micah, but she had. She loved his sense of humor, his compassion, and his perseverance. She sighed and picked up a small stack of complaints. The one on top was about a bumpy ride. How could bad weather be the fault of Char Air? She'd have to make the phone call and apologize, regardless.

Tapping a pencil against her chin, her thoughts returned to Micah. Did he know that her lifelong dream had been to marry a missionary or preacher? Would that information help him understand why she'd fallen for Chance? It reminded her of Abraham taking Sarah's servant woman when he didn't think Sarah would be able to produce the son he was promised. Settling for second best from what God intended all along.

"Megan?" Near her desk, Paige stood with a hand on her tight-skirted hip.

Megan dropped her pencil and snatched up her white ceramic cup. "Yes. I want coffee."

On the way to the snack room, Paige told her what she'd done over the weekend and then asked if Megan had done anything exciting.

"If you call instigating a church incident exciting, then yes."

Inside the coffee room, Paige shut the door. "Come on, girl. Don't leave me hanging."

As Megan told the story, Paige's expressions varied, but mostly she bore a look of frustration. "What?" Megan finally asked.

"I just think sometimes your people make a mountain out of a molehill."

With a sinking disappointment in her inability to explain things fully so that her outsider friend could understand *her people*, Megan turned away to fill her coffee cup.

"But then, I never knew a preacher personally. I guess Micah's even holier than you?"

Megan cringed and faced Paige. "Nobody deserves grace, but I suppose it appears that way." Had she fallen into the trap of believing that lie? That she wasn't good enough for Micah?

"You're a riddle. That's what I love about you." Paige fixed her coffee. "So did you see what's on the bulletin board?"

Megan walked over to a mishmash of photos and business cards, expecting to see something from the recent newsletter or a customer's thank-you note. She followed Paige's red fingernail to a sheet of lined yellow paper. Curious, she stepped closer. The signature at the bottom made her heart do a little trip. *Chance Marshall*? Her gaze scurried to the top of the page:

> *Hi, Char Air friends,*
>
> *I'm back in Shell, trying to get things in order. I suppose it's been the same with Randy picking up the pieces since I left there. Don't let him downsize the charity flights! I'll hold you accountable if I ever come back to the States.*

I hit the rainy season here, if there's such a thing. Having some downtime now, waiting for the weather to break so I can fly in and pick up a snakebite victim. A child. The missionary family from the compound assures me that God gives life and takes it away. Not to take our losses personally. I try to trust God's timing, but sometimes I just have to go with my instincts. . . .

Megan paused with understanding. How difficult that must be when it was a matter of life and death—someone else's.

Thanks for all your hard work. Remember, you keep Char Air successful, no matter what my brother claims.

I've no regrets for spending time with you all, but I'm tickled as blue skies to be back in the thick of things here where I belong.

Happy flying,
Chance

"Whatcha think?"

Megan tore her gaze from the letter. "He sounds happy."

"Yeah, but he was thinking about us on his downtime."

"With no regrets."

"What about you, honey? Because if you have them, you can still change your mind. Let your preacher and church members work out their problems while you are knee deep in jungle and love. Why, Randy would probably fly you over there, himself."

Megan grinned. "You noticed it, too? He wants to get rid of me, doesn't he?"

"Nonsense. That's not what I meant."

"I've got my heart set on Micah."

Paige nodded. "Just wanted you to admit it."

Megan was glad for the note's closure. "Don't worry. I'm over Chance. But things are complicated with Micah."

Paige brushed her hand through the air. "He's a man, isn't he?" Then she got her cup and opened the door.

Back at her desk, Megan reflected briefly on Chance's message. It validated her feelings. She was over him but wanted the best for him and his ministry there in Ecuador. And he would be fine.

As she went back to work, peace stole over her, the kind that came with agreeing with God. With it came a whisper of knowledge that shocked her. God had given her the job at Char Air for a reason. She might never understand the reason, but once her purpose was finished, He would open a different door. If she hadn't been so positive that the message came from God, she might not have had the courage to speak so boldly to Randy when he called her into his office.

"You look discouraged," she said.

His gaze flashed up at her with bitterness. "You may be my assistant, but you're not a confidante."

She rested her hand on the corner of his desk. "And I'm a great assistant. Without me, you'd have a bigger mess on your hands right now." She hoped he'd remember that he'd created his own mess and quit disrespecting her.

"So you've been here a year. Now you run the place?"

"You've worked hard to make your company successful. But I do know some things that you don't."

His jaw nearly unhinged. "Like what?"

"Spiritual truths."

He laughed out loud. "Now you sound like Chance. That why you two had a thing?"

"I guess. But we were smart enough to do the right thing."

He leaned back in his chair. "Wish I could say the same. I don't seem to know when to quit."

The pain in his eyes prompted her to say what she'd been thinking for months. "The only thing that will save your marriage is turning to God for help."

"Why would God help me? Because of a few charity flights? I do that for publicity."

That was information she regretted hearing. But Randy was hurt, and she knew people said crazy things under duress. "Because He created you. Did you know God sees right into the hearts of men? He can see into Tina's heart, too. That's why He can help you win her back."

"I don't think she has a heart. Don't try to convert us." He laughed. "I

281

can't see Tina in a bonnet contraption."

Megan felt her face heat. "There are other churches where you can find God."

"Then why didn't you leave yours and go with Chance?"

"Because I like my church." Megan pinched the inner corner of her eye to keep the tears at bay. "Just think about it."

"Oh, don't cry."

She squared her shoulders, trying to oblige him. He softened his voice. "I'm sorry I've been hard on you. You signed on here at a bad time. And Tina's jealousy puts pressure on me."

A thought flew into Megan's mind so swift and hard that it almost knocked her off her feet. She blinked, wanting to resist it, but she was sure it came from God. The missing piece of what he was already showing her. She wet her lips. "Maybe you should offer Tina my job."

Randy's eyes snapped open with interest. She watched his inward struggle. It was almost amusing to see the wheels of his mind turning over the idea.

"Just a thought."

He looked at her with gratitude. "Thanks. I'll think about it."

"Think about God, too," she said, before pivoting and leaving his office.

Two hours later, Randy emerged from his office and bent over her desk. "Would you train her?"

Biting her bottom lip with disappointment, Megan nodded. "Of course."

"Maybe we could find you another position? Assistant to Paige?"

She gave him a weak smile. It was a demotion. How would she ever get anything done sitting next to Paige? "Follow your heart. And I'll make do."

He nodded with a whisper, "Let's keep this between us. I need to think about it. I'll talk to Tina. It just might be the trick that finally wins her trust."

She cringed at the word *trick*. Randy needed a lot of help. "Don't forget about church."

Randy strode back to his office with a grin.

Megan sank back in her chair. "Aye, yi, yi."

CHAPTER 36

Micah opened his cottage door and stepped into Bill's workshop, espying a pair of tennis shoes and about six inches of blue jeans sticking out from beneath a dark blue Nova, Bill's current restoration for a lawyer from Columbus.

Not good timing. But the professor had chided him about his propensity toward perfection. Micah stood in indecision. On the other hand, this was important and needed the perfect lead in. He didn't want to pour his heart out to a pair of shoes. He put his hand back on his door handle.

"You need something?" Bill called out from beneath the vehicle.

The question sent adrenalin spurting through his veins. "Yes, if it's not a bad time for you."

The mechanic's gurney squeaked and moved until Bill's face was visible. With a grunt, he said, "I need to talk to you, too. Give me just a minute." He slid back beneath, made a few quick adjustments, and then slid back out, sitting up.

Micah reached down to give him a hand, but he brushed the offer away. "Too dirty."

Waiting patiently, Micah's gaze slid over the shop's tools without really taking them in. He watched Bill move to a sink and wash his hands with a harsh soap. "Wanna go in and see if Anita's got any lemonade for us?"

"No." Micah blurted out much too quickly. "I mean what I want to talk about is personal." He glanced at the door to his cottage. "How about my place?"

"Too dirty. Pull up a seat." Bill closed a huge toolbox and perched on it.

Seeing an empty bucket, Micah plopped it upside down and sat across from Bill, who eyed him with curiosity and what he hoped was respect. "I've been working through some things. What I once told you about Megan wasn't completely truthful." At Bill's growing frown, Micah quickly continued. "About my feelings for her. The truth is I love your daughter, sir. Have since the day I saw her on the steps at Rosedale." He sighed. "It's a long story."

"I've all the time in the world."

"She didn't return the attraction, so I learned to hide it."

"That why you came to Plain City?" Bill's harsh voice interrupted.

"No. At that time, I didn't harbor any hope that Megan would change her mind. It was more of a nuisance for both of us."

Bill nodded.

"But then we became friends and helped each other through some stuff. I gave her advice. She gave me advice."

Bill got a slight smile on his face, and Micah thought Bill was reading too much between the lines. "Anyway, I knew I'd fallen for her again, only I wasn't sure about her feelings. When you brought up marriage, I didn't want her to find out about my feelings that way. Didn't think the timing was right."

"I can understand it happened prematurely, but as far as the church is concerned, the timing could be the key to your future."

"That's just it. I started out not wanting Megan to interfere with my chance at the job, but now I don't want my job to interfere with my chance for Megan. I don't care if it means losing this position. I'm more worried about losing her."

"Have you talked to Megan about this?"

"No. We haven't been alone since the incident. I don't know if I'm reading her wrong, but I have to find out. And I wanted your permission first."

Bill rubbed his chin thoughtfully. "Permission for?"

"To pursue her." He ran his hand through his hair. "To figure everything out."

Bill's smile showed his teeth. "You have it. As long as you don't go breaking her heart. I'd be proud if things progressed and you became my son-in-law. I'm assuming that's your goal?"

"Well eventually. Long term, yes, sir."

"Your guess is as good as mine to what this congregation wants in a preacher. From what Inez told Leon today, Susanna didn't take the elders' advice. She's trying to turn the older people against you. Just being a little more subtle than normal. Pushing the idea that you'll bring too many changes."

Micah hated to hear it. He thought about what he'd done after he'd left the professor's home. How he'd gone over to Susanna's and started cleaning up her yard. She'd come out of the house, spewing, *"Don't think that's going to change my vote."*

His thoughts went over the conversation they had that day.

"No, ma'am. I'm not here to change your vote. Just to show you I'm not the bad guy you think I am."

"Same thing."

"What's wrong Susanna? What've I done to offend you?"

"For one, you stare at me when you preach."

"I'm looking at the clock. I'm sorry you thought that."

"You can just go. My son takes care of my yard every time he comes to town."

"I'm going to finish what I started."

"So am I," she'd said, marching to the house and slamming the door.

Bill interrupted his thoughts. "She's right about that. There'll be changes."

With only a week and a half until the big vote, Micah had done some planning. "I was thinking of having a communion service, then taking the vote afterward. Do you think that would be appropriate?"

"Sounds perfect. I hope the congregation doesn't make a big mistake. Because you're the right man for the job. God will have to deal with Susanna."

"He's given me a word on that, but it's not mine to tell yet."

Bill arched an inquisitive brow.

"I thought I'd ask Megan if she wanted to go with me to a fall festival out in Galena-Sunbury way." He'd wanted to take her someplace romantic, away from every reminder of church and daily grind. Some place where she might catch the passion.

"God bless you, son."

Micah reached out his hand, and this time Bill took it, shaking it firmly. Then Micah left him and strode toward the house. Now that he'd been given the go ahead, nothing could keep him from going after the woman he loved. He knew that she was home from work, and he wanted a moment alone with her before supper to instigate his plan.

Inside the kitchen Anita was humming. She turned at the sound of the door closing.

"Hi. You hungry?"

The aroma of freshly baked homemade bread wafted over him. "Getting there. Is Megan home?"

"Yeah, she's up in her room."

He moved up beside her. "I'll stir the pot for you, if you don't mind getting her for me."

Anita handed him the spoon. " 'Bout time."

It was getting hard to ignore Anita's little matchmaking attempts. He stirred the taco soup that he'd grown to love, thinking it would be nice to be a real part of this tight-knit family. He'd liked the way Bill called him *son*, earlier.

"You wanna see me?"

Anita stepped up and snatched the spoon. Probably would have pushed him, too, if he wasn't already physically drawn toward her daughter. Swallowing, he nodded. "We need to talk." Without waiting for Megan's reply, he started toward the living room. When he heard her footsteps behind him, his heart began to race.

───❦───

Megan glanced back at her mom. She gave her a frantic nod to follow Micah, who was acting strange. On the porch, she touched his arm,

"What's this all about?" One glance into his anxious face and trepidation crawled up her spine.

"Sit with me?"

Shrugging, Megan settled onto the white porch swing. When his movement swayed the swing, she grabbed the chain with one hand. Their shoulders touched, the same as they had that last time they'd shared the swing. She glanced at him. "You're not going to give another lecture about playing with fire and growing up, are you?"

He grinned. "Hardly."

Her thoughts went to the rumors she'd overheard Dad tell Mom about, rumors that he wasn't going to get an affirmative vote, and wondered if this was some sort of farewell. She didn't want to lose him now. "What's wrong, Micah?"

"Your eyes are gorgeous. When you look at me that way, it's hard to breathe, much less talk."

She shifted her gaze to the floor. "Is this better?"

"No."

She looked back up with confusion. The adoration in his gaze was unmistakable. Her heart leaped with hope. "I'm listening."

"I'd like to take you someplace romantic. I heard about a farm a county over that gives hayrides. Wanna go out Saturday night?"

The hope inside her exploded into fireworks that warmed and spread. But it seemed too good to be true. She had to hear more, to be sure of what he was offering. "Go on a romantic date?"

"Uh-huh." He fastened his soft brown gaze on her in a way that started the fireworks all over again. A corner of his mouth lifted playfully. "Want to?"

How could she convey that the prospect of a hayride with him made Ecuador with Chance inconsequential? His eyes were so boyishly hopeful, and she wanted to remove every qualm. To erase any lingering memories of her past mistakes and poor decisions. Moments passed as she groped for the perfect response. In the lapse, his gaze grew dismayed. She needed to say something before he started wheezing.

"Only if you let me kiss you in the corn maze."

His gaze opened in understanding. He beamed. Shook his head with wonder as if he'd been given a gift. "Now that's a promise."

CHAPTER 37

Megan skipped through the remainder of the week, feasting on her great-grandpa's love quotes and Micah's lovesick glances from across the dinner table. Neither of them sought out private conversation with each other, not wanting to burst their bubble of infatuation, but directing all their romantic energy toward their date on Saturday.

When the day finally arrived, Megan dressed in a warm skirt, blouse, and light wool coat. Micah wore jeans. When she slid into the passenger seat of his Honda Civic, she grinned. "This is my first ride in your car."

"First date," he reminded her with a look that held plenty of promise, a look that wasn't going to let her back down. "Hopefully, a lot of firsts tonight."

This openly flirtatious side of him was new. It was as though he'd rent the veil, and his adoration poured over her in a massive warm wave. She should have known he'd be flirtatious and fun. He'd probably be eloquently expressive in a relationship, too. After all, he was a preacher. But it was hard to believe that he was finally throwing decorum to the wind. She cast a skeptical side-glance at him. "How long do you think it will be until everybody hears about this?"

"It doesn't matter. We have your dad's approval."

"I know." She felt strangely nervous.

He sensed her hesitation. "Anyway, the Lord says not to worry about tomorrow."

"If we date, will you always quote scripture to me?"

"Not in the corn maze." He grinned. "I was thinking we'd better do that first, before it gets dark. I don't want to miss it."

Megan laughed and turned her gaze to the window. Everything familiar whizzed by, but she felt as though she was starting a wild adventure.

When they reached the farm, Micah paid their admission and raised his gaze to the jean-clad teenager who took their money. "Point me to the corn maze."

Aye, yi, yi. What was she getting herself into with such a determined, one-track man? She couldn't wait to find out.

"You can buy that ticket here, if you want."

"I want," he replied, looking deep into Megan's eyes. Blushing with delight, she clasped his hand, now stamped to get them inside the maze. They strolled along a wide path flanked with pumpkins and corn shocks. "I've waited a long time for this."

"Yes, autumn is my favorite season. Especially after a long hot summer."

"Hot and dry. Absolute drought-ridden."

They passed some food booths. It almost frightened her to imagine how such a parched man would quench his thirst, and with thoughts of her own inexperience, she slowed her pace. The pleasant aroma of kettle corn wafted over them, and he misunderstood. "Hungry?"

She paused to watch the man who ran the booth. He smiled at her. She didn't really want popcorn in her teeth for their first kiss. "There's more to life than food," she paraphrased, shooting scripture back at him.

He caressed her hand with his thumb. "I can't wait to get you alone."

A breeze swirled some fallen leaves. Megan shivered.

Micah turned to face her. He gently took her by the shoulders. "I'm only teasing you. I'm a patient man."

The tenderness in his gaze drew her. "Yes, well, I should probably tell you, about now, that sometimes I'm more words than action."

He dropped his hands, then tucked her hand in his arm and started walking. "Don't worry. I don't even know what to do in a corn maze.

I'm a city boy."

She doubted that. Micah was good at everything he attempted. They passed a stand that sold apple butter and Ohio maple syrup. "Will it be hard for you to adjust to small town? To Plain City?"

"I loved it when I was in college. In Allentown, we lived in the suburbs."

"Tell me about your grandma's house. Your house."

"It's small but quaint. In an old shady neighborhood."

"Sounds nice."

He squeezed her hand. "*Very* nice."

"You're *very* one-tracked."

He pointed at his chest. "Me?"

They reached the maze entrance. He showed another teenager the stamp on his hand. The kid motioned them in. Megan stared at the large red sign that read Enter. With a chuckle, Micah grabbed her hand and tugged her through its opening onto a path. Walls of corn instantly towered above her head. Children's voices carried to them over the beige tousled heads, and Megan relaxed. She felt almost childish again. In truth, it had been a long while since she'd actually been inside a corn maze.

Micah slipped his arm around her waist and drew her possessively to his side. "Wonder where the closest dead-end is?"

She lowered her voice and thickened her Dutchy accent. "I'll bet you do."

They followed the well-trodden path. On either side of them, sticky green and beige arms with stringy fingertips waved them along. They walked until the titters of children grew quiet around them. Rows and rows of tall brittle stalks, silent strangers except for the rustle of breeze or the thrashing of birds.

Suddenly Micah stopped. His arm still around her, he drew her close. "Thanks for coming with me tonight."

"I was thrilled you asked. I thought I had run you off for good."

"It's been complicated."

"Painfully so." She saw his eyes sadden and wanted to explain that she wasn't talking about Chance. "I've so many regrets that I didn't get to know you back in school. Things could have been different."

He leaned down and rested his forehead against hers. Whispered, "I'm not complaining. I like the way things are. You here, in my arms." He tilted his head and sought her lips.

She melted into his kiss, her hand going up to the back of his neck. She allowed him to quench his thirst, but he gave her more than he took before he drew away. He stroked her cheek then dropped his hand and gazed at her with adoration.

With his tenderness, he had completely stolen her heart. She felt like doing Lil's garbanzo dance. Or Paige's cha-cha step. She tucked her bottom lip in her teeth. "I guess that was a good idea, huh?"

He burst into laughter. His eyes lit with mischief. "Just so you know. That was your kiss. The one you requested. The next one will be mine."

Her eyes widened in speculation, his promise whetting her appetite.

"Come on." He tugged her hand, and they started back through the maze.

Megan dropped her gaze to the black soil strewn with dry matter. Like their steps, her mind covered many paths. When she looked up, she said, "It's hard to shake the feeling that we always have to watch over our shoulder."

"We aren't going to do that anymore."

She nodded, wondering about Micah's intentions for their budding relationship.

On the hayride that wound through a colorful display of woods, he brought up the subject. "By now, you must know how much I adore you. But we need to take things slow." She nodded, although she didn't fully understand, and recognized the look when his eyes took on a steely glint. "Will you trust me in this?"

Megan couldn't begin to grasp what his question entailed, but she was sure it had a lot to do with the congregation's vote. She also sensed his urgency.

"Yes, I will."

His eyes slid closed in relief. When they opened again, he said, "That means everything to me. I'll do my best not to disappoint you."

She thought he wanted to kiss her again, but he didn't. And she realized he wouldn't do that in a public setting. His steel extended beyond his gaze. Mettle ran through his veins. And from the memory of their kiss, there was hot lava in there, too. She wanted to ask him if he'd still stay in Plain City if the vote was negative, but she'd just assured him of her trust, so she squelched the question.

⸺෴⸻

Megan didn't see much of Micah the next week. Her dad mentioned Micah was spending time in his cottage, fasting and praying about the vote. But on Wednesday morning, she'd just started her Nova's heater when she noticed a small paper sack on the bench seat. It wasn't any ordinary bag with its large blue ribbon. Her heart panting with thoughts of Micah, she drew it to her lap. She shot a look toward the cottage, but the drapes were drawn tight. Relishing the gift, she slowly pulled the ribbons. Peered inside. To the delight of her soul, she pulled out a clear plastic bag of candy corn. She opened the candy and placed one on her tongue. Closed her eyes, remembering their kiss. Wondering when she was going to get the next one.

Another glance toward the cottage told her that it wouldn't be until after the vote. But in the meantime, she'd savor his gift, one kernel at a time. She stuffed the bag in her purse, thinking that with Tina coming into the office to begin her training, she was going to need all the sweetness she could get.

⸺෴⸻

Megan stood in the church foyer, looking for Micah. She'd hoped to give him a word of encouragement before the big church meeting. With disappointment, she gave in to the fact that he must be cloistered off some place with the elders or search committee.

"Not me. I don't like having the vote right after communion." Susanna shook her auburn head.

Megan retreated into the sweet-smelling library and shrank against the nearest bookcase filled with inspirational nonfictions. She hadn't set out to eavesdrop, but she didn't want to step into the middle of that conversation. She feigned interest in a book of sermons. From her hidden vantage point, she could hear Barbara's gentle protest.

"The date for the vote was set a long time ago."

Megan could imagine Susanna's eyes snapping as she argued, "Yes, but Brother Zimmerman set fall communion for the same night."

"We don't know that. It could've been the elders' idea."

"You're saying you don't know where the idea came from?"

"No. But I think it's a good one. It'll remind us to search our hearts for sin. And once our hearts are right, God's will can be done."

"That's puttin' God in a box. He can do His will with or without communion. Crackers and grape juice won't make that young man a better preacher all of a sudden."

"Susanna!"

The discussion ended, and Megan eased a peek around the corner. With relief, she saw Susanna moving toward the fellowship hall.

"She's bitter." Lori stated softly.

Megan turned, thinning her lips in disapproval. "She's not even hiding it anymore."

Lori removed the book from her hands with a grin and shoved it back into place. "Wanna sit together?"

It was an invitation to do the foot washing ceremony with her. Usually, Megan and Katy were partners, but she knew Katy would understand. "Sure."

Communion happened two or more times a year. The procedure had changed somewhat after the congregation sanctioned its integrated seating. Entering the auditorium, a quick glance assured Megan that families were going to sit together for the first part of the service, where they took the cup and bread.

Lori went to the singles' pew about halfway up the center aisle, and Megan slid in beside her. Shortly after that, Micah strode past and took his place in front of the congregation. He quietly stood, allowing his gaze to drift across the assembly. It paused on Megan and warmed. He smiled.

Megan beamed back at him, surprised and thrilled that he'd openly sought her out.

His gaze dropped from Megan to the Bible that lay open on the podium in front of him.

Lori hissed, "What was that about?"

With heat rising up her neck, Megan lowered her voice so Joy and

Ruthie wouldn't hear. "We're dating."

"I see." Lori's reproach reverberated her warning, not to rush ahead of God's timing. "Micah did the asking. He talked to my dad."

Lori's tight-lipped nod ended the conversation. The librarian fastened a stern gaze on Micah.

He reminded the assembly that communion symbolized the Lord's sacrifice at the cross, taking their sins upon Himself, so that they might have forgiveness and eternal life. He urged everyone to search their hearts for sin before taking communion. For the folks at Big Darby, it was a solemn, contemplative moment.

For an ugly instant, Susanna's remark about crackers and grape juice tormented Megan's mind. She quickly dispelled it. Felt a nudge at her arm and saw the communion tray. After she partook, she passed it to Lori without making eye contact.

Afterward, Micah instructed the women to move to the left of the auditorium and men to the right. Ray led the congregation in hymn singing as, row by row, women and men slipped into their respective side rooms.

Inside the women's anteroom, the women removed their shoes and stockings and waited barefooted, quietly whispering with each other, until one of the six chairs became available. The actual ritual was done with somberness. The foot-washing practice reflected the Lord's actions, when He washed His disciples' feet.

Lori took a chair, and Megan carefully dipped each of the librarian's bare feet into a round porcelain basin filled with soapy water then dried them with a fluffy white towel. Afterward she helped Lori stand. They kissed each other on each cheek, saying the blessing: "God's peace be with you."

The ceremony held significance for Megan in many ways. She felt acceptance and healing in her friendship with Lori and a solidarity in their desire for the good of the church and for Micah's victory.

When everyone had gathered back in the sanctuary, Micah stepped to the front. "You may take a ten-minute recess, and when you return, the elders will lead you in the voting process." He gave no parting pep talk but quietly left the podium.

An air of reverence still filled the sanctuary, and the congregation slowly came to life, milling quietly. Megan and Lori stood with the other singles. From the corner of her eye, Megan saw Barbara huddled with the widows. Above their bent, whispering heads, the clock's minute hand had only moved two marks since Micah had closed the service.

Lori nudged her. "He's coming."

She shifted her gaze, and her heart tumbled to see Micah moving toward her, but taking care to greet others along the way. He glanced up at her repeatedly, and she knew he would not be deterred.

When he reached them, he touched her arm. "Hi, Meg." Her emotions soared giddily to see his unveiled admiration and to hear the shortened endearment of her name. His brown eyes also held concern. "All I can think about is your mom's refrigerator magnet."

"Oh?" A mishmash image of her mom's garage-sale magnets ranging from ceramic flower buttons to die-cut vintage sayings gave her another delightful glimpse into Micah's complex nature. "Which one?"

" 'Either define the moment, or the moment will define you.' "

"Walt Whitman," Lori murmured.

"You have my vote," Joy Ann said softly, while toeing the hardwood flooring.

He smiled. "Thanks. That's good to know."

Lori touched Joy Ann's arm. "I believe my lip balm fell out of my purse in the anteroom. Would you help me go look for it?"

Joy Ann furrowed her brow. "Now?"

"Yes. I need it now."

Megan tucked her lower lip in her teeth until the two other women moved out of sight. "I know you and Lori make a good team, but the two of us aren't bad together, either."

"I noticed. But I hope you don't want to follow her footsteps. Whatever you do, don't switch to her brand of perfume. I love the citrusy scent you wear."

She smoothed the side of her upswept hair. His eyes softened as he followed the movement. "Thanks for the bag of candy corn you put in my car."

He sucked his bottom lip then grinned. "It was symbolic."

"Yes, I got that." She smiled.

His jaw slightly tightened. "I'm sorry I did a disappearing act this week."

"I understand."

He glanced at the clock. "I better go."

She touched his arm to detain him. "Can I come with Dad when he brings you the news?"

"Yes." He hesitated, his expression contrite. "But I may need time."

"I know."

CHAPTER 38

After the communion service, Dad continued the meeting with a short introduction and reminder that only members could vote. The process was simple. He asked those who affirmed Micah as preacher to stand.

Megan hurried to her feet. Beside her, Lori also stood. The entire singles' pew affirmed Micah. Two elders counted heads from the front of the room, allowing Megan just enough time to quickly scan the auditorium. She tried to get a general feel for the vote without honing in on individuals, lest she develop hard feelings toward those who remained seated. Susanna's row was behind her, out of her view, but she thought that Micah had the majority of votes.

"Be seated. Those opposed, please stand."

As skirts rustled, Megan wished she'd asked Micah what percentage he required to accept the calling. Some preachers required 100 percent, not wanting to take a position where there might be a rift. She kneaded her hands, remembering the church was requiring 80 percent in favor to extend the invitation. Would that be enough for Micah? She was sure the vote would not be unanimous.

"Thank you. Be seated." Dad turned to confer with the other elders, then returned to the podium.

Her dad's words had never held more significance for Megan. And then she saw the smile in his eyes and sank with relief. "He got it," Megan whispered.

"What?" Lori's hand clutched Megan's arm.

"The vote is positive," Megan's dad announced. "Big Darby Conservative Mennonite will be offering Micah Zimmerman a permanent ministerial position. We'll ask him to give us his answer next Sunday from the pulpit. You're dismissed. Go in peace."

Megan stood and squeezed Lori's hand. They knew better than to make a display of their emotions for the sake of the people who had not voted for Micah.

"Now it's up to Micah," Lori said. "Please do what you can to convince him to stay."

"He asked me to trust him."

"Just do your best."

Megan moved in a daze for the door, anxious to see the matter through, to get home to Micah. An arm snatched her in the foyer. She turned, and Barbara leaned close to her ear. "You take good care of my hydrangea bush. You hear?"

"Don't put the cart in front of the horse."

"And don't topple the cart."

Shaking her head with amusement, Megan stepped out into the brisk September evening.

"Megan."

She turned. "Mom. Where's Dad?"

"Still talking to the elders. Let your dad be the one to tell him."

"I will, but try to hurry him along. Don't let him be the last one to leave again."

"I'll do my best. Put on the coffeepot when you get home." She leaned closer. "This calls for a celebration."

They exchanged a victorious look; then Megan started toward her car. She'd only gone a few steps when Katy intercepted her. They spoke briefly and parted. She was halfway across the parking lot when she saw Susanna sitting inside her car. Mixed emotions rushed over Megan, resentment and triumph followed by guilt.

The woman looked rigid as a stone statue, and Megan wondered if something was wrong besides the outcome of the vote. Megan struggled with her conscience then veered to the left where her feet did not want to go. Even as she approached the widow's car, Susanna didn't notice her. She didn't move. Megan rapped lightly on her car window.

The widow jerked, raked a glance over Megan, then rolled the window. "What do you want?"

"Are you all right?"

"No. I'm not." Susanna gripped the steering wheel and lowered her forehead to the top of the steering wheel.

"Can I help? Drive you home?"

Susanna shook her head then lifted her gaze to Megan. "Just go home to your preacher. Someday you'll understand."

Megan sighed. "Susanna."

But the widow was done talking. She put her car in REVERSE.

Megan stepped away. For the first time, she felt pity for the widow.

Micah had been waiting in his cottage for over an hour. And after the previous week's seclusion, he was good and sick of it. He knew there was fellowship and driving time involved, but he'd hoped Bill would make an effort to bring him the results in a prompt manner. Megan's car had arrived at least twenty minutes earlier. She was doing the right thing by letting her father bring the news, but the waiting was almost more than he could bear.

He stationed himself next to the window. Even Miss Purrty paced and switched her tail. Finally the Weavers pulled into the driveway. And then they went inside the house! Micah sighed. Stood and paced, stepping on the cat. She yowled and leaped into her crate. He started after her, but then he heard the fervent rap at his door.

Diving for it, he swung the door open. He gave Bill a sheepish smile and gestured the Weavers into his apartment. From another world, Micah felt the cat's motor as it wove in and out of his legs.

The older man's eyes brightened, and he offered a congratulatory handshake. "Big Darby wants you."

Micah blew out a deep sigh and relaxed his shoulders. "That's good news."

Megan rushed to hug him. "Congratulations, Micah."

He rested his chin on top of her head, closed his eyes, and drank in the promise of love and a glorious future. There was a joyous flash of Sunday sermons, baptisms, communions, and softball picnics until he felt Megan's gentle pat on his back. Reluctantly, he released her.

Anita hugged him next. "Come in for coffee. We have to celebrate."

He nodded and choked, "I'll be right in."

As soon as they left, he sank to his knees where he'd already worn a fuzzy spot in the rug and leaned his head against the tiny bed. When he had control of his emotions, he rose with thanksgiving still on his lips. He stroked the cat. "Stay."

Inside the Weavers' home, his first clue that something wasn't entirely right was when Bill said, "I told them you'd give your answer next Sunday over the pulpit."

Disappointment settled over him like a familiar companion, but he bit his tongue until Anita finished serving the coffee and joined them at the table. "What was the vote? The percentage?"

Bill fiddled with his cup. "It was eighty-three. But given the timing, you can have every hope that a few years down the road, you'll have one hundred percent support. Change takes time. We talked about that."

Micah nodded. "I know. But I had a number in mind. It was a lot higher than yours."

Megan's face paled. Her eyes searched him over the rim of her cup. She gave a trembling smile.

He looked at Anita. Tears had sprung to her eyes, and he knew why. She didn't want her only child to move away from Plain City.

Bill gave him a forced smile. "You have all week to decide. The elders and search committee are unanimous. They want you. You have to keep in mind that it's a small congregation. That's why the margin is so big."

"I know."

Anita cleared her throat. "There's a pumpkin in the garden that's bound to be a prize winner. Have you seen it?"

Micah swiveled his gaze in confusion then caught the glint in her eyes.

"No. But may I take your daughter and check it out?"

Anita nodded. "It's getting dark, but there's a flashlight in the junk drawer."

Megan pushed back her chair and went to the drawer.

Micah stood and faced Bill. "Thanks for the news. As soon as I have an answer, this family will be the first to know."

The atmosphere was hardly celebrative. Megan followed him out the door. Without speaking, his left hand sought hers, and his right flicked on the flashlight. Its beam zigzagged across the yard but did little to lift the descending gloom.

Megan broke the awkward silence. "So what happens next?"

"I thought God and I had a number in mind. But the last couple of weeks, my thinking's changed." He knew what needed to be done. He just didn't know if Megan would support his decision.

_____

Megan walked beside Micah. Her heart leapt with joy at his words: *"I thought God and I had a number in mind. But the last couple of weeks, my thinking's changed."* Surely he was referring to their growing relationship. He was going to change his plans for her.

"It's not so much the number, anymore. I'm not staying unless I can win Susanna's vote."

"What?" She stopped walking and shrugged away. "But that will never happen!"

He flicked off the light and stuffed it in his back pocket, then took both her hands. "I have to try."

"But you only have a week. You'd need a miracle."

He caressed her hands. "I know. You still trust me with our future?"

Her mind exploded in possible scenarios of what such a trust might entail. They'd only had one date. She couldn't run off with him. "Are you staying here if you don't take the job?"

"Let's take this one step at a time."

That sounded too much like Chance's philosophy. It had ended up in a dead end. And her heart had been broken. But Micah was different.

"I have to have a job, Meg. And you know what kind of job I want."

"What about us?"

"I've waited for you a long time. I want to take it slow. I want to grow into our future."

"That's what I mean." She couldn't chase after him. "I have a job here."

"People do survive long-distance relationships."

Long distance meant periods of separation. That could stretch on for years. Was that what he'd been trying to warn her about all along? Her heart resisted, but her mind raced ahead to weigh her options now. She gripped his hands, not wanting to lose him.

She'd already fallen in love with the man. She thought he felt the same way, though he'd never told her he loved her. But now she needed to decide if she could live with and support his ministry and everything it would bring into their lives. It could be a rough row to hoe, living from one miracle to the next. She'd already faced the reality that the missionary life wasn't as she'd dreamed. Would being a preacher's wife be as disappointing?

Micah was here in the flesh now. She could either reach for her dreams or shrink back in fear. She was too invested to do that.

"I spoke with Susanna after the vote. She seemed depressed. Do you have a plan?"

"Yes." He touched her cheek. "You're so beautiful in the moonlight. Even when you're brooding. I love the way your forehead gets those little wrinkles."

His fingers traced them and sent shivers down her neck. His hand found her cheek again, and she cradled her face into his touch and breathed into his palm. "Yeah, I'll trust you."

He scooped her close, whispered against her ear, "Thank you." Then he lifted her chin and brought his lips to hers. He kissed her gently, urgently, then peppered her with kisses of promise. "Everything will be fine," he murmured.

"I know." His lovemaking made her so dizzy it was impossible to object. He might want to take it one day at a time, but she'd think of it as one kiss at a time. That would get her through. Her thoughts took her to the corn maze, comparing the kisses. "So that was the kiss you warned me about?"

He sighed. "I'm afraid so. Was it wimpy?"

"I'll make do." She stepped away and crossed her arms. She lifted her chin in determination for whatever lay ahead. Her gaze drifted to the garden, and sudden amusement bubbled up in her throat. "Bless Mom, that's the puniest pumpkin patch she's ever had."

Micah looked at the scrawny pumpkins and laughed.

CHAPTER 39

On Monday Micah trimmed Susanna's trees. When he first got started, she'd pulled her drapes closed, but just before he'd left, she stuck her head out the door and yelled, "You're doing nothing but making a big mess!"

On Tuesday Susanna's car was gone all day. He borrowed Leon's flatbed trailer and hauled off the trimmings and trash. Leon stocked him up with painting equipment to do the professor's porch.

On Wednesday morning Micah stayed home, drew the curtain and fasted and prayed. It wasn't any ordinary prayer but a struggle of sprit and flesh, for his flesh wanted to forget about Susanna, to give in and make a home for Megan here in Plain City. Late afternoon, he'd made his peace again and rose from his meditations.

On Thursday he went to the church, heartened by Barbara's kind face.

"Morning, Micah. Coffee's ready. And the professor already stopped in on his way to work. He said to tell you that Saturday does suit, after all, for painting his porch."

"Good. I want to do that before I go."

"Nonsense. I already told you you're not going anyplace. And don't be moping around and slacking off keeping up that cottage. I don't want a mess on my hands when I move in."

"Barbara, I thought I knew what God wanted me to do, but now I think I heard Him wrong."

"See, that's what I'm talking about. Moping. I heard you say it right over your own pulpit: 'Faith is unseen, but not unfelt.'"

He hadn't told anyone but Megan what he was doing at Susanna's. Or even that his decision hinged on her change of heart. He wasn't seeing any evidence of a changed heart, and now his feelings were becoming wishy-washy, too. But Barbara's faith remained intact; the woman wouldn't be deterred.

On Friday Micah unpacked his gardening tools and let himself through a creaky gate into Susanna's backyard. A flagstone walkway went from the house to a weedy, vacated garden patch. He'd noticed the grass was trodden down where Susanna veered from the flagstone to the clothesline. He'd start by clearing the walkway for her.

He sat on his haunches and moved along the flagstone, pulling weeds from the cracks and opening up the footpath. After twenty minutes, he removed his jacket and got his hoe. He headed for the worst neglected area, the garden patch.

"Just what do you think you're doing?"

Micah flinched. Bracing himself, he turned with a smile. "I'm back to finish what I started."

Susanna straightened her back and marched up to him. She was a beautiful woman, all ruffled and fierce. "You got the vote. Why are you still here?"

"I wasn't after a winning vote. I was after the congregation's love and support. But for some reason, you have hated me from the start. So I failed."

Susanna clenched her jaw, shifting her brown gaze away.

"I can still turn down the church's offer, you know."

Surprise lit her eyes. "Will you?"

"That depends on you. Don't get me wrong, I'm not worried about the damage you could do to my character or even my failure. But God never fails. So I have to obey Him. And He's telling me that I need to put my choice in your hands."

"What?" She eyed him skeptically. "Then I guess you'd better pack your bags."

"God cares more about you, Susanna, than He does about me getting the job. He sees your pain. He sent me here to give you a message. He loves you."

She lifted her chin, but her words came out shaky. "Don't make this about me."

Micah wet his lips, searched for the right words. It was another defining moment, even more important than the last, because this one defined a woman's soul.

"He wants you to love Him back."

Susanna flinched. Confusion clouded her eyes. She lowered her gaze, and it was the first time Micah had observed real weakness in the woman. Hesitant, yet feeling God's urging, Micah touched her arm. "God loves you."

Susanna looked at him. "Why?"

"Why wouldn't He?" Miraculously, her defenses shattered, and she gulped back sobs. Tentatively, Micah patted her back. There in front of the forsaken garden, God's love infused the autumn sunshine and warmed them, as Micah ministered to the woman's broken spirit.

When she could speak, she flattened her palms against Micah's chest and pushed him away. "I gave up on God a long time ago."

"But you still came to church?"

"It's all I know. It's where my friends are."

"I'm sorry we didn't realize you were hurting. Do you want to tell me what happened?"

"You know how to wear a woman down." She strode to a wooden bench near the garden. "Aren't you coming?"

Biting back a grin, Micah joined her. They sat in silence, both their gazes fixed on the tangled mass of past gardens. Then she began to talk. "When I married Charles, I had hopes of love. But he never loved me. My entire marriage, I felt like I was trapped inside a cage. But there was nothing I could do. The only people who ever loved me were my boys. But they moved away." She sniffed. "My bitterness drove them away."

It became clear that Susanna had been starved for affection and used her gossip to win a following. With a heart hardened toward God, it had been an effective tool. But it hadn't brought her love or acceptance. She was a lonely woman.

"Did God really send you here? You didn't just come because you're some perfectionist and you have to win my favor?"

"Only God's love enabled me to come here today."

"And it's up to me if you take the job?"

"Yes. I'll go away if that's what you want."

"No. I want you to stay. You're the only man who's ever been kind to me."

"Thanks, Susanna. You really need me. Your yard's a mess."

"Like me."

"Can I pray for you?"

She nodded, and holding her hand, Micah prayed for God's forgiveness and grace in her life. When they were finished, she stood and straightened her skirt. "You've got to quit going around hugging women and holding their hands. You do know that, don't you?"

Getting a glimpse of her inner loveliness and a long-suppressed sense of humor, Micah replied, "I'm making you an exception, along with my Megan."

Her eyes widened, and she opened her mouth to say something, but clamped it shut again. She shook her head. "It's going to be hard to break my old habits."

"You have the rest of your life for that. God doesn't expect perfection." He'd do well to remember that, himself.

"Well then," she said, swiping her hand across her face. "I'll go inside and get you some apple cider. Would you like that, Brother Zimmerman?"

"Why don't you call me Micah?"

"Brother Micah," she said, turning and hurrying toward the house.

Micah stooped and retrieved his hoe then looked toward heaven with a broad grin. "Thank You, Lord." He looked at the tangled mess of Susanna's garden and rolled up his sleeves. He couldn't wait to give Megan the news. And he knew just how he'd do it.

CHAPTER 40

Megan peered into the back of Micah's Honda Civic. "How did you cram all this stuff in here?"

He put his arm around her waist and shifted her to the side. "I have all kinds of talents you haven't discovered yet."

She eyed him skeptically. Ever since Friday night supper, he'd been acting like the cat that swallowed the bird. She could only hope that was a good thing, but she knew better than to press him. The stubborn man had the patience of Job, and he would do things in his timing. When he'd invited her to help him paint Noah Maust's porch, his chest had puffed out as though it was the best second date anybody had ever proposed to their girl. She didn't mind, really. He was probably just trying to give her a taste of what life with him would entail. He might even be testing her. She'd prove her mettle. Wouldn't let doubt color the decision that still loomed over them. The one he had to make before Sunday morning service tomorrow.

"Hold this?" He handed her a bag bulging with rollers, trays, and tape.

"Want me to take it up on the porch?"

He looked her in the eyes. "No, I don't." He glanced at the porch and back. "You can set it at the bottom of the steps, though."

She shrugged a brow and went to do his bidding. When she turned, he was standing directly behind her. He dropped a five-gallon can of paint at her feet like a caveman peace offering.

"What's up with you?"

The mischievous glint that shot in his eyes made her gasp and back up a step. She hit the railing.

He advanced a step and closed the distance between them. "I just wanted to make it special." His gaze never leaving hers, she felt his hands grip her waist and pull her close.

"Micah!" Without warning, he swept her off her feet and into his arms. She squirmed. "What are you doing? In plain sight of the entire neighborhood." Had he finally reached his limit and gone from discreet to throwing all caution to the wind? Of course she had no idea what he was capable of, so early into their relationship. *Oh!* He was carrying her up the steps and nuzzling her neck, and she found it hard to remember why she had tried to prevent him.

"I'm carrying you up over the threshold, sweet. Consider it a promise of things to come. No matter what happens, all right?"

His charming gesture and use of a pet name quieted her resistance. At the top of the porch, she decided to show him her mettle and swung her arms around his neck, pulling his face down. But he kept the kiss brief and set her suddenly, unexpectedly on her feet. She looked up at him with surprise.

He grinned. "Wondered how long it would take before I swept you off your feet. I thought it might happen that day the tornado came through. I'd hoped. But you got away from me. I guess it's taken about three-and-a-half years. I just want you to know that I never quit trying."

She clutched the front of his shirt. "Well, you missed a good chance that night in the corn maze. For a while, I thought you might get away."

Looking down at her, he said, "That night, I told you I wanted to take it slow. That I wanted to enjoy dating you."

She relaxed her grip. "I remember."

"But I'm giving you permission to try and change my mind. You might even find it easy to do since we won't be having a long-distance relationship."

Megan squealed. "You're staying? Oh, glory be."

"I'm staying, but I need you to promise me something."

"What?"

"Give me enough time to shower you with my love. I want to do it in a million different ways before I pop the question."

"Write me a love letter, Micah. My aunt Louise gave me my great-grandparents' love letters. My great-grandpa told my great-grandma that the poet Charles Morgan understood love. He said: 'There is no surprise more magical than the surprise of being loved. It is God's finger on man's shoulder.'"

—⌒—

Winter came. The bean patch and Brother Troyer's grave lay buried in snow. The folks at Big Darby Conservative Mennonite were adjusting to change. Bishop Heinlein came to fill in while Micah went back to Pennsylvania to wrap up some loose ends. Megan missed him but kept busy with her wedding plans.

She swept through the living room to check the mail for the Butterick patterns she'd ordered and came to a halt. Back stepping, she retraced her steps to her mom's small, round side table. A smile tugged her lips as she lifted the frame that hadn't been there earlier. It was the photograph of Mom's birth parents, and beside it was the small worn Bible. *A Christmas miracle!*

Snow swirled magically through the picture window, and Megan drew her coat up tight against her before she stepped outside. Everything was pure and beautiful, reminding her of that Christmas Eve when Lil and Katy had come over to exchange gifts for their hope chests. At the time, none of them even had a boyfriend. So much had changed since then. She'd been a bridesmaid twice over. And soon Katy and Lil would do the honor for her.

Her boots tapped down the steps and trudged through the yard to the road. She brushed the snow off the mailbox with her sleeve and pulled the latch. She bent to peer inside. No patterns. But a small parcel rested on top of some envelopes. *From Aunt Louise!* Excited, she gathered the rest of the mail and started back to the porch.

The cottage light caught her eye. Barbara waved from its window. She waved back and hurried up the porch steps to the swing. She quickly brushed off the seat with her gloves and sank into its comfort. Placing the bulk of the mail at her side, she tore open the wrappings.

She swept away the tissue paper. It was a Christmas ornament. A smile of delight spread over her face. A bride with wings. A wedding angel. She'd never seen anything like it. She remembered how excited Louise was that Megan planned to carry her great-grandmother's handkerchief the day of her wedding. Her something blue.

Sometimes she thought the day would never come. How she missed Micah. He'd only been gone for two weeks, but it seemed like an eternity. He'd already moved into the parsonage. February would be here before she knew it, and there was plenty to do. She swooped up the mail to go back inside and show her mom the bride-angel, when she saw it. A letter from Micah.

To her heart's joyous leap, she sank back into the swing. She drew out a sheet of gray stationery and read:

Dearest Meg,

I was able to spend a few days at my brother's and invite him personally to our wedding. He says they wouldn't miss it for the world, and they're anxious to meet you. I visited your aunt Louise. She says the twenty-five miles between Allentown and Reading is not a problem. She's excited about renting out my house whenever she's not traveling. Says to look for a package from her.

I miss you. It's barren and cold without you. I've thought a lot about the love letter you requested that day we painted the professor's porch. I've written at least a dozen since then but was never satisfied with any of them. They're inadequate to express my feelings. I can't compete with your great-grandfather. But if you want them, when I return, I'll give you the entire stack. Maybe they'll tide you over till our wedding night.

Megan felt her face heat, but read on:

In the meantime, some scripture from Song of Songs 4:9–11 is the best this preacher can do to keep you warm until my return: "Thou has ravished my heart, my sister, my spouse; thou hast ravished my heart with one of thine eyes, with one chain of thy neck. How fair is thy love, my sister, my spouse! how much better is thy love than wine! and the smell of thine ointments than all spices. Thy lips, O my spouse, drop as the honeycomb; honey and milk are under thy tongue."

Megan clutched the letter and fanned her face, while all around her snow swirled. *Aye, yi, yi!*

MEGAN'S JOURNAL

January

Tina and Randy are snug as two bugs in a Cessna, but working from the cubicle next to Paige is driving me bananas. She hums annoyingly, curses every time she breaks a fingernail, and gives me all the cold calls. She wants to spend every spare moment revising my wedding plans. But I guess I'll make do since the demotion came with a significant pay raise.

February

Aunt Louise sent us to San Diego, California, for our honeymoon. I'm madly in love, and Micah's obsessed with carrying me over anything that vaguely resembles a threshold. I found out that he's a hopeless romantic. Not that I'm complaining. One night we took a quilt to the beach to prove Ralph Waldo Emerson's theory: "When it is dark enough, you can see the stars." It's true.

March

Joy Ann Beitzel went with Ruthie Ropp to her cousin's wedding in Lancaster County. They had some car trouble and stayed longer than they originally intended. But when they returned, Joy Ann informed me that she's now in a long-distance relationship with the man of her dreams.

Maybe now she'll finally get over the crush she's had on my husband.

April

Micah and I are miserable with spring allergies. As much as we love the parsonage gardens, we had to suck up our pride because Barbara initiated a workday for us. It was the day that I found out Lil's pregnant. She did the garbanzo dance. Calls the baby her little bean.

May

Went to a garage sale with Mom and found a wonderful bookcase for Micah's never-ending collection of books. Jake removed a wall between two bedrooms and set up Micah's office to resemble the professor's. Even put an outside door to it. Lil thinks I should demand a kitchen update to even the score, but I'm content. Every Monday night, Lori stops by to see what he'll need for his sermon. We've become best of friends.

June

Gardens everywhere are in full bloom. Mom and I are having the discussions of my daydreams. Susanna's even got a garden this year. Micah's organized a group that helps out the widows. But he goes to Susanna's himself as long as his allergies allow it. The four of us—Mom, Barbara, Susanna, and I—are getting together to put up Lil's three bean salad.

July

One of Dad's Nova clients begged him to drive his Nova in the Plain City Fourth of July Parade. At first Dad refused, but Micah talked him into it. We watched the parade from the professor's porch.

August

It was the annual Big Darby picnic and softball game. Have I mentioned how stubborn Micah can be? He kept his white shirt/blue shirt teams. His team forgave him when he hit another home run. Now he'll have to come up with something to appease the rest of the men.

Joy Ann's boyfriend helped with the children's relays. Susanna was proud of her new quilted table coverings, and Inez admitted they were way better than rocks. There wasn't any rain this year, but Micah stole with me into Leon's barn for a few moments of reminiscing. Only this time, there were no regrets.

September

Fall allergies. Monday night Lori teased us about our his-and-hers inhalers. Micah's a hands-on preacher and keeps a "To-Do for Others" list. He employs my help whenever possible. This week we cleaned out the root cellar for Mom. He suggested we sneak back in after dark that night, light some candles, and spend the night for old time's sake, but I was having nothing to do with it. Normally, he's full of good ideas, but that wasn't one of them.

October

We went to the corn maze, and on the drive over, Micah teased me about chasing him and demanding a kiss on our first date. I told him if he didn't get the story right, he wouldn't be giving me any candy corn later. That shut him up even though he was right. I did ask for that first kiss. After that, my obstinate husband seemed to know what to do on his own.

November

Micah painted the spare bedroom blue. Stubborn man! I told him that it was too early to know what color it needed to be. I thought little Hope Marie would favor a light pink room. But in a way, I hope Micah's right. Wouldn't it be fun to raise a miniature Ichabod Crane?

December

David Miller gave us an early Christmas present. He set it up for Micah and me to go on a winter's sleigh ride. So I added horse handling to my husband's amazing talents. Afterward the entire church met at the Stucky's farm for a bonfire and ice-skating party on the Big Darby Creek.

January

Lil's little bean arrived. She's cute as a button. She still sleeps too much to tell if she's as strong willed as her parents. Something new is happening at their house. First, they traded Jezebel in on a new car. They're looking for a bigger home. It's kinda sad because the doddy house holds a lot of memories for us.

Today Aunt Louise sent us something blue for baby Isaac Michael's growing nursery. We were unanimous on the name Isaac. Micah says it means *laughter*. And we are certainly riding the giddy wings of joy these days. For me it's a precious pet name, shortened from Ichabod Crane. I never told Micah about the nickname, but somehow it lives inside me to symbolize my all-inclusive love for my husband. I envision this little life within me growing into a gangly tree climber, all arms and legs. I hope Isaac's just like his dad in every way. Well, it'd be nice if he didn't have our allergies, but that would take a miracle.

February

For our anniversary, we dressed up and went to Volo Italiano for dinner. Giavanni's anxious for Lil to return to work, though she's undecided about it. Micah held my hand and quoted Song of Songs to me across the lasagna. Honestly, I don't know how I ever made do without him.

Dear readers,

For more of Megan's journal entries, please visit my website at: www. diannechristner.net.

DISCUSSION QUESTIONS

1. Which of the following adjectives best describes Megan: principled, adventuresome, naïve, or late-bloomer?

2. Megan's family didn't have television or the internet. Imagine all you would have to delete from you mind if you'd never experienced such technologies. How did it shape her worldview?

3. Would you say Megan and her mom's relationship was close, normal, or dysfunctional?

4. Who was your favorite minor character?

5. After one of Micah's sermons, Megan tried to set her heart. Did it work?

6. Do you think Micah acted honorably around Megan? Why or why not?

7. Did you learn anything new or unusual about the Mennonite faith?

8. In line with the title *Something Blue,* what blue things were mentioned in the story? How were they symbolic?

ABOUT THE AUTHOR

Dianne Christner enjoys the beauty of her desert surroundings in Phoenix, Arizona, where life sizzles when temperatures soar above 100 degrees. She and husband, Jim, have two married children and five grandchildren. Before writing, Dianne worked in office management, in admissions, and as a teacher's assistant in a Christian school, and owned an exercise salon in Scottsdale, Arizona.

Her first book was published in 1994, and she now writes full-time. She has published several historical fiction titles and writes contemporary fiction based on her experience in the Mennonite church. Her husband was raised on a farm in Plain City, Ohio, in a Conservative Mennonite church. Dianne was raised in an urban Mennonite setting. They both have Amish ancestors and friends and family in various sects of the Mennonite church. Now Dianne and Jim attend a nondenominational church.

You may find information about her other books at www.diannechristner. net, where she keeps a blog about the Mennonite lifestyle.